THE GHOST PACT

BEN WOLF

TECH GHOST | BOOK 2

A SCIENCE FICTION THRILLER

www.AethonBooks.com

The Ghost Pact
Tech Ghost: Book 2
by Ben Wolf

Published by Aethon Books

Cover design by Kirk DouPonce
www.fiction-artist.com

Contact Ben Wolf directly at ben@benwolf.com for signed copies and to schedule author appearances and speaking events.

"Wow! *The Ghost Mine* is a phenomenal story. Ben Wolf excels at so many elements of storytelling, it's impossible to identify a single gem:

Richly developed characters; a fascinating and detailed future of machine-human hybrids and deep-space mining operations; an intriguing mystery; shocking-yet-believable twists; breakneck action; and more than a few leave-the-lights-on/eye-watering moments of sheer terror.

Now imagine all this in the hands of a deft wordsmith. *Man!*

Think *Aliens* meets *Ender's Game* meets *Rambo*. Taut, vivid, and captivating, *The Ghost Mine* will leave you breathlessly bandaging paper cuts from flipping the pages so fast. This one's a definite winner."

- **Robert Liparulo**, bestselling author of
the *Immortal Files* and the *Dreamhouse Kings* series

"A snappy, fun wild ride from hell! Wolf's knock-out novel brings all the sci-fi intensity of Ridley Scott's *Alien* movies together with a Michael Crichton-style thriller. When space colonization goes wrong in *The Ghost Mine*, it means a long, nail-biting night of sheer reading delight! Positively unputdownable!"

- **Brandon Barr**, *USA Today* Bestseller, author of the *Song of the World* series

"The Ghost Mine is dark and dangerous—sci-fi horror in the vein of *Aliens* and *The Thing*. If you like intense pressure, hazardous conditions, and a deposit of gore and treachery, then grab your pickax and a light and dig right in."

- **Kerry Nietz**, award-winning author of *Frayed* and *Amish Vampires in Space*

"Ben Wolf's latest novel, *The Ghost Mine*, is a Dantesque trip into hell, complete with demons, spirits, and plenty of evil. If you enjoy tales of fending off fiends in tight, underground places, then jump into this novel."

"As iron sharpens iron, so a friend sharpens a friend."
– Proverbs 27:17

This book is dedicated to Monét Camel.
Thanks for always keeping me sharp, brother.
GG, 1984.

Brooklyn –

The future is Now!

PROLOGUE

D r. Hallie Hayes gripped the armrests of her jumpseat as another impact rocked the *Persimmon*.

"Status report?" Captain Mitch Dawes called from the cockpit.

"Shields at 80%," replied the co-pilot and first officer, a handsome but naïve young lieutenant named Bryant Sokolov.

"Not good," Captain Dawes said in return. He guided the small Whip-Class ship through whirls and curls and spins, trying to evade their pursuers.

From her jumpseat, Hallie could see the distant stars flashing by the cockpit glass with each new maneuver the captain executed. Beams of wide red lasers streaked past them into space, and she shuddered.

This was real. Not just another drill.

Another jolt rocked the ship, and Dr. Cecilia Bright, one of Hallie's fellow researchers, gripped Hallie's hand. They exchanged a furtive, terrified glance, and both squeezed their grips tighter.

We can make it, Hallie told herself. *Captain Dawes is the best for a reason. This is why he's on this mission in the first place.*

The next shudder rattled Hallie's teeth and quaked into her bones.

"Shields at 64%!" Bryant called. "She's holding up well, but it won't last forever."

"Damn. Hold on!" Captain Dawes kept working on calculations for a jump.

Hallie held her breath. Across from her, the other two scientists on their project sat in comparable jumpseats. Dr. Angela Wainwright barely fit into her harness due to her size, but she was generally the nicest, most jovial person Hallie had ever met. Even so, terror now etched her round face.

Next to her sat Dr. Luke Messa. He was a young guy like Bryant, about the same age as Hallie, whereas both Angela and Cecilia were older by about ten years. Were it not for Luke's intellect, Hallie might've mistaken him for a soldier based on his build. He, too, clutched the ends of his armrests with white-knuckled intensity.

Another blast tore into the ship, and this time sparks rained down from the ceiling with the impact.

The loud hiss of steam escaping turned Hallie's head toward their cargo safely sealed in a cylindrical containment pod held in a transparent suspension crate. It wasn't much bigger than a thermos, and blue light from the suspension crate glinted off its chrome exterior.

It was, without question, what their pursuers were after. It was the only reason worth attacking a science vessel.

But how did they know about it in the first place? The whole project was top secret, sealed just as tightly as the containment pod itself.

The "how" didn't matter now. All that mattered was escaping their pursuers and getting that containment pod to its rightful owners.

The ship rattled again, and more sparks rained down on them, prickling the back of Hallie's neck. She brushed the sparks away, hoping they hadn't singed her skin too badly.

"We're locked," Captain Dawes shouted. "Brace for warp!"

He pressed his palm against one of the cockpit screens, and the ship lurched toward the stars.

Hallie's stomach lurched with it.

She blinked, and the stars changed. They somehow seemed closer, slightly larger.

The red laser beams no longer streaked past the ship. Cecilia released her grip on Hallie's hand, and everyone exhaled a breath of relief.

"Shields at 58%. Scans show no sign of the enemy," Bryant reported, his voice far calmer than before.

"It won't last," Captain Dawes grumbled. "They'll catch up. They always do."

Hallie's heart rate had slowed, but now it sped back up. "What can we do?"

Captain Dawes and Bryant peered back at her from their chairs in the cockpit. Neither of them spoke at first.

"Not a lot of options," Captain Dawes finally said. "Not a lot out this far. That's why we took this route—less chance of being discovered."

"No habitable planets or moons. No space stations or settlements." Bryant's crisp blue eyes locked on Hallie, and he gave a slight grin. "Wasn't supposed to happen like this. A quiet jaunt, they said."

"Not anymore," Captain Dawes said. "We just have to keep running. Jump when we can, evade when we can't. Give the shields as much time to replenish between bouts as possible. Not much else we can do until we get closer to our destination."

"And once we're in range..." Bryant held up his fist with his index finger extended and his thumb up, as if mimicking a gun. "...pew, pew! The orbital platforms will blow anyone following us clear out of the sky. Or... space, I guess."

Captain Dawes continued, "Until then, we—"

Something blipped on the screens in the cockpit, and they both turned back toward it. Hallie couldn't see the source, but she'd heard it, plain as day, and trepidation seized her chest anew.

"They found us already?" she asked.

Cecilia grabbed her hand again, and she inhaled a sharp breath. Hallie didn't blame her on either count.

"No... this is something bigger," Bryant said. "The thing's huge... giving off crazy heat signatures. Just the sheer size of it... I've never seen anything like it."

"I have," Captain Dawes said. "And it may just be that we've found our salvation. Chart a course straight for it, Bryant."

"Aye, Captain. Looks like... maybe a day? Two at the most?"

Hallie gulped. Could they last that long?

"It's our best shot," Captain Dawes said. "Our *only* shot. We've got to try."

Whatever "it" was, Hallie agreed with the captain. Their mission was too important to fail, and the contents of that containment pod were too valuable to fall into the wrong hands.

Both Captain Dawes and Bryant looked back at Hallie again.

She nodded to them. "Do it."

ONE

Less than one year after leaving Ketarus-4

"Hold 'er steady, now," Captain Enix Marlowe said over the comms. "You're almost there. Nice and easy."

Justin Barclay stood at his station in the drill chamber below, listening to Captain Marlowe talking to himself as he guided the *Viridian*, a Stinger-Class rig, ever closer to the asteroid. The closer they got, the bigger the asteroid loomed in the viewscreen on Justin's workspace console.

An array of targeting reticles, some red, some yellow, and some blue, bounced up and down over the image as the rig's sensors strained to detect stores of copalion and precious metals inside. At a preliminary glance, it looked like they might have found a good one.

"Show me those claws, Arlie," Captain Marlowe said.

"Copy," Arlie Bush, the rig's first officer said.

The grinding and creaking of the rig's articulated landing gear filled the excavation decks. On Justin's screen, eight spiderlike legs made of a hyper-strong alloy unfolded past the asteroid and promptly clamped onto its rocky surface. Drill bits emerged from the base of each leg, whirred to life, and dug into the asteroid, anchoring the rig to it.

Justin flexed the metal fingers of his right hand. Now his job would begin.

"Great landing," Captain Marlowe said over the comms, again more to himself than anyone else. "Excavation crew, we're secure. Start suckin' out that cream filling."

Justin smirked. Captain Marlowe's line was the same every time they landed on a new asteroid. But it was his ship. He could say whatever he wanted to.

[You good, JB?] Keontae's voice said inside Justin's head.

"Yeah," Justin muttered. "Not my first asterodeo."

[Chill, man. Your heart rate's elevated. Just lookin' out for you.]

"I'm fine. Might be a big score," Justin said. "And I don't need you reporting on my vitals every five minutes."

[I said *chill*, man. Just concerned for you. That's all.]

"You say somethin', Barclay?"

Justin turned to his right. His shift supervisor, Rowley Pine, was giving him his usual suspicious beady-eyed glare. The guy had a ring of long hair hanging at about ear-level, but the top of his head was shiny and bald, and he had crooked yellow teeth. All in all, he looked more like a serial rapist than a rig-runner.

"All good, Rowley." Justin gave him a metallic thumbs-up in lieu of the metallic middle finger he wanted to give him.

"Then *focus*," Rowley barked. It was his preferred tone—at least when he wasn't growling or grumbling. "Airlock doors are open. Line up the drill, and shoot your shot."

"Yep. On it." Justin gritted his teeth. He lowered his voice. "You mind helping me with this one?"

[I dunno, JB. You been givin' me some attitude. Not sure you deserve the help,] Keontae said.

Justin could almost picture his best friend's glowing green form standing at the console next to him, folding his arms. But it was just his imagination. Keontae was safely concealed within Justin's arm, as usual.

Justin placed his metal right palm on the control screen embedded in the console. It was older tech, but retrofitting new terminals and new controls for the *Viridian's* drill would've cost more than the old rig was even worth, so Captain Marlowe had decided to make do with what he had.

"We both know you've got the steadier hand," Justin said as he tried to guide the reticle, now a singular blue crosshairs shape instead of several in different colors, to find the most ideal spot to target on the asteroid's surface. The reticle bounced and wavered and shook as he moved it.

The closer he could land it to their quarry, the higher accuracy the drill would have in reaching the asteroid's biggest reserves. Higher accuracy meant more yield for their work, and more yield meant more pay in the long run.

And since they only got one shot per asteroid, he had to nail the shot the first time.

Justin had run the drill's targeting for a handful of asteroids now, but he'd only done one of them manually. The other times, Keontae had entered the system from Justin's arm and nailed the targeting with near-perfect accuracy each time.

The one time Justin tried it, he'd only gotten 84% accuracy. It wasn't a bad number, but when Keontae could hit 98% or higher each time, it made no sense for Justin to even try.

[I'm gonna need more than that, JB,] Keontae said.

Justin clenched his teeth again. "Fine. I'm sorry I got snippy with you."

[And?]

"And you're the greatest."

[Damn right I am,] Keontae said. [Now sit back and watch the master do his work.]

A familiar tingle buzzed in Justin's metal fingertips and palm, and he felt Keontae's presence leave his arm and enter the drill system. Immediately, the reticle's wobbling slowed to a soft vibration, and then it went entirely still.

"What's the holdup, Barclay?" Rowley barked.

"Don't get your dick in a knot, Rowley," Justin quipped. "I know what I'm doing."

"We don't have time for your bullshit," Rowley snapped. "Get your targeting set. Shift's over in a half hour, and I want us balls-deep in this rock before that bell sounds."

Justin was about to return fire, but Al Paulson, another member of the excavation team, sounded off first. "The only thing you've ever been balls-deep in was that holo-girl back on Yovado-2. Or... was it a guy?"

"*Shut up*, Paulson." Rowley pointed an accusatory finger at him. "Or you're gonna wake up without any balls at all."

The viewscreen in front of Justin bleeped, and the targeting reticle turned bright green—pretty much the same color as Keontae when he projected into his human form. A small percentage indicator under the reticle read "100% accuracy." The highest percentage possible, and virtually impossible for any human to hit.

Any normal human, anyway.

"Ha!" Justin whirled around. "Suck on that, Rowley."

Rowley's countenance darkened, and his perpetual scowl deepened into a mopey frown. "You are a bastard, Barclay."

"Call me what you like, you jealous prick," Justin countered. As he picked up the comms with his human left hand, the metal fingers of his right hand tingled again. He pressed the "talk" button on the comms and said, "We're clear to begin drilling... with 100% accuracy."

"Are you kiddin' me?" A woman's voice crackled over the comms—Shaneesha, who was running the containment cylinders for this shift. She was one of eight on the excavation team, including Justin, Al, and Rowley. "How'd you hit the bullseye on that shaky-ass system? Didn't think that was possible."

Justin paused to consider how best to answer that. Then he grinned. "Call it supernatural intervention."

[Finally, I get the credit I so rightfully deserve,] Keontae said.

With the targeting in place, Justin's job was done for the time being. Now he could watch as the drill positioned itself to do its work. Guided by his—well, by *Keontae's* perfect targeting, the drill emerged from a giant dome in the ceiling above Justin's position and extended down toward the containment field below and the asteroid beyond.

Normally, Justin used the viewscreen on his terminal to track the drill's movements, but not for this part. He loved watching the old machine do its work.

The drill could perform a wide range of functions, including actual manual drilling with an arsenal of metal alloy drill bits, all of them harder than diamonds, as well as via purdonic lasers. It could puncture through the solid rock of an asteroid in a variety of ways, utilizing combinations of manual and laser-based drilling when necessary.

Despite its age, the drill had yet to fail to do its job.

As the drill's long cylindrical shaft continued to descend toward the glowing orange containment field, past the various sublevels of the rig, Justin had to admit Rowley was right: it did kind of resemble a big dick. He resolved to try not to think about it.

The containment field, now their last line of defense against the vacuum of space, allowed the drill's shaft through without incident. While Justin didn't understand exactly how it worked, he knew that the drill's outer shell was made of an alloy that could pass through the containment field without breaking its seal.

Because if that seal decided to break, or if the energy couplings on the containment field faltered, they'd all be sucked into the vacuum of space.

The sight of the drill pushing through the containment field so many levels down reignited Justin's sense of vertigo. He'd mostly overcome it thanks to the shit he'd faced back at Andridge Copalion Mine (ACM)-1134, but every now and then it popped back up. His vision spun and swirled, and he blinked hard and looked away.

Don't think about any of that, Justin told himself. *Just do your job.*

[Easy, JB,] Keontae said. [Just breathe, brother.]

"I *am* breathing." With each new breath, the stink of old metal alloys, dust, grease, oil, and fuel filled his nose. Strangely, the mixture of scents stilled his churning stomach and his swirling vision instead of doing the opposite.

[Well, breathe *more,*] Keontae said.

"Thanks," Justin replied, his voice flat. "I'm good now."

Below him, a vivid yellow light flashed bright, then it dimmed. Instead of looking down again, Justin watched the viewscreen on his console. The drill's purdonic laser had fired.

Apparently, whoever was running the penetration sequence—also a terrible name for it—had decided the asteroid's geological composition would better play with the laser than with a puncture from one of the alloy drill bits.

Whatever the case, his job now was to make sure the drill stayed on course. As wannabe planets, asteroids' makeups could vary drastically from layer to layer. Those variations in asteroids' elemental structure could potentially push the drill off course, whether it was using the laser or one of the drill bits, as could any seismic instability.

It was Justin's job now to recalibrate and reposition the drill as needed. Or, more accurately, it was Keontae's job.

Justin's right shoulder ached with phantom pain. It had long since healed and fully integrated his robotic arm after the accident back in ACM-1134 on Ketarus-4, but Justin still remembered the pain of losing his arm.

Lingering aches had followed him in the subsequent days and weeks, especially in light of everything else he'd endured in that time, and they were easy to recall now, right when he really *didn't* want to recall them. Naturally.

But he'd left all of that behind. All of it except for Keontae, who'd managed to hitch a ride in his arm before Justin left the planet. And now they were bound to each other, at least until they found a better option.

The drill wobbled a bit. Justin's metal palm and fingers touched the console again, and again they tingled. Keontae righted the drill's aim, and the next instant, the drill broke through.

On the viewscreen, Justin saw the telltale teal glow of copalion, the most energy-rich and volatile fuel known to the universe.

"Jackpot," Bobby Carlisle's voice scraped over the comms.

Justin's grin returned. He'd spent almost the last decade mining the teal stuff on distant worlds, working for every major mining company in the galaxy. But after all that had happened at ACM-1134, he'd vowed never to mess with the stuff again.

The problem was, he didn't know how to do much else. When he'd happened upon Captain Marlowe's rig and his freelance extraction operation, Justin figured it was an acceptable compromise.

Now that he'd gotten his hands dirty as a rig-runner, Justin had reached a point where he didn't mind extracting copalion, even though he hated the stuff and how it drove greed across the galaxy. But that greed meant this haul was going to make them all a lot of money.

A series of joyous whoops and shouts sounded throughout the excavation decks. Even in the sparse lighting in this part of the rig, Justin saw the raised fists of at least two of his coworkers. They'd be celebrating after their shift with home-made rig hooch—something Justin had tried once and had resolved to never drink again after they'd explained how they made it.

The drill continued to lower into the asteroid and began to siphon the raw copalion up into its interior, where a network of pipes redirected it into one of Shaneesha's storage cylinders—one specifically designed for holding copalion. Others held molten silver, gold, and platinum, and others still held other precious and semiprecious metals, also molten.

But even combining all of those metals wouldn't come close to fetching the kind of price the copalion would. Then again, filling the copalion cylinder was never a sure thing. They'd gotten damned lucky to find a score this big.

The reticle on the screen flickered red, and then it flickered out. A shudder rocked through the drill, rattling the entire rig.

That's not normal.

Justin spoke to the viewscreen—to Keontae inside the system with his voice. "What's going on?"

An alert flashed onto the screen. {: Seismic Instability Detected :}

Justin's metal fingers tingled, and Keontae's voice filled his mind again. [We gotta pull out, JB. This is bad.]

Justin cursed. He deactivated the targeting system and got on the comms. "We're in trouble. Retract the drill."

"Belay that," Rowley thundered over the comms. "I'm watching the seis-mometer right now. We're well within safe ranges."

[He's full of shit, JB,] Keontae warned. [We got plenty of copalion. Don't let this leech be greedy, or he's gonna kill all of us.]

"You're sure?" Justin asked, away from the comms.

[Absolutely. Checked the data myself. Ran scenarios. Likelihood of a catastrophic failure is 68% and risin' with each gulp of copalion we take out of 'er.]

Justin hadn't been working this gig for long, but he'd quickly learned that all asteroids eventually grew too unstable for extraction operations to continue. But for the catastrophic failure potential to already be at 68% and rising—well, that was a nightmare scenario only moments away, unless they did something.

[Put me back in the system. I'll handle it,] Keontae said.

"No," Justin said. "This has to be Captain Marlowe's call."

The drill shuddered again, for longer this time, and the old rig rumbled and creaked in response.

"Shut it down," Justin repeated into the comms. "The asteroid's gonna break apart. If we lose the drill, we're done out here indefinitely, or worse."

"You're sure about this, Barclay?" Captain Marlowe asked over the comms.

Justin glanced up, though he couldn't see the cockpit above him from his position. There were too many other decks and metal implements separating them for that. "Totally sure."

"He's got shit-for-brains, as usual, Captain," Rowley insisted. "We've only gotten about half the copalion, and that drill's rated for way more seismic strain than what this rock is outputting."

"I'm telling you, Captain," Justin cut in, "this is bad news waiting to happen."

"And I'm telling you to *shut the hell up*, Barclay," Rowley shouted. "You're not gonna tank *my* payday because you piss yourself every time the rig shudders."

"Push it as far as you safely can," Captain Marlowe said. "And cut the bickering. Focus on your jobs."

Justin pressed further. "Captain, I—"

"Enough, Barclay," Captain Marlowe ordered. "We keep pulling until we can't anymore."

As if on cue, the drill and the rig shuddered again, longer and more violently this time.

"Captain, if we keep pulling, there won't be a 'we' anymore," Justin said.

"Ignore him," Rowley shouted over the rumbling. "We've just hit the halfway point. We get the rest of it, and it pays for the whole excursion twelve or fifteen times over."

[These dumbasses are gonna get us killed, JB,] Keontae said. [Well, you at least. I'm already dead... technically.]

"If I put you back into the system, can you shut it down?" Justin asked.

Before Keontae could answer, an ear-piercing *crack* ripped through the ship, followed by a klaxon blaring an alarm.

Justin looked at his viewscreen. Then, not believing his eyes, he rushed to the railing at the edge of his deck and looked down, vertigo be damned.

Below him, a huge fissure had nearly split the asteroid in two, with the drill still lodged in the center.

TWO

The asteroid was literally breaking apart beneath the ship, and chunks of rock, now broken free, pelted the *Viridian's* hull and sparked against the containment field. The drill continued to buck and bounce and wobble, and the rig danced along, following the drill's dynamic lead.

Justin stole a glance at Rowley, whose expression had shifted to sheer terror—three minutes too late.

[Put me back in the system, JB!] Keontae shouted in his mind. [Now!]

Justin smacked his palm against the console with such force that he didn't feel Keontae leave this time, but he'd gotten into the system all the same.

Keontae had already navigated the rig's network many times over since they'd boarded the ship, and now he moved at light speed through the circuits and connections to salvage not only the drill but also the entire operation.

Justin didn't know if the drill could actually *be* saved. With copalion's potential for volatility in a confined space, they might've already doomed the drill. If they couldn't extract it in time, and the asteroid blew, the best they could hope for was the drill snapping off.

At worst, the force of the shattering asteroid could tear the rig itself apart and kill them all.

Justin knew each of the workers on his shift—Rowley included—were frantically doing their part to forestall the rig's destruction, but he also knew that Keontae was already working on all of it faster than any human ever could.

"Captain," Justin said into the comms, "be ready to detach once the drill is clear. Maybe sooner, if—"

"Understood, Barclay," Captain Marlowe replied. "First Officer Bush is ready."

The asteroid was a hefty size, at least three times the size of the rig herself, but it was far from the largest they'd harvested since Justin had come on board. For all he knew, the rig's spidery legs might be all that still held the asteroid together. If that was the case, maybe they could extract the drill without it sustaining more damage.

"The drill's retracting," Rowley shouted into the comms. "It just cleared the containment field. Close the—"

The airlock doors clapped shut before he could finish his command.

The quaking persisted, now more rigorous than ever, but the drill was clear of the asteroid and encased inside the rig once again.

With his hand on the console, Justin spoke into the comms. "Now, Captain!"

The same grumbling of old parts and gears and pistons rattled throughout the rig, but then the shrieking of metal racked Justin's ears, followed by the thunder of hundreds of boulder-sized raindrops pattering on the *Viridian's* hull.

Justin refocused on his viewscreen. The asteroid had blown apart, and one entire side of the rig's spider legs hung below it, warped and useless, flopping against the void of space and getting battered by progressively smaller chunks of rock.

Before long, they'd cleared the asteroid field entirely and just floated against a black backdrop dotted with trillions of white pinpricks.

Only then did the shaking fully stop.

Only then did Justin allow himself to breathe full breaths.

[We're good, JB.] Keontae must've reentered Justin's arm at some point along the way. [Too damn close, but we're good now. Except for that landing gear.]

Justin just nodded and breathed. By this point, he'd had more near-death experiences than anyone he'd ever heard of, and he had no desire to add any more to his collection.

"Barclay, Rowley," Captain Marlowe said over the comms, "my quarters. Quick like a scorper."

Justin cursed under his breath, then he set off toward the rig's living quarters.

JUSTIN'S JOURNEY from the excavation decks to the *Viridian's* main levels took him up a series of metal staircases and through narrow corridors that made him grateful he had vertigo instead of claustrophobia.

The *Viridian* was a Stinger-Class rig, but like most ships of its type, the bottom line was ever in the forefront of the owner/operator's mind. As such, certain corners got cut. Sacrifices were made. No one aboard lived anything even close to a glamorous lifestyle. Practically speaking, the word "luxury" meant the same thing as "fantasy."

In his short duration aboard the rig, Justin had heard the *Viridian* referred to as a *Stingier*-Class ship plenty of times, and it was absolutely true.

He pushed it all out of his mind, though. He passed the bunkroom, then the meager kitchen and dining area, then the showers and toilets.

Justin hadn't seen the rig's whole system yet, but somewhere, buried beneath pipes and hoses and metal, a water-purification system recycled their waste into potable water—in theory, anyway. The water still had a weird tang to it, so he avoided drinking it when he could.

When he couldn't, he reassured himself it was just leftover chemical treatments rather than lingering raw sewage, or he tried not to think about it at all.

He reached the captain's quarters next, and he knocked on one of the few closed doors on the entire ship. The hatch wheel spun, and the door swung inward, into the chamber within. First Officer Arlie Bush, a ginger-headed firecracker compacted into the body of a forty-something, muscular five-foot-two cheerleader, stood before him.

She was also Captain Marlowe's wife, or life partner, or whatever, and they shared the captain's quarters. But instead of a ring, an ornate silver tattoo adorned the base of her ring finger and curled around to its underside.

Justin waved at her.

She scowled and motioned him inside with her head.

[Daaaaamn. It's gonna be like that, I guess,] Keontae said. [Look, if they fire you for doin' the right thing and goin' against your jackass supervisor, then walk away. Not worth those headaches.]

Justin didn't want to answer him, not in such a confined space where everyone could hear him responding. It would come across as him talking to himself. Captain Marlowe could get away with that at times—it was his ship, after all—but Justin figured he'd better not push his luck any more than he already had.

He'd only been in the captain's quarters once before. He remembered the disheveled bed with its burgundy blankets rumpled and stretched across it as if an army had marched over the mattress. Two off-white pillows lay there like two dead battered bodies left in the soldiers' wake.

Arlie motioned him toward an adjacent chamber, which in and of itself gave the captain's quarters a sort of homey feel by virtue of having more than one room. Rounded metal walls arched upward and became the ceiling, then they arched back down again on the other side of both chambers, which also made the quarters feel a bit like a jail cell.

In the adjacent chamber, Justin found Captain Marlowe and Rowley Pine sitting at a harsh but simple metal table, both hunched over steaming mugs as if meditating, or perhaps deep in prayer. At that same table, Justin had signed his employment contract with Captain Marlowe with nothing but a firm handshake and a smile.

Now they might exchange another handshake to terminate his employment at the next port of call.

[Stay cool, JB,] Keontae told him. [Ignore what I said earlier. There's no reason to fret. You were in the right, after all.]

I was in the right at ACM-1134, too, and that didn't exactly go as planned, Justin mused.

Arlie cleared her throat, and Captain Marlowe looked up. Also somewhere in his forties, he had the scarred face of a veteran soldier, with two-day-old stubble on his chin, jaw, and upper lip. Brown hair cut short, but not military short, covered enough of his head that he could pass for a civilian if needed, and he had green eyes like two dull emeralds.

He chewed on a narrow metal stick of some sort, malleable enough that he wasn't breaking his teeth, but metal all the same. How he tolerated it, Justin didn't know.

Captain Marlowe shifted the metal stick in his mouth to the opposite side and motioned toward the tortured metal chair across from Rowley. "Have a seat, Justin."

In an occupation devoid of any sort of comfort and optimized for efficiency on even the most minute levels, Justin couldn't fault Captain Marlowe for having such a chair—much less a set of four of them—around his equally industrial table.

But that didn't mean Justin wanted to sit in it after a long day of working the drill, either, especially after how bad it had been the first time.

Still, he complied.

Huh. Not as bad as it looked or as bad as he'd remembered.

"Drink?" Captain Marlowe offered. "Hot or cold?"

"Neither," Justin said. "If you don't mind, Captain, I'd like to cut to the chase on this, wherever it may lead."

Rowley scoffed and stared at Justin with his beady brown eyes. "Suits me just fine. The sooner you're canned, the sooner I don't have to look at that camel's ass you call a face anymore."

[You'd better come across this table at him, JB, or I'm gonna make your arm do it for you,] Keontae warned.

A half dozen retorts rifled through Justin's mind, both to Keontae and to Rowley, but he held his tongue... for now. In the absence of Justin's clapback, Captain Marlowe spoke.

"You don't have room to talk, Rowley," he said. "Especially when your face looks like what *comes out* of a camel's ass."

Justin granted himself a grin as Keontae's laugh filled his mind.

[I like this dude,] Keontae said.

Rowley wasn't about to retort to the captain's zinger, so he clamped his mouth shut and forced a grin. His long greasy hair hung to his shoulders, caught somewhere between loose curls and tight waves, and he looked like he hadn't shaved in half a Coalition Standard Week. The tranquil lights overhead gleamed off his bald head.

Definitely a "rapist" vibe, Justin mused. *At the end of the day, at least I don't have to look like* that.

"Arlie, join us?"

She took the seat opposite Captain Marlowe, who faced Justin and Rowley again.

"As you know, First Officer Bush and I make these types of decisions together."

Decisions? Justin's stomach churned like it had when the asteroid's instability was shaking the entire rig. *I knew it. I'm getting axed.*

"But before we make any decisions, I called you both here to honor the promise I made when you signed on: that you'll get a fair hearing with me personally if there are any major disputes."

"And when we're all about to die," Arlie interjected, "it counts as a major dispute."

"Exactly." Captain Marlowe glanced between Justin and Rowley. "As you know, we were in the bridge when everything went down, and there's only so much I can glean from the screens up there. So I want a detailed accounting of what happened, starting with Rowley."

"My pleasure, Captain." Rowley's beady eyes bored into Justin yet again.

Captain Marlowe held up his hand. "The *short* version, Rowley."

"How short? I could just say 'Barclay is a pussy who doesn't know what the hell he's doing up here and should be fired immediately.'"

[C'mon, JB,] Keontae prodded. [Knock this bitch's teeth out.]

Against his inclinations to follow Keontae's urgings, Justin held his position.

"Gonna need more than that," Captain Marlowe said.

He launched into a diatribe against Justin, enumerating not only what he thought Justin had done wrong at the end of his last shift but in practically every shift since he'd joined the operation.

Justin weathered it all until Rowley uttered his final condemnation.

"So like I said at the beginning, Barclay is a pussy who doesn't know what the hell he's doing up here and should be fired immediately." He leaned back in his chair and folded his meaty arms across his chest.

Justin jumped to his feet and reached across the table before the final word escaped Rowley's pudgy lips. His metal right hand latched onto the thick material of Rowley's shirt collar, but instead of hauling him back over the table, Justin scrambled on top of it, chasing him.

Rowley's mug toppled over and spilled off the edge of the table, but Justin didn't stop. He kept going over the table until a wide-eyed Rowley toppled backward onto the metal floor, chair and all.

Justin ended up on top of him with his left fist raised, while Rowley cowered beneath him and tried to cover his face with his hands and arms. But instead of raining down punishment on Rowley's camel-shit face, Justin left his fist elevated just long enough that Captain Marlowe and Arlie had time to pull him off.

[Why didn't you hit 'im, JB? C'mon, man! You had that bum right where you wanted 'im!]

Justin had indeed put Rowley where he'd wanted him, but he'd planned the action to go down that way.

He'd gone over the table because it gave him more time to get a stronger position. He'd gotten on top of Rowley to show he wasn't going to take any shit from him. But he'd shown just enough restraint to demonstrate that he actually did have control over his actions.

And most importantly of all, he'd shown he wasn't a pussy.

"Alright, alright," Captain Marlowe said as he and Arlie separated Justin from Rowley. "Good show, but if I wanted to see a fight, I'd visit my in-laws."

Justin stood his ground on the opposite side of the table from Rowley. Arlie's hand braced against his chest as if to hold him in place. He probably could've gotten past her, but something about her posture made him think he'd pay for it if he tried, so he stayed put.

"See? He's unhinged." Rowley pointed at Justin as Captain Marlowe pulled him up to his feet. "He's a danger to himself and to all of us. Fire his ass and drop him at the next station."

"Easy, Rowley," Captain Marlowe said. "Pick up your chair and have a seat. You had your say. Now Justin gets his."

Arlie lowered her hand from Justin's chest and motioned him toward the table again. Once everyone got seated, Captain Marlowe nodded at Justin.

As Rowley had done, Justin laid out everything he'd seen and experienced at the end of the last shift. He explained everything except for Keontae's involvement. If Justin could keep him a secret, he would. No one needed to know about that.

In many ways, Keontae was his secret weapon. He'd served as locksmith, a pathway to hacking pretty much any computer system in the galaxy. If Justin made it known he had such an ally embedded within his arm, who knew how someone might try to exploit it?

For Justin's part, ever since Keontae had made his presence known back on

Jevilos-6, Justin hadn't used him as a secret weapon, a locksmith, or to hack any systems other than those of the rig. And even then, he'd only hacked the rig as a failsafe. Keontae could make the system dance to his whims faster than human operators could issue commands to it.

That access had just played a major role in saving the rig and everyone on it.

But Justin couldn't share any of that because doing so would expose Keontae—and him—to scrutiny they didn't need. They'd had enough of that in their dealings with ACM.

So Justin explained what he could as truthfully as he could and let it linger in the captain's quarters. All the while, Captain Marlowe listened to him with an attentive, insightful expression on his face. It made Justin wonder if he somehow knew about Keontae anyway... but how could he?

Rowley eagerly filled the silence following Justin's explanation. "Bullshit."

Justin clenched his fists at his sides to keep from launching across the table again. "Or not. We're alive, and the rig is damaged."

"And we scored a *huge* haul of copalion in the process," Rowley said. "More than enough to cover the damages. And the drill's still intact and functional."

"As far as we *know*," Justin countered. "We haven't run full diagnostics on it yet."

[Uh, actually, JB,] Keontae said, [I did run some diagnostics before I jumped out, and it seemed like everythin' was good.]

Justin clenched his teeth. He couldn't exactly say that aloud. Instead, he added, "And even if the drill is good to go, we can't land on any more asteroids until the landing gear is repaired. Without half the legs functioning, we can't latch onto anything, so we can't safely drill or extract."

Rowley shrugged. "So next time we dock, we'll get it fixed. Then we'll throw your lame ass off the rig and rid ourselves of the Barclay curse for good."

"Alright, enough." Captain Marlowe leaned forward and put his hand between them. They both went silent.

[Reckonin' time,] Keontae said. [Hope we at least get outta here with enough to finally get back to Bortundi.]

Justin ignored his comment and waited for Captain Marlowe to continue.

"As you know, your rig chief, Gerald, took ill right after we left Jevilos-6," he said. "He's really supposed to be the one mediating these discussions instead of me, but in his condition, that's not gonna happen... ever again."

Justin and Rowley's staring match shattered, and they both shifted their full attention to Captain Marlowe.

"Gerald is dead."

Justin wondered if the violent shakes when the asteroid was breaking apart had played a role in doing Gerald in, but Captain Marlowe put that idea to rest right away.

"Died right after your shift started this morning." He switched the metal stick to the other side of his mouth and crunched down on it anew. "Passed in his sleep, Doc Carrington said. May we all be so fortunate."

Even as Captain Marlowe said it, Justin detected a hint of sarcasm, or perhaps even disdain in his voice.

"Anyway, now we're short a rig chief." Captain Marlowe stared at Rowley. "And I need someone to fill the role."

[Great. They're gonna fire your ass *and* promote this needle-dick?] Keontae's voice framed Justin's thoughts perfectly. [Talk about injustice.]

"And in light of the day's events, I've decided that's gonna be Justin."

THREE

"What?" Rowley stood up so fast that his chair toppled back again. "You're *demoting* me?"

"No, moron," Arlie said. "Do you even know what 'demotion' means? You're staying on as shift supervisor. No change."

Justin would've grinned, but he was still too shocked at Captain Marlowe's decree.

[Finally, a good twist for you,] Keontae said. [Really happy for you, bro. Proud of you, too.]

"Thanks, bud," Justin said aloud.

"You're welcome..." Captain Marlowe squinted at him and added, "Bud."

Justin blinked away his surprise and stood up to shake his hand. "Oh. Sorry, Captain. Thank you, *sir*, I mean."

Captain Marlowe stood as well and returned the handshake. "We can be buds as well, if you want. Eventually. Prove yourself, and we may just be friends for life."

"This is an outrage!" Rowley snapped.

"No, *you* are outraged," Arlie said, still sitting. "There's a difference."

Rowley jammed his thumb into his chest. "I've been workin' this rig for two years. Two. Years. I started as a grunt and worked my way up to shift supervisor, fourth fastest in the rig's history, by your own admission."

"Not exactly a high bar, Rowley." Arlie folded her arms.

Unfazed, Rowley continued, "Yet you promote this greenhorn before *me?*"

"He deserves it. He was right about the asteroid," Captain Marlowe said.

"But he was *wrong* about the payload!" Rowley barked. "Don't you wanna make money?"

"He had the rig's long-term interests in mind. You were only thinking in the short term. Only thinking of yourself," Captain Marlowe said. "You're like a navigator who can't see past his own nose. Not much good when charting a course through the galaxy."

Rowley's mouth hung open wide. "This ain't fair!"

"You don't like it, you're free to get off at the next stop, which'll be soon since we need to get that landing gear fixed." Captain Marlowe nodded toward Justin. "Otherwise, say hello to your new boss."

Rowley's face had been red before, but now he resembled a tomato—an ugly one, at that. He pointed a pasty finger at Justin, seething. "You... I'll get even. I *promise* you that. You won't last three full shifts in this job. It should be mine, and I'm gonna get it."

Justin glanced at Arlie, who mouthed the words, "He's never gonna get it."

"Enough of this bullshit. I'm leaving." Rowley stormed out of the chamber and into the adjacent one. Justin heard the groan of the heavy metal door opening, then it banged shut, rattling and creaking the captain's quarters.

"Sorry 'bout the ruckus," Captain Marlowe said. "I don't expect he'll stick around, and I don't think he has any cards he can really play against you. Just let 'im brood 'til we dock somewhere, and then he'll probably leave."

"Any chance you can *make* him leave?" Justin offered.

Captain Marlowe shrugged. "It gets bad enough between you two, sure. I'd pick you under any set of stars. If not, he's generally a capable rig-runner, albeit a greedy one. I'd rather not have to replace him if I can avoid it. I hate dealing with this personnel shit."

"I know the feeling," Justin said.

"Too bad for you, since it's your job now." Captain Marlowe nudged Justin's shoulder and headed over to a small refrigeration unit mounted to the wall. He popped it open and pulled out an unmarked bottle of clear brown liquid. "But hey, you got the promotion, so we're gonna celebrate with a drink of the good stuff."

He produced three shot glasses, none of them actually glass but made of metal instead, and passed them to Justin and Arlie, who still hadn't bothered to stand up. Captain Marlowe poured each of them a shot, and they shared a clink and downed the drink.

It tasted bitter and sweet and smoky all at once. Justin hated the taste, but he appreciated the camaraderie and the intention behind it. He tried not to show his disdain for the flavor, but he doubted he was succeeding.

"Good, huh?" Captain Marlowe clapped him on his shoulder and then headed to the fridge to put the bottle back inside.

"Yeah," Justin rasped. "Definitely, Captain."

Upon his return, Captain Marlowe motioned for Justin to sit again. "Look, when we're alone, in private, call me Enix. Out there, 'captain' is fine because we need some semblance of rule and authority, but in here, Enix is okay."

"Alright... Enix," Justin said.

"Gotta be honest with you, kid..." Captain Marlowe pointed down at the table, still staring at Justin. "...if you hadn't come over this table at him, I wouldn't have given you the job. I had to know you wouldn't give in when things got too tough."

Justin had to physically restrain every fiber of his being to keep from laughing in Captain Marlowe's face.

[Man, if he only knew,] Keontae said with a chuckle. [He's got no idea the shit we've been through.]

"Well, Enix," Justin said with a smile, "when it comes to fighting, you can trust that it's the one area where I'll never let you down."

[Understatement of the millennium, bro.]

Captain Marlowe nodded. "Noted and appreciated. You'll do well as the new rig chief."

"Speaking of which, where are we docking to get the legs fixed?" Justin asked.

"We've got some options. None are close. We're a few weeks away from any civilization advanced enough to be able to repair it at a reasonable price. I'm not looking to get scalped on the parts and repairs, so we'll probably just make this a short run and head straight back to Jevilos-6.

"Rowley was right about the copalion being worth a fortune. Might as well sell it, spend it, resupply, get repairs, and then get back out here right away," Captain Marlowe said. "Better than losing a bigger chunk and having to rely on junkyard parts and hack repairmen. So we're already on autopilot, heading back."

Justin nodded. It made sense.

"Until then, just get used to your new gig. You get your own quarters now, so collect your stuff and move into Gerald's old room. You'll get a nice raise, too. I'm cutting you in for his percentage for the whole trip. He's dead, so he doesn't need it, and he had no family to speak of."

Justin blinked at him. "Wow. Thanks."

[Good shit. That's a big bump,] Keontae agreed.

"Is... is Gerald's body still...?"

"Airlock," Arlie said. "Room's clear."

Justin's stunned expression shifted to her.

"Like I said, no family to speak of. It's a dignified way to put someone at rest. Military does it all the time," Captain Marlowe said.

Justin wasn't sure he'd want his body jettisoned like so much space junk and waste, but if it was good enough for the military, he supposed it was good enough for Gerald.

"For now, make the rounds, oversee the repairs to the drill, if any, and get familiar with all the shift workers," Captain Marlowe concluded.

[I know of one particular worker you're lookin' to get more familiar with,] Keontae taunted. [*Much* more familiar.]

Justin ignored him. "Sounds like a plan."

Captain Marlowe extended his hand again, and Justin shook it.

"Thanks again, Enix," Justin said. "I won't let you down."

"No, you won't. And that's why I gave you the job." Captain Marlowe smiled, and the scars on his face crinkled with the expression. "Arlie will show you out."

Arlie stood and motioned toward the adjacent chamber, the one with the disheveled bed.

"Oh, Justin?" Captain Marlowe said before he could leave. "Dinner with us tonight, in here. Don't know you well yet, but that's gotta change, especially if we're gonna be 'buds.'"

Justin chuckled. "You got it, 'bud.'"

To Dr. Hallie Hayes's great relief, the *Persimmon's* pursuers still hadn't managed to catch up with them.

Captain Dawes had employed a few of his finest tricks and tactics to keep them guessing. One of them had included a dummy rocket marked with the *Persimmon's* ship signature, which they'd launched in a totally different direction from their actual heading.

Hallie had been there when Captain Dawes insisted their employers "pony up" for the added expense, and already it had proven its worth. Their shields had crept back up to 97%. It wouldn't be much longer until they reached their alternate destination and, hopefully, safe passage to their real destination.

She poked her head into the cockpit. "How's the progress?"

"Still going well." Bryant showed her a clean, perfect smile, and she had to quell the butterflies in her stomach from becoming bats.

He was handsome, but she'd already decided they weren't compatible, even in spite of her physical attraction to him. He just wasn't mature enough for her—still had that fresh-out-of-the-academy vibe to him.

Maybe in five years, after he grows up a little bit... But after this voyage, she doubted she'd ever see him again, so she'd given up any real thought of starting something she had no intention of finishing.

She smiled back. "Glad to hear it."

"Probably eighteen hours left, assuming we need to jump again. Longer if we don't. You know I don't like to jump unless we have to. Burns a lot more fuel," Captain Dawes said.

Hallie nodded. With no viable stops along the way, it was wise to conserve as much fuel as they could, just in case something went wrong.

Captain Dawes was older, probably late forties. Also handsome, but more rugged and weatherworn than Bryant, with salt-and-pepper sideburns creeping out from under his military-issued cap. He was also definitely married to his career.

He was the best pilot Hallie had ever met—ever *heard of*. That's why she'd chosen him for this mission. That, like the dummy rocket, was also paying dividends.

"Break out the playing cards if you haven't already," Captain Dawes continued.

"Oh, we're way ahead of you on that," Hallie replied with a grin. "I usually hold my own in poker, but it turns out Cecilia played semipro back in college."

"It's how I paid for my first PhD," Cecilia called from the modest common area behind Hallie. "And I just wiped out Luke with a pair of threes."

Hallie turned back. "Chasing another straight?"

Luke shook his head. "Flush this time. I can't win."

"Maybe I can sneak away to join you for a round." Bryant glanced at Captain Dawes, who nodded.

"Sure," he said. "Take a break. I've got the helm for now."

Hallie was tall for a woman, but Bryant was a full six or seven inches taller. Broad and strong in all the right places, fit and lean in all the other right places. She gave him an awkward grin and backed away from the cockpit so he could step out.

He leaned toward her and motioned her close so he could whisper something in her ear, and she complied.

"By 'join you for a round,' I don't mean cards... at least, not necessarily," he said.

Hallie's skin shivered, and goosebumps rolled up her forearms. She inhaled a shaky breath to buy herself some time. Once she regained her composure, she whispered back, "Thank you for the offer, but I have to pass. You understand."

What, exactly, she wanted him to understand was a mystery even to her, but it would be enough to keep him at bay... at least for the time being.

His sly expression shifted to muted disappointment, but he nodded and didn't push the issue, which Hallie had to give him some credit for. Maybe he had a little maturity to him after all—or maybe he just didn't want to risk being overheard.

Either way, he joined her at the card game with the other scientists.

"Alright, alright." Cecilia dealt the clear Plastrex cards and winked at Bryant. "New seat, fresh meat."

The screens in the cockpit blared a warning alarm.

"Bryant, get back here!" Captain Dawes shouted. "Everyone else, strap into your seats. They've found us."

Hallie's heart thundered in her chest, and she rushed to take her seat next to Cecilia's.

The first blow hit the *Persimmon*, sending the cards careening into the air and the four scientists tumbling across the floor. Hallie scrambled to her feet about as fast as Luke did, and they helped Cecilia and Angela up, respectively, and to their seats.

As Hallie strapped herself in, Angela said, "I still don't understand why we aren't shooting back!"

"Doesn't work that way, Doc," Captain Dawes replied as he maneuvered the ship in complex and erratic motions. "The Whip's designed to evade and escape. Heavy armor, but she's a quick little fiend. Trade-off is that her guns couldn't even scratch their ship. We have to jump again. Everyone strapped in?"

"Yes," Hallie replied. Three more affirmations followed hers.

"Good. Calculations are nearly complete," Captain Dawes said.

The ship jolted the hardest it ever had since Hallie had been on it, and sparks rained down on the four scientists again. The whole ship continued to shudder—and that hadn't happened before, either.

Hallie's breaths came faster and faster, and this time she sought out Cecilia's hand.

"Shields at 40%! The whole ship's unstable" Bryant shouted. "What the hell did they hit us with?"

"Antimatter missile," Captain Dawes replied. "We can't take another hit like that. We jump in ten."

Bryant gasped. "With our structural damage, the ship could tear itself apart!"

"Either we jump, or *they'll* tear us apart," Captain Dawes yelled back.

Bryant looked back at Hallie, perhaps hoping she'd overrule the captain.

Instead, she shouted, "Do it!"

The *Persimmon* jumped, and the shuddering stopped in a flash of bright light.

[YOU KNOW WHAT THIS MEANS, right?] Keontae was practically bouncing in Justin's arm and mind. [That pay raise means we'll have enough to get me back to Bortundi so I can see my mom.]

"Yeah, of course," Justin said as he headed back toward the shared bunkroom to collect his stuff. "We just gotta coordinate it right so we can get you there without losing this opportunity. He said we're going back out as soon as he sells the copalion and gets the ship repaired."

[Bro, you can always get another job, 'specially with me around,] Keontae said. [But my mom's old. She ain't gonna last much longer. I need to see 'er soon, man. Gotta let 'er know her boy's not dead—not really, anyway. Give 'er some peace before she dies.]

"We will," Justin said. "I promised you we would, so we will. Just have to figure out the timing. That's all."

[Sounds like your idea of timin' ain't the same as mine,] Keontae muttered. [I ain't tryin' to be stuck in your arm forever, neither. Maybe we can find me a prosthetic body or somethin'.]

"There are billions of androids in the galaxy. Pick one, dude."

[C'mon, JB. You know it ain't that simple. We're talkin' 'bout restarting my life again. Can't just snatch some android's body and call it a day. I got standards, bro.] Keontae added, [Androids don't have dicks, either, and you know that's a dealbreaker for me.]

Justin chuckled. "I can't have you saying these crazy things in my head, Key. You're cracking me up."

"Who's cracking you up?" a female voice asked from behind him.

[Uh-oh.]

Justin whirled around to find Lora Clayton standing in the corridor. He looked her up and down, and she looked him up and down. They both grinned.

Lora gave him a white smile, stark against her brown Hispanic skin and full lips. Even wearing thick working attire, most of it a synthetic material comparable to denim, it still highlighted her ambitious Latina curves.

Long dark hair tipped with purple ends draped over her shoulders, freshly down from a ponytail. She stared at him with chocolate eyes, and her smile widened.

"Heyyy," he said.

[Smooth response, JB. Real smooth.]

Justin gritted his teeth, partly at Keontae and partly at the situation.

"So I was thinking we should try another date since last night didn't go like we'd hoped," she said.

If Justin's assurance to Captain Marlowe about fighting was the understatement of the millennium, Lora's mention of their date last night would be the first to challenge it for the title. It had gone so poorly that Justin was dreading even seeing Lora again, much less having this conversation.

Justin gave a nervous laugh. "Yeah... that's putting it... mildly."

"Exactly. So we try again. You and me, in the common room, between second and third shift," she proposed.

"I would, but I'm supposed to have dinner with the captain around then," Justin said.

Lora laughed and moved closer to him. She was definitely attractive and definitely bottom heavy—Keontae had commented on her ample booty the moment Justin first laid eyes on her—but even had last night gone well, Justin still wasn't all that interested. Their personalities clashed too much.

"You can't lie to me, hun." She ran her hands down his chest. "I know the truth when I hear it, and I know when I'm not hearin' it, too."

"It's true, though," Justin insisted. "Captain Marlowe wants me at dinner tonight with him and Arl—the first officer."

She put her hands on her bountiful hips and cocked her head to the side. "And why would he want that?"

[Be careful, JB,] Keontae said. [A woman strikes that pose, she's invitin' you to step on a landmine.]

"Because he made me the new rig chief."

"Pshht. I knew you were lyin'." Lora held up her hand and started to turn away from him. "You don't wanna try another date, just say so. I'm a big girl. I can take it."

"Lora, I'm serious," Justin pressed. "After all the shaking today, and after Gerald died, the captain said I was—"

"Wait, what?" She turned back. "Gerald died?"

"Yeah, this morning. Partway into first shift, Captain said."

She studied him for a long moment, rubbing her chin with her index finger and thumb. "Either you're tellin' me a whole *slew* of lies, or you're tellin' the truth."

Justin shrugged. "It's all true. I'm about to pick up my stuff from my bunk and my locker and go claim Gerald's room."

"You're really not jokin'?" She squinted at him and put her hands on her hips again. "This is for real?"

"Swear to God," Justin said. "Gerald died, I'm the new rig chief, and I'm having dinner with the captain tonight."

Her eyes widened. "You know what this means? It means we got our own space for a *real* date."

Oh... we're back on that again.

Justin started, "Technically, I suppose—"

"How 'bout after your dinner? We can talk, get to know each other more." She closed the distance between them again and pressed her body against him. "See where the night goes."

He backed away a half-step and took her hands into his. They were rough, but warm. He couldn't help but think of Shannon, even though he couldn't remember ever having held her hands.

"I don't know if I can commit to that right now," he said. "New job, new responsibilities... and don't you have a shift tonight anyway?"

"I'm redundant tonight, so I'm off, more or less, unless someone needs a swap," she replied. "That's why it's so perfect. So why don't we give it a try?"

[JB, don't be a flake,] Keontae said. [If you ain't into it—though with a booty like that, I have no idea why you *wouldn't* be—just tell 'er. Don't string 'er along. It ain't right.]

Justin gritted his teeth again. Keontae was right.

"Look, Lora," he began, and her countenance and posture immediately shifted to the defensive. "You're a great girl and all, but—"

"No. Mm-mmm. No." She wagged her index finger at him. "We're not doin' this. You don't wanna take another shot at having a good time? That's on you, Justin. I'm not doin' this."

Justin blinked at her. "Well, that's exactly what I'm—"

"You're right. We're not compatible. Not a good match," she continued. "I'm not doin' this again. You had your chance. If that's how you're gonna be, I'm out."

Confusion racked Justin's brain. How had she turned this around on him?

"Enough of this. I'm done. Go on, have your fun without me, *puto*." With that, she stormed off, leaving Justin alone in the corridor once again.

Once she'd gotten far enough away, Justin muttered, "You know, despite how it went, it was actually a lot easier than I'd expected."

[Told ya,] Keontae said. [Now let's pack your stuff, man.]

A FEW HOURS LATER, Justin had his new room set up, and he'd showered and dressed to return for dinner in the captain's quarters.

[Don't sweat it about Lora,] Keontae said. [She may be good-lookin', but God made 'er with a hefty dose of crazy, too.]

"I wouldn't say she's crazy." Justin shook his head. "I just think she's been burned by too many guys in the past."

[You might be right, JB.]

"Just a guess." Justin shifted his tone. "Speaking of insight, I think we should talk about our relationship."

[Uh... okay?]

"You mind coming out of my arm for this one?"

[Sure. Door's locked, right?]

"Latched, barred, and sealed shut."

[Yeah. Hold on.]

Justin's metal arm shuddered, and a glowing green form materialized next to him. It gradually took the shape of a man, and its features sharpened into the familiar face of his best friend, Keontae, the man who had literally given his life to save Justin back at ACM-1134.

In doing so, the Keontae that Justin had known had perished, but his soul had somehow lived on, preserved as a sort of tech ghost. The apparition was still 100% Keontae's personality, mannerisms, and probably even his soul, but his physical body had long since been destroyed.

Now, aside from maneuvering through circuits and networks and computer systems the galaxy over, the closest Keontae could get to the physical world was manifesting as a hologram-like image, part digital, part ethereal.

"What's up, JB?" he asked. His voice sounded the same as it had inside Justin's head, but now he could hear it with his actual ears, too.

This wasn't going to be an easy talk for Justin, but he'd given it a lot of thought and concluded that changes needed to be made. He decided to jump right in.

"We need to establish some better boundaries," he said.

"Boundaries? Like what?"

"Like… I wouldn't mind some actual alone time every now and then. You know, without you speaking into my mind and watching my every move from within my arm."

"'Watchin' your every move?' You think I'm some sorta voyeur?"

"That's not what I'm trying to say."

"You know I didn't *choose* this, right?" Keontae's voice hardened. "I was tryin' to save your ass, which I did, by the way, and I went down for it."

"I know, Key, and I'm forever grateful."

"And then I saved your ass again—at least two more times—when shit went sideways in the mine."

Justin nodded. "Absolutely. No question."

"Then what the hell are we talkin' about?"

Justin sighed. "Lora may be crazy or hurt or whatever, but that's not the only reason I didn't want to try a second date with her. I knew you'd be in my head the whole time…" He paused, then added, "…start to *finish*."

Keontae folded his glowing arms. "So you *do* think I'm a voyeur."

"No!" Justin hesitated. "Well… yes, but not intentionally."

Keontae shook his glowing green head. "It ain't like I got a lotta options here, JB."

"Right. Exactly. We're both kind of…"

Keontae pointed at him. "If you say 'stuck with each other' like this is some bullshit buddy cop NatGeo flick, I'm gonna jump into the ship and never help you again."

That *was* what Justin was going to say, so he held his tongue. He redirected the conversation. "But that's part of the solution; you just said it. You never sleep, but I do. Some of the time, could you—would you mind jumping into the rig's network and hanging out there? That way I can get better rest and maybe some privacy in crucial moments?"

Keontae stared at him with his arms folded across his chest. "Alright. Here's where I land on this. Neither of us wanted this to happen, but you were my only way outta that mine. Otherwise I'd be digital dust like Mark Brown and every-thin' else when ACM nuked the place.

"We're friends, so it's not like I'm strugglin' hard with this arrangement. Plus, you're doin' me a favor by takin' me back to Bortundi Prime to see my mom. If you want me gone after that, I'm gone. I'll find a way to stick around with her. Probably should do that anyway."

"Key, that's not what I'm—"

"Let me finish, JB," Keontae said, his voice calm, but firm. "That's all I'm askin'. I'll help you every way I can 'til we get there, but you know I wanna get back there soon. And in the meantime, I hear you. Sometimes a man's gotta be alone. I get it. So every night when you go to sleep, and any other time you tell me, I'll jump into the ship. Good?"

Relief filled Justin's chest. "That's all I'm asking."

"Then it's done, brother."

"But listen, Key," Justin said. "I don't *want* you to leave. When I get you back to your mom, you can do what you gotta do, but I'm totally fine with you sticking with me if you want. I owe you that much, at least, for what you did for me. For what you're still doing for me."

"We'll cross that slipstream when we get to it," Keontae said. "Haven't made any decisions yet. The idea of getting' a new body is appealin', but there's benefits to ridin' shotgun with you, too, so I don't know what I'm gonna do. Guess we'll see."

"Yeah. We will." Justin grinned at him. "Thanks for taking care of me."

"Don't get mushy on me, son. How can I improve your swagger if you keep goin' soft like this?"

"Going soft with you around isn't the problem. The *opposite* of that is the problem."

"TMI, bro." Keontae smiled, but shook his head. "*Way* too much information. Just put your damn boots back on so we can get you to your dinner with the captain. Unless... you'd rather I sit this one out?"

"Nah, bro. I want you there. You see things I don't. Jump back into my arm whenever you're ready."

Within minutes, they had left Justin's new room behind and headed toward the captain's quarters for the second time that day—although the word "day" had little meaning in the dead of space.

The standard Coalition day was twenty-four hours, based on Earth's twenty-four-hour day, despite the vast majority of planets in and out of the Coalition having different day and year lengths based on their rotation speeds and proximity to the central star(s) in their systems.

Someone somewhere had found a way to manage all of that and keep everything straight across the galaxy, and Justin was glad it wasn't him. Just thinking about dealing with all of those moving pieces made him want to throw up.

As he passed the common room, Justin caught a distant glimpse of Lora heading into the kitchen. She didn't make eye contact with him, probably on purpose, but there was no doubt from her rigid body language that she'd seen him.

Whatever. Not his problem anymore.

Arlie greeted Justin at the door again and beckoned him inside, and he soon found himself seated at the same table where he'd sat a few hours earlier. The only difference was that Rowley wasn't there, thank God.

Along with Captain Marlowe, another shot glass of brown liquor waited for Justin at his spot at the table. When Arlie finally joined them, they toasted again and downed the bittersweet liquid. It wasn't any better the second time.

Dinner came in the form of rehydrated salmon and rice with a sort of powdered butter flavoring. Justin hadn't eaten salmon—or fish of any kind—since before he'd arrived on Ketarus-4, and he'd managed to vomit up most of that meal while still on the ship as it was entering the planet's atmosphere. Damned vertigo at work.

But he didn't put up a fuss. Meat—real meat—of any kind, rehydrated or otherwise, on trips like this was a rarity. It beat subsisting on powdered protein and flavorless potato flakes.

"Thanks again for the invitation," Justin said. "Really nice to have someone to talk to, and nice to have a good meal for once."

"Should be the first of many more to come," Captain Marlowe said between bites. "Soon, too."

"We're already that close to the Jevilos System?" Justin asked.

"Better." Captain Marlowe smirked at him. "We're gonna catch a ride instead."

Justin glanced at Arlie, but she gave him nothing to work with. He refocused on Captain Marlowe. "What do you mean?"

"Huge colonist freighter. Coming up on our six. We're gonna dock with it and get repairs on the ship, and then we can go right back to work without having to dock on a planet." Captain Marlowe tapped the side of his head with his index finger. "Gonna save time and money in the long run."

"Oh. Good. Yeah, excellent." Justin couldn't help but wonder if it actually *was* a good plan or not, though. "Are you sure... I mean, do we know that the colonist ship will have what we need to repair the landing gear? It's pretty mangled."

"I take it you're unfamiliar with the world of professional colonization? World-building, terraforming, and all that?" Captain Marlowe asked.

"Been a laborer all my life. Almost exclusively mining," Justin replied. "In fact, this job's the farthest I've ever gotten from traditional mining."

"Mmm." Arlie nodded, but she didn't say anything else.

Captain Marlowe didn't say anything either. They just sat there, staring at Justin for a long moment.

Finally, Justin asked, "So what am I missing when it comes to—"

"Colonist ship's not just any ship," Captain Marlowe said. "Thing's a flying city. When it lands, the ship and everything inside it stay on the planet, plant roots, and grow from there. It's a fully formed capital city, complete with infrastructure, buildings, and, of course, people. They'll have what we need, for sure."

Justin could hardly fathom such a thing, but he'd heard that ACM and other copalion mining companies had created similar ships to establish new mines on uncharted or unclaimed planets. The ship would set down and essentially burrow into the ground, and then the workers on the ship would set out to establish the mine.

The ships had everything the mines needed to function, ranging from heavy machinery to alloy walls and computer networks all the way down to shovels, pickaxes, bedsheets, and soap dispensers for the bathrooms. The workers just had to put it all together, and then they could get to the actual mining part.

Apparently, colonist ships functioned similarly.

"Well, that's good," Justin finally said. "Sounds like a cool ship."

"It'll be just like visiting a city on a civilized planet. The rig-runners will get some R&R, we'll get the repairs done, and we can restock some essentials."

[Nice. New playground for me,] Keontae said.

"I like it," Justin said. "Good plan."

"Glad you approve." Captain Marlowe shoveled a sporkful of rice and powdered butter into his mouth. As he chewed, he said, "Meant to thank you earlier, but I didn't."

"Thank me?" Justin stared at him until he realized what he was referencing. "Oh, the rig, the drill, and all that. You're welcome, Enix, but really, I had to do something, or we all would've died. That's how dire it was getting."

"And that's why I'm thanking you. Part of why, at least. You've got quite the electric thumb. Like an electrician magician." Captain Marlowe nodded to Arlie, who spoke up before Justin could respond.

"You not only saved lives, but you kept the damage to the ship at a minimum. Saved us money as well. And time. And headaches." Arlie leaned forward, and her eyes narrowed. "I hate headaches."

"You shouldn't have married one, then," Captain Marlowe quipped.

Arlie didn't respond. She just stared at him, stoic.

Justin couldn't nail down their relationship dynamic. In what little time he'd been around them both, they hadn't ever really talked to each other, and they certainly hadn't shown any affection. But some people were like that—more private. He certainly couldn't hold it against them, especially after asking Keontae for more privacy.

"Anyway," Arlie continued, "thank you. By keeping me alive, you made my life much easier."

Justin could only nod and repeat, "You're welcome."

"That brings me to my next question," Captain Marlowe said. "How, exactly, did you manage to do it?"

"I already told you this afternoon. I said that—"

"I know what you told me this afternoon. I'm not asking you to rehash that," he said. "I'm asking you to tell me what really happened."

Justin gulped and tried not to sweat.

[Easy, JB. Don't get backed into a corner.]

"Just have a knack for it, I guess," he said. "When it comes to computers and networks and systems, I see things others don't see. I see them in ways others don't see. And I can move them like no one else can."

"That's all well and good, but I'm asking *how* you managed to handle all of that," Captain Marlowe pressed.

"I... I don't think I understand the question."

"That's fine." Captain Marlowe sighed and pulled a silver case out of one of his pockets. He clacked it open, revealing several rows of narrow metal sticks.

Arlie shifted in her seat, and she kept shifting as if she were perpetually uncomfortable in that chair, but she hadn't been sitting there that long, and the shifting had only just now started. Otherwise, she'd barely moved since she'd sat down, except to eat and drink.

"Let's change the topic, then." Captain Marlowe popped one of the metal sticks in his mouth, crunched down on one end, and tucked the silver case back into his pocket. Then he leaned forward. "Why'd you leave Andridge behind?"

Justin almost gasped, but he managed to choke it down.

[Impossible. There's no way he could know about what happened to Carl,] Keontae said. [He's punkin' you, JB.]

Arlie kept shifting, but Justin's focus remained forward.

"I... I don't understand that question, either," Justin stammered. He could never admit how Carl Andridge had really died. Only Shannon, Keontae, and Justin knew, and they shared an unspoken pact to never say a single word about it for the rest of their lives.

So how did Captain Marlowe know about it? How *could* he know about it? There was no way.

When Arlie finally settled, she held a plasma repeater in her hand.

It was pointed at Justin.

"Understand the question now?" Captain Marlowe asked.

FOUR

"I'm not gonna ask you again," Captain Marlowe said. "Because I can't have you endangering me or my crew. So here it is, one last time: why'd you leave Andridge Copalion Mines behind?"

Justin's thundering heartbeat calmed at those words. Captain Marlowe wasn't asking about Carl Andridge himself. He was asking about the company, ACM.

Even so, the question still bothered Justin. He'd hoped to expunge that part of his work history altogether, but Captain Marlowe had found out anyway. No sense hiding it now.

[Choose your words carefully, JB. Tell 'im how terrible they were to you, but don't play the victim.]

Keontae was right. Justin was about to walk a fine line, especially since he didn't know where Captain Marlowe and Arlie stood when it came to ACM specifically. As freelancers, their allegiance shifted to wherever and whoever would pay them.

Given ACM's size and endless supply of credits, they could very well be one of the *Viridian's* main sources of revenue. But they were polarizing, too. Before he'd ever worked for ACM, Justin had known that folks across the galaxy pretty much either loved or hated ACM. Few people occupied the chasm of feelings between.

Now, having been one of their employees and surviving what he'd survived in that mine from Hell, he understood perfectly well why so many people hated ACM. The question was, did that group include Captain Marlowe and Arlie?

"I worked there for several weeks. Got into some trouble," Justin admitted.

[Careful, JB...]

BEN WOLF

"I definitely did some things to piss off management, but I also got thrown under the hoverbus by the company in the process. And on top of all that, I lost people I cared about, including my best friend, who died saving my life when the mine became unstable."

Justin paused and tried to gauge their reactions, but neither of them moved a muscle.

"In the end, I got out of a bad situation and—"

"What planet?" Captain Marlowe asked.

"Huh?"

"The mine. What planet was it on?"

Justin wondered why he was asking that question. Before Carl Andridge's cronies had decided to let Shannon and Justin leave, they'd made it clear that in no circumstance could they discuss the specifics of what had happened at the mine with anyone.

It was a promise Justin had been glad to make at the time, but in hindsight, he realized it was a huge reach to try to do damage control. For a company as big as ACM, the loss of a single mine on a promising planet wasn't a monumental defeat, but it wasn't something they could just paint over in a single stroke, either.

The more Justin had thought about it since it had happened, the more it infuriated him. He recognized his sense of scale was different than that of one of the largest companies in the galaxy—if not the largest—but that didn't mean they could just erase the memory of what had happened there... erase the lives of all the people who had died in that horrible—

"Justin?" Captain Marlowe broke into his sequence of thoughts. "What planet?"

Justin cleared his throat and glanced again at Arlie's plasma repeater still pointed at him. ACM had told him not to talk specifics about the incident, but they'd never told him not to say what planet it had all happened on.

"Ketarus-4," he said.

That got a reaction.

Captain Marlowe's eyes widened slightly, and Arlie actually leaned forward and narrowed her eyes at him. She didn't lower the repeater, though.

"I knew it," Captain Marlowe said.

[Shit. What now?]

Justin ignored Keontae and kept silent.

"What happened there?" Captain Marlowe asked.

"I..." Justin glanced at Arlie's repeater again. "I can't talk about it. ACM swore me to secrecy under pen—"

"Under penalty of lawsuits, financial ruin, and involuntary suicide." Captain Marlowe scoffed. "Yeah, I know the drill."

Justin could tell from his tone that Captain Marlowe wasn't a fan... or that he was a good actor. Justin didn't know for sure. He *couldn't* know whether Captain Marlowe was actually in bed with ACM or not. For all Justin knew, this could be a trap.

Captain Marlowe seemed to notice Justin's discomfort. "Relax, kid. I'm not coming after you. Just wanted to know what side you're on, and if you got out of *that* mine and off *that* planet, I know you're not on ACM's payroll."

He nodded at Arlie, who stashed her plasma repeater away.

Justin found he could breathe easy again, and he nodded to Captain Marlowe. "I'm not with them. I never will be again. I've worked at a couple other big players as well, and they all give off the same kind of stink."

"It's greed, kid. Plain and simple," Captain Marlowe said. "Copalion is the lifeblood of the Coalition. Take it away, and the Coalition dies, and so do the largest corporations—who control the majority of the galaxy's wealth. But with copalion in the mix, they're behemoths feeding on anything and anyone within their grasp.

"Their greed cost you a lot. Friends, you said, and your best friend." Captain Marlowe nodded at Justin's right arm. "Cost you physically, too, 'less I'm mistaken and you were born with that."

"No. Hazard of the job." Justin shook his head and held up his robotic right hand. He huffed. "And you know, they didn't even have the integrity, the *balls* to refer to it as an 'accident.' Called it an 'occurrence' instead, like it would somehow clear them of all wrongdoing."

Captain Marlowe's stern expression curled into a modest grin. "Not much better in the military. When you're wounded in combat, they give you a medal. If it's bad enough to end your career, they discharge you with honors. You get a little pay bump, but it won't get you very far.

"Then it's off to the workforce with tens of thousands of other 'disabled veterans.' That label's a death sentence for any hope of a career. Still, we all need jobs, and we all have useful skills, but the market's flooded, so we either turn criminal and risk everything that way, or we make our own way, scratching and scraping for whatever's left over."

Justin nodded. "Exactly. It's bullshit."

[Damn right,] Keontae chimed in.

"We bleed for these bastards, and even when we try to get away from 'em, we can't, 'cause it turns out we still need 'em. They're too big for us not to."

Captain Marlowe reached toward his waist and pulled up his shirt, exposing his torso. An uneven patch of flexible metal mesh stretched from the top of his hip up to his lowest rib. It extended toward his navel and stopped along his side.

"I've bled for 'em, just like you did. Just like your friends did," Captain Marlowe said. "Got sick of bleeding for 'em, so now I just work for 'em as distantly as I can—'cause you can't ever get away from these giants. Not really. It's just a matter of how much you can keep 'em outta your life."

He let his shirt drape over his torso again and glanced at Arlie, and she planted her left leg on the table. She rolled her pant leg up and revealed a gleaming metal shinbone embedded into her skin.

How the doctors had managed to do that sort of thing, Justin would never understand. He figured it wouldn't and couldn't have worked, but he also didn't have a medical degree.

"You were both in the Coalition Forces?" Justin asked.

They both nodded.

"And did stints in private military as well, working for ACM. It's how we met. Both of us got sent to our deaths on the same mission. Piece of shrapnel tore through my body armor and carved a hole in my side, and Arlie pulled me out of there before I could bleed out. Saved my life, but it cost her a perfectly good shinbone in the process."

Justin thought he noticed a hint of a smile on Arlie's face, but it faded as quickly as it had appeared.

"They got us both out of surgery around the same time, complete with new metal parts. I've got prosthetic organs, but she's just got the one angry shinbone." Captain Marlowe smirked. "If she head-kicks you with that thing, you'll see more than stars. You'll see entire galaxies."

"Gonna avoid that, then," Justin said.

Captain Marlowe reclined in his chair and folded his arms. "I knew there was a reason I liked you, Justin. I've enjoyed our little chat."

"Me too."

"Hope dinner was good?" Captain Marlowe asked.

Justin nodded. "Haven't had salmon in awhile."

"Yeah." Captain Marlowe grabbed the bottle of brown alcohol and popped it open again. "Well, we should call it a night, but let's have one more toast before we do."

[Look at you, bro. Makin' connections. Gettin' all cozy with the captain and his lady,] Keontae quipped. [Proud of you, man.]

Captain Marlowe poured the liquor, and Arlie disbursed the shot glasses. They each held one up.

"Fuck ACM," Captain Marlowe said.

Now that was a toast Justin could get behind.

In unison with Arlie, Justin echoed, "Fuck ACM."

Then they clinked their glasses and downed the bitter liquid.

JUSTIN WOKE up to a combination of Keontae's voice, the crackling of the comms, and a persistent pounding ache ricocheting around in his head.

"Get up, JB," Keontae said. "Shit's poppin' off, and you're asleep."

Justin stirred and sat up, albeit too quickly for his head, which punished him for it. He lay back down, but that wasn't any better. He groaned.

"Docking with the colonist ship will begin in approximately twenty minutes," Captain Marlowe's voice said over the comms. "Make sure your papers are in order, so to speak, and pack up. We're leaving the ship for repairs. No crew members can stay behind. We're all going. We'll all have to sort out our own accommodations, but there should be plenty of rooms available for rent aboard the ship."

Justin squinted at the green light filling his room. Keontae must've left his arm at some point last night.

Justin cleared his throat. "You know, when I said I wanted more privacy, I didn't mean you should leave my arm and just stare at me while I'm sleeping."

"Special occasion, special reason. You heard Cap. We're gettin' off this flyin' scrapyard. Means a brand new network to play in." Keontae rubbed his ghostly hands together.

Justin groaned again and swung his legs over the edge of the bed. Like the previous bed he'd shared with his two shift workers, this one also creaked, but it wasn't nearly as bad. It also didn't stink like body odor and onions. That was the *real* perk.

He sat up again, and his head continued to pound. He clutched it with his hands and rubbed his temples with his thumbs.

"You hit it pretty hard with the happy couple last night," Keontae said. "Not surprised you're feelin' rough."

"Ugh. I remember toasting against ACM and a couple of drinks before dinner, but that's all I had, right?"

Keontae laughed. "That toast was the beginnin' of your end, bro. You, Marlowe, and Arlie finished the bottle after that, but you had fun. That's for sure."

"Oh, shit. Did I do something dumb?" Justin moaned.

"Nah. Y'all had a good time, JB. Don't sweat it."

Justin groaned yet again. "I'm gonna get some water."

"Then get dressed. We're leavin' this rocket-propelled coffin soon."

"Yeah, but we're coming back." Justin forced himself up and into his small, but private bathroom. He turned on the faucet and splashed his face with water from the archaic sink. It tasted a bit salty, as usual, and he hoped and prayed the colonist ship would offer better alternatives.

"Not 'til the repairs are done. I did some research," Keontae said. "Should take a couple days, at least, to make us whole again."

Justin turned around and considered running the shower, but he opted not to. If they were going to be on the colonist ship for a couple of days, he could shower with cleaner water wherever he found to stay.

"Should be a good time, then." His headache still thundered in his head, but he cracked his neck, rubbed the muscles at the base of his neck, and endured.

Once Justin got dressed, Keontae jumped back into his arm, and they headed up to the bridge level where the observation deck was located. He found a handful of other rig workers up there, too. Apparently he wasn't the only one who wanted to see the show.

A series of shielded windows overhead and in front of them showed the vast emptiness of space as far as the eye could see, as well as a gray object closing in on their position. As it drew nearer, Justin continually had to adjust his expectations for the thing's size.

Captain Marlowe had called the colonist ship a "fully formed capital city, complete with infrastructure, buildings, and, of course, people." Justin hadn't really been able to picture the size of such a ship, and so when it was finally right on top of them, he couldn't believe his eyes. It might as well have been its own planet.

Muted gray metal shaped its angular hull except for a dome that could've been the size of a small moon. It gleamed with a sort of reflective red-orange chrome. The color reminded Justin of an old pair of polarized sunglasses he'd owned as a teenager.

Along the ship's massive flank, the ship's name came into view, one gargantuan letter at a time: the *CSS Nidus*.

The "CSS" part stood for "Coalition Space Ship," but Justin didn't know what the word "Nidus" meant. Maybe it was someone's name.

"Means 'nest,'" Captain Marlowe said from behind Justin, who jumped in surprise. "It's Latin."

"Whoa," Justin said. "Wasn't expecting to see you here."

"Wasn't talking to you anyway."

Justin blinked at him. "Uh... aren't you supposed to be flying the ship?"

Captain Marlowe shook his head. "Simple docking procedure. Ship doesn't need me to do anything. AI takes care of that, and First Officer Bush is there as a failsafe."

"Oh. Gotcha." He refocused on the *Nidus*, but he couldn't help but glance back at Captain Marlowe again. "You know Latin?"

"I know *that* word in Latin."

Justin waited for more of an explanation, but he didn't get any.

When he turned back again, he caught sight of a pair of dark, enrapturing eyes staring at him. *Seething* at him.

Lora.

She looked away as soon as he made eye contact.

[Definitely still mad,] Keontae said.

"No shit," Justin muttered.

[The kind of broke-ass game you got with women, and you got the nerve to clap back at me when I'm tryin' to help you out?] Keontae scoffed. [If that's how you wanna play it, you're on your own when it comes to the ladies from now on.]

"I never *asked* for your help."

[Good. 'Cause you definitely ain't gettin' it now.]

"Fine by me."

Justin realized the handful of fellow rig-runners around him were casting occasional glances back at him. To them, it would've seemed like he was just muttering to himself.

Like a crazy person.

Again.

"Cool ship, isn't it?" he asked plenty loud enough for them to all hear this time.

No one responded to his question. They just turned and looked at the ship again.

And I have to lead these people. Be their boss. Great start.

Before long, the *Viridian* began to move again, and the rig drew in even closer, toward one of several shielded openings near the *Nidus's* rear propulsion rockets. Within minutes, the *Nidus* swallowed the rig whole.

"Gotta admit, I'm impressed," Justin said as he turned back toward Captain Marlowe, only to find he wasn't there. When he faced forward again, half of the workers were staring at him again... because again, it looked like he'd been talking to himself.

Perfect.

The rig shuddered to a stop, and white-blue lights gleamed through the windows from a ceiling far overhead. The sight of it stirred Justin's vertigo, and he quickly looked away before his stomach could turn against him.

"All crew, present yourselves and prepare to disembark the rig," Arlie's voice said over the comms. "We've successfully docked with the *Nidus*."

Justin didn't have any personal property of consequence that he really needed to take with him. He'd just received a promotion and a pay bump, so he'd planned to do some light shopping while on the *Nidus*, mostly for new clothes and some snacks to stash in his private room.

Now that he didn't have to worry about everything being saturated with foul smells, he didn't mind splurging a bit. Life on the rig was rough, and even the smallest comforts would make it considerably better.

A line had formed at the exit/entry hatch, and Justin lined up behind Al

Paulson and Shaneesha, whose last name he still hadn't learned. Al looked back and nudged Shaneesha, and she also looked back.

"Hey, congrats on the new gig," Al said.

"Yeah, congratulations!" Shaneesha took Justin by his wrist and pulled him into a firm hug, which Justin happily returned.

Whereas Al was a grizzled old rig-runner with close to thirty years of experience, Shaneesha was maybe twenty years Justin's senior, middle-aged, and gave off heavy "mom" vibes. Justin didn't mind that at all; his actual mom had been a waste of breathable air and not much else.

Shaneesha looked like she could've been Keontae's mom instead, with her darker skin complexion and her hair in short dreadlocks, dyed red.

Al, on the other hand, could've been the father of the entire human race for all Justin knew. He was pretty much smack-dab in the middle of the skin-tone spectrum and had a gray beard that hung low enough to cover the front of his thick neck.

When Shaneesha finally let Justin go, she held him at arm's length. "You know Rowley's as pissed as a bar toilet, don't you?"

"Oh, yeah," Justin said. "Well aware."

"Guy like that—" Al shook his head, "—wouldn't want 'im gunnin' for me. He's reckless. Got nothin' to lose no more."

Shaneesha dismissed Al's concerns with a wave of her hand. "Don't listen to this old fool. He's content where he's at in life, and you deserve the promotion. You actually care 'bout the rig and what happens to us, so I know you'll take good care of both."

"Of course," Justin said. "I'll do everything I can."

Al shrugged. "I may be content where I am, but I still know how this trade works. You take from someone, they take from you. Usually more."

"He didn't take nothin' from nobody," Shaneesha said. "Cap'n saw fit to give 'im the job, so he did."

Al shrugged again. "Don't matter what you or I think about it. What matters is how Rowley sees it. If he feels slighted, he may try to do somethin' about it."

Shaneesha shook her head and finally let Justin go. "Forget about Rowley, and forget about Father Time here. You just keep doin' good work, and the good Lord will keep rewardin' you like He did this time."

The Father Time comparison brought a smile to Justin's face, though he had to admit he'd always pictured Father Time as a man with a long white beard, white hair, and unnaturally pale skin. And maybe wearing a Hawaiian shirt and khaki shorts, just for kicks.

"Thanks, Shaneesha," Justin replied.

She gave him a white smile, and then the hatch opened and the rig-runners began to disembark.

Justin stole a quick glance back. Despite Shaneesha's encouragement, Al's warning had worried him. When he didn't see Rowley standing in the line behind him nor ahead, it worried him even more.

[She's a peach, ain't she?] Keontae asked.

"Huh?" Justin nodded.

Both Shaneesha and Al turned back to face him.

[Shaneesha. She's a peach.]

"It's nothing," Justin told the two of them. "Just curious where Rowley is right now."

"Like I said, don't waste any time on that man and his sour grapes," Shaneesha said. "You do you, and leave him to the Devil to get sorted."

Justin smirked. "I will."

The rig-runners filed out of the rig, down the boarding ramp, and into the *Nidus's* cavernous docking bay. A latticework of metal beams suspended the lofted ceiling over a sprawling sea of smooth concrete, occasionally marked with embedded strips of colored lights and paint.

Among the beams hung a web of wires, hoses, claws, and machines with pointy ends. Justin couldn't identify any of it, but he figured it had to be for repairing and maintaining spaceships. Smart to store the equipment on the ceiling in a docking bay this big—that way it was never far away.

Clean gray walls marked with various numbers and symbols framed countless clear entry fields, all of them far larger than the rig. The same orange glow of the containment field at the base of the rig's drill surrounded each of the openings. It doubtless functioned similarly, too, as it had let the rig pass through without any issues.

Beyond those shielded entry fields twinkled trillions upon trillions of stars pinpricked against the black canvas of space. Justin decided not to look out there for too long. No sense giving his vertigo a chance to act up again if he could easily avoid it.

Altogether, the docking bay probably could've held hundreds—if not thousands—of copies of the *Viridian*, but at that moment, she was the sole occupant of the space.

Well, aside from the welcoming party of a dozen armed soldiers in forest-green fatigues. Each of them wore a protective mask over their face. They approached in a hovercraft, which Justin was already thankful for because it meant he wouldn't have to traverse the entire docking bay by foot.

A man in a burgundy Coalition uniform with close-cropped gray hair accompanied the soldiers, and he approached the two lines of rig-runners that had formed. Like the soldiers, he also wore a face mask.

"Which of you is the captain?" he asked in a whiny voice.

From somewhere behind Justin, Captain Marlowe called out, "Here."

"Come forward, please," the official said, and Captain Marlowe and Arlie both complied. "That's close enough. My name is Charles Wendell. You may refer to me as Officer Wendell. Perhaps this isn't quite the warm welcome you were expecting, but I'm sure you understand that ships like ours have thorough quarantine protocols that visitors must adhere to."

[Quarantine?] Keontae asked. [What for? They think you're sick or somethin'?]

Justin shrugged, unwilling to reply verbally in this setting. The more he stood in the docking bay, the more exposed and helpless he felt. The rig, with its narrow corridors, small rooms, and tight confines, had reshaped Justin's perspective on size. Now he actually preferred smaller spaces.

Here in the wide-open space of the docking bay, he couldn't help but feel… off.

"Each member of your crew must submit to a full-body scan, and your ship will be searched in accordance with Coalition Law. Anyone who does not submit to testing will be quarantined by force for a period of no fewer than fourteen Coalition Standard Days."

[They're gonna scan you *and* search the ship? Talk about government overreach, man.]

Probably all routine. Justin didn't know for sure because this was their first stop since they'd left Jevilos-6, and he'd never worked on an asteroid-mining rig before.

It didn't matter to Justin. He had nothing to hide, and he wasn't sick, at least as far as he knew.

"No problem," Captain Marlowe replied.

"Very well. Then if you'll have your crew please form two single-file lines, two of our soldiers will administer the scans while the rest search the ship." Officer Wendell nodded back at the soldiers.

Ten of them headed past the crew and into the rig, while two remained outside with their rifles slung onto their backs and with some sort of medical scanners in their hands. The scanners looked like something Dr. Handabi had used back in the medbay at ACM-1134.

The soldiers scanned the rig-runners one by one, from top to bottom. The scanners glowed white for everyone, meaning everyone passed the scan, including Justin. Apparently, their scans couldn't detect Keontae, which was good.

When all the rig-runners had passed, Officer Wendell directed them to stand in two lines again, this time facing the rig. Against the clean lines and pristine interior of the docking bay, the rig looked like a piece of scrap metal that had been chewed up by a grinder and spat back out. The mangled metal spider legs underneath it didn't help any.

Stranger still, despite its name, the rig didn't have a dash of green paint or color anywhere on it. The whole thing was dark-gray, with some spots even darker from rust and grime. The sight of it only served to make Justin feel even more out of place in the expansive docking bay.

As they all stood there, Justin glimpsed a patch on the shoulder of one soldier's fatigues. It was a logo he recognized immediately—Farcoast Mining, one of ACM's chief competitors.

[Noticed that, too,] Keontae said. [Maybe they're co-sponsoring the colonists' voyage or somethin'. Heard about partnerships like that happenin' before. Companies will cozy up to the Coalition on colonization ventures to try to lay down roots before their competition does. Then they get first shot at settin' up shop.]

It made sense from a business perspective... but they'd sent troops, too? The more he thought about it, the more it also made sense. After all, most of these corporations had fought galaxy-spanning wars over copalion resources throughout the last century.

Farcoast Mining ranked either second or third overall when it came to copalion mining, energy production, wealth, and overall power among similar corporations in the galaxy. ACM still held the top spot and had for the last couple of decades, and it hadn't even wavered after Carl Andridge's death.

To Justin's knowledge, Farcoast wasn't actively attacking ACM, but with the Fourth Copalion War still ongoing, sometimes hot and sometimes cold, he couldn't be sure what was really going on. After all, it spanned the entire galaxy, as did the energy empires of all of the companies involved.

But seeing Farcoast soldiers here, aboard the *Nidus*, meant Farcoast was at least on good terms with the Coalition—for now, anyway.

Another few minutes of awkward silence and waiting passed, and then the Farcoast soldiers began to file out of the ship just as they'd entered. One of them approached Officer Wendell and said something in his ear that Justin couldn't hear.

Had they found something?

Officer Wendell nodded, then he turned to face the group. "It appears our soldiers have discovered some contraband aboard your ship."

[Oh, snap. Someone's gonna get fried,] Keontae quipped.

No kidding, Justin mused.

Officer Wendell held up a clear Plastrex bag of glowing red rocks. They looked like dying embers from a fire.

Tyval. A popular drug with homeless addicts and the incredibly wealthy alike. Justin had never seen it in person.

These rocks only gave off a faint light, which meant they were lower grade—cheap because they wouldn't do as much as the brighter, more vibrant rocks. Either way, the drug was definitely still illegal, so as Keontae had said, someone was gonna fry for this.

Officer Wendell passed the Tyval back to the same soldier and pulled out a handscreen. "I take it your crew staff list has been properly and consistently updated, Captain?"

Captain Marlowe nodded. "Of course. Just updated it yesterday, in fact. Member of the crew died."

"I see." Officer Wendell scanned through it. "The drugs were found in a private chamber belonging to one of your crew. According to your records, the room belongs to..."

Private chamber? There were only a handful of those to begin with. Dr. Carrington, the ship's doctor had one. Captain Marlowe and Arlie shared one. The ship's science officer, a guy named Carey Hughes, had one as well. Aside from those, the only other person who had a private room was—

"Justin Barclay," Officer Wendell said.

FIVE

"What?" Justin nearly shouted. "Impossible. It's not mine."

"Said every person ever in possession of illegal drugs," Officer Wendell countered. "Take him away."

[Oh, *hell* no,] Keontae said. [I'd tell you to fight this, but they got you way outgunned, JB.]

"I said it's *not* mine. I've never seen them before. Hey!"

A pair of the Farcoast soldiers grabbed him by his arms, pulled them behind his back, and clamped magnetic shackles around his wrists with ridiculous efficiency.

Justin looked back at Captain Marlowe. "Captain, come on! It's not mine!"

Captain Marlowe just stared at him with an eyebrow raised.

Had Gerald stashed them before he died? Or had someone else dropped them in Justin's room?

He scanned the crowd of rig-runners until his eyes met those of Rowley Pine. The bastard was smirking at Justin.

[That motherfucker,] Keontae said. [He set you up.]

"Scan him," a female voice said.

"Who said that?" Officer Wendell surveyed the crowd until, to Justin's absolute surprise, Lora stepped forward.

"Scan him. For the drug. You can do that, right?" Lora pressed. "You can test to see if it's in his system."

"They're also capable of scanning his skin for trace amounts of the drug as residue," Dr. Carrington added. He was a taller guy with short blond hair and glasses.

Officer Wendell hesitated and looked Justin over.

[Bastard's decidin' your fate right before your eyes.] Keontae added, [*Our* fate.]

"Sir." Now Captain Marlowe stepped forward as well. "I think you should do the scan. If it's not him, then I need to know who on my crew is bent and using so I can deal with them."

Officer Wendell cleared his throat. "That's all well and good, Captain, but it isn't your call what happens from here on out." He nodded to one of the soldiers holding a scanner. "Scan the suspect first. If he charts for usage or residue, there is no need to scan further, as far as I'm concerned."

"Yes, sir," the soldier, a woman, said.

She approached Justin and held the scanner up to his head. It rightfully glowed white the whole time.

"He's clean," she reported.

Officer Wendell released an exasperated sigh. "Then release him, and scan the rest of them."

As the soldiers removed the magnetic cuffs from Justin's wrists, the other soldier with the scanner joined the first and began scanning the rest of the rig-runners. Now free, Justin turned back, determined to find out who'd left drugs in his room.

By that point, the smirk on Rowley Pine's face had soured to a tense frown. And sure enough, the scanner's light turned red when it swept over Rowley.

"It wasn't me!" Rowley barked. "I'm innocent! I've never even touched the stuff!"

The same pair of soldiers who'd clamped shackles on Justin started toward Rowley, and Justin grinned.

"Hey—hey! You stay away from me, you hear?" Rowley unslung his pack and tried to swing it at the soldiers, but they batted it away, and it fell from Rowley's hands.

He proceeded to try to run away—where to, Justin had no idea, since the docking bay was just a massive open space—but the soldiers caught him a few steps later and tackled his pudgy body to the hard concrete floor.

"Ow! Get off me, you bastards!" he yelped.

[No less than the prick deserves,] Keontae muttered.

"You said it," Justin muttered back. Justice had never felt so good.

Rowley had devolved into a spitting, swearing mess, and though the soldiers had shackled him and gotten him back on his feet, he still strained and struggled against them.

"I've called another hovercraft to come and escort the three of you to the ship's detention center," Officer Wendell told the soldiers escorting Rowley. "Book him there, and then return to your usual duties. In the meantime, walk him toward the exit, and if he continues to resist, feel free to *inspire* him to be more cooperative."

At that, Rowley's mouth clapped shut, but only for a few seconds. He stared Officer Wendell dead in the eyes and said, "Go to Hell."

Officer Wendell nodded to the two soldiers, and one of them brandished a stun baton. It activated and arced with swirls of purple electrical currents, and he whacked it into Rowley's thigh.

Rowley jerked and then went slack, and his protests silenced indefinitely. Then they dragged him toward the exit and toward a now-approaching hovercraft.

"Scans are complete," the female soldier reported. "Everyone else is clean."

"A drug dealer *and* a user," Captain Marlowe said to Arlie. "Looks like I made the right call after all."

She remained silent and motionless, with her arms folded.

"Now that that's resolved," Officer Wendell motioned toward the hovercraft, "outside the docking bay, the hovertram line will take you to the ship's main thoroughfare through Nidus City. From there, you are free to go where you wish. Please note that all Coalition laws apply equally here as they would on any Coalition planet. Welcome to the *Nidus*."

———————

HALLIE BLINKED, and the light from the jump dissipated, leaving her vision scarred with the light's negative, now a ghostly blur of non-color.

She quickly realized the ship was no longer shaking, and she was still alive and breathing—all good signs. Very good signs, given their situation only moments earlier.

"What happened?" she asked.

"We jumped," Bryant said. "Successfully."

"Everyone alright?" Hallie asked the other scientists.

They all muttered or mumbled affirmations, and Cecilia squeezed Hallie's hand. She'd forgotten she'd taken ahold of it in the first place.

"What about you, Captain?" Hallie called.

She got no response.

"Captain?" she called again, this time a bit louder.

"Oh, shit!" Bryant yelped.

"What?" Hallie blinked, and some of the scarring in her vision dissipated— enough to see the captain slumped to the side in his cockpit chair. Enough to see that the control screens in front of him were not only dark, but burnt and blackened with jagged edges. "Oh no…"

"Shit!" Bryant yelled again. "Oh, God… he's… all that blood…"

Hallie hadn't even noticed the blood at first, but then she saw a pool of it on the floor under Captain Dawes's chair.

She tore at her harness to free herself. Once it released her, she rushed to the cockpit to check on him.

Bryant was on his feet as well, working the straps of Captain Dawes's harness, trying to get him out so they could better examine him.

When Hallie got there, she saw the chunk of metal protruding from Captain Dawes's chest and the blood running down into his lap, melding with the burgundy of his Coalition-issued uniform.

"Oh no," she repeated. She turned back and shouted, "Luke! Get the medkit, now!"

"On it!" Luke replied.

Hallie already knew it would be too little, too late.

She helped Bryant get Captain Dawes out of the chair and out of the cockpit. Cecilia had gotten free of her harness as well and brought the hover-stretcher over for them. With Bryant handling most of the heavy lifting, they laid Captain Dawes on the stretcher, and then Hallie brought it up to waist height with a single tap on its control screen.

"What happened?" Cecilia covered her mouth with her hands.

"Cockpit screens and the console must've exploded somehow. Captain took the brunt of it," Bryant said, his voice shaky. "I… I don't know that I can do anything to help here. I've only had basic medical training…"

"You're doing fine, but I need you back in the cockpit," Hallie said. "Make sure they're not following us. Get us flying again."

Bryant gave her a small but resolute nod. Better for him to focus on something he was good at right now.

Luke produced the medkit—a blaze-orange case loaded with everything from basic medical supplies all the way to a smattering of surgical-grade medical tools.

The hover-stretcher displayed Captain Dawes's vitals—or rather the total lack of them—on its control screen. Everything was flatlined, but Hallie checked his pulse with her fingers anyway. Sometimes these fancy medical devices didn't always function properly…

But she felt no pulse.

"Epinephrine, and then we start compressions," she told Luke, who grabbed a prefilled syringe from the medkit and handed it to her.

Hallie wasn't a medical doctor—not in the classic sense of the word—but she understood human physiology better than most medical doctors ever would.

She'd built her career on it, written volumes on it, helped to create procedures and technology that would reshape it forever... but even she couldn't resurrect a man from the dead.

Still, if there was any chance to save Captain Dawes, she had to try. She pulled on some disposable gloves and got to work.

Fifteen minutes later, after compressions, epinephrine, and even defibrillations, nothing had changed. Captain Dawes's blood dripped off the sides of the hover-stretcher onto the cold floor below, and his face had gone pale from exsanguination.

He was dead.

Hallie stepped back and pulled her gloves off. She set them next to Captain Dawes's body on the hover-stretcher. She glanced at the blood on the cockpit floor. Perhaps she should've left the gloves on; they had a lot of cleanup to do.

"He saved us," Cecilia said. "He saved us, and it cost him his life."

"A true hero," Luke added. "It should've been me instead."

Hallie shook her head. "That's a noble thought, Luke, but we need you. You're a part of this project. Captain Dawes's sacrifice won't be in vain."

"It might be if we're stranded here," Angela said.

"Don't have to worry about that," Bryant's sullen voice called from the cockpit. "We're on backup power until I can restore total power. Gonna take another few minutes, but we should be up and running soon. In the meantime, at least we're still drifting in the right direction... more or less."

"What do we do with him?" Luke asked.

"I... I don't know," Hallie replied as Bryant stepped out of the cockpit. "Are there regulations about this sort of thing?"

"Soldier's last ride," Bryant said. Everyone stared at him, so he added, "Burial in space. Not a fancy funeral, but that's what we do. Keeps the bodies from stacking up."

Hallie's stomach churned at the thought. Perhaps that policy was advisable for periods of conflict or during wartime, but it didn't seem right to treat Captain Dawes that way. He'd given his life to save theirs. He'd been someone Hallie could trust, absolutely, to help her get that cylinder where it needed to go—perhaps the only person she could truly trust.

And now they were supposed to expel him from the ship like trash? It wasn't right. It just wasn't right. He deserved so much better.

Bryant must've read the concern on her face. He looked down at her and said, "I'll handle it. You don't have to worry about it."

"No," she said. "We need you to get us on the move again. We don't have any time to spare. They keep finding us, and now it has finally cost us big time. We need to get where we're going, and fast. We'll take care of the cleanup and Captain Dawes."

"You got it," Bryant said. With that, he headed into the aft section of the ship, past the suspension crate, and descended the metal staircase into the ship's engine room below decks.

"Come on," Hallie told the others. "If we do this, let's do it right. We'll send Captain Dawes off with as much honor as we can."

About five minutes later, Bryant had the power reestablished throughout the ship, and he joined them for Captain Dawes's send-off via the airlock. The sight of his body jettisoning into space made Hallie shudder, but she told herself to accept it as the harsh reality of this life.

It didn't help.

Once the deed was done, Bryant returned to the cockpit and put them back on course.

While the others began cleaning up the hover-stretcher and the floor around it, Hallie began working on the pool of blood in the cockpit. The metallic scent soured in her nose and twisted her stomach, but she pushed through it.

"How close are we?" she asked.

Bryant set the autopilot, donned some gloves of his own, and bent down beside her to help sop up the captain's blood with another rag. "A few hours. Six, at most."

"Do we have that much time?" Hallie was afraid to hear his answer.

"No way to know for sure, but if not..." He gave her a sad grin and took her gloved hand in his. "...it's been a hell of a ride."

She matched his sad grin with one of her own and gently pulled her hand away. "Yeah. I hope it doesn't end like that. It can't. We're so close to making it."

"I still have hope," Bryant said. "You should, too. I don't think we would've come all this way, endured so much, only to fail now. I don't think that's our destiny."

"Destiny isn't real, Bryant," Hallie said. "It's an illusion. It's not quantifiable or measurable in any way. It's wishful thinking and optimism if things go well, and it's pessimism and defeatism if things don't."

"Spoken like a true woman of science," Bryant said. "Believe what you want. You won't change my mind."

Even though Hallie disagreed with his belief, she had to admit he had given her hope.

But would that hope be enough to see them through to the end?

The bloody rag in her hand said no. It was a physical manifestation of the random chance of the universe at work. Captain Dawes hadn't expected to die before they'd jumped, but he'd died all the same. And he'd demonstrated more hope than any of them—after all, he'd initiated the jump.

Now he was gone, killed because of the intersection of his actions, the actions of their pursuers, and a freak explosion in their ship.

Hope was as fleeting as ever.

Even so, she still wanted to believe otherwise.

THE HOVERCRAFT RIDE from the docking bay toward the *Nidus's* central area proved as clean yet as stale as the docking bay itself had been. But that all changed when the corridor opened up, and the ship's red-orange dome came into view through the shielded windows on the hovercraft's ceiling.

Justin still couldn't see through it, but within moments, he was about to enter it and see it from the inside. He had some idea what to expect, but as they passed into the dome via an opening large enough for the hovercraft to fit through, all of Justin's expectations blew out the airlock.

An entire city came into view, complete with skyscrapers, paved streets, and hovercraft darting to and fro in no discernible traffic pattern. Neon blue, purple, and green lights glowed from countless windows, buildings, and scrawling signs, casting a welcoming, if not alluring vibe throughout the space.

Overhead, the red-orange dome sealed everything in under a canopy of blue sky with sporadic clouds and even a distant, yet glowing sun. None of it was real, Justin knew—just a concerted effort to provide the illusion of fresh air and sunshine.

If he had to guess, the dome's interior would shift throughout the course of the day and night, following the trajectory of the sun and providing appropriate light for a standard Coalition twenty-four-hour day. Justin had never seen anything like it.

The hovercraft stopped, and the Farcoast soldiers beckoned them to exit the vehicle and venture into Nidus City. Some of Justin's coworkers tried to ask the soldiers for directions or information, but none of them offered any help. They just boarded the same hovercraft and disappeared deeper into the city.

"Look," Captain Marlowe addressed them, "I don't know how long the repairs will take. Just keep your portable comms handy so I can reach you when we're getting ready to leave. Otherwise, you have some R&R time, so make the most of it."

The *Viridian's* crew looked at each other and then dispersed into the city on foot, each more or less taking their own path. To Justin's surprise, not even

Captain Marlowe and Arlie stayed together. They each went their separate ways as well.

As Justin set out down a busy thoroughfare, a voice called his name. He turned back and saw Lora standing there. Her purple-tipped hair stood out among the myriad of people passing by.

"I was thinking," she said as she approached him, "we're in this nice setting. City lights and all that. Maybe it's a good chance for us to try again? We gotta find rooms for the night anyway. Maybe we get dinner, see some sights, and then share a room? Would save some credits, too."

[Don't fall for it, JB. This ain't Paris. It's a random colonist ship city that they're gonna plant on some un-terraformed planet to start a new civilization,] Keontae warned. [And trust me—splittin' a room for the sake of savin' money is the *last* thing on her mind.]

Justin agreed with Keontae on this one. He'd planned to just grab a quick local meal, find a place to hunker down, and then maybe do some exploring. He could appreciate the idea of sharing those experiences with someone else, but given how everything had gone with Lora thus far, he had no desire to spend that time with her.

"Lora..." Justin started.

A hopeful smile brightened her pretty face.

[Be decisive, man, or she'll turn it back on you like she did before.]

"...I'm gonna pass. I appreciate the offer, but it's better that we don't entangle ourselves like this," Justin said. He wanted to add, "especially since I'm your boss now." He figured saying something like that aloud would be akin to detonating a bomb in his own face, so he held off.

Lora's optimistic expression soured. She slung a slew of curses at Justin, some in Spanish, and then disappeared into the city.

[Good enough.]

"Yeah. She left, anyway." Justin walked in the exact opposite direction.

For the first hour, he roamed Nidus City's downtown area, taking in the imposing structures and wondering whose brilliant idea it was to build and launch an entire city onto a new planet all in one shot. Hovercraft continued to soar overhead, some of them loud and rumbling and others as quiet as a whisper.

Men and women in fine clothes, most of them also glowing with some sort of neon light, usually in the lapels of their coats or along the seams of their sleeves, strode in and out of the buildings like colorful ants coming and going from a nest. Most hardly noticed him, but those who did looked him up and down with no small amount of disdain in their eyes.

The panes of glass—or whatever it was—that made up the buildings reflected

Justin's haggard appearance. He wasn't one of these people, and he didn't belong there. That was for sure.

The first restaurant he happened upon served only vegan food, grown aboard the ship, and the prices were astronomical. He didn't even need to come up with a third strike against the place, and he moved on.

A few other restaurants offered either fine dining or cookie-cutter fast-food options, but Justin wanted something more niche, more local, if he could find it. Problem was, he didn't even know where to begin.

He stopped a man in the street—middle-aged and with a decent-sized belly hidden under his glowing orange coat. Didn't look too rich, but looked well fed enough. Justin figured he would know some good spots.

"Excuse me," Justin said. "Love your jacket, friend."

"Out of my way, vagrant." The man huffed as he tried to get around Justin. "Panhandling is illegal, you know."

"Sorry…" Justin stepped into his path again. "Not trying to panhandle. Got plenty of my own credits. Just wanted to ask if you could point me to some good local food."

"Local?" The man huffed again. "Nothing here is 'local.' This is a colonist ship. Now move."

Justin positioned himself in front of the man again. "Really sorry. Something ethnic, then? Unique?"

The man growled at him. "Head down this street, then take a right on 34th. Take it all the way down to the Asian District. Plenty of options there. Now I'm rushing to a meeting. Will you let me go, please?"

Justin stepped aside and let the man pass.

[Asian District, huh?] Keontae said. [I used to come down *hard* on some Asian food back in the day. You know… when I wasn't incorporeal.]

"Well, maybe you can at least catch a whiff when we find a good spot." Justin's stomach rumbled. Asian food sounded pretty amazing. He set out for 34th Street and took his right turn.

The farther away from downtown he traveled, the smaller and less opulent the buildings became. Rather than covered in mirrored glass, they were constructed of concrete and metal, and he didn't have to look up forty stories to see the tops of these buildings.

He noticed what looked like apartment complexes and shops, as well as a handful of restaurants. Some were chain stores, but a handful of unique stops were mixed in, too.

He almost caved and stopped at a small Greek restaurant with a blue neon "GYROS" sign in the window next to an image of someone he could only assume was a high-tech Julius Caesar, but he decided to follow through on his original plan and kept heading toward the Asian District.

Before long, the buildings took on a different tone. They looked to be about the same size as the buildings outside downtown, but they had a distinctively Asian flare. Justin had visited a couple of large cities on some of the planets where he'd worked for mining companies, and he'd visited similar Asian districts there, albeit only briefly.

Beyond the architecture, the neon Asian symbols and characters in the windows and on the sides of the buildings added to the effect. Justin spoke precisely zero words in any Asian language, so he couldn't differentiate between Chinese, Japanese, or any other language. It all looked more or less the same to him, even though he knew it wasn't.

Bamboo—possibly real, but possibly some sort of synthetic lookalike—adorned many of the shops and buildings, and red tiles that resembled dragon scales covered the tops of several of the buildings. Others had the same style of tiled roof, but in other colors—some blue or green or brown.

The deeper into the Asian District he went, the more the delicious aromas of food threatened to overwhelm his hunger. A series of food carts along the street, which had at some point shifted to a sort of cobblestone surface instead of standard concrete, beckoned him over.

Seared meats and vegetables, rice, and varieties of sauces, some hot and some mild, tantalized his senses. He found a vendor selling dumplings of some sort, but when he asked what was in them, he quickly realized the short, older man operating the cart didn't speak English. Justin only got lots of head-shaking and shoulder-shrugging, both of which he returned.

"Please allow me to translate," an unusual voice behind him said.

Justin turned back to find, of all things, an android approaching. It looked to be a standard human-shaped model like the ones at ACM-1134 had been, but it had a metallic blue body and limbs instead of chrome. The lights in its wrists, ankles, and chest glowed red, and a shining gold star on its chest told the rest of the story.

Justin's first impulse was to extend his energy sword from his robotic arm and cut the thing down, but this security android wasn't going to harm him. Still, he didn't exactly trust it, either.

"Sure," he agreed. "I just want to know what's in the dumplings."

Every culture ate different meats and vegetables, and even though Justin was exploring, he didn't want to venture *too* far into the unknown.

The android translated for him, and the vendor replied.

"He says they contain pork, cabbage, and carrots," the android relayed. "He has others that feature beef and chicken as well."

[JB,] Keontae said, [if you don't try 'em all, we can't be friends anymore.]

Justin's stomach growled in agreement. "Tell him I want three of each, with a side of rice. And sauce."

The android translated again, and the vendor smiled at him and nodded. He packed everything into a trio of paper containers, stuffed it into a paper bag, and dropped a pair of chopsticks in there.

Justin hesitated. "Fork?"

As he pantomimed using a fork, the vendor just shook his head and laughed.

Well, guess that's my answer. Justin paid the vendor a modest amount of credits—super reasonable for all the food he'd gotten—and threw in a few extras as a tip for the vendor, who smiled and nodded again, and then he bowed.

Justin gave him an awkward half-hearted bow and a thumbs-up.

"If that will be all, I must continue my rounds," the android said.

"Yeah, sure. Thanks," Justin said to him.

"I am happy to serve," the android replied, then it walked away with clanking steps.

[More of that shit again,] Keontae said. [A machine bein' happy to serve.]

"Hey, don't begrudge the machine its happiness," Justin said. "You're pretty much one of them at this point."

[Say that again, and I'll turn your next shower into an icy rain. We'll see who's happy then.]

Justin picked up a sweetened green tea from another vendor and carried his dinner over to a stone bench near a shop selling what appeared to be Chinese or Japanese lanterns. Even with the handicap of using chopsticks, he devoured all of it within a matter of minutes, and he savored every glorious bite.

[You done stuffin' your face?]

Justin puffed his bloated belly out and grinned. "I wasn't stuffing my face."

[I'm right here. Saw all of it,] Keontae said. [You should be prosecuted for war crimes.]

Justin slurped down the rest of his tea. "You're just jealous."

[Damn right I'm jealous.] Hurt, and a bit of anger, lined Keontae's voice.

"Look... I'm sorry I said that," Justin began. "I was just trying to keep up with your banter. I didn't mean to—"

[It's fine. Can't be helped,] Keontae said. [Ain't mad at you. Just mad at the situation.]

Justin nodded. "Well, I'm sorry anyway."

[Like I said, we're good. Don't worry about it.]

As Justin sat back, a flurry of bright neon lights materialized into a huge hologram before his eyes. The lights knitted together in a rainbow of colors, forming intricate patterns and images that gradually joined together as scales, limbs, and a massive head.

It was a classic Chinese dragon, the kind Justin had seen depicted in art countless times throughout his life. Here it was again, as a hologram, weaving and floating up and down above the street without a care in the world.

[Wow...] Keontae said. [That's somethin' you don't see every day.]

"Incredible," Justin said. "Looks almost real."

[I love Asian culture, man,] Keontae said. [If I hadn't been born black, I woulda wanted to be Asian. Chinese, Japanese, Korean, Thai... don't matter which one. It's all legit, and their food is bangin', too.]

"Got that right," Justin said.

Justin continued watching as the dragon's tail writhed into view, lithe and strong and brilliant with colors. The dragon wafted down the street, away from them, and it turned a corner instead of traveling out of the Asian District.

"You, guy," a voice broke Justin out of his trance.

He turned. In the entrance to the shop stood an Asian guy about Justin's age, wearing a white apron over his clothes.

"You go," he said in broken English.

"Huh?" Justin stared at him.

"You go now. Stop talk to yourself and go," the man said.

"Oh. Sorry." Justin collected his garbage from dinner and stuffed it all into the paper bag. He looked around but didn't see anywhere to drop his trash. He did, however, notice a group of four young men, all of Asian descent, staring at him from across the street. He ignored them. "Uh... is there a garbage can somewhere I can—"

"I take." The man in the store entrance motioned Justin forward with his hand outstretched, and he took the bag from Justin. "Now you go. Big trouble, you stay. Go."

Justin had no idea what he'd done to invite such treatment, aside from talking to himself, but he didn't want to argue. The artificial sun had sunk toward the dome's horizon, and night was descending over Nidus City. He needed to find a place to crash for the night anyway, and any further conversation wouldn't be worth his time or the Asian man's.

He started walking down the street. "What was that about?"

[Beats me. Probably nothin'.]

As he walked, Justin noticed the four Asian guys keeping pace with him, but staying on the other side of the street.

"That's not a good sign."

[Just stay over here. Forget about them.]

Hard to forget about someone—or four someones—who were practically stalking him like prey. Three of them wore short-sleeved black shirts with slits cut into them on the torso, revealing their glowing undershirts beneath. One glowed blue, another glowed green, and the third glowed with a violet color, like so many of the neon lights marking the various establishments in the Asian District.

The other one wore the same attire, only his outer shirt was white, and his undershirt glowed orange, making his torso almost look as if he were on fire. Maybe he was the leader?

Whatever the case, it was immediately clear they were not only together and unified in purpose, but they were organized, too. Maybe a gang.

Tattoos ran down the lengths of their lean arms to their knuckles and fingers, and more tattoos crept up their exposed necks to their jaws. Portions of their tattoos gleamed like shining metal in the light, but Justin couldn't tell whether they were some sort of augmentation or prosthesis like his arm or if they were just really fancy tattoos.

[Don't look at 'em, JB. Just keep walkin'.]

"Trying, Key."

With everything in Asian writing, he couldn't decipher what was what, so he'd been heading back down 34th Street toward the area surrounding downtown. In the distance, the downtown skyscrapers glowed. If he could get back to the English-speaking part of town, he could find a place to stay and put this very mixed experience in the Asian District behind him.

But as he advanced, the group of four guys sped up and stepped into the street ahead of him, blocking his path.

Justin stopped and stared at them, and they stared right back, unblinking.

The one in the white shirt had blond hair, definitely bleached and dyed and probably bleached again. The others had black hair, and all of them stared at Justin with dark, probing eyes.

"Can I help you boys?" Justin asked. He immediately regretted calling them "boys," but it was too late now. He just hoped he'd come across as pleasant enough that it wouldn't sound like an insult.

The sun now barely crested its digital horizon. Before long, it would be night, and everything about Nidus City would completely change, as happened in most cities at nightfall. Already, several streetlamps had begun to glow with golden light, each of them adorned with Asian ornamentations and symbols.

The one in white with the blond hair stepped forward. In accented English, he said, "You came to the wrong place tonight."

[I swear, you're a magnet for bullshit, JB,] Keontae said. [No wonder I'm dead. I hung around you too much.]

"You're not dead... not exactly. And *thanks*."

"What did you say? You trying to get smart with us?"

"No, sorry. Just talking to myself," Justin said. "If you'll let me past, I'll get out of your way."

"Too late for that," the guy in the white said. "You're already in too deep. Only way out now is to buy your way out."

Yep. Definitely a gang.

"Guys, I barely have any credits in the first place," Justin lied. "I work on a mining rig. Almost all of my money goes into my savings account. Gotta make a trip to Bortundi Prime to see a family friend, so all my credits are going toward that."

"Don't care," the guy in white said. "You're on our turf. You want to leave? Then you pay."

Justin despised these types of situations. He hated to lose control, to feel powerless, to be extorted.

He glanced down at the street and realized that the cobblestones were actually translucent—possibly Plastrex, even. Below them, soft light shone upward, and the colorful silhouettes of koi fish swam in an underground tank of some sort. It was a really neat touch, but he couldn't appreciate it. Not right now.

He countered, "Then I guess I'll stick around."

The guy in white shook his head. "No. You got to go."

"But... I have to pay you before I leave?" Justin clarified.

"Yes." The guy in white stepped closer to Justin, and his three friends followed. "Right now."

"And what happens if I don't pay?"

[They're gonna kick your ass. You never saw any old martial arts movies?]

Justin waited for the guy in white to respond.

"You will pay one way or another. That is for certain."

"You got a name, chief?" Justin asked. "Chief" might've been a derogatory nickname as well, but at this point, Justin didn't care. He wasn't going to just roll over and let these thugs take what was rightfully his.

"Quan Yazhu," the guy in white replied. "Remember that name before you come in here next time."

"I'm just passing through, Quan. I don't want to fight with you about this. Just let me go, and I'll never come back, okay?"

Quan shook his head. "No. You're in *Ikari* territory. Now you will pay. Make your choice."

Ikari? Justin glanced around. Where was that damned police android when he really needed it?

"No one is coming to help you, miner," Quan said. "Time's up. What do you choose?"

The three other thugs encircled Justin, blocking any hope for a clean escape.

[Too late to run,] Keontae said. [I don't think you got enough credits with you to satisfy 'em. You might be fightin' either way.]

"Then I might as well do it from the start," Justin mumbled, and he squeezed his right fist hard and fast.

Quan opened his mouth to say something else, but he went silent at the sight of Justin's orange energy sword extending from his robotic wrist.

SIX

"Is this really how you want this to go?" Justin asked. "Because I've been through a hell you couldn't even begin to fathom. You want a taste of that, then come on over."

[That's right, JB,] Keontae said. [Don't take any shit from these bastards.]

Quan glanced back at the other three, all of whom stood their ground, well trained, disciplined. Waiting for Quan's direction.

He nodded to them, and they each pulled plasma repeaters from the back of their waistbands and pointed them at Justin.

[Uh... I take it back.] Keontae yelled, [Run!]

Justin took off and ran to the side, deeper into the Asian District. As he ran, he released his clenched fist, and the energy sword fizzled to nothing once again.

Plasma blasts sheared into buildings as he passed them by, but his legs didn't stop moving. Shouts sounded behind him, and they made him run even faster.

That's what I get for bringing an energy sword to a gunfight.

He turned off the main street, rounded a corner, and found himself facing an alley with a dead end and no more glowing cobblestones under his feet.

[On your right,] Keontae said.

Justin looked to his left and saw nothing.

[No, your *other* right!]

On his right, Justin found a side entrance to some sort of business. Orange Asian symbols glowed from the metal door's surface. Justin put his hand on the door. His fingers tingled, the symbols turned green, and the door slid open.

"Thanks," Justin said.

[Got you,] Keontae replied.

More shouting behind him. Definitely not in English.

Plasma crackled toward him, and Justin ducked into the shop just in time. The blasts sizzled past and smacked into the back wall of the alley.

The door shut behind him, and he placed his hand on it again so Keontae could lock it. Similar characters on the inside of the door went from green to orange.

[Don't stop. That door's not very strong. They'll get through.]

"Great."

Justin stood in a room lined with shelves of food—everything from sacks of rice to boxes of produce and crates containing... something. They were all labeled with Asian characters, and Justin didn't have time to explore.

It looked like some sort of storage room, and he saw another sliding door ahead, between two shelving units.

Pounding sounded on the side door, another reminder that he had to keep moving. He bolted for the door, and it slid open on its own.

On the other side, Justin found a grocery store of sorts. The same food and boxes lined the shelves out here, but it had a more inviting, welcoming feel, and it was smaller than the storage room had been—more homey. Blue-white light shined throughout the whole store, giving it an almost clinical feel.

A clerk, or perhaps the proprietor, stood behind a counter, wearing a white apron stained with blood. Embedded in the counter, a case displayed various meats. Dead chickens and ducks, both plucked clean of feathers, hung from hooks on the ceiling around him.

The proprietor gawked at Justin, pointed, and said something Justin couldn't understand.

"Hi." Justin waved, then he rushed toward the front of the shop.

But as he made it to the front, two of the four Ikari thugs strode into the store. They both noticed him immediately and raised their repeaters.

Shit.

The proprietor ducked behind his counter, and Justin dove behind the nearest shelf as plasma blasts sheared into the back wall and the bags of rice stacked there.

On his hands and knees, Justin scrambled across the other two rows of shelves and took cover behind one of them.

The two thugs spoke to each other—Justin made out distinct voices, but as usual, he couldn't understand them.

[They're tryin' to box you in,] Keontae said. [One on your left, one on your right.]

"You speak their language now?" Justin joked.

[Actually, yeah, I do,] Keontae said. [It's Chinese. Learned it from the door I just hacked. Only some, but it's enough to make out what they're saying.]

"Nice that you've become a sentient Rosetta Stone, but that doesn't help me get *out* of here. What do I do?" Justin hissed.

[I'm gonna scare the shit out of 'em,] Keontae said. [When you see me move outta your arm, use your stun gun to take the first one down. Stay low, aim well. Headin' to your right.]

"Okay. Damn good idea."

[I know.] Keontae quickly added, [*Now*.]

Justin's arm tingled, and Keontae materialized to the right of the shelf, wreathed in green light.

An obvious gasp sounded from the first of the two thugs, and then Justin curled around the shelf, took quick but careful aim with his palm, and shot a stun blast.

The thug seized, went rigid, and went down. His repeater clattered away, but not toward Justin. But he was out... for now.

His friend rushed over to him, spouting off something in Chinese, but he stopped when he saw Keontae still standing there. Then Keontae started to hover toward him.

Justin followed, but he stayed low.

The Ikari thug shouted and yelled and fired his repeater at Keontae in erratic shots, each of which passed through Keontae as if he were... well, a ghost.

With his green arms spread wide, Keontae descended toward the thug, who now cowered in fear at the apparition before him. He covered his face with his arms and looked away, quivering.

When next the thug looked up, Justin stood in Keontae's place, pointing his metal palm at the thug.

"Lights out," Justin said. Then he stunned him.

Keontae jumped into Justin's arm again with a tingle.

"Good work, Key." Justin reached down to grab one of the plasma repeaters.

Behind them, the door to the storage room slid open, and the third thug in black stepped into the store. Justin froze.

[Don't celebrate yet, JB!]

The thug fired fresh blasts at Justin, who abandoned his hope of grabbing one of the repeaters. Instead, he ran for the store entrance.

[The cage!]

"What?"

[Control panel. Touch it, and I'll lock all three of 'em in the store,] Keontae explained.

Justin saw it and dove for it with his right hand extended. His fingers smacked the control panel, and Keontae jumped into the store's network with another tingle in Justin's fingertips.

The metal cage in the store's wide front opening rattled down and locked in place. The thug kept firing, but the blasts continued to miss Justin, who'd stepped clear of his line of sight. Then the cage rattled again, and the bars twisted to the side, revealing that they weren't bars at all but rather metal panels that formed a solid wall of metal, locking everyone inside.

Another panel on the outside of the store blinked with a green light. A signal from Keontae.

Justin touched the panel and felt the familiar vibration of Keontae reentering his arm. All the while, the metal wall rattled as the thug trapped inside tried to get out, but he couldn't.

[*Now* you can tell me I did well.]

"What about the back door?" Justin asked.

[Cage is down over that, too,] Keontae replied. [So like I said, you can tell me—]

"*Hey!*" a shout interrupted Keontae's words.

Justin turned back to the street.

Quan stood there, still clad in his white shirt and glowing orange undershirt. The light from the irradiated koi pond under the street gave him a ferocious appearance, especially now that night had fully fallen. He looked like a phantom bent on revenge.

But instead of holding a repeater in his hand, he held a gleaming whote sword. It was curved and looked more like a katana than any Chinese sword Justin had ever seen.

[Those dudes were speakin' Chinese, and so was Quan earlier,] Keontae replied. [Sword's definitely Japanese, though, and so is the word *Ikari*. Means 'fury,' loosely translated. But I'm not surprised. You've seen this place. It's a blend of lots of Asian cultures. Even included some Arabic ones, too. Probably why it's called the 'Asian District' and not 'Chinatown,' or somethin' like that.]

"So what do you think he's gonna do with the sword?" Justin asked.

[Probably wants to cut off your other arm,] Keontae said. [And you're welcome, by the way.]

"For what?"

[My cultural insight.]

"Yeah. I feel more informed than ever."

Quan pointed the white sword at Justin. "You and me. Man to man. Your sword against mine."

[I'm gonna go out on a limb here and guess he probably knows what he's doin' with that thing. Probably a bad idea to fight 'im.]

"I think I agree with you."

"Quit talking to yourself and accept my challenge," Quan demanded.

Justin started toward him. "What do I get if I win?"

"I let you leave."

[JB, you're not seriously considering doin' this?]

Justin ignored Keontae. "And if you win?"

"You die."

[Yeah... don't do this, JB. He'll cut you into sashimi.]

"I've got a plan," Justin muttered. "One swing of that sword, and mine will cut right through it. Boom. End of fight."

[Not much of a plan.]

"Why complicate things? Occam's razor scooter, and all that," Justin muttered.

[That's not the term.]

"Close enough." Then, louder, Justin said, "I accept."

Quan beckoned him into the vivid blue street, which was now empty aside from the two of them. Everyone else must've fled once the shooting started.

The glow from the cobblestones beneath their feet provided ample light for Justin to see his opponent, and the abundance of neon lights on the buildings around them cast Quan's angry face and his blond hair in various colors.

Justin stood about six feet away from Quan, clenched his right fist, and extended his energy sword. It burned orange like Quan's undershirt, only brighter and hotter.

"Let's go," Justin said.

Quan inched closer with the sword cocked near his shoulder, ready to swing.

Justin didn't move.

The white sword flashed toward Justin's head, and he took a step back and brought his energy sword up to defend.

But instead of his energy sword shearing through Quan's blade, the white sword sliced clean through the orange energy, briefly interrupting its flow, and slammed into the side of Justin's shoulder.

The blow sent vibrations ricocheting into Justin's chest and down his arm, and he stumbled back, shocked that Quan's sword was still intact. He looked down at his arm and saw a noticeable groove in the metal where Quan had struck him. Had Justin not stepped back, the blade very well could have sliced through his neck instead.

With his mouth hanging open, Justin asked, "How?"

"Galvanized heatproof alloy," Quan replied with a cunning smile. "Can't be destroyed by weapons such as yours."

Shit.

[You may wanna consider running again.]

But before Justin got the chance, Quan attacked, swinging his sword like a demon. Justin clumsily dodged about three-quarters of the blows, somehow managing to stay on his feet while he did. The other quarter he batted away with his metal arm itself.

Fury indeed.

None of Quan's strikes actually hurt his metal arm—he'd barely ever felt any pain in it since Garth had lowered his pain settings down to their minimum level back at ACM-1134—but he knew he could only last so long before Quan outmaneuvered him and cut him somewhere else. Then the fight would really be over.

[Your arm's strong, JB,] Keontae reminded him. [Use that!]

Good idea. Quan's sword may have been impervious to heat and energy, but it was still only a thin piece of metal. Justin waited for his moment, and on Quan's next swing, he blocked with his metal forearm and quickly grabbed its white blade with his metal fingers.

He squeezed and wrenched all at once, but instead of the blade bending, it shattered into shards under the force of his grip.

Now it was Quan's turn to back up with a stunned expression on his face while Justin gloated.

Quan's surprise vanished in a blink, and he leaped at Justin with his foot extended.

Justin took the kick square to his chest, and it knocked him flat on his back. In his periphery, a big orange koi floated under the left side of his head and emerged from under the right side of his head.

At the same time, Quan's left foot screamed down toward Justin's face, and he rolled to the side.

CRACK.

As Justin launched up to his feet, he realized that Quan's foot had actually managed to crack the faux-cobblestone street. Was his leg prosthetic, like Justin's arm?

He was wearing baggy black pants, so Justin had no way of knowing. But Justin's chest felt like he'd been hit with a sledgehammer, and if he hadn't moved, his head would've been reduced to mush on the street.

Quan engaged Justin again, this time with a series of kicks and punches, most of which Justin took as blows on his arms and occasionally to his face. They all hurt, but they weren't enough to take Justin down. Quan was the smaller of the two, and he wasn't hitting very hard.

Then Quan's left foot lashed up at his head, primed to take his head clean off, but Justin's right arm went up to defend. A muted metallic clank sounded upon impact, and Justin got his answer. Quan's lower leg, if not his entire leg and hip, was prosthetic.

The kick sent Justin reeling anyway, and he staggered to keep from falling. Quan's attacks persisted, but Justin didn't want to get pummeled anymore, so he focused on avoiding as many of them as he could.

Quan moved faster and had way more actual skill than Justin did, but Justin had one advantage: his arm's enhanced strength. Time to put it to use and end this.

Another devastating kick from Quan's prosthetic leg launched toward Justin's head, but this time, Justin's right arm blocked the attack, hooked around Quan's shin, and locked his ankle in place. Then Justin took one huge step, leveraged all the strength his arm could muster, and twisted hard.

He'd hoped to throw Quan a mile down the street, but instead Quan's back crashed into one of the food vendors' carts, knocking it over and spilling its contents all over the street.

[*Day-um*, JB!] Keontae hooted. [I thought that boy was gonna kick your ass. You must've picked up some fighting shit after all.]

"Learned everything I know from you," Justin said. "That, and after the mine, I'm just not afraid anymore."

[I hear that. Still, nice work, bro.]

As Keontae finished saying it, Quan slowly rose from the wreckage of the cart. He wobbled a bit, dazed but somehow still standing. Justin was impressed. He had to admit it.

Food stains marred Quan's white short-sleeved shirt on both the front and back, and dark sauce dripped from his tattooed hands and forearms. Justin had to do a double take to be sure it wasn't blood.

"I will *kill* you," Quan seethed at him.

[I think we're done here, JB. Sleep this bastard, and let's go.]

The ache in Justin's chest and in sporadic other spots on his human arm and torso echoed Keontae's sentiment. Quan rushed forward with a barbaric yell, and Justin opened the palm of his right hand and shot him with a stun blast.

Quan slumped to the glowing street, quivering, but alive, with koi swimming all around his body. If Justin were honest with himself, Quan probably *would've* kicked his ass if the fight had continued, so Justin had done what he needed to do to end it.

"Sorry, but I'm not gonna fight you anymore," Justin said. "I'm gone. You won't see me again. Be good, Quan."

With that, Justin turned back toward downtown and left Quan lying in the street.

IF HE'D WANTED TO, Justin could've booked a room at one of the ultra-posh hotels downtown, but it would've shredded his credit balance. In the end, he'd settled on a modest place outside of downtown but plenty far away from the Asian District —just in case Quan and his friends decided they hadn't had enough.

The thought occurred to Justin that an environment like this, aboard a colonist ship with its own city inside, shouldn't have any use for hotels, or at least very little. Unless they got regular traffic from random ships like the *Viridian*, which seemed unlikely given their empty docking bay, who was meant to stay in these hotels?

He supposed that people from one part of the city might want to visit another part without feeling the need to head home for the night, or perhaps the hotels offered more of a getaway experience for patrons. And even on colony ships, people probably still went out, got hammered, and couldn't get back home. Maybe the hotels helped out there, too.

Even so, the one he'd chosen seemed pretty empty. He was the only one in the lobby when he walked in, until the concierge emerged from an office behind the front desk. She was a young lady with deep brown eyes, cute, and with dark hair. Might've been Asian, in fact, but Justin couldn't tell for sure.

And even if she was Asian, she didn't *have* to live in the Asian District. That kind of segregation based on race was mostly a thing of the past, especially where the Coalition was concerned. They didn't tolerate that sort of bullshit.

She booked Justin for a basic room and directed him to the grav lifts, and he headed up to his room on the top floor for the night. After a quick shower, during which Justin discovered several new bruises, courtesy of Quan, he retired for the night.

As promised, Keontae jumped out of Justin's arm and into the hotel's system, leaving Justin alone and in perfect solitude. Exhausted, he fell asleep in no time.

"*JUSTIN.*" A voice dragged him out of his dreamless sleep and into the darkness of his room. "Wake up, man."

The voice was Keontae's, but the room around Justin and the comfortable bed he lay on made no sense.

Then it clicked into place—the hotel. The colonist ship. Repairs to the *Viridian*.

"What?" he asked, still groggy and unwilling to move from the softness of his bed, even as the green light from Keontae flared ever brighter.

"Get your *ass* out of bed, JB," Keontae said. "You got trouble comin'."

"Pshhht. What trouble?" Justin mumbled.

"Quan and the Ikari," Keontae said. "Only there's like twenty of 'em this time."

SEVEN

Justin jerked upright. "*What?*"

"No joke, JB," Keontae said. "They're in the lobby now, headin' toward the stairs. I already shut down the grav lifts to buy you some time. You gotta go, man."

That concierge girl *had* sold him out after all.

Maybe. It didn't really matter now.

Justin threw on his clothes and yanked on his boots, then he headed for the hotel room door.

"I'm gonna stay in the system 'til you get to the roof," Keontae said.

"Wait, *what?*" Justin almost shouted.

"Quiet, man!" Keontae hissed. "You can't go down. They got guys waitin' in the lobby and out the back of the hotel, too. Only way outta this is on the roof."

Justin's vision wobbled at the thought of it. "This building's seven stories high."

"So is the one next to it. You either gotta get over your fear of heights and get across, or you're gonna be dragon food."

Justin swore a litany of curses, but he had to trust Keontae on this. "Which way do I go when I get out of the room?"

"Hang a right, and then a hard left. There's a roof access door down the hall and on the left side. I'll make sure it's open for you."

"Got it."

"And when you get to the roof, follow my lead. I snatched a map of the city. I'll direct you."

"Good."

Justin pulled the door open, thankful he hadn't brought anything with him from the rig, and turned right. He took the first hard left and found the roof access door. As he reached it, the door slid open, and Justin walked through. It slid shut right away and locked behind him.

The ladder before him ascended a good ten feet up to the roof, but he steeled himself, grabbed the bottom rung, and pulled himself up. A minute later, the hatch at the top opened on its own, and he climbed onto the roof.

Around him, Nidus City glowed blue, purple, and green against the stark black of the night sky. The downtown skyscrapers still loomed in the distance and still radiated their tranquil lights. Hovercraft flowed through the city like blood cells through arteries, albeit slower and less frequently than they had that afternoon when he'd arrived.

Justin briefly wondered if the dome overhead had just gone transparent, and if the stars he could see above were actually there, or if the whole thing was just a continuation of the sunny sequence he'd seen earlier. Ultimately, it didn't matter; if he didn't escape, he'd never see another sunrise—real or otherwise —again.

The roof hatch closed behind him, again on its own. Then a control panel on what might've been a roof-mounted climate-control unit began to glow with green light. He hurried over to it and slapped his metal palm on it, and his hand tingled as Keontae leaped into his arm.

[Edge of the roof, straight ahead. You'll see the next one,] Keontae said. [It's even a bit lower. You can make the jump.]

"Jump?" Justin shook his head. "You didn't say it was a *jump*."

An explosion sounded behind him, and the hotel's roof shuddered under his feet. When he looked, the hatch to the roof hung open, nearly twisted off its hinges.

[Time to go, JB,] Keontae said.

A voice shouted something behind him, but Justin couldn't make it out.

What he *could* make out was the sight of Quan's blond head emerging from the hatch opening. He scanned the roof until his dark eyes locked on Justin's.

He brandished a pulse rifle and took aim.

"Shit!"

Justin ran toward the edge of the roof as pulse rounds scorched the air around him. As he barreled toward the edge of the roof, he could see the next roof was lower, but he still couldn't gauge the size of the gap between them.

Too late now. When he reached the edge, he sprang off it with all of his strength.

Only then did he see how wide the gap was beneath him, and vertigo thrashed in his mind and in his stomach.

But he cleared the jump anyway. He landed hard on his boots and skidded, then he lost it and tumbled head over heels to a stop on the roof.

[Get up, JB!] Keontae shouted. [They can still shoot you!]

Keontae was right. Justin pushed through the pain and the confusion, got up, and kept running.

"THERE IT IS," Bryant announced. "We've made it, and with no sign of anyone behind us."

Hallie hurried to the cockpit and stepped inside so the others could peer in past her. In the distance, a long gray colossus of a ship cruised through the void of space.

It had a huge red-orange dome in the center, and it was the most beautiful sight she had ever seen.

"See?" Bryant looked up at her. "Hope and destiny. Not just the names of my two favorite strippers at the club back home."

Hallie rolled her eyes. "This still doesn't mean you're right."

Bryant shrugged and gave her a perfect smile. "Like I said, believe what you want, but you won't change my mind."

"Get us there, and maybe you will have changed mine." Hallie turned to the others. "Strap in. We're landing soon."

PULSE BLASTS BATTERED the rooftop all around Justin, but none managed to hit him. He followed Keontae's instructions, fully trusting his view of the city. At this point, Justin's lungs were burning too much to even question where Keontae was leading him.

He skidded to a halt and ducked behind a ventilation unit.

[JB, you can't stop!] Keontae yelled inside his head.

"This won't last. I can't outrun them."

[You don't have to. Next roof over is our solution.]

Justin looked, but apart from much of the usual machinery atop these roofs, he didn't see much. The shooting behind him had stopped, now replaced by shouts in an Asian language.

[But you gotta go now.]

"Okay." Justin sucked in a deep breath, rose to his feet, and barreled toward the next edge.

The shouts behind him escalated, and pulse rounds streaked through the air around Justin yet again. Once more, at the edge of the roof, he vaulted forward, but this time it wasn't enough. Fatigue stole some of his power, and his jump didn't carry him as far as he needed it to.

His chest and legs slammed into the side of the building, pushing the air from his lungs and replacing it with pain. The grip of his left hand on the ledge faltered, but his right hand held fast.

Damn right it held. He hadn't lost his arm back at ACM-1134 and gotten a new one for it to be worse than the one he was born with.

Despite the agony he'd put the rest of his body through, his prosthetic arm pulled him up onto the ledge with ease, then he consciously rolled over and lay behind it for a moment to catch his breath and recuperate.

[You got ten seconds, JB, and then they'll be too close for this to work.]

"For what to work?" Justin wheezed.

[Get up and get movin', and I'll show you,] Keontae said. [You're not dyin' here, not after all the shit you already survived.]

Justin's many weaknesses tried to overcome his will, tried to stomp out its fire and make him yield to his fragile body, but he'd been forged in the darkness and death of that damned mine, and he refused to give up.

Keontae was right. He wasn't going to die here.

So, again, he pushed himself up and started running on shaky, aching legs. His bruised knees wobbled, and his chest burned from the series of hits he'd taken that night, first from Quan and then from the side of this building, but he didn't stop. He *wouldn't* stop.

[Ahead of you,] Keontae said. [Water tank.]

"And?" was all Justin could manage to get out, even as he adjusted his course toward the water tank on the roof.

[Cut that bitch down.]

Then Justin saw it. The water tank stood on a tripod of three alloy legs—perfectly stable as it was, but if one leg faltered, the whole tank would topple over. A smirk graced Justin's tired face, and he picked up speed.

The rattling of pulse blasts had ceased, but it soon picked back up again. Either these guys were miserable shots, or their weapons were off, or maybe God was looking out for Justin for once. Whatever the case, nothing had managed to hit him yet.

He clenched his fist, and the familiar orange blaze of energy erupted from the top of his wrist and formed into a glowing blade. Now within range, he swung at the water tank's front leg, and his energy sword carved a clean line through the rigid metal supporting it. The tank overhead jolted.

In the sword's wake, the molten metal crackled and sparked, but then it molded together and began to cool—and it began to solidify again.

"Shit."

[Hit it, JB!] Keontae shouted in his head.

With pulse blasts pinging the water tank and zipping past him, Justin slammed his metal fist into the side of the leg, right where he'd cut through, where it was still weak.

The leg buckled fast, and metal groaned overhead.

[Get out of there!]

Justin would've done it even if Keontae hadn't yelled at him. He ran under the falling water tank and made it to the far side just as it crashed into the roof and burst open, sending torrents of water screaming at the Ikari.

The water launched all of them off their feet, silencing their shooting as it swept them toward the edge of the roof and then over it.

And they were still seven stories up.

Had Justin just sent them all to their deaths?

[Best not to linger, JB. We still gotta find somewhere safe for you to stay the rest of the night.]

Justin shook his head. "No way I'm going back to sleep after all of this."

He couldn't help but think about how he'd washed away a group of men trying to kill him. He'd never killed anyone before—not anyone still alive, anyway. He hadn't even killed Carl Andridge; Keontae had done that through his prosthetic arm, against Justin's will.

They'd had a long discussion about it afterward, and in the end, Justin had cleared his conscience of it. But now...

[Don't sweat it, JB,] Keontae said, as if he could read Justin's mind. [It was you or them.]

"Yeah," Justin said, but he still felt a hollow pit in his stomach. He could've killed Quan or the other three back in the Asian District and possibly avoided all of this, but he hadn't. He'd thought he was showing them mercy, but it had only resulted in more dead.

[Look, you can feel guilty anywhere,] Keontae said. [But if the android cops or those Farcoast soldiers show up, you won't be able to explain your way outta this. And they *will* show up, too, to deal with all the collateral damage.]

Keontae was right... again. About all of it. Justin tried to pump steel into his nerves and ignore it, and it sort of worked. Maybe this was how guys like Stecker and Gerhardt and Captain Marlowe got to be so strong and decisive.

Justin's legs moved him along the roof before the tide of water could slosh back to him, and he decided to focus on deadening his emotions about what had happened.

They had attacked *him*. *They* had wanted *him* dead.

And *they* paid the price for it. That was all there was to it.

[There's an old-school fire escape on the side of the building. You can get down that way.]

Justin did, and he found his bruised chest and knees didn't like climbing any more than they'd liked running for his life. He resisted his vertigo with every step down, and before long, he rediscovered the ground again.

As his boots hit the pavement, the first sound of approaching sirens reached his ears. He tucked his chin down, adjusted his shirt collar, and walked at an even clip away from the building and toward the ethereal blue of downtown Nidus City.

Despite his curiosity, he didn't bother to try to round the building for a look at the damage he'd caused. Better to not risk it, and better to not risk a crisis of conscience over it.

Instead, he turned his attention to the city lights and the skyscrapers.

And that's when he saw the telltale glow of a spaceship streaking across the domed sky. But rather than its thrusters emitting a glow, the whole ship seemed to radiate a sort of angry aura and a noticeable amount of smoke. Then it disappeared beyond the edge of the dome.

"Did you see that?" Justin stopped in his tracks.

[See what?]

I guess Keontae doesn't see everything. "A ship. It just flew across the dome. You think it was part of the programming, or…"

[No. Missed it.]

If Justin had his bearings correct, that meant the ship was heading toward the *Nidus's* docking bay. "I think we just got company."

[So?]

"The ship was smoking. Looked like it was in rough shape. Something happened to it. Maybe it got attacked," Justin said. "We've got time to kill before sunrise, and I'm curious. Let's go check it out."

[If you want. You know I don't sleep anyway, and it's better than roamin' the streets all night lookin' over our shoulders,] Keontae said.

"Then let's go."

The journey back to the docking bay took Justin through Nidus City on foot until he reached the hovertram line. He boarded a hovertram, and it took him to the docking bay alone.

When he got there, the doors were sealed, but the hovertram left him there all the same. When he was done exploring, he'd have to wait until it came back to hitch a ride back to the city.

With Keontae, locked doors didn't matter much anymore. Just about anything controlled by a computer, Keontae could bend to his will.

Justin placed his hand on the control screen next to the door, which displayed the words "Restricted: Authorized Employees Only" in red capital letters. Employees or not, they were about to authorize themselves. Keontae jumped into the network and began doing his thing.

Justin waited for a long time while Keontae worked, but instead of the docking bay doors sliding open, the console flashed with green light. Justin touched it, and his fingers tingled as Keontae returned to his arm.

"What's up? Couldn't you get it open?"

[I can,] Keontae replied, [and I will, but I had to tell you this before we got in there.]

"Okay…?"

[Hold on. I snagged a piece of an audio recordin' from the network,] Keontae said. [Couldn't get the whole thing. Security on this network is legit, bro. As good as the mine's, at least, but fifty times bigger. Maybe more. Lots of cyberspace to navigate.]

"Is that a problem?"

[No. Just a bigger job. I can do it, but it's gonna take longer until I can bypass more of the security protocols. It's a lot like ATMs; I *could* break into 'em, but not in time to stop 'em from alertin' the authorities.]

"Don't remind me. We nearly got caught the one time we tried," Justin muttered.

[Here… I gotta play this audio for you. You're gonna trip.]

"…stated cause of the damage was…?" a male voice asked.

"We were attacked," a new voice crackled into Justin's ear. Female. Pleasant. Articulate.

"By whom?" the first voice asked.

"By a—" the woman started, but someone else cut her off.

"Pirates," a guy's voice cut in. "Space pirates, or marauders, or whatever you call them these days."

"But you said you're a science vessel. Why would they bother to—"

The recording cut off.

"Huh," Justin said.

[There's more,] Keontae said. [I heard it, but I couldn't grab all of it. Basically, their ship is worth a mint. The kind of ship diplomats and generals use to escape hostile situations. Heavy armor. Fast. Expensive.]

"Makes sense that pirates would want it, then."

[Yeah, but those pirates managed to kill the ship's captain in the process, too.]

"Ugh. That's terrible." Justin shook his head. "Damned pirates."

[You said it. Alright… load me back up, and I'll get you inside.]

BEN WOLF

Justin glanced around, careful to make sure no one else was watching, but the area was dead. It was one of those in-between areas where people neither cared to nor even could congregate if they'd wanted to. But a place like this, with a locked door leading to the *Nidus's* docking bay...

"Cameras?" Justin asked.

[Already handled,] Keontae said. [Obviously. And I made sure any record of you jumpin' across rooftops disappeared, too.]

"Smart move." Justin touched the console again, and with a tingle, Keontae shifted back into the *Nidus's* network.

It took another couple of minutes, but sure enough, the docking bay doors did slide open, and Justin made his way inside.

As before, a sprawling cavern of a room expanded before him, and in the distance he could see the *Viridian's* distinct shape. Across from it sat the new ship.

From such a long distance, he couldn't make out any damage on it, or really any details, for that matter. He realized he couldn't actually see the *Viridian's* details either; his brain was just filling in the info he'd already seen and knew.

He also realized he was standing there, out in the open, where he wasn't supposed to be standing. And if the Farcoast soldiers or anyone else happened to turn and look his way, they'd see him.

Justin glanced around and remembered an opening in the wall near the docking bay doors—it was another set of doors, but smaller. He'd seen them on his way out of the docking bay the first time.

He strode over to them and read yet another "Employees Only" notice emblazoned on the doors in bold red paint. Keontae was already in the system, working his magic, and the doors opened upon Justin's approach.

The inside of the room was dark except for the faint green glow of a screen on a console near a viewing window. Justin stole over to it, crouched down, and pressed his metal hand against it.

Keontae dashed back into his fingers. The screen reverted to a bluish color and displayed a diagram of the science ship that had just entered, which was apparently named the *Persimmon*.

[Take a look at that, JB,] Keontae said.

Justin rose a bit higher to get a better view.

The diagram showed significant damage to the rear portion of the ship, which made sense if pirates had been chasing them. But the extent of the damage surprised Justin. Parts of the ship were seared black from something scorching its hull, and chunks of it were missing entirely.

Either they'd gotten lucky, or the ship really was as beastly as Keontae had described. Whatever they'd survived had certainly tried to take them down but failed.

Justin reached up to try to make the image zoom in, but as he did, Keontae loosed a warning in Justin's mind.

[JB, behind you!]

A hand clamped over Justin's mouth from behind, and another jammed something hard into his lower back—possibly a plasma repeater.

Then a voice hissed into his ear, "Don't move a muscle."

Justin froze.

EIGHT

Even though the command came at him as a harsh whisper, it felt familiar. Something about the cadence of the speech, the way the guy enunciated the words... he knew that voice.

"I'm not gonna hurt you," the voice said in hushed tones, "unless you scream or yell, so stay quiet. Crystal?"

Justin gave a slight nod.

When the hand finally loosed from around Justin's mouth, he slowly turned back. From out of the shadows of the room emerged Arlie Bush, first officer of the *Viridian*.

But it wasn't her voice Justin had heard. He peered into the darkness some more until Captain Marlowe showed himself as well.

[Not cool,] Keontae said. [Thought you were about to get shivved by an Ikari.]

Justin ignored Keontae's comment. "What are you two doing here?"

"Could ask you the same thing," Arlie countered.

"I was curious about the ship," Justin said.

"Which one?" Captain Marlowe asked.

Justin blinked at him. "Huh?"

"The rig, the *Nidus*, or the science vessel?"

"Oh. The science vessel. And the rig, too, I guess. And also the *Nidus* is pretty interesting, so all three."

Arlie was still pointing her plasma repeater at him.

"Uh... you mind putting that away?"

Her voice flat, Arlie responded, "Yes."

"A little corporate espionage, then?" Captain Marlowe suggested.

"What? No," Justin asserted. "Why does everyone always think I'm spying on stuff? I don't know anything about that."

"Figured you might still be on ACM's payroll after all," Captain Marlowe said. "Sent here to look into what Farcoast has going on with the Coalition and their joint venture."

"No. No chance." Justin shook his head.

[Man, *stop* answerin' him,] Keontae warned. [His lady's got a gun on you. Say the wrong thing and you're just a red stain in this office.]

"You just admitted you were interested in the *Nidus*," Captain Marlowe countered.

"Yeah, but not like that," Justin said.

"Then what is it like?"

"Well, I just wanted to be friends, not go steady with the ship or anything."

Neither Captain Marlowe nor Arlie gave so much as a chuckle.

[Further proof that your jokes aren't funny, my dude,] Keontae said.

Justin wanted to tell him to shut up but restrained himself. Instead, he said, "Just curious. I'm good with computers. Wanted to see what their security is like."

"And now we know why you got in trouble back at ACM's mine."

"No. Not the same thing," Justin said.

[Ehhhhh... it kinda is, though, JB.]

"Definitely different. *Way* different," Justin added to address both Captain Marlowe and Keontae.

"And what about the rig?" Arlie asked.

"Was gonna see if any of the repairs got started."

"In the early hours of the morning?" Captain Marlowe challenged.

"Well, no. I saw the science vessel coming in for a landing. That's what drew me here," Justin admitted.

Captain Marlowe looked at Arlie, and she looked at him. Without saying a word or even so much as blinking, they somehow communicated with each other and both faced Justin again at the same time. Then Arlie's plasma repeater lowered.

"We saw it, too," Captain Marlowe said. "Saw it was damaged. Good thing it came in when it did. Now the *Nidus* can keep it quiet."

"Why would they want to do that?" Justin asked.

"Because the damage on that ship didn't come from pirates," Captain Marlowe replied.

"You know about the pirates, too?" Justin asked.

"Yes, except like I said, there were no pirates." Captain Marlowe folded his strong arms across his chest, and Justin caught a glint of the chrome ring tattooed on his ring finger, just like Arlie's. He'd never noticed it before. "That damage is from an antimatter weapon. Probably a missile. Pirates don't have that kind of weaponry—at least, I've never heard of any that do."

"If it wasn't pirates, who was it?"

"Only ships that carry antimatter missiles are warships—actual, bona fide warships—and they're technically not supposed to have 'em either."

Justin's eyes widened. "Really?"

"Think about it, kid." Captain Marlowe numbered his points on his fingers. "If pirates wanted the ship for the ship's sake, they'd try to board it and capture it instead of shooting it down. Even if they were after something aboard the ship, they wouldn't risk blowing it up for fear of losing the treasure."

"But a warship would?"

"Warships have better tech than most pirate vessels. They can calculate their attacks better, they hit their targets more frequently and more accurately, and they generally deliver all sorts of precision ass-kicking that a pirate ship cobbled together from spare parts couldn't even dream of."

"I see," Justin said. And ACM and the other huge mining companies had countless warships spread across the galaxy, all of them ready for all-out war at a moment's notice. It was a miracle the human race still existed at all.

"Point being," Captain Marlowe stopped counting his fingers, "whoever or whatever was after them is bad news, and if it tracks them here, we could all be in a world of hurt really soon."

Justin decided then not to mention his run-ins with the Ikari. That probably wouldn't bode well for him or the rest of the rig-runners, and Captain Marlowe and Arlie didn't need to know about it. It wasn't any of their business anyway, and Justin had already handled it, so what did it matter?

"It's clear they wanted something, but I dunno what it is," Captain Marlowe continued. "Or, at least, I won't know until I get on the science vessel and find out."

Justin's eyebrows rose. Captain Marlowe intended to board the ship? And, what? Just have a casual look around with Arlie like a couple searching for a new apartment to rent?

"How're you gonna get there?" Justin asked.

"Miracle of the good Lord above," Captain Marlowe said. "Or magicking of days long since passed. Take your pick."

"We were going to borrow employee uniforms and sneak aboard," Arlie said.

Captain Marlowe said nothing else, but his face ever so slightly betrayed that she'd ruined his fun.

"What are you hoping to find?" Justin asked.

"Having good intel is crucial to winning the battle, at best, or at the worst, surviving," Captain Marlowe said. "The point is, if I can figure out who or what is coming for them and why, I can position us to get out of here, perhaps with a little bit of profit, too, if it all lines up nicely."

"As in, you'd steal whatever's aboard the ship?" Justin shook his head. "Don't you think whoever's following them could turn around and find us and the rig, too?"

"Don't get too far ahead," Arlie said. "We don't even know there *is* anything of value on the science vessel."

"Hence the need to do more research." Captain Marlowe nodded toward the window. "But now that you're here, the mission's compromised, and we'll have to abort, regroup, and try again later."

Justin looked through the window and saw a hovercraft full of people drifting toward them, and he ducked out of reflex.

"Easy, kid," Captain Marlowe said. "It's mirrored glass on the outside. They can't see in here."

"Oh. Right." Justin straightened up again. "Well, since they're leaving, can't you get over to the ship now?"

Arlie shook her head. "Cameras. The patch we dropped into the system won't last long enough. We could get in okay, but we'd be seen getting out."

"Oh, well... I can figure out—"

[Careful, JB,] Keontae's voice interrupted. [Better if I stay unknown, right?]

"—why that would frustrate you," Justin finished. Keontae was still a secret, as were his powers to shut off the cameras.

They both eyed him, particularly Captain Marlowe, but neither of them said anything.

"I still think it's worth the risk of being seen," Arlie said. "If something wicked this way comes, we don't want to be anywhere near the *Nidus* when it arrives."

"Then *you* go and do it." Captain Marlowe turned to her.

Arlie's stare could've torn a space station in half. Through gritted teeth, she said, "Fine. I will."

With that, she tucked her repeater in the back of her waistband and stood.

"You're serious?" Captain Marlowe looked down at her.

Justin peered through the window again, unsure if the hovercraft had passed them by yet or not.

"What are they gonna do if they catch me?" Arlie challenged. "I'll say I'm checking on our ship if anyone finds me."

"That's a good way to get shot out of an airlock." Captain Marlowe shook his head and stood. "I think we should abort."

"No," Arlie said, resolute. "You told me to go. Practically gave me an order. So I'm going."

"I was being—"

"I *know* what you were being, Enix."

Captain Marlowe's mouth clamped shut, and he and Arlie stared at each other for a long time in stone-cold silence.

[This is awkward,] Keontae muttered.

"Should I... go?" Justin asked.

[You should definitely go,] Keontae said.

"No," both Captain Marlowe and Arlie said in unison, but neither of them turned toward Justin.

"Oh... kay," he said quietly, and the silence persisted another moment.

[Didn't she say the cameras would only be out for so long?] Keontae asked.

Good point, but Justin wasn't about to bring it up.

"We're both going," Captain Marlowe finally said. "We need you to stay here as a lookout."

With his eyes still locked on Arlie, he pulled something out of one of his pockets and tossed it to Justin, who caught it.

It looked like a flesh-toned bean, but it was solid and not otherwise bean-like at all. "Uh..."

"It's an earpiece. Two-way, single-channel comms on an isolated frequency." Now Captain Marlowe broke his staring contest with Arlie and looked down at Justin. "Left or right ear. Doesn't matter. Talk normally. It'll pick up your voice specifically once it's calibrated."

"Okay... what if I want it to pick up other voices?" Justin asked. "Like if I'm overhearing something?"

Now Arlie looked at him, too. "Like what?"

Justin shrugged. "Maybe a classical aria, or some spoken word poetry?"

They stared at him with the same intensity they'd just been staring at each other.

"I mean, I could also keep those types of things to myself."

"If you feel inclined to share, tap the earpiece while it's in your ear and it'll pick up more. You'll have to tap it again to recalibrate it to your voice again," Captain Marlowe said. "So share wisely. Last thing I want to hear is spoken word poetry."

"Keep watch," Arlie said. "Let us know if someone's coming."

Justin stood up and pressed the earpiece into his ear. "Sure."

Captain Marlowe clapped him on his shoulder. "We know we can trust you. Otherwise we wouldn't have made you rig chief. And I'm not regretting that decision. Probably not, anyway. I guess we'll see."

In light of all that had happened in the last day, Justin had completely forgotten about his promotion. It hadn't mattered as much to him when he was dueling Quan, or jumping across the rooftops trying to escape the Ikari's wrath, or sending a dozen of them cascading off the edge of a seven-story building.

"I won't let you down," Justin said with more confidence than he felt. But when he considered it again, they weren't asking him to do much—just to let them know if anyone came in and headed toward the ship. "I can definitely handle this."

"Wouldn't be much good if you couldn't," Arlie mumbled.

"Thanks for the vote of confidence," Justin said.

"Tap your earpiece," Captain Marlowe said. "Make sure it works."

Justin tapped it. "Can you hear me?"

A faint voice in his ear said, *Vocal calibration complete.*

"Try again," Captain Marlowe said.

"Can you hear me now?"

"Yes. Alright. We're going. It's terrible timing, but we're going." Captain Marlowe locked eyes with Arlie again, and then the two of them headed for the door.

Once it closed and Justin could see them going, he headed over to the console and pointed to it with the index finger of his robotic hand.

[You want me in there?] Keontae asked.

Justin nodded. He didn't want to get caught talking to Keontae over the earpiece.

[I'm guessin' you want me to see about the cameras?]

Justin nodded again. He touched the console with his metal hand, and Keontae vibrated into it.

Captain Marlowe's and Arlie's forms shrank smaller and smaller as they ventured farther and farther away. Their dynamic weirded Justin out. He never knew if they were going to throw down for a fight or throw off their clothes for a f—

A series of images appeared around the perimeter of the window in front of him, which he then realized was also a screen. All of them glowed green around the edges—probably Keontae's way of showing Justin he had control of the camera feeds.

Most of them showed Captain Marlowe and Arlie progressing toward the science vessel, but two others showed the entrance to the docking bay, both the exterior of the doors and those same doors from the interior.

"I got the screens in here working," Justin said in a hushed tone. "I'm watching the camera feeds."

"You can talk at a normal volume, Justin," Captain Marlowe said. "I told him that, right? I definitely said that to him."

"Sorry," Justin said, still in that same hushed tone. Then he repeated it, but louder. "Sorry."

And that's when he saw her onscreen—a young blonde woman approaching the exterior door with one of the Farcoast soldiers aboard a smaller hovercraft—some sort of hoverbike. He dismounted and approached the control panel.

"Enix!" Justin yelped.

"I told you to talk at a *normal* volume, kid," Captain Marlowe growled.

"Someone's about to open the docking bay doors!" Justin said it with as much energy but far less volume.

"Shit. Give me details."

"One soldier and one woman. She looks like she might be from the science vessel," Justin said.

"The science vessel is sealed. Can't get in quick enough," Captain Marlowe said. "We're taking cover in the rig. Let us know when we're clear." Then he added, "I knew we should've aborted."

Justin could barely see that far with his naked eyes, but the camera feeds showed them creeping aboard the rig via the boarding ramp. He glanced to another screen and saw the docking bay doors opening at the same time.

The soldier remounted the hoverbike and urged it into the docking bay. Their trip to the science vessel took less than a quarter of the time it had taken Captain Marlowe and Arlie to reach the pair of ships.

When they got there, the woman dismounted the hoverbike and lowered the science vessel's boarding ramp while the soldier stayed put. Then she went inside.

She returned a few minutes later carrying a knapsack of some sort. Just some forgotten piece of luggage. The soldier nodded, and the woman, whose face Justin had finally gotten a good look at, climbed onto the hoverbike again.

Justin liked what he saw. She was pretty—like, *really* pretty, especially for a scientist—with blonde hair and light-colored eyes, either blue or green. She wore brown trousers and a baggy dark-blue sweater made of some sort of heathered fabric. Her clothes didn't look new, but they weren't old grubby work clothes like what Justin was accustomed to seeing aboard the rig every day, either. It all looked good on her.

The hoverbike looped around and headed back toward the docking bay doors, but Justin realized she'd left the science vessel's boarding ramp down—wide open for Captain Marlowe and Arlie. It was perfect.

"Good news, guys," Justin said. "They're leaving, and they left the ramp down. You can just walk right in."

"When they're out of the bay and the doors are shut, let me know," Captain Marlowe said.

A moment later, the docking bay doors shut behind the hoverbike. "All clear."

Captain Marlowe and Arlie trickled out of the rig, dashed across to the science vessel, and clambered inside.

All the while, Justin wondered why he wasn't in there as well. He'd come to investigate the ship, too, but somehow he'd been left behind.

Then again, Captain Marlowe and Arlie seemed to know what they were doing, and had Justin gone with them, no one would've been able to tell them that someone was coming.

Still, Justin couldn't shake the feeling that he'd been here before—that already, within a day of arriving aboard the *Nidus*, he'd ventured where he didn't belong more than once. He'd done that back at ACM-1134, and then everything had quickly unraveled.

Unraveled wasn't the right word. It had deteriorated into the worst kind of shit show—the kind where people died. Lots of them.

Lightning wouldn't strike the same place twice, though. Or in his case, the same person. Captain Marlowe and Arlie would gather the intel they needed, and they'd be on their way, aboard the repaired rig, heading for more juicy asteroids.

A few minutes later, Captain Marlowe and Arlie exited the science vessel.

"We still clear?" Captain Marlowe asked.

"Yeah. No one else is in here."

It took them another few minutes to make it back to the office, and before they got inside, Justin placed his hand on the console so Keontae could jump back into his arm.

"Good work, team," Justin said as Captain Marlowe and Arlie entered the office. He gave them both a thumbs-up, but neither of them offered one in return.

Instead, Captain Marlowe eyed the screen behind Justin, which was now blank. "Thought you said you had the cameras going?"

"I did. Shut 'em off before you got here," Justin said.

[That might've been the smoothest lie you ever told, JB.]

Technically, it was only a partial lie. That's what had happened, but Keontae had been in control the whole time, not Justin.

"Nothing there worth stealing, anyway," Captain Marlowe said. "So why would anyone attack a ship like that?"

"You saw the suspension crate, same as I did," Arlie said. "Whatever was in there is probably what they were after."

"Even if that were so, it's not there now. Might never have been anything in there."

"Then why put a suspension crate in there in the first place?" Arlie pressed.

"Maybe it was left over from a previous trip. Or from previous owners."

"You don't really believe that, do you?" Arlie put her hands on her hips.

"No." Captain Marlowe sighed. He returned to staring at Arlie, who stared at him.

Silence followed until Justin broke in. "So we're done, then?"

"Not remotely." Captain Marlowe turned and held up a small silver box about the size of his palm. "Gotta analyze this first. It should give us some answers."

"I assume that's some sort of hacking device?"

"Practically magic, because I can't explain how it works—nor would I want to, and nor do I even care how it works. But it does." Captain Marlowe looked at Justin. "Though you probably know, don't you?"

[Careful, JB.]

"I might." Justin gave Captain Marlowe a smirk and a wink.

Captain Marlowe studied him for several long seconds, then he continued, "Have to decrypt the intel. It'll take some time, but then we'll know what's coming."

"As long as it's not already too late," Arlie muttered.

"Anyway, we're done here. You covered your tracks in the system, right?" Captain Marlowe asked.

"Yep," Justin said. "All clear."

"Good. Then let's get out of here before morning dawns and work crews start filing in." Captain Marlowe added, "Last thing I need is to get caught by a bunch of wrench-heads."

THEY RODE the hovercraft back to the city, and when they got there, Justin tried to give them back the earpiece. But Captain Marlowe insisted he hold onto it, just in case he needed to reach them more securely. It felt a bit cloak-and-laser to Justin, but he went along with it.

"Two taps to shut it down or turn it back on," Captain Marlowe said. "Press and hold to send a ping to us, even when we have ours turned off. We'll come to you if you get into trouble."

Justin gave him a thumbs-up and then gave his earpiece two taps. Then they headed their separate ways.

The artificial sun had begun to rise from the edge of the dome to Justin's right, creating a mosaic of beautiful hues along the horizon. Even though it wasn't real, it gave Justin a sense of peace and helped him to relax.

Sunshine or otherwise, fatigue from Justin's lack of sleep the night before had caught up with him, and he found himself dragging as he continued to walk downtown. But the rumbling in his stomach also demanded his attention. Running and fighting and running some more had left him hungry, so he decided to gratify his gut first.

As he walked deeper into downtown, a flash of blonde caught his eye. He turned toward it and noticed the woman from the science vessel staring at a clothing storefront with its main lights off, although neon signage advertised the latest fashions at the lowest prices.

She still wore the same blue heathered sweater and brown pants, and she still carried the satchel she'd retrieved from the science vessel as well. The sight of it made Justin wonder if she'd taken something from the suspension crate Captain Marlowe and Arlie said they'd seen, but he doubted it.

Who would carry something of value in a shoddy old satchel like that? It wasn't safe. Wasn't reinforced or protected. One good bump, and whatever was inside there might never be the same again. Or what if she got robbed? So much for keeping it safe.

No, it was probably just clothes and a toothbrush and some specialized shampoo or whatever chicks used on their hair these days.

[Another blonde, huh?] Keontae teased. [You definitely do have a type.]

"She's from the science vessel," Justin said. "Maybe I could get close to her, try to get some intel for us."

[Yeah. *That's* why you wanna get close to her,] Keontae quipped. [*Intel*.]

"Shut up, Key."

Keontae just laughed.

The woman turned and walked away from the store, apparently satisfied for the time being. Justin followed her about ten paces back.

The early morning streets were mostly empty save for a few dedicated joggers and workaholics in business attire rushing to their offices. She led him on a zigzagging path through the downtown area, occasionally stopping to peer into windows of restaurants and other storefronts.

Justin kept up with her, careful not to get too close, careful not to make it seem like he was following her.

[What, exactly, is your plan here, JB?] Keontae asked.

"Follow her until she stops, then casually approach and introduce myself."

[That ain't gonna work.]

"What? Why not?"

[How'd that work out with Shannon?]

Keontae's jab hurt. Justin gritted his teeth and replied, "That was different."

[Which time was it different? 'Cause you approached her like eight separate times, and each time she shot you down.]

"It was *four* times, not eight." Justin fumed. "And she didn't 'shoot me down' all four times. We had a really good conversation in the club back on Ketarus-4 before Dirk and his idiot friends showed up."

[Yeah, and how'd it all work out in the end?]

"Well, it *might've* worked out differently if you hadn't used my arm to rip Carl Andridge's throat out."

[We've been through this, JB,] Keontae's voice took on a sullen tone. [You know why I did that.]

"Yeah, but the end result with Shannon was still what it was."

[And I already apologized for that, too,] Keontae said, [even though we both know you had no chance with her anyway. So maybe we should drop this conversation.]

"You brought it up."

[Bro, I'm just tryin' to keep things light and fun.] Keontae's tone brightened. [I'm basically dead, right? Watchin' you squirm whenever I bring up your track record with the ladies is one of my few joys in this digital afterlife.]

"Well, find a new hobby."

[I would, but this is the gift that keeps on givin'.]

As Justin rounded a corner with a cunning reply on the tip of his tongue, he froze.

The blonde woman stood before him, facing him with a sour expression on her face.

She held some sort of small device in her hand. It flashed purple.

Justin's teeth rattled with a burst of electricity, and he blacked out.

NINE

Oh, God... what have I done?

Hallie stared down at the man whom she'd just shot with a stun pulse. She quickly tucked the stun gun back in her pocket and glanced around. No one seemed to have seen it—but no one was around, either.

He'd been following her along her absolutely random pattern throughout Nidus City for the last ten minutes. Every turn she'd made, he'd made as well. Every long stretch of street she'd walked, he'd followed.

And since she didn't have a definite destination, that meant he didn't, either. It meant *she* was his destination.

I wish I had let Bryant stick around with me after all. He would've been able to handle this much better.

Why, then, did she feel guilty about having stunned him? The guy was being a creep and following her. He deserved it. At this point in mankind's history, men across the galaxy *had* to know what did and didn't constitute stalkerish behavior. There was no excuse anymore.

So, yeah, he'd gotten what he deserved.

Then why weren't her feet moving her away from the scene?

Something about his face... he looked handsome, despite the obvious strain on his face as he lay there, convulsing. Well, jittering, more like. But tens of thousands of volts of electricity ratcheting through a man's body tended to have that effect. And aside from his grubby worker-style clothes, he looked like a decent enough guy.

Then again, white males between the ages of eighteen and their mid-fifties still produced the highest percentage of serial killers than any other demographic. That had been true for hundreds, if not thousands of years at this point.

Hallie, what are you doing? Make a decision. And that decision needs to be to get the hell out of here.

The man lying there stopped convulsing, stirred, and his eyes blinked open. As he began to move, Hallie yanked out her stun gun and pointed it at him again. Only as he sat up did she notice his prosthetic arm.

She'd invested a lot of her early years in academia studying prosthetics. Years later, she'd worked to develop newer, more efficient technical components in some of the most advanced prosthetics on the market. They had improved the lives of so many people over the years, and their ever-advancing technology had informed her own innovations and research in considerable ways.

Hallie recognized the model that had replaced his right arm. The sight of it made her want to stick around even more.

So she did. She stood there, waiting for him to wake up and notice her.

JUSTIN AWOKE to the sound of raucous laughter. He immediately recognized the voice as Keontae, but he couldn't figure out what was so funny.

Then he realized he was on the ground. On asphalt, or some other paved surface. Glass buildings towered overhead, clawing at the morning sky like shining fingers glinting with orange sunlight, but something about it just didn't seem... right. The sunlight wasn't quite the right color, and neither was the morning sky.

Yet it was all somehow so familiar.

Where the hell am I?

Keontae's laughter persisted.

Justin sat up and blinked, trying to get his bearings. When he looked up at the person standing before him and saw the device in her hand, his memories all clicked back into place.

The *Nidus*. The city. The blonde woman. The flash of purple.

He'd been following her, and she'd turned around and stunned him.

And that was why Keontae couldn't stop laughing.

"Real funny, Key," Justin muttered.

[Damn right, bro!] Keontae managed between laughs. [You got *no* game at all with these women! This will never *not* be hilarious to me!]

The blonde woman stared down at him, tense, but not running away. Why she'd stuck around after zapping him, Justin had no idea.

She had blue eyes—light-blue eyes with maybe a hint of green around the irises. Justin would have to get a lot closer to confirm, but he doubted that would happen any time soon... if ever.

"Hi," he said to her. "Is it okay if I stand?"

"Not yet," she replied. "Not until you tell me why you were following me. What do you want?"

Keontae's laughter renewed. [I *told* you, bro! I *told* you!]

Justin ignored it as best he could. "I'm sorry. I didn't mean to freak you out."

"You didn't 'freak me out,'" she said.

"I mean, I'm sitting on the sidewalk because you stunned—" Justin stopped. "Look, I don't blame you. I was an idiot, for sure."

"You still haven't answered my question."

"Sorry," Justin repeated. "I was following you because... well... you're pretty. You're blonde. And I wanted to see if I could talk to you. Maybe invite you to breakfast."

She still hadn't lowered the stun gun. "You could've just asked."

Keontae laughed some more. [Oh, man. I need to write a book about this shit.]

Justin scoffed, both at Keontae and at her. "And what would you have said?"

"Probably 'yes.' It's morning, and I'm hungry."

Justin stared at her, bewildered. He hadn't expected an approach that simple could've worked.

"You can stand now, but don't come any closer."

As Justin stood, the aches and pains from dealing with the Ikari the night before reawakened, but he gritted his teeth and endured them.

"If you were freaked out, why'd you stick around?" Justin asked.

"I said I *wasn't* 'freaked out.' I was... unnerved that you were following me." She sighed. "As a woman, you get used to it, but also... you never *really* get used to it."

In his head, that actually made sense to Justin, but he kept his mouth shut instead of voicing his opinion. Instead, he said again, "I'm sorry."

Her light-blue eyes narrowed as she searched his gaze. "I'm inclined to forgive you."

Keontae's laughter had slowed considerably by that point. Now all Justin heard were a few sporadic chortles here and there.

"That would be great, especially if you're interested in that breakfast," Justin said. "I'm Justin, by the way."

"I'm Hallie."

Justin nodded at the stun gun in her hand. "That thing kicks like a Grostonian racehorse."

"Good," Hallie said. "I've never used it on anyone before, so I'm glad it works."

"Oh, it works alright. Laid me out flat in no time."

A smirk curled Hallie's lips. "Yes, it did."

"I actually have one, too." Justin held up his robot arm. "It's embedded in the palm of my prosthetic arm, here. Seems like it's at least as strong as yours. Recharges in three seconds."

Hallie waved her stun gun. "One second."

Justin nodded. "That's... impressive. Didn't know they could recharge that fast."

"When you're a woman in a bad situation, you may not have three seconds to spare between pulses," Hallie said. "You may not even have *one* second, but anything portable with decent range and enough kick will have some sort of recharge time."

Justin could relate to all of that, too, thanks to ACM-1134, but again, he kept quiet. Instead, he said, "Look, I won't stick around. I made it weird, so I should go. Have a nice day."

As Justin turned to leave, Hallie said, "Wait."

He turned back.

"I've decided you don't seem like a creep or a weirdo. Misguided in your approach, sure, but not threatening." Hallie gave him a small grin and lowered her stun gun. "If you want to get a bite, you can continue to prove me right... or I guess you can prove me wrong. Know any good breakfast spots around here?"

Justin grinned in return. "Not a single one. But I'm up for looking around if you are. And I'll walk next to you instead of ten paces behind you. Good?"

"Mmmm... You can walk ten paces in *front* of me so I can see you at all times," Hallie said. "And then, when you find somewhere to eat, somewhere nice and public, you can hold the door open for me. You can prove that chivalry isn't dead—just that sometimes it needs to get stunned onto its ass every now and then."

Justin's grin widened into a smile. "Deal."

"Lead the way." Hallie motioned toward the street with a wave of her hand.

[Huh. Color me impressed,] Keontae said. [But hey, Stockholm syndrome is a thing, so...]

"Fuck you," Justin murmured as he started walking, and Keontae laughed again.

***

ON A DAY-TO-DAY BASIS, breakfast was the meal Justin tended to eat the least, but if he could figure out how to replicate what he'd been served at the downtown restaurant, he'd totally reconsider his life choices on that front.

The restaurant, an upscale place called LaBorn's, located on the street level on the exterior of a tall skyscraper, had menus printed on old-fashioned sheets of paper rather than displayed on handscreens. They served semi-cold water out of a carafe with a plug-type lid on the top.

Justin selected a meal that looked hearty by its description, but when it came, it was a fraction of the size of meal he would've normally eaten. However, the taste had more than made up for it.

His fluffy two-egg omelet had bacon and cheese and green peppers in it, and he'd never tasted a better one. Likewise, they'd provided him with only a meager side of hash browns, but they'd been perfectly seasoned and cooked to an ideal crispiness that left Justin wanting more.

Altogether, breakfast had impressed him... or perhaps it was that he'd enjoyed the company more so than the food.

Hallie, he'd learned, was actually Hallie Hayes, a moniker she'd rolled her own eyes at.

"Who names their kid Hallie Hayes?" she'd lamented, and then they'd both shared a good laugh about it.

She had a handful of PhDs in scientific fields, including biology, robotics, engineering, and biomechanical engineering, and yes, she'd had no life growing up. All she'd done was work and study, and study and work, and then do it all over again for the first twenty-four years of her life. But it had paid off, and now she was essentially working in her dream job.

Despite all of that, she hadn't actually said what she did, what her dream job was, or where she worked. Justin didn't press the issue... not this soon into the conversation, but he noted it and listened intently to everything she had to say.

He had to admit, at least to himself, that her success made him feel pretty insecure. She was about the same age as him and had achieved far, far more than he probably would in his entire life.

Then again, Justin doubted she would've survived the shit he'd gone through back at ACM-1134. Everyone got dealt their own hand in life, and she was playing hers a lot differently than he was playing his, and that was okay.

Later, when the android server cleared their empty plates, Justin just shook his head at the sight.

"What's on your mind?" Hallie leaned forward with her elbows on the table and her hands under her chin, smiling at him.

Justin blinked away his puppy-dog eyes and tried to remember what she'd just asked. "I just think it's ironic that a restaurant would have both paper menus and android servers."

"Why is that ironic?"

"Well..." Justin found he could more easily focus on her if he wasn't actually focused *on* her, so he did a lot of looking around the room instead of meeting her captivating eyes. "If you think about it, what does having paper menus say?"

Hallie shrugged. "You tell me."

"It says 'we're an expensive, top-of-the-line place,'" Justin continued. "Which is ironic, at least to me, because if they're such an expensive place, why would they have android servers instead of hiring real people instead?"

"Ohhh." Hallie nodded. "Because they're not paying for 'real' employees?"

Justin hesitated. Something about the way she'd said the word "real" made him worry he'd walked into a trap. "I mean, androids are fine, but why not give a human being a job instead?"

"Lower margin of error, easier to ensure quality standards, overall cost savings, all of which leads to increased profitability for the business, which is undoubtedly owned by humans..." Hallie rattled them off and numbered them on her fingers. "Reduced food waste through precision preparation and cooking, streamlined and error-free communication..."

Justin nodded. "Okay. That proves my point. Expensive place, but they're using androids to save money. I get that there are benefits, but I guess what I don't like is that they're putting machines before people."

Hallie's eyes glinted with mischief. "What about the people who work in the factories who helped to build those machines? And before you tell me they're automated, let me say that I've been to most of the big ones in the galaxy, and while there's a lot of automation involved, they still employ plenty of human workers as well."

"What about them?" Justin shrugged. "How far back into the supply chain do you need to go to justify androids working here instead of people?"

As soon as he said it, Justin bit his tongue. Already, he'd overstepped, pushed too far.

"You look embarrassed," she said. "Don't be. Don't back down, either. This is my field, so I don't mind a hearty discussion if you don't. And besides, it's not like you're sitting on a high horse with no skin in the game."

She nodded toward his right arm—his prosthetic arm.

"You gonna tell me you designed this, too?" He held it up.

"Even if I did, I couldn't tell you because of these companies' nondisclosure agreements. They're ironclad and brutal on anyone who violates them." Hallie gave him a wink. "But don't try to change the subject on me now."

"It's your move. I asked a pointed question, and you said you were fine with that kind of discussion, so let's have your answer."

"That's what I like to hear." She took a sip of her water and refilled both of their glasses with the carafe. "My answer is that your question is inherently flawed, because without that supply chain, nothing in this restaurant would even exist. This whole ship wouldn't exist. So the answer is that it doesn't matter how far back I go in the supply chain since everything is so interconnected."

[Damn. I like her, JB,] Keontae said.

Justin folded his arms and smiled. "Wouldn't that also mean your question is flawed? You asked about the workers who built the androids. If everything's interconnected, then...?"

"Don't take this the wrong way, but..." Hallie's smile widened, big and bright white. "...you're a *lot* smarter than you look."

Justin laughed, and so did Keontae. "I'll try to take it as a compliment."

"It is, truly," Hallie said. "And you're right."

"So where does that leave us?"

"Right back where we started."

"Which is?"

Hallie leaned forward again. "We're a part of a much larger system, a galactic economy that's never going to change on a macro level, no matter how much we want it to. So we can either get on board with it, we can complain about how it could be better, or we can try to do something that actually causes change on a micro level."

"So I was complaining?" Justin jabbed. "That's what you think?"

Now Hallie laughed. "Yeah, a little. I won't hold it against you, though, because your words are only a part of who you are. Your actions are much more important to what makes Justin who he is."

"And what do my actions say?"

[Oh, you just walked into this one.]

"Aside from you being a stalker?" Hallie quipped.

Justin bit his lip. "Damn. I really *did* walk into that one."

"I'm kidding. Mostly." She winked at him again, and he loved it. "No, your actions say that you're hardworking, resourceful, and willing to give more than you get. Hence your arm."

Justin huffed, but only because her assessment was so accurate. "That's kind of you to say."

"I think it's true." She nodded at his arm again. "Mind telling me how it happened?"

"I would, but someone recently told me that these companies and their non-disclosure agreements can be brutal for anyone who violates them." Justin winked back at her, and she laughed.

[Alright, JB. I take it back. You're doin' well now, son.]

Keontae's comment made Justin smile all the more.

He realized he hadn't had this much fun since he'd finally broken through to Shannon back in that club on Ketarus-4, and even then, that whole experience had combined all seven herculean labors into one insane night. Thus far today, he hadn't gotten his ass kicked—well, aside from getting laid out by a stun gun—so this was already better, if only for that reason.

But it wasn't just that one reason—everything about his interaction with Hallie since they'd arrived at the restaurant had been positive. No, *great*. Better than great.

He'd never connected with a woman like this, ever, and he'd never expected to connect with a woman as gorgeous as Hallie. Not to mention she was a thousand times smarter, too.

"Here's what I can tell you," Justin finally said. "There was a mishap at a mine I used to work at. A mech suit went bad, and one of the mining lasers cut my arm off at the shoulder. Had to get a replacement."

Hallie shook her head, and her pleasant countenance went solemn. "Sorry. That had to be rough."

"It was, but now I can give that company the most metal middle finger you've ever seen."

Hallie rolled her eyes. "Class 4 purdonic laser, right?"

"Yeah..." Justin tilted his head. "Most people don't know anything about mining equipment, but you nailed that one."

She shrugged. "I told you, this is my field."

"From the sound of it, you have so many degrees that *everything* is your field."

"You're not far off, actually."

The serving android approached and presented a bill for the meal, also printed on fine paper. The android said, "At your leisure, kindly remit payment for your breakfast. I trust everything was to your thorough satisfaction?"

Both Justin and Hallie nodded and uttered affirmations.

"Splendid. I will pass your feedback on to our chef," the android said. "It has been my pleasure to serve you. Thank you for your patronage, and we hope you'll return again soon."

As the android left, Justin looked at Hallie. "You think the chef's a human or an android? I'll bet it's an android."

She shook her head. "I'm not taking that bet."

Justin reached for the bill, but Hallie snatched it away before he could grab it.

"Hey!" Justin said. "Give me that."

"Not a chance," she said. "Rarely do I have this much fun talking to anyone, so breakfast is on me. And besides, I guarantee I make at least ten times what you make."

"Ten times? Really?" Justin eyed her.

"Yeah. At least that." She eyed him back. "By the way you're dressed, it might be twenty."

"Ouch. Well, I don't care what you make." Justin shook his head and pointed his thumb at his chest. "Your stalker deserves the right to buy you breakfast, at least, to make up for all the... you know, stalking."

"If my stalker really wants to make it up to me, he can buy me dinner here tonight." She stared right at him, unflinching.

Justin stared back, stunned. Had she really just—

[You *dumbass!*] Keontae shouted. [Say *yes!* Say it before she realizes the terrible mistake she's just made and changes her mind!]

Justin would've killed Keontae if he could've. Then again, he kind of already had.

He ignored Keontae's quip and answered Hallie. "Deal."

"Seven in the evening, then?" She slung her satchel over her shoulder.

"I'll be here," Justin said. Literally nothing would keep him away. Even if the rig got repaired and Captain Marlowe wanted to head out, Justin would convince him to stick around at least through dinnertime. Or hell, he might just quit his job and stay behind.

That's how determined he was to meet her for dinner. That's how much fun he'd had with her, how much he'd enjoyed talking to her.

"Good." She leaned forward again with her eyebrows scrunched down. "You think I should leave the android a tip, or...?"

"Can I walk you back to where you're staying?" Justin offered as they exited the restaurant. "I mean, as your stalker, I'm gonna find it eventually anyway, so you might as well let me make sure you get there safely."

Hallie laughed, and Justin decided he'd never get tired of the sound of her voice.

"Sure," she said.

"Good. I also happen to know these streets aren't the safest place. And not just because of potential stalkers."

"Oh?" She turned toward him, and her expression told him she wasn't sure if he was joking.

"Ever heard of the Ikari?" he asked.

She shook her head.

"An Asian gang. Multiethnic, but all Asian in descent. I've been told they've got a presence on this ship, in this city."

"Oh, really?" Hallie's tone suggested he still hadn't convinced her.

"I'm actually dead serious," he said. "I don't know how long you're planning on being here, but I wouldn't head into the Asian District if I were you. I went there last night and nearly lost my wallet. Maybe even more than that."

[Look at you,] Keontae said. [Tryin' to low-key strut your badass self in front of your new girl.]

"You're not joking?" Hallie stopped and looked at him. She was only a couple inches shorter than him, and she had such flair to her personality that she seemed brighter than almost anyone he'd ever met.

"Like I said, dead serious."

"Sounds like there's a story that I need to hear," she said. "And don't give me that nondisclosure line again. Street gangs don't use those."

Obviously Justin couldn't tell her the extent of what had happened, so he decided on a detail-free version of the truth. "Some guys approached me and forced me to leave. I found out later they were Ikari, and that was enough to keep me from ever going back there."

"Sounds scary," she said as they continued walking.

"It was," Justin admitted. "A little."

[Liar.]

"Any idea how long it'll take to complete the repairs on your ship?" Justin asked.

She glanced over at him, and her eyes narrowed slightly. "I'm not sure. Hopefully not too long."

"Our rig's supposed to be done in a day or so, and then I'm gone again, back to chewing up asteroids."

"It's nice that you can make a living even way out in the middle of nowhere."

Now Justin eyed her. "Is that supposed to be a dig?"

"I see what you did there." She wagged her finger at him. "But no, I'm being serious. I'm glad this is working out for you."

"I guess so," he said. "Truth be told, I'm saving up so I can make a visit to Bortundi Prime. Gotta visit my best friend's mom."

"Oh?"

"Yeah. He—died back at the mine I worked at. I promised him I'd check on his mom for him."

"I'm sorry to hear that."

Justin nodded. He didn't like having to feign sadness whenever he mentioned Keontae, especially since he still existed, albeit not in physical form. "Thanks. He's a—he was a good guy. Still is, I'm sure, wherever he is now."

[You're not so bad yourself, JB. That's why I stick around.]

They'd walked out of downtown now, and though the buildings had gotten smaller, they made up for it in grandeur. Fine stone houses loomed overhead, most of them three or four stories high and built in an old, regal style Justin loved but could never dream of affording.

Stone steps led up to their imposing front doors, giving them the look of small castles like those Justin had seen in shows and movies. Old-fashioned silver door-knockers gleamed with amber light from the artificial sun, beckoning Justin to try them out—were it not for the reinforced metal fences and gates blocking his path to them.

Even so, despite the houses' large sizes, hardly anything separated them from each other. Their perimeter fences extended down the sides as well, but the homes were built so close together that Justin probably could've reached out the window of one of them and high-fived a guy doing the same thing in the house next door.

What was the point of having this kind of money if a person couldn't even get space to themselves? Then again, Justin had lived in much tighter quarters than these places his whole life. Perhaps the whole idea was that the houses were big enough to afford people extra space on the inside instead.

"Bortundi Prime is nice," Hallie said. "I've been there a few times for work. What will you do after that?"

"Not sure. Might collect a half dozen PhDs of my own. I gave you enough of a head start. Now it's time to catch up."

Hallie grinned at him. "Even if you had three lifetimes, you couldn't catch up to me, handsome."

[Oh, shit. She just said you were handsome,] Keontae said. [And maybe stupid, too, but focus on the handsome part. That ain't nothin', JB.]

They walked a few more blocks until Hallie stopped them in front of a regal white mansion with a bronze door. A bronze fence surrounded the property, tipped with pointed ends that looked decorative but were definitely functional as well. It was a fence Justin wouldn't be trying to climb over any time soon.

"This is your place?" Justin asked.

Hallie faced Justin. "Well, we're renting it. The crew's splitting the costs. We wanted something with a bit more comfort."

[Maybe a bit more privacy, too,] Keontae suggested.

"It's…" Justin paused. "I wanna say 'nice,' but I'm gonna go with 'huge' instead. And 'decadent.'"

"Yeah. That's why we picked it."

"If you say so."

Hallie met his gaze, and the sight of her light-blue eyes sent his stomach fluttering. In that moment, under the artificial sunlight, he confirmed that she did, in fact, have a small ring of green around her irises. Like everything else about her, it was amazing.

"This has been fun," Justin said. "The last woman scientist I met tried to kill me, so this has been an improvement all around."

"What?" Hallie laughed, and Keontae snickered, too.

"Just ignore me. Making jokes."

"Well, as far as my experiences with stalkers go, I can only hope they all end up this positive," she said.

"So I'm your first?" Justin asked. "I'm honored."

Hallie tapped the screen attached to the fence, and when it glowed to life, she pressed her palm against it. The gate in the fence unlatched and swung open.

"You want me to pick you up here tonight, or...?" Justin asked.

"Just meet me at the restaurant." Hallie looked him up and down. "And while I don't mind the handsome, rugged type, I wouldn't mind seeing the handsome, rugged type in some nicer clothes if you've got them."

Justin smirked. "I've been meaning to go shopping anyway."

"I look forward to seeing what you come up with." She showed off her marvelous smile again. "Have a nice day, Justin. See you tonight."

"Yep. Bye." Justin wished he would've thought of a more eloquent way to send her off, but that's just what came out of his mouth.

Hallie closed the gate behind her and headed up the walkway toward the house. Before she got to the bronze door, it opened, and a man stepped outside. He was younger than Justin, and also taller and well-built. His haircut and his posture suggested he might be a soldier.

He gave Justin a stern stare and then stood aside for Hallie to enter the house.

Justin matched his stare and waved with his prosthetic arm.

The other guy didn't wave back. He just headed back inside and closed the door behind him.

[Don't think he's gonna be your friend any time soon.]

Justin shook his head. "No, Key, probably not."

[But look, dude, you nailed it. I mean, I was seriously impressed. Your game was perfection today. Like a damned sharpshooter.]

"Thanks." Justin started to say something else as he turned back, but he stopped when he saw a curvy Latino woman with purple-tipped hair standing on the sidewalk several yards down the street, staring at him.

Glaring at him.

Lora.

Then she turned and stormed away.

[That's bad news, JB,] Keontae said. [It's more than romantic interest with her. It's obsession now. Better watch your ass.]

Justin sighed. "I will. Wouldn't mind your help with that."

[You already know I got you.]

"I do." Justin shook off his concerns. "Let's head back into downtown. Find a place to crash for the day, do some shopping. You've always had a better sense of style than me. You can help me find some new clothes for tonight."

[You know it,] Keontae said. [My sense of style is classic and refined. You're gonna look pimp by the time I'm done with you. Don't even worry about it. Just get me in the store, bro, and I'll take care of the rest.]

JUSTIN WASN'T sure exactly how much he'd spent on new clothes, but it was a lot. Most of the cost came from the one killer outfit Keontae had helped him put together, and the rest was a bunch of basics like socks, underwear, denim pants, and long-sleeved shirts, all of which he could wear when working on the rig.

With four shopping bags in tow, two in each hand, Justin checked into one of the nicer downtown hotels. That, too, cost him big time, but if the Ikari were by some chance still after him, it would be worth it to have the added security and distance from the Asian District that night. He'd sleep better knowing they couldn't get to him there.

Inside his room, Justin dropped the shopping bags on the soft comfortable bed and then he flopped down on it as well. "You can come out now, Key, if you want."

Justin's arm shuddered, and green light mingled with the artificial sunshine pouring in through the windows. They'd nabbed a spot on the thirteenth floor, about two thirds of the way up the hotel, and the view was pretty great.

Justin didn't care, though—he just wanted to get some rest.

"Yo," Keontae said.

"Yeah?" Justin replied.

"I appreciate what you said back there."

"When?"

"With your girl. You told her you had to get back to Bortundi Prime to see my mom. I know we already talked about that, but I was glad you re-upped on your commitment. Meant a lot to me."

"Happy to do it, bro." Justin waved his hand and sat up. He was exhausted, but he'd never fall asleep with the curtains open—not with all that light pouring in.

As he began to pull one side of the curtains shut, the sound of his hotel door unlatching caught his ears. His first thought was that housekeeping was coming in and that he needed to hide Keontae.

But when he saw a plasma repeater pointed at him instead, Justin realized exactly how wrong he was.

TEN

"Justin Barclay," Captain Marlowe said, chewing on another of his metal sticks. "And... your green friend, whoever he is."

Arlie stood at his side. As usual, her repeater pointed at Justin.

By now, she'd done it enough times that the sight of it no longer surprised Justin, but it still unnerved him to have to stare down a deadly weapon.

Justin glanced at Keontae, who didn't move either. He continued standing there, aglow in his usual green light. They'd been caught. The secret was out.

"I knew something about you was off." Captain Marlowe nodded toward them both and folded his arms across his burly chest. "You couldn't possibly be as good with tech as you are while also not knowing a damned thing about what you were doing. I think an explanation's in order, don't you?"

"Yes," Arlie agreed. "Definitely. And no lies."

Justin looked at Keontae again, who met his gaze. Fighting back wasn't an option, nor did Justin even want to. And there was no escape, either. Hopefully Captain Marlowe and Arlie would recognize the value of what Justin and Keontae had to offer and not decide to do anything rash.

The thought crossed Justin's mind that Captain Marlowe might try to kill him and take Keontae for himself if he knew Keontae's true value. Even though Keontae would never go for it or go along with it, that didn't mean Justin wouldn't pay the price anyway.

Well, I'll just have to make it clear.

"This is Keontae." Justin gave a half-hearted wave toward him. "Remember the friend I told you about who died back at the mine? This is him."

Arlie aimed her repeater at Justin's face. "I said *no lies*."

Justin recoiled a step. "Easy! I'm not lying. It's true."

"He's not lyin'," Keontae echoed.

"You're some sort of hologram," Arlie snarled. "An AI program, at best."

Keontae shook his head. "No. I'm a lot more than that."

"Explain." Arlie's icy gaze landed back on Justin.

Over the next few minutes, Justin described the sequence of events that led to Keontae's death and resurrection—so to speak—and Keontae filled in what details he could. The whole time, neither Captain Marlowe nor Arlie changed their incredulous expressions.

When Justin finished, Arlie still hadn't lowered her repeater, but she wasn't talking anymore, either.

Captain Marlowe finally said, "Suppose I choose to believe you're telling the truth. That would mean you stumbled upon something that, as far as we know, is unprecedented in all of history, and it happened to turn your friend into this 'tech ghost' thing."

"That's exactly what I'm saying," Justin said. "There is no better explanation for it."

"Or he's an AI, like I said," Arlie muttered.

"I'm *not* a damned AI," Keontae insisted.

"Prove it," Arlie countered.

"How?" Keontae asked. "I got a mother back on Bortundi Prime. I had a work history before I 'died' workin' for Andridge. I'm a real person, or I was, anyway, 'til the accident."

"I'm not convinced." Arlie shook her head. "All of that could be taught to an AI program, along with your entire personality matrix."

"I can't be copied or replicated," Keontae said. "AI programs can be."

"Even if that were true, we got no way of testing it here and now."

"Look," Keontae held up his green hand, "I don't gotta justify shit to you, lady. I know who I am, and I know what happened to me because I was *there*."

"You *do* have to justify it if you want your friend to stay alive." Arlie's grip on the repeater adjusted, and she took more careful aim at Justin.

Okay... this is getting out of hand.

"Hey, easy," Justin coaxed. "In the end, what does it matter whether he's AI or not? I've been nothing but loyal to you both, and—"

"Except for completely lying to us about your capabilities," Captain Marlowe interjected.

Damn. Good point. "Well, if I had told you, would you have given me a chance in the first place?"

"We give idiots, assholes, and freaks a chance all the time." Captain Marlowe pulled the metal stick from his mouth and flicked it across the room. It clacked against the hotel room window and disappeared somewhere on the floor. "How else do you think we ended up with Rowley Pine on staff?"

Justin cursed under his breath. "I can't argue with that. But can you try to see why I wouldn't want it getting out that I've got my best friend living in my prosthetic arm? I had no idea you'd be okay with it or that you'd take me seriously. And even if you did, I didn't want the rest of the crew knowing.

"After everything that happened at that mine on Ketarus-4, and with ACM still breathing down my neck from across the galaxy, the fewer people who know about this, the better," Justin continued. "My concern isn't about myself as much, though that factored in, of course. My main concern is making sure Keontae gets back to Bortundi Prime to see his mother one last time."

Both Captain Marlowe and Arlie stayed quiet for a long time, and Justin reacclimated to the prolonged silence as he had the last few times they'd given him this kind of treatment.

Finally, Arlie shot a glance at Captain Marlowe. Again, they only made eye contact and didn't convey any other visible or audible communication, and then Arlie lowered her repeater and tucked it in the back of her waistband.

How she'd known to put the repeater away instead of shooting, Justin had no idea. Had they practiced this beforehand or something?

Whatever the case, the tension in Justin's chest subsided, and he exhaled a long breath.

"We're not sure we believe everything you've told us," Captain Marlowe said, "but thus far, aside from this lie, you've given us no reason to distrust you. And, for what it's worth, I do understand why you'd want to keep it a secret, especially if your friend is what you say he is.

"His existence is potentially devastating for Andridge, knowing what he knows and having seen what he's seen. On top of that, he's probably worth a mint to their R&D department. Having a sentient life form who can manipulate virtually any network and computer system is a powerful tool."

"A *weapon*," Arlie added.

"Better if he didn't end up in their possession," Captain Marlowe concluded.

"Couldn't agree more," Keontae said.

"So suffice it to say, your secret's safe with us—under one condition," Captain Marlowe said.

"And here's the ask," Keontae mumbled.

"Which is?" Justin held his ground.

"You keep working for us. With your friend's targeting accuracy and technical knowhow, there's no reason we can't all make a fortune together and finally break free of all the oppression in the marketplace."

Justin hesitated. "That's not my agreement with Keontae."

"Yeah," Keontae agreed. "No disrespect, but my only priority is keepin' this kid alive so he can get me home to Bortundi to see my mom before she passes on."

"And then after that," Justin said, "I can't speak to what his plans are gonna be. He's mentioned finding a body of his own instead of staying in my arm forever."

"Jump into the rig, then," Captain Marlowe suggested. "What better body than an entire spaceship?"

"Not exactly what I had in mind, Cap'n," Keontae said.

"Why not?"

Justin began, "It's kind of a touchy subje—"

"I got this, JB. Let me put it to you this way..." Keontae held out his hands as if to frame the circumstance for Captain Marlowe. "You got this fine lady with you. You love 'er. That's clear as day. You wanna make 'er happy. You with me so far?"

"Sure." Captain Marlowe folded his arms.

"Now imagine you died but your soul lived on, and your options were to either find a new body with all the anatomical parts that you need to make 'er happy... or you could jump into a damned spaceship."

No one said anything for a long moment.

"I'm sayin' your spaceship doesn't have a dick," Keontae clarified.

"Yes. I know what you're saying." Captain Marlowe waved his hand. He glanced at Arlie, who shrugged. "Point taken."

"But that does not leave us with much incentive to keep your secret," Arlie added.

"How about because you're decent people?" Keontae said. "Or, if not, how 'bout because you hate Andridge as much as we do and don't want 'em gettin' ahold of me?"

"That doesn't do much for our bottom line," Arlie said.

"Perhaps this time, our bottom line isn't as important as keeping something like this quiet," Captain Marlowe countered.

Arlie squared herself with him. "So it's better for us to sleep in that vermin-infested rust-bucket you call a rig? Better for us to scrape by with meager rations and even fewer amenities?"

Captain Marlowe remained silent and let her talk.

"I want *toothpaste*, Enix!" Arlie snapped. "Just some damned toothpaste! Is that too much to ask?"

"This is a nice hotel," Justin said. "I'm sure they provide it. You could just steal some from here."

Arlie's wrathful eyes shifted to Justin, and he regretted speaking.

"Or not."

"It's not *just* the toothpaste." She turned her scorn back onto Captain Marlowe. "This is *not* the life I was promised when we bound our fates together."

"This isn't a conversation we can have right now, Arlie," Captain Marlowe said, his voice calm.

"The hell it isn't," she almost shouted.

"Not in front of our subordinates."

"I don't care." Arlie stomped her foot. "This has gone on for long enough. We finally catch a break, and you aren't *man enough* to take advantage of it!"

Captain Marlowe didn't utter a word. He just stared at her with sad anger in his eyes and a rigid, albeit somewhat hunched-over posture.

Justin glanced at Keontae, who returned his look of uncertainty. They'd gotten caught in the middle of this marital spat, and neither of them wanted to be there.

What surprised Justin the most wasn't Arlie's venomous words but rather Captain Marlowe's tempered reaction to them. He didn't fight back. He just stood there and took it.

Justin doubted he would've been able to hold his tongue half as well.

"Nothing to say?" Arlie hissed. "Just gonna stand there like a mute?"

Finally, after an interminable silence, Captain Marlowe replied, "I don't have anything kind to say in response, so I'm choosing not to say anything at all."

Arlie fumed, her fists clenched, and she stormed out the hotel room door, leaving the three of them alone.

Captain Marlowe turned toward Justin and Keontae again. "Sorry about all that. But look—I think I may have thought of a way to make use of your friend's abilities without having to restrict the both of you to the rig forever. And it'll be another chance to re-demonstrate your loyalty to me."

Justin and Keontae exchanged another glance. Justin asked, "What is it?"

LATE THAT AFTERNOON, after a solid nap and once they were certain the docking bay mechanics had left for the day, Justin and Keontae accompanied Captain Marlowe aboard the *Persimmon*.

All the while, Justin kept checking the time. It was a bit after 5:30pm now, and he was supposed to meet Hallie at the restaurant at 7:00pm. Hopefully he could do what needed doing and still make it back into the city in time to catch her.

Inside the *Persimmon*, Justin admired the ship's clean lines and sleek design—a stark contrast from the rough, grimy interior of the rig. Jumpseats lined the small cabin area, replete with harnesses and straps and everything else that was supposed to give the impression that flying was safe.

A series of metal panels along the back wall had handle slots in each of them. Probably pullout cupboards or drawers or something.

Justin placed his metal hand on one of the ship's dark screens, and his fingers tingled as Keontae jumped into its system. The screen began to glow with green light, and two lines in the center wriggled as Keontae spoke, his voice quiet and tinny from the small speakers embedded on either side of the screen.

"Security's tight in this network," he said. "Gonna take me a bit to penetrate the shields. Lotta layers here."

"Go as quickly as you can," Captain Marlowe said. "Our time of being unseen is short."

"Yup," Keontae confirmed. The two lines swirled together and formed a rotating circular symbol.

Justin approached a cylindrical container on a stand. It was mounted to the floor on the opposite end of the ship from the cockpit, but before the back wall. The cylinder's curved metal wall held up a rounded black top, but the wall only reached about halfway around. A matching base extended from the half-wall on the bottom.

"I think I found your suspension crate," Justin guessed aloud.

"Yep." Captain Marlowe nodded. "When it's powered on, the beams create a force field around whatever's inside. Impenetrable, they say, but not impossible to bypass, of course."

"Whatever was in here, it's already gone."

"Right now, I'm less concerned about whatever was in there and far more concerned about the surprising amount of blood on the cockpit floor."

"What?" Justin headed across the ship's interior toward Captain Marlowe, who stood at the cockpit entrance, staring down.

"I'm ashamed to admit I missed it the first time around." He pointed down at the metal floor, but Justin didn't see anything. "You gotta look closely. They cleaned most of it up. It's subtle, but it's there."

No matter how closely Justin looked, he couldn't identify even a single drop of blood. The lack of adequate lighting in there wasn't helping, either.

"You don't see it, do you?" Captain Marlowe asked.

Justin considered lying, but he decided against it. "No. I don't see anything."

"Don't worry. You'll learn." Captain Marlowe nodded toward the cockpit's console. "See that?"

The left side of the console looked as if someone had detonated a small grenade inside it. Metal stabbed and twisted outward, curled and tinged brown around its edges.

"Whatever did that, it killed the guy whose blood is all over the cockpit floor."

"Or girl," a female voice said from behind them.

Justin whirled around with his metal arm outstretched, ready to send a stun pulse into whoever was there, but he stopped when he saw Arlie's telltale red hair.

He glanced back at Captain Marlowe, whose reaction was virtually nonexistent. He hadn't even turned back. Had he known she would be joining them?

When he finally did turn back, he gave her a nod. "Nice of you to join us."

She held up one finger. "Don't start with me."

Captain Marlowe raised his hands. "I'm just glad you're here."

"That makes one of us."

"We were just talking about what might've gone down," he continued. "Nothing good."

Justin started to ask, "How do you know the guy—"

"Or girl," Arlie cut in.

"—or girl died?"

"Didn't see anyone come out of here on a stretcher," Captain Marlowe said. "None of the crew had visible injuries, either, so he probably stiffed before they landed. If he was in the captain's chair, he was probably a military man, so they probably buried him in space like we did with Gerald."

"You were watching when the crew left the docking bay?" Justin asked.

"Of course. Recon." Arlie shook her head at him. "A ship like this docks, you find out everything you can about it."

"That's why we're here," Captain Marlowe said. "Because the damage this ship sustained isn't normal. It has me worried."

"Worried how?" Justin asked.

The remaining screens in the cockpit flared to life with green light, and Keontae's voice sounded, this time considerably louder than before.

"Good news, bad news," he said. "Good news is that I'm through their shields. Bad news is that most of the data's corrupted somehow. Scrambled, almost."

"A security feature? To prevent hacking?" Arlie suggested.

"Nah. Would've picked that up," Keontae said. "This data was wrecked before I got here. Either they did it themselves, or whoever or whatever attacked them did it. So far, no luck on figurin' out what kind of cargo they were carryin', and the crew roster is fragmented worse than the inside of that console. Did find some video, though."

The screens crackled with snowy static, all in hues of green. As the images sharpened, the coloring changed to black-and-white with just a hint of green around the outer edges.

The resolution was crap, but Justin managed to make out the shape of a star in the background. Then beams of white light streaked toward the screen at a furious pace, and the whole picture quaked with each impact.

Then, in the background, a dark silhouette broke into the star's light.

"Freeze it there," Captain Marlowe said. Something about his voice sounded different. Less certain, perhaps, than usual.

They all stared at the nearest screen, examining the shape of the thing blocking out a good chunk of the star's light. It was probably a ship of some sort, but Justin couldn't tell anything about it from its shape alone.

Captain Marlowe and Arlie, on the other hand, straightened up and shared a look of concern.

No—it wasn't concern. As he stared at them, Justin recognized the emotion for what it was. He'd seen it more than enough times back in the mine on Ketarus-4 to know it.

It was fear.

Terror. Restrained, but terror nonetheless.

"We need to leave." Captain Marlowe's voice was every bit as resolute as it usually was, but now a sense of alarm edged his words. "Now."

Justin placed his hand on the screen, and Keontae tremored his way back into Justin's arm. "What's wrong?"

"No time to argue. We need to get off this ship." Captain Marlowe nodded to Arlie, and they both headed toward the *Persimmon's* ramp.

"Is someone coming?" Justin called after them as he followed their quick pace. "If someone's coming, maybe we shouldn't just storm off this ship like a marching band."

"Not this ship," Captain Marlowe said back to him, over his shoulder as the three of them hurried down the ramp and onto the docking bay floor. "The *Nidus.* We need to leave this whole place right away. An hour ago. Three hours ago. Hell, we never should've come here in the first place."

"Why? What was that thing in the video?" He muttered to Keontae, "Do you know what their problem is?"

[Some sort of ship. A big one. Beyond that, no idea.]

As Keontae finished speaking, the earpiece in Justin's ear screeched to life with a relentless beeping noise. He'd reinserted it before they returned to the docking bay, but that annoying beeping made him want to rip it from his ear and smash the earpiece under the heel of his boot.

Justin reached for it, but the beeping stopped, replaced by Captain Marlowe's voice instead.

"Attention rig-runners of the *Viridian,*" he said. "Sorry to disturb you this evening, but our time aboard this ship has come to an end. Report to the docking bay in thirty minutes or less. Anyone not here in time *will* be left behind. Do *not* test me on this."

Justin hurried to catch up with Captain Marlowe and Arlie. "Are the repairs even done? The legs? Are they fixed?"

Captain Marlowe shook his head but didn't look back. He was heading for the rig instead of toward the docking bay doors. "Doesn't matter. We're leaving either way."

"Why?" Justin repeated. "What did you see?"

Captain Marlowe stopped at the base of the rig's ramp and turned back. He pointed to Arlie first. "Prep the cockpit. Fire everything up. Get her up and running."

She nodded and bolted past them into the rig.

[Guess you're not gonna get an answer, JB.]

Captain Marlowe pointed at Justin next. "Can your friend run a diagnostic of the rig for me and tighten up anything that's loose in the network? We need to be legs-up before that thirty-minute deadline is up, if possible."

"Yeah, of course, but—"

"No time to explain. Get him in the ship, and do what he says. Got my own problems to worry about." Captain Marlowe clapped. "*Move*, Barclay."

Without another word, Captain Marlowe bolted up the ramp into the rig.

TWENTY MINUTES LATER, the majority of the *Viridian's* rig-runners had answered Captain Marlowe's summons, as had the *Nidus's* welcoming team of soldiers and Officer Wendell, whose face seemed to have gotten stuck in a perpetual scowl.

Justin and Keontae had finished the majority of the diagnostics and optimizations, with Keontae handling the majority of the work, as usual. Meanwhile, Officer Wendell and Captain Marlowe argued about something just outside the ship, loud enough that Justin could hear their voices but not their words from just inside the boarding ramp, even over the hum of the rig's engines.

The remaining stragglers from the crew continued to gradually board the rig, all well within that thirty-minute limit that Captain Marlowe had imposed. Like Officer Wendell, each of them wore frowns and angry expressions.

Justin didn't blame them. He'd had to totally abandon his plans to meet with Hallie again at the restaurant, and it soured his stomach.

Worse yet, not only would he probably never see her again, but he also had no idea how he could possibly let her know that he wasn't going to make it. So her final impression of him, despite the great morning they'd shared, would be that he was the kind of jerk who would just ghost a girl.

To make matters even worse, the last of the rig-runners to board was Lora. Amid Officer Wendell's protests about the *Viridian's* abrupt departure and Captain Marlowe's curt responses, Lora stormed up the boarding ramp. She noticed Justin right away, and it was too late to hide, so he got a full measure of her dagger-eyes.

It made him regret bailing on Hallie all the more.

"*Enough*," Captain Marlowe snapped. "We're leaving, and that's final. You've got no legal authority to keep us here, so we're going. Take the damned credits and get the hell away from my rig."

Justin shifted his attention back to the confrontation in time to see Captain Marlowe tromping up the boarding ramp, shaking his head and muttering to himself.

Their eyes met, and Captain Marlowe asked, "Everyone aboard?"

"All except Rowley." Justin pressed his hand against the nearest console, and Keontae tingled back into his arm.

"Forget him." Captain Marlowe waved his hand. "He made his choice. He's in their custody, and it's not worth fighting to get 'im back. One more dick buried in a mountain of 'em. Retract the boarding ramp. We're done with this godforsaken—"

An alarm wailed throughout the docking bay, and all the overhead lights began to flash red. The sight of it took Justin back to ACM-1134, but the sound of the alarm was so different that he didn't have to linger in that memory for long.

Even so, this couldn't be a good thing... whatever it was.

[The hell is that?] Keontae asked.

Justin just shook his head and stole a glance at Officer Wendell and the Farcoast soldiers. Each of them held a hand to one of their ears, as if listening to something amid the screech of the alarm.

"*Shit*," Captain Marlowe spat. He rushed back down the boarding ramp and looked out the nearest set of entry fields.

Justin followed him, also peering into the void of space but seeing nothing.

Arlie's voice crackled over the comms in Justin's ear, asking the very questions on Justin's mind. "What is it? Are they refusing to let us leave?"

"*Shit*," was Captain Marlowe's only response. He clenched his fists and stopped short of the nearest entry field. "*Shit!* We're too late."

Justin still couldn't see whatever Captain Marlowe was seeing.

[The hell?] Keontae asked. [What's he so freaked out about?]

Justin continued to close the distance to Captain Marlowe's position. "Maybe it's a bunch of ships."

[Even so, a ship this size can probably handle a damned armada.]

Now only a few feet from Captain Marlowe's position, Justin caught a glimpse of something large and dark gray drifting by outside the *Nidus*. He slowed his approach as more and more of the new ship cruised into view, blotting out the countless stars behind it.

It was much bigger and much closer than it had been in the video Keontae played aboard the *Persimmon*, but its shape was unmistakable. Unique. Whatever this ship was, it was the same one from the video.

[Oh... shit...] Keontae uttered.

"What is it?" Justin found himself asking aloud.

Dozens of massive guns and turrets ran along the ship's surface, along with several other implements that Justin couldn't identify. The vessel looked both heavily armored and well armed—perhaps excessively so. And the ship itself looked pristine and new, as if it had never even seen a battle before.

The truth of it hit Justin as Captain Marlowe said it aloud: "It's a warship."

And as it drifted along, Justin saw a familiar orange-and-teal logo emblazoned on the ship's side—

The logo for Andridge Copalion Mines.

Justin added his own thoughts to those of Keontae and Captain Marlowe.

"*Shit.*"

ELEVEN

The ACM warship wasn't even a quarter of the size of the *Nidus*, but Justin had no doubt it could obliterate the colonist ship four times over.

"You see it, Arlie?" Captain Marlowe asked.

"I see it," she replied over the comms.

Justin finally understood Captain Marlowe's frantic behavior and the terror underpinning his actions. "We need to get out of here."

Captain Marlowe shook his head. "I said we're too late. Take off now, and they'll shoot us down. They won't even bother trying to stop us. They'll think we're trying to run."

[We *would* be tryin' to run,] Keontae muttered.

"Right now, our only play is anonymity," Captain Marlowe said. "They don't have a reason to chase us. In fact, they're definitely after the *Persimmon*, so we're not even on their scanners. I intend to keep it that way."

"So what do we do?" Arlie asked.

"Remain calm. And get everyone off the rig again. Fast."

"You're asking for a mutiny," Arlie mumbled. "Hurry aboard. Hurry to get off."

"No choice. If we're all aboard the rig when the soldiers board the *Nidus*, it'll look suspicious. Can't say we're about to leave while we still have a busted landing gear and records on why we showed up in the first place, and we can't say we just got here, either.

"There's no good solution." Captain Marlowe popped open his silver case, removed a metal stick, and crunched down on it. "We need everyone to disperse

127

throughout the city. Remain anonymous 'til we get a chance to get out of here, or until Andridge leaves."

"How long will that be?" Justin asked.

Captain Marlowe shook his head. "Depends how quickly they find what they're looking for. I'd bet my military pension they want one of two things: either someone from aboard the *Persimmon* or whatever was stored in that suspension crate."

"Or both," Arlie said. "I'll give the order."

As they stood there, watching the ACM warship match its flight pattern with the *Nidus*, the rig-runners began to disembark once again.

The thought of ACM grabbing Hallie shook every fiber of Justin's being. She was clearly brilliant, and whatever had gotten her aboard the *Persimmon* was important enough that ACM had sent an entire warship after them.

It made Hallie all the more alluring. But more importantly, Justin realized he had to do something about it.

He had to warn her.

Or did she already know? Had the same alarms in the docking bay sounded throughout the rest of the *Nidus*?

It would be hard to miss the huge ship cruising alongside them. Perhaps Hallie did already know, and perhaps she and the rest of her crew had already sought shelter.

Good thing, too, because the entry fields all around the rig rippled and warped as dozens of transport vessels soared into the docking bay, each of them bearing the orange-and-teal ACM logo. They hummed in a chorus of optimized, copalion-burning engines and set down on the docking bay floor.

"Shit," Captain Marlowe said again. He called out to the rig-runners leaving the *Viridian*. "Arlie, shut 'er down. Everyone else, look busy. Don't run. Don't hide. Comply, keep quiet, and this will pass."

['This will pass?'] Keontae repeated. [The hell does that mean?]

The hatches on the sides of the ships opened up like dragons spreading their wings, and dozens of soldiers filed out. They wore dark-blue camouflage armor that reminded Justin of the rocks back on the desolate surface of Ketarus-4, tactical belts loaded with equipment, and helmets with reflective gold face shields.

Each of them carried a pulse rifle that looked comparable to the ones carried by the Farcoast soldiers, but there were hundreds of ACM soldiers, compared to the handful of Farcoast soldiers who had accompanied Officer Wendell.

The ACM troops swarmed throughout the docking bay like locusts, and they quickly overtook the *Viridian*, her rig-runners, and the Farcoast soldiers. Justin stood there with his hands raised, complying, hoping they wouldn't be able to identify him.

As far as Justin knew, ACM was done with him and had been ever since they'd released him after the incident on Ketarus-4. They'd even told him outright they weren't going to prosecute him for his role in what happened at ACM-1134—not that they knew anything about it anyway since Carl Andridge had ordered the site destroyed before his death.

But even so, they'd released him with a warning that he was a person of interest to the company and always would be. The term "person of interest" didn't have a good connotation attached to it. It meant he was on their "shit list."

And being on the shit list of a galaxy-spanning corporation was never a good thing.

Enough ACM soldiers had entered the docking bay that several of them each took individual people aside and began to question them, including Justin. Still others surrounded the distant *Persimmon* and stormed up her boarding ramp like pirates.

But for now, the *Persimmon* and Hallie were the least of his concerns. The six ACM soldiers standing before Justin, separating him from Captain Marlowe, constituted a far more pressing issue.

He caught a quick glance and a slight nod from Captain Marlowe, and it somehow set him at ease. More nonverbal communication, again not discussed in advance, but Justin got the message all the same: "Play it cool."

That, Justin could do. Probably. If these guys were assholes, it would be harder.

"I said show me some identification," said the lead soldier, who wore a sergeant's bars on his shoulders. His voice came through his helmet sounding tinny and distant.

"Under whose authority?" Justin figured a bit of pushback would be normal. Too much cooperation might get them wondering.

The sergeant raised his pulse rifle slightly, not as a threatening measure but as a reminder of who the big dick in the conversation was. "ID, or I'll tell my men to hold you down while I shove the business end of my rifle up your ass and liquefy your insides."

Justin scoffed. "Someone wasn't hugged enough as a child."

That actually got him a few chuckles from the other ACM soldiers, and Keontae laughed too.

"C'mon, man. I've got a job to do," the sergeant said, his voice lighter now. "Sooner you cooperate, sooner you can go free."

"Same here," Justin countered.

"Then show us some ID, and you can get right back to it."

[Probably enough pushback, JB. Best to comply at this point.]

"Yeah," Justin said aloud. "Okay, fine."

He held out his right hand, palm up, and produced a holographic image of his personal details. It displayed his name, his date of birth, and some of his vital statistics—but only the bare minimum required by Coalition Law. After all the shit ACM had put him through over the last year, he'd made it a point to learn his rights and stick to them.

Once he finished looking over Justin's ID, the sergeant asked, "What's the nature of your work here in the docking bay?"

Justin nodded toward the *Viridian*. "I'm part of a team that operates the drill on that rig."

"Drill?"

"Yeah," Justin said. "We latch onto asteroids, use a high-powered drill, and extract resources from inside. Gold, precious metals, copalion. That type of stuff. Then we sell it. Not fancy, but it's a living."

"I get it." The sergeant nodded. "My old man worked in an ACM mine in the early days."

"Done that, too," Justin said.

"For ACM?" the sergeant asked.

[Careful, JB...]

"All over," Justin replied. "Got tired of it. Decided it was time for a change."

"Sure."

The sergeant seemed pleasant enough. Despite the armor, his weapon, and his face shield concealing any hint of expression, he could've passed for a decent human being.

Too bad he was working for the most treacherous company in the galaxy. That alone made him untrustworthy.

He nodded toward the *Persimmon*. "Know anything about that ship over there?"

Justin glanced at it. This would be his first real lie to these guys.

"Not much. Saw it flying in. Got up close for a look since I'd never seen one like it before. Lots of charred spots and damage on the hull." Justin glanced between the soldiers. "I'm guessing that was your doing?"

"Can't comment on that, Mr. Barkley," the sergeant said.

Justin wanted to correct him on his pronunciation—*Bar-clay*—but he held off. The less he had to engage with these guys, the better.

"Anything else?" Justin asked. "If not, I'm supposed to head into the city to grab some supplies."

"Can't let you do that just yet, sir," the sergeant said. "Gotta keep you here just a bit longer. We appreciate your cooperation."

Justin scowled. Was it really cooperation if guys with guns weren't giving him a choice?

It had to be close to 7:00pm by now. He'd never make it to dinner with Hallie in time.

Then again, he really ought to let go of that whole idea. She was on her own now, and he couldn't do anything about it. But she'd understand why he couldn't come, what with the ACM soldiers aboard the ship now.

At least he hoped she would understand.

He stole another glance at Captain Marlowe, who continued speaking with the six ACM soldiers who'd confronted him. Beyond him, closer to the rig, stood Arlie and another group of soldiers. She stood there with her arms folded, lips welded shut, her face as cold and emotionless as any of the soldiers' reflective face shields.

From the docking bay exit sounded a commotion. Justin looked, as did the soldiers attending him. When the soldiers turned, Justin considered snatching one of their pulse rifles away, but only for an instant. It was a terrible idea, and it would only get him killed if he tried it.

Several dozen Farcoast soldiers had entered the docking bay, all of them armored, outfitted, and as heavily armed as the ACM soldiers, only they wore their forest-green colors instead. But they weren't shooting—just marching, loud and in unison.

With them walked several Farcoast soldiers in battle mechs, also painted forest-green. The sounds of their heavy, unison footsteps reverberated throughout the docking bay.

As the sea of forest green marched closer, half of the ACM soldiers who'd been interrogating people abandoned their positions and moved up to form ranks before the approaching Farcoast soldiers.

Thus far, no one had opened fire, but with so much firepower all in one place, and with the two companies being vicious rivals on virtually every level, Justin had to wonder how long a cease-fire could even last.

From the opposite end of the docking bay approached another group of soldiers, these from the ACM ships. Their number easily matched or exceeded those of the Farcoast soldiers, and they had mechs as well, and more of them.

The two forces met near the center of the docking bay, and only then did Justin see how many more Farcoast soldiers had entered behind the original group that he'd seen. The numbers were still weighted against Farcoast by far, but this was no slouch of a force.

If the two armies came to blows, things would get ugly fast. Worse yet, the two forces seemed to be converging in the vicinity of the *Viridian*, meaning Justin and his coworkers would be caught in the middle if anything went wrong. He was no tactical genius, but he knew that spelled disaster for the rig and its crew.

From within each of the groups emerged nearly matching sets of men and

131

women in official-looking uniforms rather than combat armor, except that the ACM half wore dark-blue uniforms and the Farcoast side wore forest-green. Each of them bore their respective logos on the shoulders of their sleeves.

With the Farcoast officials stood a handful of people wearing burgundy Coalition uniforms. One of them, an older man with white hair, stepped forward with Officer Wendell and a middle-aged woman in burgundy close behind.

From the ACM side, a trio of officers approached, led by a fifties-something man in the center. He had gray hair and a matching beard, well manicured, and darker skin that reminded Justin of Pradeep Handabi, the now-deceased doctor from ACM-1134. He also wore black gloves over both of his hands, unlike either of the officials following him.

Justin glanced back at Captain Marlowe again, but he only made brief eye contact with Justin, then he refocused on the meeting playing out before them.

"Admiral," the Coalition official said, extending his hand, "I am Captain Wilson James, captain of the *CSS Nidus*. I regret that we are being introduced in such a manner, especially since our *repeated* attempts to hail your vessel went unanswered."

The admiral smiled and shook Captain James's hand. "It's a pleasure to meet you, Captain. I'm Admiral Siroch Sever of the *ACMS Avarice*, and I apologize for the intrusion. I usually don't like to be this flashy, but I'm afraid the situation warrants it."

Admiral Sever's voice came out smooth and crisp, and his tone conveyed a sense of superiority, which, all things considered, wasn't unfounded.

"Then you're prepared to explain your reasons for boarding our vessel with such a show of force?" Captain James asked.

"If only it were possible, Captain, I would explain everything I know to you in thorough detail, but I cannot. I have a mandate to follow, and I refuse to violate that sacred trust. That's why we couldn't respond to your hails." Admiral Sever's smile persisted. "I'm sure you understand, what with being a Coalition officer."

Justin glanced at the sergeant, who remained focused on the conversation between his admiral and Captain James. He still held his rifle so casually. With the added strength in Justin's robot arm, he was sure he could wrench it away if he had to.

"This is most irregular," Captain James said. "Had you communicated with us, we could have prepared for your arrival in a more hospitable manner."

"Hospitality is the least of my concerns," Admiral Sever said. "I am here to fulfill my mandate, and I intend to do so in the most expedient way possible. All I ask is that you and your band of 'tree people' allow us to do what we must do, unhindered. If you comply, we will complete our task and be on our way in short order."

Captain James's brow furrowed, perhaps at Admiral Sever's comment about the Farcoast soldiers being "tree people." But Justin actually had to agree—they really did resemble a forest of evergreens.

"With respect, Admiral, it is difficult for me to acquiesce given that I don't know anything about why you're here or what you must do," Captain James said. "So at the moment, I'm not inclined to be accommodating."

"And as I already said, I am not permitted to discuss my mandate," Admiral Sever said. "But I can assure you that it is our intention to leave this fine colonist ship thoroughly untouched."

Captain James held up his hand. "Forgive an old military man for being direct. I'm... what? Ten years your senior? I've been in countless stalemates like this over the years and resolved the vast majority of them peaceably. I'm flying this ship as a cushy last hurrah before retirement, and then it's pension payments and sunny beaches for the rest of my days.

"Suffice it to say, I'm not going to do anything to jeopardize that future, which draws nearer with every breath. Not only does that include refusing to play word games with you, but it also means refusing to risk my career by allowing a rogue force to take control of my commission without a damned good explanation.

"So, Admiral, let's skip to the end. Either you tell me what you mean to accomplish here, or I'm going to have to insist that you leave my ship," Captain James said.

Admiral Sever's smile faded into a smirk, and disappointment etched lines around his eyes.

"And before you decide," Captain James continued, "I implore you to consider that even though Farcoast is sponsoring the *Nidus's* journey to a new world by providing military and security forces, you are still speaking to a representative of the Coalition itself, and your actions will be taken into account on behalf of all of ACM by the Coalition. So what's it going to be?"

Admiral Sever nodded and began tugging off his gloves. "I regret that you have drawn such a hard line, but I deeply respect your conviction, and I'd like to thank you for your many years of service to the Coalition. The galaxy is a safer, more just place because of good men like you."

Silver metal gleamed where Admiral Sever's human hands should have been. Either he had prosthetic hands, or he was wearing something overtop of them. From his current distance away, Justin couldn't tell for sure.

Then Admiral Sever said, "But unlike you, I am not a good man."

He pointed his right hand at Captain James. It split apart, revealing a cylindrical tube of sorts, and it rattled off three quick pulses.

The first two struck down the Coalition woman and Officer Wendell, and the third seared through the left side of Captain James's chest.

Justin's mouth dropped open.

[Oh, shit!] Keontae bellowed into Justin's mind.

He glanced at the sergeant's rifle again. He might have to go for it after all.

Captain James clutched at the wound as the woman and Officer Wendell slumped down beside him, dead, and he stared at Admiral Sever with wide, terrified eyes. Then Captain James crumpled to his knees and onto his side, and his eyes went vacant.

"Kill them all," Admiral Sever ordered.

TWELVE

R ather than diving for cover, Justin stunned the sergeant with his robot arm and snatched the pulse rifle from his shuddering hands before he could hit the floor. Around him, pulse rifles rattled and mechs roared as the docking bay erupted in mayhem.

Though he managed to get the pulse rifle into his hands, Justin fumbled with it at first, trying to find his grip and get his finger in the trigger guard. By the time he got a handle on it, the other two soldiers guarding him had realized what he'd done and raised their rifles to fire, well before he could've shot them first.

Why am I so terrible at this stuff?

His chest seized, and he stiffened as the pulse rifles clacked with a flurry of rounds.

Then both the soldiers dropped before him, their backs issuing steam from multiple cauterized holes in their armor. Behind them stood Captain Marlowe, who also held a pulse rifle. Around him lay the three soldiers guarding him, also dead.

How he'd managed to take them down so fast, Justin had no idea, but it didn't matter now. He was alive, holding a pulse rifle, and had to get the hell out of there.

Arlie, also wielding a pulse rifle, led a frantic group of the *Viridian's* crew over to Captain Marlowe. It looked like most of them, from what Justin could tell. Without so much as a word, all of them ran away from the rig, toward the docking bay exit, skirting along the wall of entry fields on their left.

In the main area of the docking bay, the battle raged on. Swaths of ACM soldiers fell and died, but they kept coming. Farcoast soldiers perished, too, in about equal numbers, but their forces dwindled with each passing moment.

Justin followed Captain Marlowe closely, his rifle raised and ready for action, but thus far, he hadn't fired a shot. Hadn't needed to. None of the Farcoast soldiers had even taken notice of them.

Arlie brought up the rear, and the few times Justin glanced back, she'd been firing her pulse rifle into the ACM soldiers behind them. She wore a mischievous grin on her face as she battered ACM's ranks. Must've been cathartic for her. A release. A way to vent her pent-up frustration at Captain Marlowe, at ACM, at this whole situation.

Her shooting, however, didn't prevent stray pulse rounds from reaching them. Several times, Justin heard his fellow rig-runners cry out, and when he'd glance back, someone would be lying on the docking bay floor, dead or wounded.

His chest ached each time someone went down, but the sight of Dr. Carrington taking a round to the side of his head twisted Justin's stomach. He went down hard and fast, gone in an instant.

Others from the crew grabbed their wounded comrades and helped them along, and Justin tried to keep his focus forward in case he needed to use the pulse rifle in his hands.

[JB, three o'clock!] Keontae's voice ratcheted through Justin's mind.

Justin turned, his rifle raised in time to see a helmetless ACM soldier pulling a pin from the grenade in his hand. He stood several yards away, staring right at them with a wicked sneer on his face. Then he plucked the striker off with his thumb and drew his arm back to hurl the grenade.

Focus.

Justin skidded to a halt, lined up the shot, exhaled a quick breath, and squeezed the trigger. His rifle spewed pulse blasts at the soldier, and a few of them hit. The blasts racked the soldier's body, twisting and contorting him, and he fell backward with the grenade still in his hand.

It was still live.

"Run faster!" Justin shouted as he resumed his charge.

The grenade exploded behind them and to the side, and a chorus of screams sounded from the soldiers around the one Justin had shot dead.

Another scream sounded, this time much closer. Right behind Justin. He glanced back in time to see Al Paulson, one of the rig-runners he knew better, on the docking bay floor, clutching his bloody thigh. A small piece of shrapnel protruded from the meat of his leg.

Justin had to help Al. Shaneesha was already crouched beside him, trying to help him get back on his feet, but she couldn't manage it alone, so Justin ran back and hooked his arm under Al's arm and dragged him upright.

"Come on, Al," he hollered over the fracas around them. "You're old, but you're not dead yet!"

Al managed a pained chuckle, and with Justin and Shaneesha's aid, he hobble-jogged after the group.

"Hurry up!" Arlie shouted at them from ahead, still firing her rifle like a space barbarian. Justin hoped she was covering them and not firing at random.

Then Lora ran at them from the back of the group. "Give him to me! You need to cover us!"

Justin would've argued with her about it, but it made sense. She slipped between him and Al, who was much taller than her, and helped him along while Justin found his grip on his rifle anew.

They moved far slower than the rest of the group, but by that point, they'd progressed far enough from ACM's front lines that several layers of Farcoast soldiers—some of them dead—separated them from ACM's attacks.

As Justin advanced, he got a close-up look at one of the Farcoast mechs. It was about one and a half times the size of the mechs ACM had used in the mine back on Ketarus-4, both taller and wider. Only about ten yards away, Justin could see it clearly.

Rather than a simple alloy skeleton with some protective shielding, the battle mech had thick armor plating and metallic cockpit glass. A rectangular box with four fist-sized holes in it was mounted atop its right shoulder, and a long plasma cannon launched occasional blasts from its left, all while the rifles welded to each of its arms roared with light.

Justin couldn't help but want to try one of them out. His fascination with it subsided, though, when a rocket slammed into its left leg and sheared it clean off. Despite the mech's thick armor and the commotion around them, Justin could hear the Farcoast soldier inside shrieking.

They'd almost made it to the docking bay doors by that point, but perilously few Farcoast soldiers remained alive. Given the number of motionless forest-green bodies littering the docking bay floor compared to those standing, Justin estimated that probably only 10% of the original force was still alive and fighting.

ACM might've lost just as many men, but despite the countless dead soldiers on their side, their ranks didn't seem to have suffered nearly the level of loss that Farcoast had. And the disparity in the size of their forces meant Farcoast would either surrender soon or be overwhelmed.

Worse yet, ACM's soldiers were advancing while the Farcoast soldiers pulled back. Justin, Shaneesha, Lora, and Al had to get out of the docking bay fast, or they'd get caught in the aftermath of this onslaught.

By the time they reached the docking bay doors, they found Captain Marlowe and Arlie waiting there, aiming their pulse rifles past them and shooting toward

ACM. Once they got Al through the doors, Justin went through as well. Captain Marlowe and Arlie brought up the rear, and then the doors whooshed shut behind them.

Of the rig-runners, a rough count showed that only ten of them had survived, not including Justin, Captain Marlowe, and Arlie.

"Where are the hovertrams?" Justin asked.

"No idea," Captain Marlowe said. "Might be shut down because of the invasion. Unless you can help with that...?"

[Damn right we can help,] Keontae said.

"On it." Justin slung the rifle over his shoulder and hurried to the nearest access terminal.

Rather than just pressing his palm against the screen and letting Keontae do his thing, Justin made a show of bringing up the operating system on the screen. Keontae still jumped into the terminal and did all the work, but Justin refused to give the surviving rig-runners any reason to doubt that he was manipulating the system instead. Better safe than sorry.

Moments later, the screen displayed the words "Hovertram Operational," and the low whir of an approaching hovertram sounded in the distance.

"Got it," Justin said as Keontae trembled back into his robotic arm.

"We need to cover the docking bay doors." Captain Marlowe pointed his rifle at them. "At least until we're on that tram. Everyone else, take cover."

"Better yet, I can seal them..." Justin said. "I think."

[Yeah, I got you, JB,] Keontae confirmed.

He hurried over to the same terminal he'd used to break into the docking bay last night, and Keontae got to work once again. When Keontae finished and jumped back into Justin's arm, Justin turned back to the others.

"It's not gonna hold for long," he said. "They're just doors. ACM has enough firepower to get them open one way or another, but it should buy us some time."

But the threat never manifested. The hovertram arrived, and the *Viridian's* survivors boarded it and cruised toward Nidus City, leaving the carnage in the docking bay behind them.

As they glided toward the city, one question permeated Justin's mind, brought to life by Keontae's words spoken only to him:

[What the hell do we do now?]

AFTER KILLING CAPTAIN JAMES, Admiral Siroch Sever casually pulled back and waited in his transport until the resulting battle concluded.

His men had shielded him so well that the pulse-resistant shield emanating from his left hand didn't even take a single hit. If it had, he would've felt it.

Decades earlier, in the Third Copalion War, he'd lost his hands while trying to defuse a copalion bomb planted aboard a transport vessel full of ACM troops. Sever, then only a lieutenant, only had basic bomb-defusing training, but he'd managed to pull it off, saving the lives of everyone on board.

That is, he'd managed to extract the detonator from the bomb, thus preventing it from igniting the copalion and vaporizing the entire ship, but it had still exploded in his hands.

The protective armor he'd donned had saved his life and preserved most of his body, but the force of the blast had reduced every bone in his hands and forearms into powder. The best doctors in the galaxy with the best medical tech and training couldn't have saved them, so they were amputated and replaced with prosthetics.

Fitting, in hindsight, for a man whose last name was "Sever."

As the symphony of gunfire and explosions slowed to occasional chatter, Sever knew the fighting had concluded. Now his soldiers would sweep through the docking bay, looking for stragglers. They'd take the healthy ones who'd surrendered and any important-looking officials in for questioning, and they'd finish off the injured survivors quickly and cleanly.

In the years since the bomb incident, Sever had risen through the ranks at a breakneck pace. His ruthless decisiveness and calculating mind had earned ACM countless victories over the last two decades, and they'd rewarded him with the *Avarice* and an admiralty as a way to thank him.

Now, at long last, he truly had the status he'd long sought after and the power to go with it. The *Avarice* was a cunning, devastating ship, a testament to everything that a warship should be, and it was fully his to control. Sever doubted he could've harpooned a vessel as massive and valuable as the *Nidus* with a lesser ship.

"Admiral."

A voice pulled Sever out of his reverie, and he looked up from the screen in his hands. Commander Caustus Falstaff, the *Avarice's* third-in-command officer and Sever's right hand when it came to troop operations, stood before him at attention.

"Report," Sever said.

"The enemy is routed. A few dozen survivors, half of them wounded. Interrogations are already underway."

"And what of our commission?"

"Still unfulfilled," Falstaff replied. "We've located the science vessel, and I've got a team of specialists scanning it as we speak. If it's there, we will find it."

Of the thousands of soldiers aboard the *Avarice*, only Sever and Falstaff knew the nature of the quarry they sought. Not even Captain Gable knew anything about it.

While he technically outranked Commander Falstaff, Captain Gable was relegated to commanding the *Avarice's* day-to-day operations. He didn't need to concern himself with the bigger picture—that was Sever's job, and Commander Falstaff was there to execute his will for him.

"Fine," Sever said. "Any sign of the vessel's crew?"

"They don't seem to be among the dead, as far as we can tell," Falstaff replied. "Some of our soldiers reported interrogating the crew of the other ship, a Stinger-Class drilling rig. They are now unaccounted for, but several of our men saw them fleeing the docking bay once the shooting started."

"Scattering like the insects they are." Sever leaned back in his chair and folded his hands. "What's their affiliation? Farcoast?"

Falstaff shook his head. "Independent. Freelance. The men performed a basic search of their ship and found nothing of note, but if you want, I can have another team scan it more in-depth."

"Fine. But don't let it distract you from your focus on the science vessel."

Falstaff nodded. "Understood, sir."

When Falstaff didn't leave, Sever asked, "There's more?"

"Permission to speak freely, sir?"

Sever granted himself a grin. "It must be important if you asked me that, Commander. You rarely ever do."

"Usually there is no need to, sir, and I'd rather not come across as insubordinate by virtue of asking."

Above all else, Sever appreciated his commander's loyal regard of the chain of command. Rather than pushing back or questioning orders, generally he opted to get things done and provide updates later. It made him an ideal officer in Admiral Sever's eyes.

Given that, Sever had no problem with granting his request this time. "Speak freely, Commander."

"I think it was a mistake to attack the Coalition's representatives," he said.

The second trait of Falstaff's that Sever appreciated was his blunt, no-nonsense approach to everything. He got to the point without delay, and Sever preferred that. It kept conversations concise and clear.

"Why?"

"I'm worried about the repercussions it will have for the company, like Captain James said."

Sever nodded. "I won't go so far as to say my decision was the only viable option in that situation, but I will say it was the most expedient way of getting us total control over this colonist ship—and thus control of our commission and the prize that we seek. It was the quickest way to overcome that obstacle."

"We lost a lot of men, sir."

"We're at war," Sever replied. "Casualties are inherent. But now no one else needs to die since we have seized control of the ship. Before long, we'll have our quarry, and we'll be on our way."

Thanks to various peace treaties following the Third Copalion War, ACM wasn't at war with anyone at the moment—not officially, anyway. But that didn't stop either ACM or rival companies like Farcoast from operating in the shadows and dueling with each other in secret. After all, what good was a ship like the *Avarice* without a target for all that firepower?

"Even so, I expect we will be made to pay for this. Whether personally or at the corporate level, this will not go unpunished," Falstaff said.

Sever looked Falstaff up and down. He was a younger man, especially for his rank. Mid-thirties. Tall, lean, strong. Blond hair, dark eyes, and a good, solid soldier's jaw.

"We'll let the corporate offices worry about that," Sever replied. "With the *Avarice*, we can handle just about anything that comes our way. If the Coalition does come after Andridge for this, the company will pay the fine, skirt the sanctions, and operate as usual. And that's assuming there's any evidence of wrong-doing left to find."

Falstaff's chin rose slightly. "If you give that order, I'll obey, though I'd prefer not to have the deaths of the tens of thousands of people aboard this colonist ship on my conscience."

"Noted, Commander," Sever said.

If Falstaff had any weakness, it was the presence of his conscience. Rarely did it come into conflict with what they had to do, but Sever would've preferred that Falstaff forgo his conscience entirely, just as Sever had. It would make both of their jobs so much easier.

The day that bomb took his hands, Sever gave up his conscience, and he hadn't looked back since.

From the pensive look on Falstaff's face, Sever could tell it wasn't enough to satisfy him.

"In any case, Andridge has made it perfectly clear to me that our quarry is more important than anything else. They put no limits on what I was permitted to do in order to obtain it."

"*If* it exists."

"The only people who run are those who have something to hide, Commander," Sever said. "The science vessel ran. In that ship, they thought they could get away, but they were wrong. And soon, we will possess that which they're trying to keep from us."

"Aye, sir." Falstaff nodded, then his hand went to his ear, and he nodded again. "Sorry, sir. I'm told the scans have come back negative aboard the science vessel, except for trace amounts of blood resulting from an explosion in the cockpit."

Sever sighed. "Then we must expand our search. Take the science vessel back to the *Avarice*. Pull it apart, piece by piece, until we're absolutely certain it isn't hidden somewhere aboard.

"Also, send your men into the city. Have them search and question everyone, house by house, until it is found. Give them just enough information to know what to look for, and tell them to focus on finding the crew of that science vessel. Pull the manifest from the vessel and use that to locate them."

Falstaff's fingers still pressed against his ear. "I'm being told that our technical team is already aboard, but the manifest is fragmented and mostly unreadable. Only two names are decipherable. One is the captain, Mitch Dawes."

"Finding him would be a boon. Focus your efforts primarily on him." Sever asked, "Who is the other?"

"Dr. Hallie Hayes."

"Then find her, too."

"Aye, sir," Falstaff said.

"You're dismissed, Commander."

"Aye, sir." He saluted Sever and turned to leave.

"Commander?" Sever barked, and Falstaff turned back. "Kill anyone who gets in your way."

ONCE THEY GOT off the tram, Justin replaced Shaneesha in helping Al walk. Their hopes of catching a hovercar or some other transport to take them farther into the city had dropped to zero thanks to ACM's invasion. Their next move might prove to be a life-or-death decision, and it made Justin all the more wary.

"Where do we go?" Shaneesha asked, looking around.

Nidus City, once bustling and thrumming with life, had gone silent as a crypt. Its vibrant, multicolored lights still glowed, casting that blue hue everywhere, even as the artificial late-afternoon sun sank toward the faux horizon. But no one moved through the streets, and only a handful of vehicles zoomed between the towering buildings.

"Gotta figure the hotels and businesses are closed," Captain Marlowe said, still holding his pulse rifle. He, too, scanned the cityscape before them. "And we don't know anyone here. So no one's gonna put us up willingly."

"So we need to break in somewhere and hunker down." Arlie crouched down next to Al's leg with some bandages from her pack in her hands. "Hold still. I'm gonna wrap your leg so it doesn't keep bleeding."

"Thanks," Al said down to her.

"Maybe we can break in," Captain Marlowe replied. "Either way, those soldiers will come here next. If they're willing to massacre an army of Farcoast soldiers, they damn sure will rip this city apart 'til they find what they're looking for."

"What are they looking for?" Lora asked.

Justin looked at her across Al's chest, and their eyes met, albeit briefly. She'd helped him out by getting Al off his back, literally, but now they supported Al together, one on each side.

Her eyes narrowed at him, and her lips tightened, and then she looked away.

Apparently, she was prepared to hold onto her grudge even though they'd been thrown into the middle of a war zone... as if Justin didn't have enough to worry about already.

He rolled his eyes and sighed.

"You say somethin'?" Her head snapped back toward him.

"No," he replied quickly—perhaps a bit too quickly. "We're just in a rough spot."

"That's puttin' it mildly."

Justin bit his tongue.

[She just won't let this go, huh?] Keontae muttered.

"You know what?" Lora continued. "We *do* know somebody here."

Everyone turned their attention to her.

"At least, Justin does."

[Oh, *shit*. She's callin' you out, son.]

All eyes fell on him, and he wanted to shrivel up into a ball and roll away. If he'd wanted to suggest taking everyone to the house where Hallie was staying, he would've done it by now. Amid all the commotion, he'd completely forgotten that Lora had seen him leaving there, and now it was coming back to bite him in the ass.

Even so, maybe it really was their best option. Al needed medical attention for his leg, more than what they could provide there, in light of Dr. Carrington's demise. Hallie wasn't a medical doctor, but she clearly knew something about biology, so perhaps she could help. Or maybe one of her crew could.

In any case, it made sense to find her anyway. She and her crew undoubtedly had whatever ACM was looking for, and that meant she might have some answers. More information might lead to more choices for them, and possibly a way to get out of this with their lives.

"Well?" Arlie pressed.

"Yeah," Justin finally said. "I know a place."

WITHIN HALF AN HOUR of sluggish steps thanks to Al's injury, they'd reached the ritzy neighborhood where Hallie's rented house was located. As with the rest of the city, the entire block of grand stone houses remained silent and sullen, yet behind them, Justin could hear the distant sounds of rifle fire and explosions announcing ACM's arrival.

[So much for a simple search,] Keontae said. [They're gonna ravage this whole ship 'til they get what they want.]

The idea that they'd inevitably come face-to-face with ACM again, this time with soldiers who would stop at nothing to get whatever it was they came for, sent terror ratcheting into Justin's chest, but he resisted it.

After all, he'd survived a hell of a lot worse than this back on Ketarus-4. If he was careful, he could survive this, too.

Several houses later, they stopped in front of a familiar white mansion with a bronze door. The same spear-tipped bronze fence surrounded the property, now with its gate shut and locked. Earlier, Justin had decided he was glad he'd never have to climb over it. Maybe he'd been wrong.

"This is it," Lora said for him.

He eyed her across Al's chest. "Thanks."

"Will you two cut it out?" Al snapped. "The simmering between you is making me sweat. I feel like I'm a piece of fresh roadkill stuck between two badgers."

Justin didn't know what a badger was, but he got the idea. "Sorry, Al."

"Not yet, but you're gonna be," Lora quipped.

"I take it back," Justin said. "I'm sorry I ever met *her*."

"That's right. Make jokes. See how far that gets you."

"Both of you, shut up," Captain Marlowe barked. "We're on the same side. Fight all you want when we get off this ship, but until then, I don't want to hear any more squabbling. Crystal?"

"Clear," Justin replied.

"Oh, we're clear," Lora said. "'Cause I don't need to say it for him to know how it is."

Justin just sighed again.

Captain Marlowe ignored her. "You're up, Justin. Get us inside."

Justin glanced between him and the gate, and Shaneesha took his place in helping Al stay upright. He wasn't exactly sure what he was supposed to do in this situation.

"You know someone inside, right?" Captain Marlowe said.

"You'd better believe he does," Lora said.

"*Quiet*," Captain Marlowe snapped at her. "Try calling at the gate. See if they'll let us in."

"O—kay..." Justin approached the bronze gate. A small screen affixed to its bars glowed with blue light from a rectangle in the center, but there were no directions.

He pressed the rectangle with his right index finger, and Keontae jumped in. Rather than waiting for any sort of answer, Justin decided to let Keontae handle the work, as usual. Within seconds, it turned green, and the gate slid open, occasionally squeaking as it rolled on its track.

Justin turned back to the others. "Guess it worked."

On his way through the gate, Justin rested his hand on the screen again so Keontae could jump back into his arm, and he did. Everyone else followed him inside, and they ascended the stone steps toward the large bronze door at the front of the house.

Justin got it open as well, again thanks to Keontae, and everyone carefully and quietly ventured inside.

The door opened into a large receiving area, sort of like a lobby, Justin supposed. Smooth stone floors shone underfoot, and twin staircases crawled up the walls on both sides, leading to the second floor. Openings to the left and the right of the lobby led into additional rooms, both as grand and huge as the lobby, if not more so.

To Justin's surprise, there were no lights on, but a decent amount of golden afternoon sun still streamed through many of the windows—enough to see, but not enough to see much detail. Under the stairwells, matching doors led deeper into the house, but he couldn't tell much beyond that due to the low light.

Overall, his initial impression of this and the other houses on the block had been right: the space inside was plentiful, with high ceilings and sprawling rooms, especially compared to the narrow boundaries between the houses on the exterior.

To their credit, the others hadn't uttered a word since entering the house. Even Lora, who never kept quiet for long, had managed to stay silent.

But that all changed when an orb of orange plasma zipped into the lobby and shattered a vase near Captain Marlowe's head.

THIRTEEN

E very one of the rig-runners yelled and either dropped to the floor or darted around, desperate to find cover.

By contrast, Captain Marlowe and Arlie crouched down, found cover, and raised their pulse rifles, ready to return fire.

Justin's response landed somewhere in the middle. He shouted an obscenity, crouched low, and raised his weapon, but he stayed out in the open like an idiot.

The error only lasted for a couple of seconds, and he promptly dove toward Captain Marlowe's position and slid across a section of the marble floor. Another plasma blast tore into the wall where he'd just been standing.

"It's me!" Justin scrambled to his feet in one of the doorframes under the stairs next to Captain Marlowe. "It's Justin! Don't shoot!"

"Justin?" a familiar female voice called. "As in the stalker?"

Despite barely avoiding being eviscerated by a plasma blast a few seconds earlier, Justin had to chuckle. "Yes! We had breakfast at the all-android restaurant. You told me about your dozens of PhDs and decided not to leave a tip because they're just machines."

"Bryant, stop shooting," Hallie said from somewhere in the darker parts of the house.

"What if this is a trap?" a man's deep voice asked from around the same spot.

"Then we've sprung it, and we're going to die horrible deaths at the hands of these monstrous people." Hallie added, "Trust me. We're safe."

She got only silence in response.

"Justin, I'm coming out," she called. "Don't shoot me, or you can kiss your chances at a second date goodbye."

Heat hit Justin's cheeks, though he supposed that bit of info was going to come out sooner than later. Might as well be now.

Hallie stepped into view with her hands up and empty. The sunlight streaming in through the windows backlit her, crowning her blonde hair with a golden glow. Even though Justin couldn't really see her face, her silhouette was delectable all the same.

She stepped forward, and a new bit of light caught her face. Definitely Hallie… and she was smiling, too.

"What's a girl gotta do to get permission to put her hands down?" she asked.

"Sorry," Justin said as he stepped forward, still holding his rifle. "You're good."

When he reached her, she held out her hand, palm facing him, stopping him short. "Didn't give you permission to touch me yet, stalker."

Justin smirked. "My bad."

"No, your 'bad' was breaking into my house. Well, my rented house, anyway." Her smile turned into a frown. "So, stalker, what the hell are you doing here?"

"ACM invaded the ship. They've got an army, and they're searching the city."

"Tell me something I don't know," the male voice said from the darkness beyond. Then a tall, younger guy walked into the lobby as well. He was the guy who'd scowled at Justin from the front door when he'd dropped Hallie off there.

Bryant.

He still held a plasma repeater in his hand, but it remained at his side, harmless. Nothing else about him looked harmless, though.

He stood probably about six-foot-four or -five, broad in his shoulders yet lean in his midsection, and built like a premier athlete—the kind of guy who could move fast and make you hurt if you were off your game.

Except Bryant was clearly a soldier. He wore the same burgundy Coalition uniform that Officer Wendell and Captain James had worn, only his fit more snugly over his robust arm and chest muscles. He hadn't been wearing it when Justin saw him the first time.

The look in his hard eyes reminded Justin of Dirk Hammer from back at ACM-1134, but thus far, he'd proven far less talkative and coarse. Maybe he wasn't as huge a dick as Dirk had been, but it was too early to gauge his personality.

Justin could tell one thing for sure, though—from the way Bryant looked at him that morning when he'd dropped off Hallie, and from the way he was glowering at Justin now, he saw himself as her protector. He might've even had a thing for her.

"We need a place to hide for awhile," Captain Marlowe said, casually holding his rifle. "And we were hoping for some medical help for one of my rig-runners. We had a doctor on our crew, but a stray pulse round from ACM took him out."

"You got a name?" Bryant's attention shifted to Captain Marlowe.

"Yeah. Why?"

"I'd like to know who I'm talking to," Bryant said.

"Feeling's mutual, kid."

"Sure." Bryant's stern expression didn't change. "Lieutenant Bryant Sokolov, Inter-Planetary Marines."

"In your dress maroons?" Captain Marlowe asked. "They didn't send you with tactical gear?"

Justin wondered at Captain Marlowe's question and at Bryant's attire. When the IPMs had shown up back at ACM-1134, they were all wearing black tactical armor.

By contrast, the IPMs he'd seen at the Ketarus-4 spacestation were wearing blue camouflage fatigues, closer in color to what the ACM troops in the docking bay had been wearing. Then again, the rocky terrain of Ketarus-4 was blue, so perhaps the IPMs had worn those fatigues to match the planet.

"We're not on a combat mission," Bryant explained. "We weren't expecting to—"

"Less is more, Bryant," Hallie interjected. She nodded toward Justin and the rest of the *Viridian's* crew "I'm sure you're all very nice people, but we really can't say anything else."

To his credit, Bryant didn't resist her instruction. He continued staring at Captain Marlowe. "Still didn't get your name."

"Enix Marlowe, captain of the *Viridian*. She's the other ship that was in the docking bay when you arrived."

Bryant nodded slowly. "And now you can't leave because ACM has you trapped here, just like us."

"Exactly." Captain Marlowe nodded toward Arlie. "This is Arlie Bush, my first officer."

She and Bryant exchanged curt nods.

"Ex-military?" Bryant asked.

"Ex-Coalition Forces, and some private work," Captain Marlowe replied.

Justin noted that he hadn't mentioned doing merc work for ACM in the past. Probably a wise decision, given the lingering tension in the room.

"Enlisted, not an officer, like you," Captain Marlowe continued. "Decided I was done with that life and promoted myself to captain of my own ship."

"If only it were that easy in the Corps," Bryant said.

"I'm sure we could exchange war anecdotes all day, but you said you have someone who is wounded?" Hallie said. "We don't have much by way of medical supplies, but one of our team, Angela, is an MD. I can ask her to take a look."

"Send 'er my way," Al said from the back of the rig-runners. Lora and Shaneesha helped him hobble forward. "Leg's pretty jacked up. Could use some TLC, for sure. Some strong drugs wouldn't hurt, neither."

Hallie grinned. "I'll fetch Angela. In the meantime—" She eyed Justin. "—I need you to explain to Bryant how you bypassed the house's security system."

"You mean your bronze fence and a locked door?" Justin eyed Hallie right back. "Not exactly something I'd need a PhD to figure out."

"Oh, stalker-boy, she's equipped with far more than that." Hallie grinned at him.

[She ain't lyin',] Keontae said. [Found some pretty nice stuff in the system, but I shut it all down before we made our approach. Didn't want anyone gettin' fried on the way to the front door.]

"In any case, this house is as fortified a position as we can muster, so we need the security system back online in case ACM tries to get in here," Bryant said. "Can you help or not?"

Justin wanted to ask them about whatever it was ACM was looking for, but he figured that could wait until the rig-runners had dispersed and Al was getting treatment. No need for everyone to be involved in that conversation.

For the time being, Bryant had a point. ACM would eventually come knocking, and ensuring they couldn't get in, or at least that they'd have a hard time getting in, was in everyone's best interest.

"Yeah. I can help," Justin replied.

As Hallie escorted Al and the other rig-runners into an adjacent room, Bryant holstered his repeater and gestured Justin over. Captain Marlowe and Arlie came with, too.

"Main screen's this way." He motioned with his head toward one of the doorways under the staircase, and they all followed him.

The doorway led to a staircase that descended into the house's basement. The space was unfinished, with scrap panels of carpet forming a trail over a hard cement floor. Exposed wires, conduits, and pipes ran along the ceiling and disappeared up into it at various points.

Justin scanned the space for anything unusual, but nothing stood out to him. He wondered if the metal walls that framed the basement could move or if they concealed hidden rooms, but only until Bryant led him to a screen mounted to one of the walls.

"I'm locked out. And on top of that, this is far from my area of expertise," he admitted. "Give me a ship, and I can fly it pretty damn well, but this stuff…"

"I can give it a shot." Justin glanced at Captain Marlowe and Arlie. "Got any fun war stories you can tell while I'm working? Helps me to concentrate."

What he really wanted was for them to distract Bryant so he wouldn't get curious about *how* Justin was doing what he was going to do. Fortunately, Captain Marlowe got the message.

"You're a baby," he said to Bryant. "Fresh meat. Out of the academy... what? Two years ago?"

"Four, actually." Bryant turned away from Justin and faced Captain Marlowe and Arlie. "Did two years of flight school after that."

Justin tapped the screen and tried to shield as much of it with his body as he could. Keontae jumped into the network and set to work while Justin tapped harmlessly on the screen.

"Admiralty track?"

"That's the theory, but it's competitive." Bryant folded his arms and leaned against the wall next to Justin and the screen, but he didn't look over. "Most guys never make it past captaining their own ship."

"Never made it past master sergeant, myself," Captain Marlowe said. "Arlie here was a corporal when she got out. Spent the first half of my career with the Coalition, a couple of years bouncing around doing merc work, and finally gave it up to get the rig. Arlie and I pooled our life savings and bought 'er outright, so anything we make goes to us, not to some cutthroat bank."

"Living the dream," Arlie muttered.

"I'll bet." Bryant looked over at Justin. "How's it going?"

Justin stopped tapping and looked up at him. Somehow Bryant felt even more imposing than Dirk had, even though Bryant hadn't done anything all that threatening to Justin.

Still, if surviving ACM-1134 had proven anything to Justin, it was that he was nobody's bitch. "It'd be better if you didn't have to look over my shoulder while I'm working."

Bryant's stare persisted, and then it hardened.

Justin didn't relent. He'd stared death itself in its wretched, malformed face. Bryant was nothing by comparison.

Finally, Bryant looked away, and Justin mocked as if he were continuing his work.

"You mentioned a mission," Captain Marlowe said. "If it's not a combat mission, and if Andridge is after you, then it's something top secret, no doubt."

Bryant shook his head. "Can't talk about it. I already said too much upstairs."

"But Andridge *is* after you," Captain Marlowe pressed. "They took a keen interest in your ship, specifically. Damn near shredded its back half trying to get you to stop, but somehow you still made it here. Antimatter missiles, right?"

"Captain," Bryant held out his palm, "I said I can't talk about it, and I won't. Please change the subject."

Keontae buzzed back into Justin's hand. [All good. Everything's back online. I restored user access, too, so he can mess with it some more if he wants.]

"All done." Justin backed away from the screen and motioned for Bryant to take a look.

Bryant peered down at the screen, but he didn't touch it. "If you say so. Like I said, it's not my area."

"You're not even gonna check to make sure everything's up and running?" Justin asked.

Bryant shook his head. "I'm sure you put it all back the way it belongs. If you did a shitty job, we're all dead once ACM shows up."

[We might all be dead soon anyway,] Keontae said.

Justin wanted to ask Keontae if there were any hidden rooms tied to the network or anything else out of the ordinary, but asking aloud now would blow his cover, so he kept quiet.

They made their way out of the basement and up to the main level again. The artificial afternoon sun must've sunk beyond the horizon because it no longer shined golden light into the house. Instead, only a handful of small lights burned in the innermost rooms, away from the windows. They were probably trying to make ACM think no one was there.

Decent strategy, but that hadn't stopped ACM from entering both the *Persimmon* and the *Viridian* when no one was aboard. If whatever they were searching for was important enough to massacre all those Farcoast soldiers, then they wouldn't pass by a house just because the lights were off.

On the main floor of the house, everyone gathered in a grand living room space with plush leather couches and chairs. The room was larger than Justin's entire house had been when he was a kid, in height, depth, and width. A fireplace flickered with digitized flames but gave off real warmth, providing some of the only light in the room.

Al sat on one of the couches with his wounded leg freshly bandaged and propped up on a fancy leather ottoman. Shaneesha sat on one side of him. Lora sat on the other, and she gave Justin a glare, as usual, but he ignored her. It was much easier now that he was around Hallie. He could just stare at her instead.

The two groups exchanged introductions, but Justin couldn't hope to remember all of their names—he still had trouble remembering the names of the folks who worked opposite shifts from him aboard the rig.

Hallie sat across the room from Justin, along with the other scientists in her crew. There were only five of them in total, including Bryant, which seemed like a small number, but their ship was a lot smaller, too.

"So explain to us how you got stuck in this debacle," she said.

"I got a better idea," Lora said. "Why don't you explain why ACM is after you, instead?"

Hallie's pleasant expression faded. "That's not something I can talk about."

"Then maybe you can explain to us what you and Justin talked about on your little date this morning."

Justin's eyes widened, and Hallie glanced at him. All he could do was shrug.

"I'm sorry... have I done something to offend you?" Hallie asked Lora. "I mean, other than allowing you to stay in this house, away from the soldiers, and getting someone to treat your friend's wound, that is."

"Oh, *chica*." Lora shook her head. "I got no problem with you. It's all a problem with him."

Her fiery gaze landed on Justin.

[Here we go again,] Keontae muttered.

"Enough, Lora," Captain Marlowe broke in. "We already had this conversation."

"All due respect, Captain, but you can butt out. This has got nothin' to do with you, just like it's got nothin' to do with this blonde bimbo, neither."

Hallie chuckled. "You're a little firecracker, aren't you?"

"That some kinda racist comment, bitch?" Lora fired back.

"Well, gunpowder was created by the ancient Chinese, so... maybe? Are you Chinese at all?" Hallie asked. "I mean, if you want, I can *try* to be racist more specifically to your heritage, but I'd need to know more about your background."

"So she's smart *and* a smartass," Lora said. "Keep talkin'. Bitches like you get cut where I'm from."

"Okay." Justin stood. "Clearly, the livestock is being unruly. I can stun her and put us all out of our misery."

"What the *fuck* did you just call me?" Lora stood as well, but as she approached, Justin raised his robotic hand, palm out, toward her. She scoffed at him. "You don't scare me. I'll rip that metal arm off and beat you over your damn head with it."

[I know you want to, JB, but *don't* stun her. It's a bad look,] Keontae warned.

"Alright, alright. Back off. Both of you." Arlie wedged herself in between them.

"Don't touch me, Arlie." Lora tried to swat Arlie's hands away, but Arlie persisted and shoved Lora back into her spot on the couch. Lora gawked up at her. "Hey! What the hell?"

"Look at me, and listen up." Arlie leaned in close to Lora. "You may say you're not afraid of Justin or Blondie, here, but you damn sure better be afraid of me. I got no problem thrashing you in public or in private. You keep running your mouth, and pretty soon the only thing running from it's gonna be blood. Crystal?"

Lora's jaw clamped shut. After a long pause, she replied through clenched teeth, "Clear."

Without so much as another word, Arlie returned to her seat and plopped down into it.

Justin sat back down, too, and he caught Hallie's pleased expression. She mouthed the word, "livestock?" to him and then smiled, ear to ear. He smiled too, unconcerned if Lora saw him or not.

"Despite her shitty approach," Captain Marlowe said, "Lora raised a good question. Why is ACM after you?"

"Again, Captain," Hallie said, "we can't talk about that."

"You might as well. The damage to your ship from their antimatter missiles already says a helluva lot about what kind of shit you're in."

Hallie cast a nervous glance at Bryant but didn't say a word.

Captain Marlowe pulled his silver case from his jacket pocket and popped it open. "Look, Miss Hayes—"

"*Doctor* Hayes. Several times over, in fact," she corrected him.

"Dr. Hayes," Captain Marlowe repeated.

He plucked a new metal stick from the case, positioned it between his teeth, and bit down with a faint *crunch*. Then he let out a small sigh and closed his eyes for a second as he tucked the case back into his jacket.

When he opened his eyes, he said, "We already know you've got something in your possession that ACM wants. Or they're after one of your number, or both. Frankly, I don't give two twisted tankards what the situation is, but I do care about what you mean to do about it."

Justin watched Hallie's every move. Despite Captain Marlowe's pressuring, she remained poised, her posture straight, on the edge of her chair.

"For the time being, we're safe here," she replied. "It's part of the reason we rented this specific house. We couldn't be sure they wouldn't catch up, so we petitioned Captain James, who captains the *Nidus*, to secure it for us. He also promised us that Farcoast soldiers would assist us should ACM show up."

[She's in for some bad news, huh?] Keontae said.

"Hate to break it to you, but Captain James is dead, and so are the Farcoast soldiers. Probably all of them," Captain Marlowe said. "Saw it happen before my very eyes."

Hallie's eyebrows rose at that. She looked at Justin. "How?"

"When ACM showed up, the admiral of their ship, a guy named Sever, tried to negotiate with Captain James, probably to find you," Justin said. "Captain James wouldn't budge, so Admiral Sever killed him, right there, on the spot. That sparked a firefight, and ACM had way more men, so they overran the Farcoast soldiers. Game over."

Bryant had been standing next to the fireplace near a bookshelf embedded into a wall. At that, he stepped forward. "You mean to tell me that *every* Farcoast soldier is dead now? They're not fighting the ACM troops as we speak?"

"Maybe not all of them," Justin said, "but most of them, yeah. It was a hell of a battle."

"We barely escaped with our lives," Captain Marlowe added. "Some of our crew weren't so lucky."

"Knowing ACM, they will have torn your ship apart by now looking for what-ever you're hiding," Arlie said. "So you're stuck here 'til they find you."

"This ship has a bazillion escape transports," Hallie said. "We can escape on one of those."

"And go where?" Captain Marlowe asked. "The ACM warship will shoot you down or incapacitate any vessel before you make it very far, and even if you could make it past, those transports won't have warp capability, and there's nothing else out here."

Hallie glanced at Bryant, whose frown had deepened.

"You don't have a lot of options here," Captain Marlowe continued. "So maybe you oughta consider giving up your prize."

"Absolutely not. Out of the question." Hallie shook her head.

"So it's a person, then," Captain Marlowe said.

"I never said that," Hallie countered.

"You're being too defensive for it not to be." Captain Marlowe scanned the faces of each of the crew. "One of you is more important than you seem."

Was it a person? Justin couldn't be sure. After all, he'd seen Hallie leaving the ship carrying something, and whatever had been in that suspension crate aboard the *Persimmon* wasn't in there anymore. Then again, had anything been in there in the first place?

"I won't entertain conversation of this sort." Hallie folded her arms.

"This is the only kind of conversation you *can* entertain," Captain Marlowe said. "This conversation is literally determining your fate as we discuss it."

Bryant squared himself with Captain Marlowe. "What's that supposed to mean?"

"It's not a threat. We're not the bad guys." Captain Marlowe held up one palm in surrender. "But the bad guys are coming, make no mistake. And what you decide now will determine what happens to all of us."

"You don't want to be here, then leave," Bryant said.

"Dying to protect your friends is very noble, but it's better not to die at all," Captain Marlowe said. "All you can accomplish by staying here is dying. This place could be an impenetrable vault—and we've already shown it's not—and you'd still lose. Eventually, you'll run out of food and water, and then it'll be over. Staying here forever is not an option."

"Neither is handing it over," Bryant said.

"*Bryant!*" Hallie snapped.

"Shit..." He turned toward her. "Sorry, Hallie. Shit."

So it wasn't a person after all. It must've been whatever Hallie had with her when she'd left the *Persimmon* for the second time.

"Like I said, I don't care what it is. But now that we know it's an *it* rather than a *him* or a *her*, that makes it a lot easier. Just deliver it in a package to ACM, and let them go on their way. No one needs to get hurt."

"Don't you think that's a little naïve?" Luke, the other guy from Hallie's ship, challenged. "You just told us how ACM took out everyone in the docking bay, including Captain James. I could see them justifying killing the Farcoast soldiers because they're armed, aggressive rivals, but they also killed a high-ranking Coalition official.

"Do you really think they'll let this ship keep floating toward its destination without its captain and with that many already dead? Especially when they have the firepower to wipe the whole ship from existence? That's their next play once they get what they're after."

Captain Marlowe gave a nod. "You raise a good point, actually. There may be no way to win in this situation."

"Nah," Lora blurted. "Forget this. Give it up, and let's take our chances with them being merciful. They might let us go. We got our own ship anyway. We can be gone and outta sight before they do whatever they're gonna do here."

Arlie stared daggers at Lora, and Lora noticed.

"What? I'm talking about the issue at hand, not the other thing."

Arlie's stare persisted, and Lora shrank back into her seat with her arms folded.

"No." Captain Marlowe shifted the metal stick to the other side of his mouth and continued chewing. "His point is valid. They're behaving this way because they don't intend to leave any survivors. I hadn't considered that."

"In any case, we can't give it up," Hallie said. "And yes, it is an *it*, but I'm not saying anything else about it. Anyway, it's too valuable to the Coalition. Captain James understood that. And now he and Captain Dawes, our pilot, have both died because of it, along with countless Farcoast soldiers. Their deaths won't mean anything if we just hand it over."

"Then jettison it into space," Captain Marlowe said. "Or destroy it. Be rid of it somehow. That way, whatever it is, ACM won't get ahold of it."

"I can't do that. I won't. This is my life's work," Hallie said. "And if there's even a chance that we can get it away from here safely, we have to try for it."

[Well, she's dedicated. You gotta give 'er that.]

"Even if that means it falls into ACM's hands?" Justin asked.

"I wouldn't let that happen. There's a failsafe, but again, I really can't say more than that."

"Those damned nondisclosure agreements, huh?" Justin quipped.

Hallie gave him a melancholy smile. "Something like that."

Damn. Thought that would've gotten more of a rise out of her.

"Well, we've talked ourselves into a pit with no obvious way out," Captain Marlowe said. "I don't know what other solution there is."

An idea hit Justin.

A really, really dumb idea.

But it was crazy enough that it just might work.

"I think..." he began.

Everyone turned their attention toward him.

"I think I have a plan."

[Oh, shit. This doesn't sound good...]

"Our problem is that there are too many troops, right?" Justin said. "And the other problem is that even if we did get past them, we could never get the rig past the *Avarice*."

"The what?" Bryant asked.

"The *Avarice*. That's the name of ACM's ship," Captain Marlowe explained.

Hallie scoffed. "Fitting."

"Yeah," Justin said. "Like I was saying, we've got to get past them both... but what if we didn't have to?"

"What are you suggesting?" Captain Marlowe asked.

"Okay... this is gonna sound batshit crazy, but bear with me, okay?"

WITH EACH PASSING MINUTE, Admiral Sever grew more and more perturbed at his soldiers' inability to locate their quarry. By now, a few hours had gone by, and he had yet to receive any actionable intel from his men spreading throughout the *Nidus*.

He'd hoped to retrieve it and be off this damned colonist ship within a day or less, but the utter lack of success thus far had dashed those hopes into oblivion. Commander Falstaff was doing his best, Sever knew, but perhaps that wouldn't be enough.

He knew of a way to possibly speed up the process, but Andridge's corporate offices had told him he wasn't permitted to pursue such an option unless there was no other viable alternative. It was only a prototype after all, and it hadn't been thoroughly field-tested. Even corporate didn't really know what it was capable of.

Yet they'd also told him to succeed by any means necessary. They couldn't have been clearer about it. Given that, why wouldn't he use every asset available to him to ensure his success?

He grinned. Ever since corporate had installed the pod aboard the *Avarice*, Sever's morbid curiosity had burgeoned. He wanted to see what it could do, and there was only one way to find out.

He had to deploy the asset.

And that's exactly what he was going to do.

Sever tapped his handscreen, and it blazed to life, along with the main viewscreen in his private transport ship. Captain Gable's image materialized onscreen, with the clean, white bridge of the *Avarice* behind him.

"Admiral," Gable greeted him with a salute and a steely gaze. "How goes the search?"

"Fine," Sever replied. "But not fast enough. I am issuing the release order on the prototype."

Captain Gable paused for a moment, as if reflecting. His face contorted slightly, perhaps in thought—or disgust—and then it reset. "Understood."

"Launch the pod toward the *Nidus* and direct it to the docking bay near my transport's position. I will handle it from there."

"Aye, Admiral," Captain Gable said, his tone flat and tinged with disdain. "Commencing launch now."

Sever ignored it. Captain Gable would have to deal with his own sour grapes. "Over and out, Captain."

He ended the transmission and stood.

As he exited his private transport, a pod the size of a small hovercar drifted into the docking bay through the nearest entry field. It landed on its own next to his transport, hissing as it settled on the docking bay floor. It was sleek and chrome on its bottom half, and its top half continued its oblong shape but in black, opaque glass instead of chrome.

Sever approached the pod and entered his personal access code onto the screen, still cold to the touch from the frigid vacuum of space. The screen requested physical verification, so he pressed his palm flat onto its icy surface. It read his prosthetic just as it would a normal hand. When it finished scanning, it requested audible confirmation.

"Admiral Siroch Sever," he said to it. "Passcode: Crimson Flame."

The screen displayed the word "APPROVED" in bold green letters, and then the pod began to hiss again. First, a chrome drawer slid out from the bottom of the pod, under where the glass ended. Within the padded foam casing inside the drawer lay a small black orb topped with a red thumb-switch. Behind the orb lay a narrow metal tube about six inches long.

Sever picked up the orb first and then the tube. From his briefing, he already knew what the orb was, but he activated the metal tube anyway. A small hologram emanated from a pinprick-sized lens in its center, displaying an image of a pretty young woman with red hair and wearing a white lab coat.

"Hello, Admiral," she said. "Thank you for agreeing to help the company's Research and Development branch with this field test. We're glad you saw fit to deploy this asset during your current mission.

"As you know, this is a prototype model, and it is the result of generations of scientific research, study, and testing. We are confident of the kind of results you can expect, but of course we are eager to track the asset's efficiency in a real-time combat situation."

I'll bet you are, Sever mused.

"We have already briefed you on the full range of this asset's capabilities as well as the failsafe protocols should anything go wrong, though we do not expect anything of the sort," she continued. "You have already activated the unit, and the black failsafe orb—which we have lovingly nicknamed "the Pilkington," after the head of the company's R & D department—may be activated via the red switch in case such protocols must be observed.

"In order to properly function, the Pilkington must be within fifty feet of the asset. The frequency it emits will not harm humans, cyborgs, or androids within that range, though in some tests, subjects mentioned experiencing mild discomfort from the sound the device produces." The woman smiled. "Rest assured, all subjects were perfectly fine following subsequent wellness tests.

"Please be sure to keep the Pilkington in a secure location so as to safeguard the asset and the company's intellectual property. In closing, we at R & D thank you again for your willingness to participate in this exciting venture. This message device will self-incinerate in ten seconds."

The hologram winked out, and streams of bright sparks promptly spat out of both ends of the tube. Sever tossed it aside, even though it likely wouldn't have harmed his prosthetic hands to continue holding it. The tube clanged against the docking bay floor and burned itself to ash.

Sever studied the Pilkington's smooth black reflective sheen and the crisp red switch on top. He didn't expect he'd need it, but he tucked it into the front pocket of his trousers all the same for safekeeping.

As he did so, the black glass pulled away from the chrome part of the pod, and plumes of violet vapor erupted from the widening space in between.

Sever stepped back and watched as the pod continued to separate. He tried to peer inside the pod, but all the vapor and mist obscured his vision.

The decompression process lasted another few seconds until finally the last of the violet vapor dissipated into the docking bay. But when Sever looked down into the pod, all he could see was a black speckled sheet draped over a massive form.

Was the thing dead? Had corporate done this as a sick joke? Or were they just thoroughly incompetent?

Had it died at some point between Andridge's genetic engineering facilities and the *Avarice*? Or had he somehow accessed it improperly and accidentally killed it?

As he considered the variety of possibilities, he caught a bit of movement from under the sheet. It wasn't dead after all.

Then a large violet-colored hand reached up and out of the pod. The hand grabbed the edge of the black glass, and another hand grabbed the edge of the chrome and started to pull itself upright. When it pulled the black sheet off its head and rose to its full height, Admiral Sever smiled.

Perhaps corporate wasn't solely populated by idiots after all.

FOURTEEN

As Admiral Sever sat in a chair just outside his transport's personal armory, Commander Falstaff entered and saluted.

"You summoned me, sir?" Falstaff said.

"Yes, Commander." Sever folded his hands and looked up at Falstaff. "I take it you still haven't found that which we seek?"

"It is only a matter of time, sir," Falstaff replied.

An indirect answer. An evasion of sorts, and usually Falstaff prided himself on being direct. Was he actually worried about his chances for success?

Sever chose to let it slide. "What can you tell me?"

"Our men are gradually searching the city but…" Falstaff hesitated. "…but it's a large city. If we had more men, it would go faster."

"As you pointed out, we lost many in the last battle," Sever said. "And those that remain aboard the ship must remain so as a contingency."

Falstaff's jaw tensed. "Then we will make do with the forces we have."

"What kind of resistance are we facing?" Sever asked.

"Minimal. Disorganized. Though I suspect it will intensify the deeper into the city we progress. They will have had more time to prepare."

"This is why civilians shouldn't be allowed to own guns," Sever muttered.

"I agree, sir."

"Surveillance?" Sever asked.

"We're running our own, sir, but the city isn't moving except when we make it move. Not a lot of intel there."

"And the *Nidus's* surveillance systems?"

"Not bulletproof, but damn good, sir. Resilient," Falstaff said. "I've got our finest techs working on it now. If we can get in there, we should be able to zip this up much faster."

"Fine."

Something clanked behind Sever, from inside the armory.

Falstaff's expression changed to one of confusion and wariness as he looked between the door and Sever, who grinned.

"I didn't say you would be leaving empty-handed." Sever rose to his feet and knocked on the outside wall of the armory. Heavy footsteps sounded from within, advancing closer to the armory door. "Rather than mustering more infantry from the *Avarice* to aid in your search, I decided to recruit some special assistance for you."

As Sever finished speaking, the asset emerged from the armory door and stood before Commander Falstaff, who gawked at the sight.

"Commander, meet the newest soldier under your command. His name is Vesh."

Vesh stood close to seven feet tall, had violet skin that was translucent enough to show off his dark, bulging veins, and raven-black hair, slicked back. His eyes were black like the void of space, yet they somehow shined like twin blazing stars. Layers upon layers of muscle sheathed his body, and he wore a perpetual scowl on his half-tattooed face.

"What in God's name...?" Falstaff managed to say.

"I assure you, God has nothing to do with it," Sever said.

Vesh wore special black-and-blue armor across his chest and midsection, and it wrapped around his back. It also covered his legs but left his arms bare, and he wore no helmet.

Rather than a standard-issue pulse rifle, Sever had granted Vesh access to his private armory, and he'd rightfully selected a handheld, rapid-fire pulse cannon. It was meant to be wielded with two hands and a torso harness due to its weight, but Vesh held it solely in his right hand as if it weighed nothing.

"Several months back, we received a specialized pod containing Vesh, who has been in an induced hibernation for close to a full year," Sever explained. "The contents of that pod were a strict company secret, one I had to conceal from everyone but Captain Gable, whose rank and clearance authorized him to know about it.

"Vesh is a prototype soldier created at Andridge's secret genetic engineering facility on a small moon in the Zhevalia System. While he has had extensive training, he has never seen real combat or performed in any real mission. We have been granted the opportunity to field-test him, so to speak."

Falstaff blinked. "Aye... Admiral."

"Have no fear, Commander," Sever continued. "He is perfectly loyal, capable, and effective... or at least that's what corporate has assured me. You have only to set him loose in the city and allow him to do his work. He will help root out our quarry, or aid you in suppressing insurgents, or do whatever you command him to do."

Falstaff straightened his back. He was fairly tall, but no matter how much he straightened his spine, Vesh still dwarfed him and always would.

"Very well, Admiral," he said. "Thank you for the additional help."

"Use him to end this quickly so we can be on our way. When we retrieve what we came for, we will deal with the cleanup and then promptly return to the core Coalition planets to pass off what we've found to them, along with Vesh."

"Aye, sir." Falstaff nodded to Sever and then looked at Vesh again. "Follow me, soldier."

"Commander," Sever said as Vesh thumped across the room and took his place at Falstaff's side. "Do not squander this resource. I'm told he is capable of things you couldn't even imagine. Use him wisely."

"Aye, sir," Falstaff repeated. Then he turned and left, and Vesh followed him.

Sever grinned again, and he closed the armory door via the screen mounted next to it. Wherever the crew of that science vessel was hiding, Vesh would find them. Of that, Sever had no doubt.

"Hey," Hallie said from the kitchen door.

Justin turned away from the refrigeration unit and looked at her. Damn, she looked good.

"Hey!" He cleared his throat and made his voice deeper. "I mean, *hey*."

[Nice save, JB,] Keontae quipped.

She giggled. "A little excited?"

"More hungry than excited." He held up a Plastrex package of sliced roast beef. "You think this is real beef or the stuff they grow in labs?"

Hallie headed in closer, her arms crossed and hands tucked into the extra-long sleeves of her shirt. "The stuff they grow in labs *is* real beef. They grow it from the cells of prime eatin' cows. There's nothing artificial about it."

"Did you just say 'prime eatin' cows?'" Justin chuckled at her.

"Well, if they're not called that, then what do you call them?" she pushed back. "Dairy cows produce milk for dairy products, so that's not accurate."

Justin thought about it, but he couldn't think of the term either. "I got nothin'."

"I figured. Make me a sandwich, too?" she asked.

[Oooh. That's a good sign. Work your mojo, son.]

Justin wished he'd made Keontae head into the house's security system for the night, but he hadn't. Now would've been the perfect chance for some actual alone time.

"Sure." Justin set the package of roast beef on the kitchen island's granite countertop. A package of cheddar cheese lay nearby, along with the bread, and mayonnaise. The tomatoes and lettuce were still in the sink. He'd already rinsed them off.

Truth be told, he didn't even like making sandwiches. For all the trouble it took to make one, the end result was pretty much always lackluster, at best. But he didn't feel like trying to figure out how to cook anything in this fancy kitchen, and he didn't want to make a huge mess and have to clean it up.

Plus, now that Hallie was there to keep him company, maybe he might actually enjoy making sandwiches for once.

Justin pulled out four slices of bread and set them on the counter.

"Want plates?" Hallie asked.

"Uh… yeah. I didn't want to go digging for anything and be noisy while people are trying to rest."

Hallie retrieved two ornately painted ceramic plates from one of the cabinets and set them on the countertop.

"What brings you to this 'valley of plenty' at such a late hour?" Justin asked as he laid the bread out on the plates and popped open the package of roast beef.

Everyone else had decided to call it a night early since they didn't know when they'd next get a chance to rest. That is, everyone except Bryant and Arlie, both of whom had insisted on keeping watch in addition to relying on the house's security system. Captain Marlowe was due to switch out with Arlie in a few hours after he'd gotten some sleep.

"I wanted to catch up with you," she said. "We missed our dinner date because of the invasion, so this is a make-up date."

"How romantic."

[I like the way this girl thinks. She's makin' it easy for you.]

Hallie leaned on the counter with her elbows and rested her chin on her hands, which were still covered by her extra-long sleeves. "I don't think we're quite at the romance stage yet, stalker."

"And we won't be as long as you keep calling me that." Justin plopped a generous helping of roast beef on the first sandwich and then matched it on the second. Hallie didn't say anything, so he assumed he was doing well.

"Does it bother you?" she asked.

"I mean, I deserve it. I definitely *was* stalking you." Justin opened the package of cheddar cheese.

[Damn right, you were.]

Justin gritted his teeth and ignored Keontae's extra commentary. He added a slice of cheese to each sandwich. "But we need to move past that at some point, don't you think?"

"That depends." Hallie straightened up, her fabric-covered palms flat on the countertop. "Are you going to keep stalking me?"

"Of course not." Justin sealed up the cheese and the roast beef and tossed both to the other side of the counter.

"Yet I find you here, in my rented house, eating my food."

[She's got a point.]

Whose side are you on? Justin wanted to say it aloud, because Keontae couldn't read his thoughts, but Justin restrained himself. Instead he refocused on Hallie.

"I mean… there are only two things I can say in my defense…" he began, "and at least one of them is true."

"Alright." Hallie nodded, feigning extreme interest. "Please go on."

"First of all, after the invasion, we had nowhere else to go. Literally, we were on our own and had no other options."

"Mhmm." She nodded with exaggerated concern on her face.

"Second… cutting board?"

"What?"

"For the tomato. It's not the second thing. I just need a cutting board and a knife."

"Ah." Hallie abandoned her post at the end of the counter and dug out a Plastrex cutting board and a sharp carving knife for Justin.

He set to work on cutting the tomato, and its red juices briefly reminded him of some of the carnage he'd seen back at ACM-1134. When the little green seeds popped out the side of the tomato, he thought they looked like guts.

Morbid imagery, but easy enough to push away. He kept slicing.

"Second," Justin continued, "you're irresistible."

"Oh." Hallie's posture straightened. "Am I?"

"Completely and absolutely," Justin confirmed.

Hallie tilted her head and smiled. "While I appreciate the compliment, that's exactly the type of thing a stalker would say."

"Or someone with eyes. You know… basically everyone," Justin said. "Hell, I'd bet blind people even know you're gorgeous when you walk by."

[Nice line. Did I teach you that one?]

Justin considered it. Actually, Keontae might've said that one first. Justin could hear his telltale deep voice saying it in some distant memory.

"Uh-huh." Hallie folded her arms and leaned up against the refrigeration unit, now much closer to him than she'd been since they'd arrived at the house that afternoon. "So let me get this straight: you came here because you had nowhere else to go and because I'm irresistible?"

"Yep." Justin added a slice of tomato onto both sandwiches and then moved on to the lettuce.

"So which of them is true?" she asked.

"Hm? Oh. Right." Justin pretended to have to think about it. "Tough choice, but... they both are, I suppose."

"You're not sure?"

"Not sure that we had nowhere else to go? Yeah. We probably could've found somewhere else if we'd looked a bit harder. As for you being irresistible, though... that one is definitely true." As Hallie's cheeks turned tomato red, Justin held up the mayonnaise jar. "Mayo?"

"Are you having some?" she asked, still red.

"Yeah."

"Then go for it."

Two identical sandwiches. At least she was easy to please.

[You're just gonna leave it there? Bro, you got 'er on the hook. Reel 'er in!]

"*Easy*," Justin muttered.

"What?" Hallie asked.

"Huh?" Justin looked up at her. "Oh. Nothing. Just making sure I don't put too much mayo on the sandwich."

"You're weird," Hallie said.

"And your..." Justin crowned the sandwich with the other piece of bread and picked up Hallie's plate. He held it out for her. "...sandwich is ready."

"Thanks." She shook her head. "But I'm not hungry."

Justin's sense of satisfaction at having nailed that sandwich fizzled to nothing. Why the hell had he just made a sandwich for her if she wasn't going to eat it?

"I figured you'd want two."

Justin looked down at her sandwich and then back at his, which still sat on its plate on the counter. Actually, he did want both.

"Well... alright." He set her plate next to his and picked up her sandwich first.

But before he could take a bite, Hallie was there with her hand on his chest, freezing him still, looking up at him with those light-blue eyes with rings of green around her irises.

Justin's mind went blank. He couldn't move. Had she somehow stunned him again, like she had in the street?

No... he was still standing. Still holding the sandwich in the air, too.

She was up on her tippy toes, leaning in toward him, her lips getting closer and closer to his.

Was this actually happening?

[What the hell are you waitin' for?] Keontae shouted at him.

He was right. This was Justin's chance. He leaned in, too, ready to kiss her.

And then, as their lips were about to meet, she turned her head away and bit down hard on the sandwich in his hand.

When she faced him again, it was with a mouthful of sandwich, which she was chewing with one hand covering her mouth.

Justin just stared at her in disbelief.

[What the hell just happened?] Keontae's question was the same as Justin's.

"Sorry," she said amid her chewing. "Changed my mind. It just looked so delicious."

Justin exhaled a quiet, tense breath to chill his heated blood. His voice flat, he said, "No problem."

"Ohhhh. Sorry!" She swallowed her bite of sandwich, and her eyes widened. "Did you think...?"

Justin frowned. She was toying with him.

But maybe he deserved it.

He sighed and lifted the sandwich to his mouth.

[Damn. Maybe next time, JB.]

Again, Hallie stopped him from taking a bite. She blocked his hand with her wrist, leaned into him, and kissed him full on his lips.

She tasted like sunshine—and a roast beef sandwich with lettuce, tomato, cheddar, and mayo. But Justin could've stayed in that moment all day.

[Oh, *FUCK YEAH!*] Keontae let out a whoop. [My man *finally* scored! Look at you!]

Hallie ended the kiss less than two seconds after it had started, leaving the inside of Justin's chest a flurry of dragon riders at war.

[What? Why'd she stop?]

"Have to be brief," she said. "That way, you'll want more."

"Huh?" He gawked at her. Why couldn't he have more now?

"That way, you'll survive your asinine plan and come back to me," she added.

[Put that sandwich down already. You look like a damn fool.]

Justin set it on the plate and looked back at Hallie, still trying to process what had just happened. The girl sure knew how to mess him up in the head.

"You don't think it'll work?" he asked.

She shrugged and leaned against the refrigeration unit again. "It might. But it's so risky. Anything could go wrong."

"I think it's our only shot," he said.

"I know. And I hate to agree with you, at least about this, but I think you're right."

"But you're... looking forward to me coming back?"

"If it works, I definitely want to see you again," she said. "Yes."

"I want that, too," he said.

"So don't get yourself killed, alright? I'm hoping for an encore later on." She gave him a wink.

"You got it," he said.

They talked and flirted some more while Justin scarfed down both sandwiches. Turns out, he was more than hungry enough to eat both. He was considering making a third when Bryant stormed into the kitchen, stopped, and stared at them both.

Then his stare became a scowl directed solely at Justin.

"Hi, Bryant." Hallie waved to him. "What's up?"

Bryant cleared his throat and shifted his attention to her. "The soldiers are close. We don't have much time."

So much for that third sandwich.

Bryant looked back to Justin. "You ready?"

"As ready as I'll ever be."

"Pack your things," Bryant said to Hallie. "We're leaving in ten."

With that, he shot Justin another glare, and then he left the kitchen.

"I don't think he likes me," Justin told Hallie, his voice low and quiet.

"I *know* he doesn't," she countered, her voice also low and quiet. "He told me as much."

"Well, what'd I ever do to him?"

"He's jealous. I think he knows I like you."

Getting kissed had been a great experience, but hearing Hallie say that out loud sparked a joy in Justin's chest that he hadn't felt in years.

More importantly, it filled him with renewed determination to succeed. Having a real shot with someone like Hallie was a once-in-a-lifetime chance. He had to make it out of this drama alive so he could see where this little flirtation was going.

"Well, he's just gonna have to deal with it," Justin said.

"That's more or less what I told him." She touched his arm with her hand, now out of its sleeve. "Hey, I have to go get ready to leave, but I'm serious—come back alive, okay?"

"I will," Justin said. "Probably. Maybe. Well... I'll do my best."

She gave his arm a squeeze.

"You do your part, too, and make sure *you* come back," Justin said.

"I've got the easy part. I'll be fine." She gave him a wink and then left him in the kitchen with a final wave.

Justin exhaled a long sigh as he brushed breadcrumbs from the countertop into his hand and deposited them in the sink.

[JB,] Keontae said. [I don't think I've ever been more proud of you, man.]

"I survived a mine infected with radiation-mutated monsters, malfunctioning killer androids, and a vengeful tech ghost out for blood," Justin said, "but *this* is the proudest you've ever been of me?"

[Absolutely,] Keontae said with a smile in his voice. [You just charmed the most dangerous creature mankind has ever known, and you did it like a damned pro.]

Justin grinned. "Thanks, man."

[You'd better drop me in the security system before those soldiers reach this house. You're gonna need me.]

Keontae was right, so Justin headed downstairs to the main screen once again.

FROM HIS VANTAGE point at the end of the hovertram line, high above most of the buildings, Vesh could freely scan Nidus City with his augmented eyes.

It had taken him awhile to reacclimated to his enhanced body, but he'd rediscovered his stride, remembered his training. As promised, he couldn't remember any of the gene therapy treatments that had transformed him into... whatever it was that he'd become. He figured that was for the best. He doubted it had been a pleasant experience.

Something behind his eyes burned and tingled, but he blinked hard, and the sensation faded.

Vesh's vision cycled through a variety of types as he scrutinized the cityscape before him.

Infrared. 40x zoom. Ultraviolet. 60x zoom. Biometric. 100x zoom. Night vision.

He could see almost everything. His X-ray vision wouldn't function from so far away, but he'd seen plenty all the same.

But seeing the present wasn't nearly as good as seeing the past.

Admiral Sever, his new commanding officer, had asked Commander Falstaff about the ship's surveillance. Apparently, the tech crew available to the *Avarice* couldn't break through.

That didn't mean Vesh couldn't.

He abandoned his perch and found the nearest control panel. He knew what he was supposed to do when he got there, but he couldn't remember *how* he knew... or how he could even do what he was about to do. How was that possible?

He looked down at his hands. Thick veins and arteries under his violet skin pumped enhanced blood throughout his hungry body. He could see them most clearly on the backs of his hands, where his skin was thinner and the veins were closer to the surface. But his veins weren't what he was looking for.

He flipped his hands over, palms up, and inspected his fingertips. Fine metal lines, golden in color, flowed beneath the skin of his fingers.

Upon closer inspection, he realized they weren't just metal lines—they were circuits. Circuitry of some sort ran from his fingertips down into his palms, and it gradually faded to nothing in the center of his hands.

Had they implanted circuits into his hands? What did that mean?

His training reminded him what it meant.

It meant he could perform the tasks he needed to perform.

Vesh pressed his hand against the screen, and warmth from his hand flooded the console. His fingertips emanated soft golden light as his mind engaged with the ship's network.

He raced down wires and through memory blocks and into various operating systems until he found his target: ship security's surveillance records. The security sub-network tried to keep him out, but Vesh tore through its shields in seconds.

Before long, he was scrolling through hundreds of hours of video from various cameras around the city and the rest of the ship.

Vesh stopped his search on a series of videos from a select sequence of source cameras. He strung their feeds together and played them at double speed.

Several docking bay cameras captured the science vessel, the *Persimmon*, docking aboard the *Nidus*. Those same cameras captured the ship's crew as they exited their vessel and headed toward the docking bay doors atop a hover transport.

The view followed them, still jumping from camera to camera, all the way until one of the crew ventured back into the docking bay, escorted by a Farcoast soldier driving a hovercraft.

But as soon as she entered, the camera feeds from within the docking bay shut off. Vesh found that odd. Perhaps someone had tampered with the cameras or deleted the footage.

In any case, when she returned, she was holding a sack of some sort. From what Commander Falstaff had told him about the object they were seeking, Vesh supposed it could've fit in there... though he'd expected it to be larger.

In any case, these people were his target. If he could find them, he could find the prize, one way or another.

He watched them through the ship's various cameras around the city as they boarded a hovertaxi of sorts and cruised into an affluent section of the city with big stone houses and wider streets. They stopped at a specific house surrounded by a bronze fence and went inside.

Vesh scrolled through several more hours of footage in a matter of minutes, confirming that the woman with the sack had left once, gone to breakfast at a restaurant downtown with a man with a prosthetic arm, and eventually returned to the house. She hadn't left since, and the sack she'd had with her hadn't left the house, either.

That was enough for him. He knew where he was heading, so he extracted his mind from the network and pulled his hand away from the screen.

He'd found them. And in a few minutes, he would reach them.

The slow, tingling burn behind his eyes started up again, and again, he blinked it away.

Then he turned toward the city and stormed forward with his pulse cannon in hand.

BY THE TIME the first soldier approached the gate in front of the house, everyone inside was already gone except for Justin.

They'd used an escape tunnel in the basement to get out the back and disappear into the city. As it turned out, there had been a secret wall in the basement after all, and that's what it had been hiding.

The thought of just picking off these soldiers with the house's security system both appealed to Justin and sickened him. With Keontae at the helm, it would be so easy—*too* easy.

Justin hadn't actually killed anyone before he'd shot down the soldier with the grenade back in the docking bay. Sure, he'd shot his fair share of androids and mutations back at ACM-1134, but that was totally different. And technically, even though it had been his arm that did the deed, he hadn't been the one to kill Carl Andridge, so he didn't count that as his first kill.

He wished he hadn't needed to shoot the ACM soldier with the grenade, but he'd done what he had to do to survive. The thought of unceremoniously carving through more soldiers did nothing for him personally, but he knew that by killing them off, he'd give his escaping friends more time to get away.

So he and Keontae set to work.

The first soldier to reach the gate reached out and tried to pull it open. A jolt of 10,000 volts of electricity sent him seizing to the ground, and his fellow soldiers gathered around him.

To Justin's surprise, another idiot tried the gate as well and suffered the same fate. It didn't happen a third time, though. One of the soldiers pulled a grenade from his pocket, lobbed it at the base of the gate, and fell back.

BOOM. Just could feel the explosion through the basement, and it rattled his teeth. When he looked up, he saw the remnants of the gate lying in a twisted heap off to one side as ACM soldiers poured onto the property.

The soldiers who chose to walk on the grass encountered small explosive charges buried there. Whenever the bombs went off, men usually lost a foot and the lower half of a shin. But on the whole, the ACM soldiers still advanced.

Some of them went down with missing limbs, and others went down with twisted ankles from stepping into the holes carved into the lawn by the charges, but all in all, the house managed to take out several more of the soldiers that way.

Still others fell thanks to the occasional turret that would pop up from under plants in the garden or from on the roof. The house—and Keontae—was effectively turning the front yard into a warzone.

When they made it to the front door, the ACM soldiers tried to kick it down and break it open, but it refused to budge. Thanks to more turrets, they, too, perished before they could make much progress.

But despite how easily they had all fallen, some of the soldiers hadn't moved beyond the gate. Instead, they radioed for reinforcements.

A long period of peace followed as more soldiers began to arrive. Mechs, too, with better firepower.

By then, Captain Marlowe had radioed over the comms that they'd gotten away. Justin responded in the affirmative, and he set out to begin phase two.

He pulled Keontae back into his arm to let the house deal with the additional ACM soldiers and their mechs, and then he left through the same tunnel that the others had used to flee.

He popped out of a manhole cover a few houses away and a couple blocks over. He glanced back and saw flashing lights and explosions as the soldiers made war against the house. The air thundered with booms and gunfire, both from the house and ACM, but that wasn't his concern anymore.

All he had to do now was—

Something slammed into him from the side, hard, and he found himself tumbling and skidding across the asphalt street until he landed in the grassy front yard of one of the houses.

Pain racked his body. Had he been hit by a hovercar or something?

But when he looked up, he didn't see a hovercar.

Instead, he saw an impossibly large man with purplish skin striding toward him.

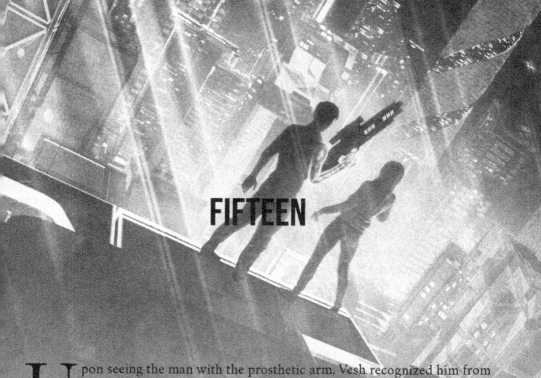

FIFTEEN

Upon seeing the man with the prosthetic arm, Vesh recognized him from the footage of the woman heading to breakfast. He'd been accompanying her at the time.

When the man popped out from a manhole cover a few blocks away from a surprisingly well-fortified house, alone and apathetic to his surroundings, Vesh moved to detain him. He might have valuable information about the woman's whereabouts, or perhaps he even knew the location of the item Admiral Sever wanted recovered.

So rather than shooting the man down, Vesh closed in silently, charged ahead, and knocked him over. All told, he hadn't put much behind the collision aside from his girth. After all, if he accidentally killed this person, Vesh couldn't extract any information from him.

But as Vesh approached, the downed man scrambled to his feet. He swayed for a moment when he got upright, but he'd managed to get up nonetheless. That alone impressed Vesh.

Then again, Vesh had taken it easy on him. Perhaps *too* easy.

The burn behind Vesh's eyes returned, and he blinked it away. It was annoying, but not debilitating, so he would endure. Once this mission was complete, he would log the sensation in his report and request an examination.

For now, though, he had to collect this man and interrogate him.

[Ho-lee shit. That's a *big* motherfucker,] Keontae said.

"Understatement of the millennium," Justin muttered.

After seeing what phichaloride gas and radiation from copalion could do to people back at ACM-1134, not much horrified Justin anymore. It was part of why he'd succeeded in making a life on the rig, despite its lousy, disgusting, cramped living conditions.

But the sight of the mammoth man, his bare tree-trunk arms, and the black-and-blue armor canvassing his broad chest and huge legs proved more than enough to set Justin on edge.

Had there only been one or two weird things about him, Justin wouldn't have thought twice. But this guy looked like a walking science experiment gone wrong —or perhaps perfectly right.

His skin was translucent and violet, and Justin could see thick veins and arteries running up and down his bare arms. On top of that, his eyes were black voids, yet they somehow seemed to emanate some sort of arcane glow.

The combination made him look alien, but in all of mankind's travels throughout the galaxy, they'd never discovered intelligent life. That left a possibility Justin had only heard rumors of: genetic engineering.

Maybe Justin's flippant science-project thought was closer to the truth than he'd imagined. Was this guy some sort of super soldier, made or modified in a lab somewhere?

Even though it might've explained his size and his appearance, genetic engineering in humans was unquestionably outlawed. The Coalition had passed legislation against it decades ago.

Justin scoffed. Then again, when had following the law ever been one of Andridge's priorities?

Then he noticed the pulse cannon strapped to the big guy's back. Could he actually carry that thing *and* shoot it? Justin doubted it was just there for looks... and that meant the big guy was at least as strong as he looked, if not more so.

[This is some shit you don't need, JB,] Keontae warned.

Justin found himself wishing he hadn't given his pulse rifle to Bryant. He should've just held onto it in case of a situation like this. *Too late now.*

As the big guy drew nearer, Justin realized he was much bigger than even Dirk had been, both upward and outward. This dude might've weighed close to 400 pounds. Had to be 350, at least, and all of it powerful muscle and bone.

But that much heft would mean he couldn't be fast. So instead of fighting back, Justin took Keontae's wisdom to heart. Without so much as a word, he turned and ran deeper into the city, away from the big guy and the sounds of mayhem from the ACM soldiers nearby.

He glanced back a couple of times. The first time, he saw the big guy following him, running, albeit much slower. The second time, the big guy just wasn't there anymore... but Justin hadn't taken any turns or darted down any alleys... so where had the big guy gone?

Whatever. Justin had gotten away, at least for now. Now he had to get to the—

A huge object dropped in front of Justin's path with a thunderous impact. It hit so hard that chunks of asphalt erupted from the street and pelted nearby buildings and houses, leaving scars and gashes in their façades.

[Look out!] Keontae shouted.

Justin skidded to a halt as concrete dust and gravel stung his face and his good hand, which he used to shield himself from the cloud hissing over him. Had ACM dropped a bomb in the middle of the street?

When the dust cleared, a long, muscle-coated arm lashed toward Justin and grabbed his shirt collar. Justin noticed the arm's dark veins first, then he noticed its violet color.

[...the hell? How'd he do that?]

Justin already knew. The big guy had gotten a running start and then jumped. How else could he have done it? He'd been genetically engineered to be stronger, not faster.

And with that enhanced strength came one hell of a grip.

Justin tried to pull away, but all he succeeded in doing was popping the top button off his shirt. It skittered across the pavement and disappeared, and Justin's shirt hung half off his shoulder, exposing his undershirt.

[*Run*, JB!] Keontae shouted at him.

"Trying!" Justin fired back. He yanked on his shirt with both hands, but the big guy held on and began to reel Justin in closer. Then he reached with his other hand, too.

Justin's right hand pushed forward, palm open, and he stunned the big guy square in his chest. It should've knocked the big guy out, or at the very least made him let go, but all it did was give him a sharp jolt.

When the big guy looked down with those vacant black eyes, Justin sensed anger where he hadn't before. The big guy was fuming now.

[Aw, shit... you pissed 'im off.]

Justin yanked on his shirt again and let it stretch out, then he squeezed his right hand into a fist. His energy sword blazed to life with orange light, and he sliced through the shirt fabric and staggered back, now free.

The big guy dropped the piece of fabric to the street and kept striding forward. He wasn't fast, but he wasn't slow, either.

Justin started to back up.

[Why the *hell* ain't you runnin'?] Keontae asked.

"He'll just jump again and catch me. I can take him."

[The hell you can! Look at this dude! He's gonna eat your dumb ass for breakfast!]

"Not if I cut him down to size." Justin held up his sword.

The big guy reached for him again, either oblivious to Justin's sword or ambivalent toward it. That gave Justin pause, especially after clashing blades with Quan in the Asian District, but it was too late. Justin was already swinging.

His sword clashed against the big guy's arm, and it sparked and crackled as it deflected harmlessly off his skin, which rippled with some sort of yellow shield.

"Shit!"

Justin ducked under the big guy's grasp, but his follow-up grab caught hold of Justin's left wrist—his human wrist. The big guy yanked him back and grabbed hold of Justin's collar with his other hand again.

One squeeze would reduce Justin's wrist to jelly.

"Stop resisting," the big guy said in a deep, haunting voice.

"No chance," Justin replied. He balled his metal hand into a fist, and with all his prosthetic's enhanced strength, he slammed it squarely into the big guy's freaky face.

Another jolt, and nothing more. He hadn't even scratched the surface.

But that familiar anger returned to the big guy's face and his soulless black eyes.

[Oh, shit,] Keontae said.

Then the big guy yanked Justin forward and bashed the crown of his head into Justin's forehead.

A flash of white light leaped across Justin's vision, and then everything went dark.

JUSTIN DIDN'T KNOW how long had passed when he finally came to, but he quickly acclimated to his familiar surroundings. He lay on the docking bay floor, staring up at the countless lights and repair machines hanging from the high ceiling.

[Careful, JB. Move slow,] Keontae said. [They got you. Don't give 'em a reason to shoot you.]

"Great," Justin mumbled as he pushed himself up to a sitting position, clutching his forehead with his left hand. There was definitely a lump there now, and it hurt to touch it. It also hurt not to touch it.

Around him, dozens of ACM ships sat throughout the docking bay. He craned his aching head and saw the telltale gray color of the rig in the distance, too, but there was no sign of the *Persimmon*. It was just... gone.

Even more surprising, apart from some bloodstains on the floor and some damage to the walls and floor, there was no indication that a battle had even taken place there. All the bodies were gone, Farcoast and ACM alike.

Had they dropped them out one of the entry fields and left them to the void of space? Or had they done something else with them? Justin didn't want to think about it.

[Heads up, JB. You got company.]

Good. It would help take his mind off the question of where the dead had gone.

As Justin rose to his feet, he noticed a group of several other people walking toward him, escorted by ACM soldiers. Some of the people had dirty faces and wore workers' clothes, while others in fine attire looked as if they'd just come from some sort of fancy evening event.

None of them wore shackles or cuffs, and neither did Justin. But he supposed there were more than enough soldiers around to prevent anyone from doing anything stupid. With so much manpower, they didn't need to shackle their prisoners.

On Justin's other side stood the big guy who'd brought him in. Justin scowled up at him.

"You know," he said, "the least you could do is bring me some ice for my head."

With those freaky black eyes, it was hard to tell if the big guy was looking at Justin or beyond him. Either way, the big guy didn't move.

[Don't get yourself killed. That ain't a part of your plan.]

"Neither was getting bulldozed by a giant purple dude, but here we are," Justin muttered.

As the group of people—folks from Nidus City, Justin guessed—lined up beside him, he noticed a man approaching. He wore a dressier type of ACM uniform compared to the armor the soldiers had on, and he had rich brown skin and gray hair.

Admiral Sever.

Great.

Altogether, there were about twelve men and women lined up along with Justin. Admiral Sever stood before them, looking each of them up and down, studying them like a predator examining its prey.

Justin ignored the intimidation tactic and instead focused on Admiral Sever's hands and arms. How much of him was prosthetic? With his gloves back on and long sleeves, it would be hard to tell.

Admiral Sever consulted with one of the ACM soldiers, who pointed at the various people lined up with Justin. Then Admiral Sever turned and faced one of the men in nicer clothing.

"I am told you are a person of some importance on this ship," he said. "I have a few questions for you."

The man's face hardened with anger. "I won't tell you anything."

"I think you'll find that it is far better for you to cooperate than to be obstinate."

"Fuck you," the man spat.

Admiral Sever didn't move for a moment. He just stood there, staring at the man, studying him. Then he pulled off his gloves, exposing his metal hands. His right hand split apart as it had before, and the plasma cannon inside emerged.

He raised it to the man's head and fired.

The blast sheared the top of the man's head clean off, just above his eyebrows. He went wide-eyed, his jaw slackened, and he crumpled to the floor, very dead.

[Oh, *shit*. This thug ain't playin'.]

Justin's heart shuddered. Playing up his usual smartass nature would just get him killed. He'd have to approach this differently—and more carefully.

Admiral Sever's hand clamped shut, concealing the plasma cannon once again.

He moved two people down the line, closer to Justin. Now he stood in front of a middle-aged woman, whose face and clothes were dirty. She was a good fifty pounds overweight and had brown hair.

"And you, my dear," he said. "Are you more willing to help?"

She nodded, and tears streaked down her cheeks, through the grime.

"What's your name?"

"Jeroma," she replied with a slight lisp. "Please... I've got five kids."

"Cooperate, and you'll see them again."

"I... I don't know anything."

"Not exactly starting out on the right foot, are you?" Admiral Sever shook his head. "You were caught while trying to resist our troops. You wanted to keep them from searching your house. Why would you do such a thing? What are you hiding?"

"I-I'm not hiding anything. I just..." She whimpered, and her whole body quaked.

"You what?" Admiral Sever leaned in closer.

"I just didn't want them there. It's not right." Her voice hinted at indignation. "*You* don't have the right."

Admiral Sever nodded. "'Might is right.' You know the ancient saying, don't you?"

"That's not... you can't..."

"I can, and I did. And I will continue to do so." Admiral Sever held up his right hand, but it didn't open up. It remained a cold metal hand instead.

"Oh, no... please don't!"

"Are you hiding something for the scientists?" Admiral Sever asked.

"What? No." She shook her head, resolute. "I don't know what you're talking about. I don't know any scientists."

"You're certain? No one contacted you and asked you to conceal something for them?"

She nodded. "Positive."

"Because we will tear your home apart at even the slightest suspicion that you're lying. And your family will suffer the most for your dishonesty here today."

"No... no! I swear, we haven't done anything like that. We've got nothing to hide," she pleaded. "Please don't hurt my children. We're just trying to get to a new world, to get a new start."

Admiral Sever nodded. "If you don't have it, then you're of no use to me."

His hand opened up again, and the plasma cannon blew a hole through the woman's chest. She slumped to the docking bay floor, just as dead as the man missing the top half of his head.

Justin considered making a run for it. Staying here and getting killed wasn't what he'd planned—not by a long shot. But failing to escape—which he most certainly would—and getting killed anyway wasn't part of his plan, either.

"Run identity checks on the rest of them," Admiral Sever said. "I want to know who they are and what interactions they've had with the Coalition and Farcoast over the last three years."

"Produce your identification," one of the soldiers said as several of them approached. Two of them produced handscreens and tapped at them.

Justin frowned. He'd been through this already when ACM first arrived. But now that they were checking histories with Farcoast, Justin's work experience with them might show up.

While the scanning began, Admiral Sever walked over to the big guy and initiated a conversation with him. They spoke in hushed tones, and the big guy nodded at Justin. Then Admiral Sever started toward him.

[Shit.]

"Couldn't have said it better myself," Justin murmured.

"You there." Admiral Sever pointed at Justin with his metal hand.

Justin had to force himself not to flinch.

"Come here."

"Do I have to?" Justin asked. He regretted it immediately.

"You saw the alternative, didn't you?" Admiral Sever motioned toward the dead man and woman on the docking bay floor.

Justin started toward Admiral Sever. He wondered if it would be worth it to brandish his energy sword and cut him down right then and there.

"Wait, Admiral." The big guy stepped between them and held out his gigantic right hand. "Take the modification cartridges out of your arm and hand them over."

Justin hesitated. Without them, he'd be defenseless except for his arm's enhanced strength.

"Do it now, or I will remove the entire arm," the big guy warned.

[Better do it, JB.]

Justin cursed under his breath. He held out his arm and popped open a chamber on the back of his hand. He disconnected the stun gun mod from there. From his wrist, he pulled out the energy sword mod, and he removed the purdonic resistance shield emitter from his forearm. He dropped them all into the big guy's hand.

"You're sure that's all of them?" the big guy asked.

For good measure, Justin popped open the three other mod spots along his arm—one just above his elbow, another in his metal biceps, and a third in his shoulder. They were all empty. He hadn't ever gotten mods for those.

The big guy turned to Admiral Sever. "You may proceed, Admiral."

"Thank you, Vesh," Admiral Sever said.

[What the hell kind of name is "Vesh?"]

"What the hell kind of name is 'Keontae?'" Justin muttered back.

[It's a family name. Don't be racist.]

"Did you say something?" Admiral Sever asked.

Justin shook his head. "Just talking to myself."

Admiral Sever fingered the seared edge of Justin's shirt. "Vesh tells me you were quite troublesome to capture. More importantly, he tells me he saw video of you with a certain young lady at breakfast this morning. What can you tell me about her?"

[Shit. Careful, JB.]

"Her name is Hallie. We met yesterday morning while we were both out for a walk. I invited her to breakfast," Justin said. So far, it was all true. "We had a good time, so we were gonna meet up again tonight, but then you guys showed up and tanked that idea."

Admiral Sever grinned. "A poet once said that life tends to happen while you're busy making other plans."

"I wouldn't call what you're doing here 'life.'" Justin glanced at the dead man and the dead woman still lying on the floor. "Seems like the exact opposite."

"I am doing what must be done in order to fulfill my mandate," Admiral Sever said. "And now I'd like to hear from you where I can find this 'Hallie' person."

"Why?"

"That is none of your concern."

"It is if you're gonna kill her."

"As I said, that is none of your concern," Admiral Sever insisted. "Surely you've seen how these conversations go in movies. You resist telling me, and then I torture you. Eventually you *do* tell me, and then I kill you anyway. But there is good news, Mr.—?"

"Barclay. Justin Barclay."

"Mr. Barclay," Admiral Sever repeated. "The good news is that I will guarantee you a swift, clean end if you cooperate. I'd offer more, but that's the best you will get, given your situation, so help me and die quickly, or resist and die very slowly and very painfully."

Justin's heartbeat accelerated. This wasn't what he'd wanted. He couldn't die now. Too much hinged on him staying alive. "Not much of a choice."

"In this galaxy, choice is an illusion for all but the highest echelon of the wealthy and powerful," Admiral Sever said. "The only choices you have are the ones that other people give to you."

Justin kept quiet. Hallie and Captain Marlowe hadn't told him where they were going on purpose. That way, if ACM tried to force it out of him, he wouldn't be able to tell them anything. All things considered, he'd hoped to avoid being tortured, though.

"I don't know where she is," Justin said. "And that's the truth."

"Then I suppose you've bought yourself a few more hours, Mr. Barclay," Admiral Sever said. "Although by the end of them, you will wish you hadn't."

"I'm telling you the *truth*," Justin insisted.

"Even if you are, I obviously can't trust you. But I *can* trust that your pain will make honest men of us both."

Admiral Sever turned away, and Vesh started toward Justin again, who backed up.

"Wait!" Justin called.

Admiral Sever turned around, and Vesh stopped his advance.

"I don't know where she is," he said, "but I know something else that's of value. To Andridge on the whole."

Admiral Sever approached Justin again. "And what would that be?"

Justin smirked. "I know what really happened to Carl Andridge at ACM-1134."

[What the *hell*, JB? Why would you throw yourself under the hoverbus like this?]

Admiral Sever squinted at Justin. "And what, exactly, happened to him?"

Justin shook his head. "No way I'm telling you. You gotta take me back to the core planets. To ACM headquarters. I'll tell them."

A new grin spread across Admiral Sever's face. "A valiant attempt, to be sure, but I will decline. High marks for creativity, though."

Again, Admiral Sever turned away.

"You know I know the truth," Justin called. "It wasn't made public that Carl Andridge died on Ketarus-4. So how would I know that?"

Admiral Sever stopped, and once more, he turned back to face Justin. "Perhaps you have good connections and, thus, good intel."

Justin shook his head. "To be frank, I suck at networking. I'd rather dig or drill all day. No, the reason I know is because I was there. I survived ACM-1134."

Admiral Sever looked Justin up and down, wearing a mask of incredulity.

"If you don't believe me, look me up. Scan my ID, and do your illegal deep-dive into my past."

"We will. And I can assure you that if you are anything less than who you claim to be, your death will be the longest, most agonizing experience that any man in history has ever endured."

"Deal," Justin said.

Admiral Sever motioned for one of the ACM soldiers with a handscreen to come over and look into Justin's past. The soldier scanned his virtual ID badge with the handscreen. After a few moments of tapping, the soldier looked up.

"Well?" Admiral Sever asked.

The soldier flipped his handscreen around. "He's right. He's one of only two survivors of the incident at ACM-1134 on Ketarus-4. Says here he's a person of interest to Andridge corporate, and we are to detain him if possible for further questioning."

Being a person of interest to Andridge corporate wasn't news to Justin, but being wanted for further questioning surprised him. ACM had asked their questions and let him go with a symphony of warnings, but now they wanted him back? Why?

Admiral Sever examined the screen and then looked at Vesh again. "Send him over to the *Avarice*. Have them lock him in a cell and question him about the woman scientist. When we're done here, we'll take him back to Andridge corporate and let them question him all they want."

[Shit, JB. I can't believe that worked.]

Justin hardly believed it, either.

Then Vesh grabbed Justin by his triceps, and his long, thick fingers wrapped all the way around to his biceps. Justin felt like an unruly child being escorted out of a restaurant as Vesh hauled him over to one of the ACM transport ships.

But hey... at least he wasn't dead.

WHEN JUSTIN ARRIVED aboard the *Avarice*, he didn't see much of it. The transport ship had docked in the *Avarice's* version of a docking bay, which was considerably smaller than that of the *Nidus*, yet still huge overall. They were both gigantic ships, after all.

Vesh had stayed aboard the *Nidus* with Admiral Sever, and as far as Justin knew, he'd held onto Justin's arm mods as well. A handful of nameless, faceless ACM soldiers had escorted Justin to the *Avarice*. Now they escorted him through the ship's clean, yet narrow corridors toward, he presumed, the *Avarice's* brig.

He tried to pay attention to his route from the docking bay to the brig, but they made a bunch of turns and went down multiple gravity lifts—he'd never be able to remember it all.

They ended up in a wide room that resembled the waiting room of a doctor's office, only it had a dark, oppressive feel to it. Justin had never been in prison, but he'd certainly been arrested and "detained" before, both on his home planet growing up and elsewhere. He knew the heavy, despairing feel of jail cells, and this place felt like that, only worse.

A pane of what he guessed was reinforced two-way glass served as the back wall, all except for a doorframe with a glowing red energy field instead of a door. It looked like a gateway to Hell itself.

The soldiers passed him off to a pair of guards not wearing face shields or armor. Instead, they wore medium-blue-colored fabric uniforms, tactical belts, and frowns. They deactivated the glowing red energy field and led him into the brig's processing area.

While one guard supervised with a stun baton, crackling with arcs of purple energy, in hand, the other booked him in the system, including taking fingerprints from his human hand, scanning his eyes, and swabbing his mouth for DNA.

Then they made him strip down to his underwear and sent him through a full-body scanner, which was only half as humiliating as when they patted him down afterward anyway.

[Welcome to my world,] Keontae said. [Cops done that shit—and worse—to me more times than I can remember, whether I was guilty or not.]

Satisfied that Justin had no contraband or weapons jammed into any of his orifices, they let him dress in his own clothes again and escorted him through another red energy field and into the cellblock.

The term "cellblock" wasn't wholly accurate. There was a small common area with some Plastrex benches and rounded Plastrex tables bolted to the floor, and... that was pretty much it. A few people milled about, but otherwise, there wasn't much else to see. Then again, it was the middle of the night in Coalition time, so perhaps everyone was asleep.

At chest height, hexagon-shaped panes of dark-blue glass marked the walls at consistent intervals all the way around the common area. Justin had no clue what they were for until he saw one of them open.

A man crawled out, bare feet first, and landed on the floor about a yard below. Behind him, in the hexagon, lay a small pillow and some orange light, but nothing else.

Sleeping pods? That would account for why Justin couldn't see any beds or cells anywhere—there weren't any. Prisoners just hopped in a hexpod, and that was their own private space, cramped as it was. Made the most of the available brig space, for sure.

Good thing Justin only had a fear of heights and not claustrophobia.

"Sleep with your boots on," a man's voice said.

Justin blinked out of his thoughts and back into the brig. The barefoot guy who'd just climbed out of his hexpod was staring at Justin—specifically at his feet, with a longing look in his deep-blue eyes. He had a few days' worth of gray stubble collecting on his chin and jaw, almost as long as his gray buzz-cut hair.

Probably mid-fifties or older, Justin guessed, by the wrinkles on his face. He wore a plain blue jumpsuit that matched the color of his eyes, and it had a faint reflective quality to it. Whenever the light shined on it, the fabric almost shimmered.

"Socks, too," the man said. "Anything you part with in here tends to grow legs and disappear."

"I'll keep it in mind," Justin said. "Thanks."

[So those pods are all you get, huh?] Keontae said. [I can just imagine the ship designers tryin' to cut corners and save on costs, and this is the shit they came up with. Meanwhile, they're probably livin' in penthouse apartments on New Germania-7 or some other rich-ass planet with plenty of space.]

Keontae was probably spot-on, but it didn't matter much at the moment. Just another of the galaxy's endless injustices.

"Uh…" Justin gingerly rubbed the lump on his forehead. It still hurt, but the swelling had gone down. "How does this work? Do I just… pick one?"

"Simple as that. One of the open ones. Once you're inside, it'll sync to your biometrics, and it's yours 'til they find a reason to reset it."

Justin looked at the pods again. He hadn't noticed at first, but some of them were indeed open, while others were closed. He counted three staggered rows of twenty pods around the room. Of those, the majority were closed, and maybe eight of them were open.

Did that mean there were more than fifty prisoners locked in the brig with him? Or did the brig keep some of them closed all the time? Justin didn't want to be locked in such a small area with fifty other people, especially if they were criminals, even if only by ACM's definition.

"Thanks," he told the barefoot guy.

"Name's Jonesy," the guy said. "Full name is Fennimore Jones, but folks just call me Jonesy because 'Fennimore' is too long, 'Jones' is too boring, and 'Fen' is a girl's name."

[Can't argue with the man's logic,] Keontae said.

"I'm Justin Barclay. 'Justin' is fine." He extended his hand toward Jonesy, who didn't return the gesture.

"No offense, but I won't be shaking your hand, son." Jonesy fingered a hole in the fabric of his jumpsuit just above his waistline instead. "Last man's hand I shook decided to bury a shiv in my side while he had me close. Earned me half a week in the medbay, shackled to my bed, of course."

Justin noticed the remnant of a slightly darker stain around the hole in Jonesy's jumpsuit. Probably blood.

[Welcome to prison,] Keontae muttered.

"Between the boots and the handshakes, it must sound like I'm a slow learner," Jonesy said with a huff.

Justin had been thinking it, but he hadn't dared to point it out.

"I promise, it's just in here. Never done time before this. Never done anything wrong in my life 'til my commanding officer decided to trump up some malarkey to ruin my career."

Justin had no interest in hearing this guy's sob story. For all he knew, it might not even be true. Then again, if he could make a friend out of Jonesy, that was better than making an enemy, even if the old guy seemed harmless enough.

"For what it's worth, I know exactly how that feels," he said. "ACM tried that on me, too, awhile back."

"I was the best mechanic they had, too," Jonesy continued as if he hadn't heard Justin. "They're screwed without me. That's for sure. I just hope none of our boys get killed because of piss-poor maintenance on their Strikers."

Truth be told, Justin didn't care either way. He didn't want anyone to die if they didn't have to, but these guys *were* all working for ACM. As far as he was concerned, they all deserved whatever they got.

Justin nodded at Jonesy. "Hope you get it sorted out. It's late, and I'm gonna find a pod for the night."

"Okay. Thanks for listening." Jonesy gave him a wave. "Good luck with the pods. They usually stay shut, but some of these guys have jiggers that can pry them open. You ought to sleep with your feet toward the door in case they try to pull you out. That way, at least you can throw a punch or two before they get at you."

That did *not* help Justin's sense of calm, but it was good information to know all the same.

"Thanks," Justin repeated, and he headed toward an open hexpod ninety degrees away from Jonesy's.

He climbed into the tight space with absolutely zero finesse, but he managed to get inside all the same. On the ceiling, which was only about a foot up from his head, a screen glowed down at him. He tapped it with his human fingers, and it glowed to life.

A thick layer of transparent Plastrex covered its surface, like a shield. These things probably took a lot of punishment from unhappy prisoners.

A message on the screen instructed him to press his hand against the screen to confirm his identity, so he did. The screen scanned his fingerprints, and the glass at his feet gradually slid shut, sealing him inside. A soft orange light glowed along a singular track on the right side of the ceiling.

He couldn't sit up, and he didn't have much room to move to either of his sides, but he was secure and alone... at least for now.

"Think there's an in-flight movie?" Justin muttered.

[Good luck with that,] Keontae said. [See that dot at the top of the screen? That's a camera. Means *you* are the in-flight movie.]

"Can you...? You know?"

[Of course. Load me up.]

Justin pressed his metal fingers against the screen, and he wondered if Keontae would be able to get through to the tech inside, given the extra Plastrex protection. But his fingers tingled as usual, and Keontae got in no problem. The light from the screen took on a green hue.

Rather than talking to Justin out loud, Keontae sent messages to him on the screen.

{: I'm in, but these shields are insane, man. Gonna take some time to work through. :}

Justin nodded. "How long?"

{: Not sure, :} came another message. {: This protection is serious, though. Top-of-the-line shit. Best plan to get comfortable. Could take me a day. Hopefully less. :}

"A *day?*" Justin hadn't accounted for that much time.

His plan all along was to get aboard the *Avarice* so Keontae could sabotage it from within, but would the others be able to last a full day aboard the *Nidus* with hundreds of ACM soldiers searching for them? And would Justin be able to last a full day in the brig with whoever else happened to be in here, too?

"It has to be faster than that."

{: I'll do my best, ofc. :}

"Thanks. You mind hitting the light so I can catch some sleep?"

The orange light bar flickered off, and the screen went dark as well.

"Thanks. Be safe."

The screen flared to life once more. {: You too. :}

JUSTIN AWOKE to the sound of groaning metal and scraping glass. He jerked upright, only to smack his head on the low ceiling above him, and he flopped onto his back again.

The groaning and scraping continued, and he realized it was coming from his feet. Someone was trying to break into his hexpod.

Shit.

He had nowhere to go. Once that glass door opened, he'd more or less be at the mercy of whoever was breaking inside.

He craned his neck for a look and saw several sets of hands reaching for him. They grabbed his ankles and the fabric of his pants and began to haul him out. He didn't bother to fight back... not yet.

God, I hate prison.

As he cleared the end of the hexpod, Justin cocked his metal arm, ready to throw the first punch.

Then he froze, confused, when the first face he saw belonged to Jonesy.

SIXTEEN

Justin had missed his chance to fight back. Two men grabbed his arms and locked them in place. One guy was the size of a small hovercar and perfectly round in his midsection. He held Justin's right arm, which made sense given Justin's augmented strength, although the fat guy couldn't have known about it in advance.

The fat guy wasn't all that unusual to look at, but the guy holding Justin's left arm freaked him out a little bit… mostly because he was missing the lower half of his face.

A black breathing apparatus had replaced his nose and mouth, now a slab of metal that formed a chin that was disproportionately small compared to the rest of his head. Chrome tubes ran from each side of the apparatus, along his jawline, and they sealed to two metal panels on his upper back, visible through two holes cut into his shirt.

He had albino-white hair, short and spiky, and he stared at Justin with jaundiced yellow eyes and manic golden irises. A low electronic voice issued from his face apparatus. "It's not polite to stare."

Justin blinked and looked back at Jonesy, who looked the same as he had the night before, still barefoot but far more relaxed. It probably helped that a dozen men and women now surrounded him, their arms folded as they scowled at Justin.

"Mornin', Jonesy."

"Good morning, Justin." Jonesy now wore a smirk instead of a nervous smile. "Warned you about the jiggers, didn't I?"

"Yep," Justin replied. "Not much I could've done about it anyway, though."

"You could've swung as soon as you came out."

"I think we both know how that would've ended. Twelve—no, thirteen against one makes for a tough fight," Justin said. "I mean, you'd need at least double that number for it to be fair."

Jonesy's smirk widened into a smile. "You've got a sense of humor. I like that about you."

"Enough to let me go?" Justin proposed.

Jonesy shook his head. "Sorry, but no."

"Worth a try."

"It was. You're either very brave or very foolish."

"Honestly?" Justin shrugged, and the two goons holding his arms immediately gripped him tighter. "I'm a good mix of both. It's how I've stayed alive this long."

Jonesy's pleasant timbre darkened, and his face went sullen. "Keep talking, and your run ends today."

"You got me all wrong. I'm here to listen," Justin said. "What's on your mind?"

"I've got some questions for you." Jonesy reached into his jumpsuit and produced a shiv. "And I'm going to get answers one way or another."

Justin glanced around the small common area, hoping the guards—or Keontae —would see what was happening and intervene. He doubted the guards cared, but if Keontae was seeing this...

"The guards aren't coming. They wouldn't get here in time anyway, so you might as well stay focused on me." Jonesy pointed the shiv at Justin's midsection and took an impossibly small step forward. He was about six feet away, but even with those microscopic advances, he'd make it to Justin soon enough.

"I'm gonna guess you're not actually a flight mechanic," Justin said.

Jonesy's smirk returned. "Matter of fact, I am. But that's hardly a way to earn a good living, even with all the years and seniority I got under my belt."

"So... drugs, then? Probably Tyval? That's what all the cool kids are huffing these days."

"I believe the term is 'criminal enterprise.'" Jonesy took another tiny step forward, still pointing the shiv at Justin. "Means it's a big operation. It's a big ship, after all. All sorts of wants and needs to be met. Drugs, sure. But also women, simulated and otherwise. Men, too. Even children, if the price is right and the client is discreet."

The mention of children being involved sickened Justin to his core. If he survived this encounter, he promised himself he'd kill Jonesy before he got out of this cell. He clenched his jaw tight and tried not to show his fury on his face.

"Then there's gambling, loans, contraband, weapons, blackmail, and good old-fashioned extortion. You could say I've got my fingers in a lot of dirty little pies."

Jonesy took another measly step. "Speaking of pies, I even control what food comes into the cafeteria and what goes out."

Justin cleared his throat. "Seems like they oughta hire you to do something more than just being a mechanic."

"I'm content with the current arrangement, all except for one little part of it." Jonesy took another step forward, this one as equally small as the others.

"Like I said, I'm here to listen." Justin stole another glance around the room and spotted a woman in one of the hexpods who didn't seem to be part of the group.

She was bald, with tan skin. Tattoos ran from her neck down as far as Justin could see, which wasn't much. She lay in the pod on her belly, watching the scene unfold while resting her chin on her hands. Probably would've been pretty cute if she had some hair.

"I'm stuck in here," Jonesy said. "I should be out there, overseeing my domain, but here I am, locked up."

"I can see how that would be frustrating," Justin said. "I mean, I'd rather be out of here as well, so I get it."

Jonesy's stalking ceased. He held up his shiv, looking it over. "This one is very special to me. You know where I got it?"

"I figure if you eat enough prison cereal, you can send the box tops away with your receipts, then you get one in the mail in a few weeks," Justin quipped.

"Close." Jonesy's smile returned. "That was a good one, by the way."

"I'm nothing if not entertaining when my life is being threatened."

"No, I took this from the man who tried to kill me with it." Jonesy patted his side, near the hole in his jumpsuit. "Happened right after I got here. He thought he had me. But he was an amateur. Held onto the shiv too long. So I bashed his nose with my forehead, yanked the shiv out of my own gut, and returned it to him via his left eye."

Justin nodded. "Solid choice."

"I left this place on a stretcher, but he left in a body bag." Jonesy smirked. "I'd make that trade any day."

"Again, solid choice."

Jonesy's advance began anew with yet another small step. "And now we come to you, my new friend, and what you can do for me."

"Let me have it." Justin grimaced. "Scratch that. Poor choice of words. I mean I'm listening."

"You can be my hostage and my leverage for getting out of here."

"What?" Justin blinked. That sounded like a terrible plan. "Hold up. How long have you been in here?"

"Close to three months. And it's killing my business." Another tiny step.

"And you're just now taking a hostage?"

"You're different than any of these baboons. You have value. They're nobodies, like me."

Justin chuckled. "I don't know where you're getting your information, but I'm not worth the processed air I'm breathing."

"Don't sell yourself short, Justin Barclay," Jonesy said. "Sole survivor of the accident at ACM-1134, but more importantly, the only living person with information about Carl Andridge's death."

Justin didn't say anything in return, but he should've kept up his comedy routine. Now that he'd stayed silent, he'd given himself away. Well, might as well lean into it now. "Not strictly the sole survivor. One other person survived, too."

"Ah, but they're not here. You are."

"Wherever you're getting your information, good for you," Justin said. "Probably wasn't easy, and it probably didn't come cheap. Either that, or ACM really is as incompetent as I thought."

The bald woman huffed from behind Jonesy, but no one turned to look.

"Since you have value to the company, they'll be willing to bargain for your life. I'll get out, and you'll be saved. It's a perfect plan." He stepped forward again. Now he stood about three feet from Justin's position, well within striking distance.

"And they're just gonna let you go back to everything you were doing before?" Justin scoffed. "Wouldn't be too sure about that."

"No, you're right. I'm done here. But they will give me a transport and let me take my accumulated wealth with me when I leave."

"Yeah... then they'll shoot you down the first chance they get."

"Wrong," Jonesy said. "Because I'll still have you with me."

"That long, huh?" Justin sighed. "Well, if we're in this for a long-term relationship, you'd better at least buy me a ring."

"The time for jokes is coming to an end, Justin. The time for blood is at hand."

Justin recoiled a bit, but the goons held him in place. "Uh... what?"

"I can't claim you're a hostage if you're in here doing fine. They won't care," Jonesy said. "But if you're bleeding from what could easily become a mortal wound if not treated, or perhaps the first of many wounds, then they're more likely to pay heed to my demands, and quickly."

A flicker of green light caught Justin's eye. Something on the ceiling. He glanced up and saw a few dozen nozzles lower from the ceiling at scattered yet even increments. Sprinklers? Fire suppression? Or... something else?

The bald woman had noticed the nozzles too, and she'd pulled back into her hexpod and shut the glass.

Justin had no way of knowing for sure, but her reaction, the green light, and the lowering nozzles were a good indication that Keontae was at work. Maybe Justin could find a way to survive this after all.

"This next part is the trickiest of the entire plan." Jonesy's shiv glinted under the prison lights. "But if you hold still, it'll be less likely that I'll hit something important."

Time was up. Justin yelled, "Now, Key!"

White gas hissed out of the nozzles and descended into common area, gradually filling it with clouds of the stuff.

Jonesy lunged forward, but Justin was ready. The two goons had tightened their grip on his arms, but they'd left his legs unchecked. Justin pulled both legs up, caught Jonesy in the chest with the soles of his boots, and pushed with all his strength.

Jonesy's small frame launched halfway across the common room and disappeared into the fog, and Justin felt the grip on his right arm go slack. The fat guy was wobbling, already affected by the gas.

Justin yanked his right arm free and promptly slammed it into the half-face of the guy holding his left arm.

Already, though, the gas was getting to Justin as well. It smelled sickeningly sweet with a bitter after-scent, like burning cotton candy. And it was making him feel woozy.

There was really only one place he could go—back to his hexpod.

But if he did that, then how could he ensure Jonesy wouldn't just come for him again later?

He couldn't. That meant he had to make a different choice, and fast.

He dropped low, covered his mouth and nose with his shirt, and took one last breath of mostly clean air. It still smelled weird, and his vision began to wobble and swirl, but he wasn't out yet.

Justin scrambled along the floor in the direction Jonesy had flown, still holding his breath. He climbed over unconscious bodies, searching each of them as he frantically tried to outlast the tainted air toxifying his lungs and the malaise settling into his head.

Finally, he found Jonesy, who stared up at him, still conscious but bewildered and confused.

With his last exhale, amid the clouds of smoke all around him, Justin said, "Kids for discreet clients, huh?"

Jonesy just blinked at him.

Then Justin pulled his metal fist back and drove it into Jonesy's sternum so hard that his whole chest caved in with an earsplitting *crack*.

Jonesy convulsed once, and then he went limp. His wide jumpsuit-blue eyes glazed over, and his blackened soul dissipated into the clouds of white gas.

Justin's lungs forced him to inhale, and he used the last of his cognition to stumble away from Jonesy. Better not to be found on top of his victim's body if he could help it. He landed atop two other prisoners, and then he fell asleep to the scent of burning cotton candy.

JUSTIN AWOKE to a female voice and a stinging sensation alternating on his right and left cheeks. Someone was smacking him, and not lightly, either. The last one hit him so hard that his teeth clicked together.

He moaned and swatted at his attacker's hands, but he hit nothing.

"Wake up," the female voice said.

Justin's eyes cracked open, and a feminine form overhead blocked out some of the harsh prison lights. He noticed a silhouette of a bald head next. It looked familiar, but he couldn't remember why.

He began to cough, and hard. Hacking coughs out, wheezing breaths in, repeat.

Justin turned on his side and gave into the fit until white-tinged mucus oozed out of his mouth and onto the floor. The familiar scent of burnt cotton candy now tinged the back of his throat and tongue.

He spat a few times, then he sat up and blinked until his vision cleared.

Aside from the bald woman with the tattoos and Justin, everyone else was still out cold. She looked at him with dark, mysterious eyes, and he tried to take in her awesome tattoos, but his mind still couldn't focus enough to identify most of them.

She wore a tight black tank top without a bra and black cargo pants. Rugged black boots covered her feet, and tattoos covered her neck, shoulders, and arms all the way down to her hands.

Now that he was closer to her, Justin noticed she had piercings in her face, too. She had one through her septum that ended in two red orbs, one in her lip, and another in her left eyebrow. Each of her ears had about a million piercings running up and down in a scattered rainbow of colors.

"Ouch," Justin said, still seated on the floor.

"You'll be fine," she said in a voice that was deeper than he'd expected.

"No. All your piercings," he said.

"You get used to it. Some of the tattoos hurt worse." She crouched beside him. "Whenever the tattoo is close to bone, that's what really stings."

"I bet."

"You did well back there."

"Well at what?"

"Dealing with Jonesy." She motioned toward his body with her bald head.

"Oh. Yeah." Justin glanced at Jonesy, who still lay there with his chest caved in. Then his eyes widened. "*Shit*. You saw that?"

"I saw how you kicked him away. Then the gas came down, and he disappeared in the fog. Now he's dead, with his chest caved it. Your kick couldn't have done that." She shrugged and eyed his prosthetic arm. "But hey, accidents happen. We're in a brig aboard a military ship. People die in here all the time."

An accident? Either she *had* seen Justin kill Jonesy and didn't seem to care, or she was being truthful and hadn't, and she still didn't care. Justin had to trust that the cameras hadn't seen anything thanks to Keontae, but the last thing he needed was Jonesy's goons coming after him if they figured out what happened. He looked at her expectantly.

"Your secret's safe with me," she assured him. "Would've done it myself, but I never got the kind of opening you did. He was an asshole."

"Selling kids as prostitutes? Yeah. 'Asshole' isn't a strong enough word."

"You think that's bad... you don't know how he got rid of those kids when they were done." She shook her head. "Know how an airlock works?"

Justin closed his eyes. "Fuck."

"Don't worry about it. You more than avenged them, and he'll never hurt anyone—children or otherwise—again." She extended her tattooed hand, and Justin caught sight of tattoos on her palm, too. "Name's Valkyrie Moon. Call me Val."

"Justin Barclay." Justin took her hand and started to shake it, but instead, she stood and hauled him up to his feet. It made his head swim. "Whoa."

"Man like you deserves to be standing upright on the battlefield. You were great." She eyed him. "Not sure how you managed to get the gas to turn on, but good for you. Good planning, and nearly perfect execution."

"Uh..." Should he keep the lie going? He couldn't exactly tell this person about Keontae, and taking credit was still pretty close to the truth, so he decided to roll with it. "Yeah. Thanks. I didn't know if it would work, but it did."

"Well worth the risk, in my opinion. And one less asshole in the galaxy. A major one, at that."

With both of them standing, Justin guessed she was right around five-foot-six. The boots might've given her a bit more height, though.

"Right."

"Interesting that you had it voice activated. I don't know that I would've gone that route."

"Only way I could time it right," Justin lied.

"What if they covered your mouth?" Val asked.

Justin blinked at her with his mouth open. He managed to say, "Like you said, worth the risk."

She nodded and then sauntered over to the nearest Plastrex bench. She stepped up onto it and sat on the edge of the table instead. "So what's your plan for when the rest of these cockmunchers wake up?"

Justin suppressed a grin. He already liked Val. She wasn't really his type as far as romantic potential went, but in another life, he could see them being friends. Hitting up bars, throwing back a few, maybe having each other's backs in fights in the parking lot. She seemed cool.

"I figure I'll stay quiet and let them slowly realize their leader is dead. Then I'll watch as one by one, they realize *how* he died. Then I'll deal with any pushback after that."

Val frowned. "Shit. You're not here to take over Jonesy's book, are you?"

"Huh?" Justin shook his head. "God, no. I'm just biding my time until I get out of here."

"What about that mine stuff? He said you were with Carl Andridge when he died or something?"

"Long story," Justin replied. He really didn't want to get into that now. Sure, Val seemed cool, but they *hadn't* actually been friends their whole lives, hadn't gone drinking together, and hadn't gotten in fights together, so he felt no obligation to tell her anything else. "I don't work for ACM anymore, though. I'm here for other reasons."

"Which are?" She leaned forward with her elbows on her knees and her chin in her hands.

"None of your business," Justin answered. "No offense, but I don't know you."

"It's the tattoos, isn't it?" she asked. "Or maybe the piercings."

"Hell no. Don't care about any of that. I think it suits you."

"You might not think so if you knew about *all* my piercings. Including the ones you can't see." She winked at him.

Justin resisted his urge to flinch at imagining the pain of what she was insinuating. He probably wouldn't have had a problem with how it looked.

"Hmm. Not even a blink. Usually I can get most guys with that one."

Justin inhaled a long, calming breath. "You were close. I'll say that. But my cold heart is basically a frozen rock at this point. Takes a lot to unnerve me."

Keontae would've taunted him for that one. Good thing he was somewhere in the ship instead of in Justin's arm.

"Looks like they're starting to stir." She nodded toward some of the other prisoners behind Justin. He looked, and they were indeed waking up.

Great. Now what? His big talk about sitting back and letting them realize he'd killed Jonesy was all well and good, but if they rushed him, he couldn't take them all at once—not a chance.

Several of them began coughing and hacking just as Justin had. The cacophony of retching sounds made Justin want to throw up. So much for nothing fazing him anymore.

"Sit over here, with me." Val patted the Plastrex table next to her. "They'll think twice about causing trouble if the two of us are both sitting here, looking fine and healthy when they wake up. It's psychology."

Justin saw no reason not to. If she'd wanted to do him harm, she could've done it while he was out from the gas. Instead, she'd helped wake him up first so he'd be prepared when the others woke up. So he went over and sat down next to her.

"Here." She smacked something hard and metal against the table between them. It was Jonesy's shiv. "Show this off, and they'll fear you. Aside from your arm, it's the only weapon in here… least as far as I know, and I've been watching for a long time."

Justin picked it up. Another sign of friendship, of cooperation, sure, but he was mostly glad he didn't have to worry about someone jabbing at him with it. "How long have you been in here?"

"Hmm. Hard to keep track, but maybe five or six months? All the days run together."

"What for?"

She blinked at him with those dark eyes. Really beautiful dark eyes. "You mean my crime?"

"Yeah. You innocent, like everyone else in jail?"

"No." She gave a small laugh. "No, I'm guilty."

"Of what?" Justin asked.

"Assassinating someone important."

Justin's eyes almost bugged out of his head. Who was this person?

"Got you that time," Val teased. "If the 'pierced lady bits' joke doesn't get 'em, the 'lady assassin' part usually gets the job done."

"Guess I'm not the coldhearted bastard I said I was." He rubbed the back of his neck with his human hand.

"You're still alive in here after the ship's most dangerous criminal came for you. I'd say you're a straight-up badass." She gave him another wink.

He wanted to ask her more about the assassination, but the other prisoners were beginning to rise like the undead from their graves.

By then, the prisoners' coughing had devolved to a lot of spitting and even more cursing.

"What the hell was that?" the fat guy asked as he sat up.

"Thought it was a nitrogen leak at first," another guy said.

Instead of human eyes, two orange orbs protruded from a pair of black goggles clamped over the top of the guy's head. The orbs danced on articulated metal tubes, extending and contracting and moving freely and independently of each other—which normal eyes weren't supposed to do. He looked like a giant insect.

Several others woke up shortly after, but the guy with the lower half of his face missing stayed down. Had Justin's punch killed him, too?

The fat guy waddled over to him and shook him a few times, then he jerked upright and shook his head like a dog covered in water. In his electronic voice, he asked, "What happened?"

"We got gassed," the fat guy replied. "Some sorta prisoner-suppression stuff."

"Unlikely in my case. My prosthesis is optimized to filter out all contaminants. My lungs can't handle anything but perfectly mixed air." His golden, jaundiced eyes fixed on Justin, and he pointed a pale finger at him. "He punched me."

"You deserved it," Justin countered.

"Wait a sec..." the fat guy said. "Where's Jonesy?"

The first guy froze in place, but his robotic bug eyes kept moving. They zeroed in on one specific spot—where Jonesy lay, dead from Justin's fist crashing through his chest—and his mouth dropped open.

"Here," he said.

"Oh, dang," the fat guy said as he approached. His pudgy face contorted with concern. With great difficulty due to his size, he crouched down next to Jonesy and looked him over.

Justin hadn't noticed before, but the fat guy's hair had a purple tinge to it. Justin had just thought it was black and that the light was hitting it weirdly, but he'd been wrong.

"Oh, daaaaang," the fat guy repeated. With even more difficulty than crouching down, he managed to stand back up. "Y'all know what this means?"

No one responded.

The fat guy's anguished face morphed into a joyful expression, and he raised both of his thick arms into the air. "We're free of that bastard once and for all!"

He let out a whoop, and most of the others followed suit. The guy with the breathing mask raised his hands halfway, still with a crazed look in his eyes, and said in monotone, "Yaaaay."

The guy with the bug eyes danced a little jig and bounded around the small room, offering high fives to anyone and everyone who would humor him. He even got one from Justin, because why not?

But despite the bug-eyed guy's revelry, Justin still didn't know what was going on. These guys had all been working for Jonesy, yet now that he was dead, they were celebrating?

When he looked over to Val for answers, she just shrugged. "No one wants to have a master. You serve one if you have to, and if you don't, then you don't."

Slowly, they all turned toward Justin, recognizing him. The majority of the other prisoners gave him a wide berth, but the bug-eyed guy, the half-face guy, and the fat guy all tentatively approached him.

"Hey, uh..." The fat guy glanced between Justin and Val—more so at Val, though. "Look, I hope you don't hold it against me that I was holdin' your friend in place for Jonesy. You know how it goes. Didn't really have no choice. It was either cooperate or see my guts spillin' onto the floor, y'know? Without my mech suit, I ain't good for much of anythin'."

Justin tilted his head. The fat guy was talking to Val, not to him. Did he think Val had killed Jonesy?

"Same here," the guy with half of his face said. His crazed golden eyes focused on Val most of the time as well. "I mean about restraining him. Not about being useless. 'Cause I'm pretty skilled in a lot of different areas."

"Wait..." Justin interjected. "You all think *she* killed Jonesy?"

All three of them nodded, including the bug-eyed guy.

Justin looked at Val, and she shrugged again.

"What can I say? I told you I was an assassin."

Justin gave a small nod. Probably best to let her have the credit on this one. The less attention he drew to himself, the better—and he'd already drawn more than enough. Better to slip back into obscurity until Keontae finished everything on his end.

"This is Justin." Val motioned toward him. "But you already know that. Introduce yourselves, boys."

"Name's Arthur Henry." The fat guy extended his equally meaty hand. "But everyone calls me Bear on account of my size."

"Justin Barclay." Justin shook his hand, but it felt like shaking a cold, clammy dead fish. "Nice to meet you."

"Again, I'm real sorry 'bout all that before," Bear said. "Didn't have no choice. Bein' locked in here is... hard."

"Apology accepted," Justin said. "No harm done."

"Thanks, Justin. Really 'preciate it." Bear moved aside, and the guy with half a face stepped forward.

"Zed Cavale," he said in his electronic voice. He motioned to his artificial chin. "And since I know you're gonna ask—everyone does—I'll tell you how this happened. When not incarcerated like a street dog, I like to play with chemicals. Sometimes they go boom, and one time they went boom when they weren't supposed to.

"Probably shoulda killed me, but it didn't." His golden eyes widened slightly.

"Tore off the bottom half of my face, ruined my mouth and nose, and the fumes trashed my lungs. So now I breathe and eat—liquids only—through this thing." He tapped his chin again. "Anyway, I've said what I had to say, so don't talk to me about this again. Ever."

With that, he turned and retreated toward Bear, who frowned at him.

"You didn't apologize," Bear said.

"Yes, I did," Zed insisted. "I said, 'Same here.'"

"That ain't no apology." Bear's tone was corrective, but it reminded Justin of a kindhearted grandfather's correction. "I think you should try again."

A low groan issued from Zed's breathing apparatus, and he rolled his golden eyes. Without looking at Justin, he said, "Sorry."

Justin figured that was as close as he was going to get, so he didn't push it any further. "I forgive you. We're good."

When Justin looked to the bug-eyed guy, both of his eyes were extended and pointed in two different directions. How that wasn't scrambling his brain, Justin had no idea.

Val cleared her throat, and the bug-eyed guy's eyes snapped back forward and receded into his skull.

"Sorry. Wasn't trying to get you killed, but I'm still sorry. Would much rather be friends than enemies." His words came out quickly, almost frantically so. "Name's Ritzveld Townsend. Ritz's fine. I don't suppose I can call you 'Justy,' though? If I could, that'd be swell."

"Uh... no. Justin is good, though."

"Alright. Alright, I see." He snickered. "I mean, literally, I see. That's my thing."

"Let me guess," Justin said. "An accident as well?"

"Nope. Elective surgery. Thought it'd make me more valuable to the military. Turns out, I was right... mostly. But one wrong move, and I got myself thrown in here."

"What did you do?" Justin asked.

"It's... embarrassing."

Justin shrugged. "Well, I guess you don't have to—"

"Tell him," Zed said, "or I will."

"Don't you *dare*, metal-mouth." Ritz jabbed a finger at Zed. "You know I can kick your ass from downtown to Chinatown and all around the merry-go-round... so don't *fuck* with me."

"He pissed in his commanding officer's soup," Zed said.

"You bastard!" Ritz raised his hands and balled them into fists. He made small circles with them, and his left bug eye also started circling while his right eye remained fixed in place. "Put 'em up. I'm gonna knock the rest of your ugly face off."

Justin covered his mouth to keep from laughing, but that proved impossible.

As Zed lifted his hands and squared off with Ritz, Val clapped her hands once, and they both turned to look at her. "Enough."

At that, they both lowered their hands and pulled away.

Once he managed to stop chuckling, Justin addressed Ritz again. "So you were working for ACM?"

"Yeah. And my CO was a major cockatrice, if you know what I mean," Ritz replied. "And I mean he was a dick of legendary proportion. A real man-banana."

Justin thought back to Oafy and Gerhardt from ACM-1134, and to Carl Andridge himself. "Must be a theme with ACM."

"I've never worked for ACM a day in my life." Zed folded his arms and raised his chin. "Hate 'em. Always have."

"Then what got you thrown in here?" Justin asked.

"Tried to blow this ship up."

Justin's eyebrows rose. "Is... that possible?"

"Cram enough explosives into a sealed metal tube in the vacuum of space and light a fuse... oh, she'll blow alright. Like a trombonist in the background of an amateur adult movie."

Justin cocked his head at the analogy, but he got the idea.

"But they caught me, took away my gear, and threw me in this dump."

"I was with Farcoast," Bear said. "I was runnin' one of the mechs in that battle the other day, but they blew out my mech's knee joint, and I went down. Was doin' fine 'til that happened, but then I couldn't move." Frowning, he quietly added, "Too much weight."

"You were aboard the *Nidus*?" Justin asked.

"Yeah. They captured me and brought me here. Not much I could do 'bout it, but at least I ain't dead."

At this point, that might as well be the mantra for Justin's life—*at least I'm not dead.*

Around that time, the guards noticed Jonesy was still lying there and had been for awhile, so they ordered everyone back to their hexpods over the comms, locked them inside remotely, and came in to collect him.

Justin marveled at the sight of Bear squelching into his pod. He fit, but only just barely.

All told, the guards didn't seem to care that Jonesy had been killed. They removed his body and returned with meager lunch portions for everyone, which they left out on the Plastrex tables in stacks of trays.

While he was in his hexpod, Justin checked his screen for updates from Keontae.

{: You okay? :} was Keontae's first question.

"Yeah, I'm good," Justin said. "Your timing was perfect."

{: Yours more than mine. Saw that kick, bro. Fire. :}

"Thanks. Where are we at?"

{: Still need some time. I'm outta the brig, and I'm between the ship's subnetworks tryin' to squeeze through the cracks into the main network. Once I do that, we're golden like grahams. :}

"Good. I think I'm safe for now, but the sooner we can get out, the better. I can't imagine what Captain Marlowe, Arlie, Hallie, and the others are doing right now to survive."

{: They'll be alright. Captain Marlowe's a beast, that Bryant guy seems good, and Arlie's more dangerous than the two of 'em put together. :}

"Still…"

{: I know, I know. You're worried 'bout your girl. Don't blame you. She don't have enough booty for me, but I get your attraction to 'er all the same. We'll get you back there soon enough. :}

"Thanks, Key."

When the guards finally left and the hexpods reopened, Justin slipped out. But rather than heading toward the stacks of trays of food on the tables, he found Val instead. He motioned her off to the side, and she met him away from the others, who were tearing into the food trays like wild animals—especially Bear.

"What's up?" she asked.

"I've got a plan to get outta here," he said. "But I could use some help. Someone to watch my back."

She shook her head and scoffed. "You're not getting out of here."

"Yes, I am."

Her head continued shaking. "No. No chance. This place is locked down."

Justin didn't want to argue with her. "Okay. Suppose I do get out. If I manage it, do you wanna come with?"

"You won't."

"But *hypothetically*, if I did, purely in your *imagination*, would you come?" Justin asked. "The fantasy version of me could use your help."

Val stared at him with narrowed eyes. "If you were to get out, and I could get out, too, then yeah, I'd back you up."

"Great. That's what I needed to know."

"But you won't get out."

"Yes, you've made that very clear." Her certainty was getting on his nerves, but he couldn't exactly explain Keontae to her.

"What makes you think you can get out?" she asked.

"Nothing."

"You wouldn't be asking these silly questions if it was nothing."

Justin lowered his voice even further. "I have a friend on the inside. That's all I can say."

"Well, unless he outranks the admiral, we're not going anywhere."

"In that case, you've got plenty of time to tell me about who you assassinated."

She scoffed. "Which one?"

Justin couldn't tell if it was bluster or if she was serious. "The one that landed you in here."

Val frowned. "The one that landed me in here was a failed attempt. Got caught before I could even pull the trigger."

"Who was the target?"

"Admiral Sever."

Justin blinked at her. "Really?"

"Really."

"Why him?"

"It's a job." Something about the way she said it wasn't wholly convincing.

"No. It's more than that. I can tell."

She stopped making eye contact with him. "Fine. It's... personal."

Should he pry more? Or should he leave it at that? Justin opted to leave it alone for the time being.

"Oh. Sorry. I don't need to know anything else abo—"

"He had my parents executed," Val interrupted.

SEVENTEEN

"Long time ago. Ten, fifteen years, maybe. I lost count," Val continued. "Been a rough life since then. Orphanages, mostly, 'til I was sixteen. Lit out and never looked back. Found some ex-military guys willing to train me in exchange for... you know. And cleaning. I had to clean up after them, too.

"But in the end, it was worth it. I made a career out of what I learned. Set off on my own, did a few simple hits, made some credits. Paid for more advanced training. Got that. Did a few more jobs. Got some ink. Got some piercings. Got more ink and more piercings. You know, the cycle continues.

"All the while, I'm looking for the guy who did it. The guy who ordered my parents killed. I knew his face, knew he was with ACM. Finally found him and started making plans. Then, when I had my best chance, I blew it," she finished. "Now I'm in here."

Justin stared at her. His childhood had sucked, but hers sounded worse. Then again, if someone had executed his parents, he might've been better off in the long run.

Still, he could empathize with her to a certain point. She'd gone through some shit, just like he had, and she'd come out the other side stronger and better.

"Sorry," she said. "I know it's a downer of a story."

"No, no. It's fine. I get it," Justin said. "Sorry you didn't get him."

"Yeah. Maybe someday." She quipped, "Like when you break us out of here."

"Make fun of me all you want, but it's gonna happen. Mark my words."

"'Mark my words?' What are you, a medieval baron? No one says that anymore."

"Well, I just did." Justin smirked. "So mark 'em, and mark 'em well."

"C'mon." She motioned with her head. "We'd better get some grub before Bear thinks he's entitled to our breakfast."

EVER SINCE THEY'D left Justin behind, Hallie wondered if his plan was going to work. It was, on the surface, the dumbest possible idea she could've imagined. For him to willingly get caught with the hope of somehow accessing the *Avarice's* network and hacking into it...

Suffice it to say, it was farfetched, but he'd been *so* certain he could pull it off when he pitched the idea. Had Captain Marlowe and Arlie and their surviving crew members not backed him up, she probably wouldn't have agreed to it.

Then again, his assessment of the situation was still correct. Eventually, ACM would've breached the house's defenses, and then they'd have no means of escape. Leaving and staying mobile would at least buy them more time.

Most importantly, their only way out of this was to either get past ACM or to take them down. They couldn't escape if ACM had any significant presence on the *Nidus* or was waiting for them once they left.

She tugged her satchel higher on her shoulder. The asset was heavy, but she would bear it forever if she had to, especially if it meant keeping it out of ACM's hands.

The idea that she might use it against them had crossed her mind as well, but...

No. That was a bad idea. She wouldn't do that unless she had no other choice. And even then, once she opened that cage, she could never put the canary back inside.

By now, almost a full day had passed. Thus far, they hadn't noticed any change in ACM's collective behavior. The soldiers' search continued full force, and Hallie's group hadn't heard anything from Justin, either.

So was he dead? Captured and locked up? Helpless to do anything?

Or was he still working on it, making progress, and about to turn everything in their favor?

Hallie and the others had no way of knowing. All they could do now was stay on the run and try to buy time, so that's what they were doing.

Her satchel weighed on her shoulder more with each passing step. Bryant, Luke, and Captain Marlowe had all offered to carry it for her, but she'd declined. She refused to entrust its contents to anyone else. She preferred to be the one in control of what happened to it.

Plus, even though Luke, her fellow scientist, knew what the satchel contained, the other two didn't, and she wanted to keep it that way. If it was with her, she controlled who knew what it was.

As they hunkered down in an alley, Luke pointed at the dome over the city. "Look at that."

From Hallie's vantage point, several tall buildings blocked her view of whatever he was pointing at. She leaned forward and tried to line up her view with his.

"There, between the two tallest skyscrapers," he clarified.

By now, she wasn't the only one trying to get a look. The rest of her fellow scientists and the *Viridian's* crew strained to see as well. Only Bryant remained behind, watching the entrance to the alley with his rifle held at the ready.

At first, she didn't see anything. Then a small glowing orb shot upward, sort of on a curling trajectory. It looked like it might've been a signal flare, but then a beam of harsh red light dashed through the sky and hit the orb. It flashed bright orange, and then it was gone.

A second later, another orb launched into the night sky. It, too, was hit by a red laser, and it exploded. That's when Hallie realized what she was seeing.

"Escape pods." Her gut twisted at the thought of all those people dying because of ACM's invasion. "Launching from an auxiliary docking bay, maybe."

Luke nodded. "ACM is shooting them out of the sky."

The fact that she'd lured ACM here, albeit inadvertently, gnawed at her insides. So many people had perished because of her decision to sign on to this project in the first place. How many more would die before the end?

No. You can't think like that, she chastised herself. *What you're doing will end the fighting and put the control back in the Coalition's hands once and for all. No matter how many die here, you're saving millions of lives across the galaxy. Maybe even billions.*

"We should keep moving," Bryant said from his position at the end of the alley.

"We should get underground," Captain Marlowe said.

"We're on a spaceship," Cecilia said. "Is there such a thing here?"

"Sewers," Arlie said. "Maintenance tunnels, maybe."

The idea of traipsing around this city's sewers wrinkled Hallie's nose, but getting caught wasn't an option. "If that's what we have to do, let's go."

"There's a grate here, but it's locked." Captain Marlowe crouched down in the alley and nodded toward a grate at his feet. He pulled a silvery tin out of his inner coat pocket and popped it open. "Looks like pretty standard steel and not some fancy alloy. We *could* shear through it, but it might be noisy."

"We either find another way in, or we risk cutting through it here." Captain Marlowe pulled a narrow metal stick out of the case, put it in his mouth, and bit down hard. Then he shut the case and tucked it back into his coat pocket.

"Would any of these buildings have access to the maintenance tunnels?" Luke asked.

"Maybe," Arlie said. "No way to know for sure without checking."

"And that'll take time," Captain Marlowe said. "And we might get cornered or trapped inside one of them in the process."

"Wait. I have an idea," Luke said. "Bryant, let me have your plasma repeater for a sec."

Bryant didn't move. "Why?"

"Just trust me. I know what I'm doing."

Bryant's stillness continued for another few seconds, then he relented and held it out. "You shoot yourself with this, I'm not responsible."

"Please. I served in the military, too." Luke took it from Bryant, hooked his index finger in the trigger guard, and spun it around in a series of fancy moves. "Spent a lot of time playing with these things and picking them apart."

Luke had a PhD in weapons engineering, and he'd proven to be one of the finest weapon designers Hallie had ever worked with, despite his youth. Aside from his intelligence and capability, his attention to even the smallest details had impressed her the most.

He stopped spinning the repeater and deftly deconstructed it with his bare hands, revealing its insides. Hallie hadn't even known that was possible, but he'd just done it right in front of her as easily as shucking an ear of corn.

"These repeaters have limiters designed to inhibit the amount of energy they project," Luke explained as he worked the repeater's insides with his fingers. "Modify the limiter, and they project more or less. The problem is, they're delicate mechanisms and hard to manipulate."

Hallie marveled at his lightning-quick movements.

Luke snapped the repeater's outer shell back in place. "Do it wrong, and the whole thing might blow."

"Blow?" Captain Marlowe eyed him.

"Blow," Luke repeated, again spinning the repeater on his finger. "As in, it could explode in your hand like a grenade when you pull the trigger, and with just as much kinetic energy."

Everyone recoiled, and several of them gasped.

Luke just laughed. "Fortunately, I'm a genius with this stuff. Literally."

He crouched down, took aim at the locking mechanism on the sewer grate, and fired.

An orange light burned in the alley like a star going full supernova, and a brief but deafening hiss sizzled in the air.

Most of the group yelped and gasped, but as the light faded to nothing and Hallie's vision returned, she saw the aftermath of Luke's blast: not only had the repeater's blast shorn through the lock in the grate, but it had also seared half of the grate itself and some of the concrete around it into oblivion.

Hallie checked her satchel, mostly to make sure it hadn't somehow gotten damaged. The last thing she needed was its invaluable contents slipping out onto the street or into the sewers while they were on the move.

Luke himself was fine. He stood there, gawking at the results of his handiwork. He turned and chuckled to the rest of the group, most of whom were still blinking away the negative image of the light flare or rubbing their eyes.

"Well..." he said, "I may have loosened her up a tad bit too much, but we should have no trouble getting into the sewers, at least."

"We'll be lucky if the whole ACM army isn't heading our way after that blast." Bryant snatched the repeater from Luke and tucked it into his holster.

"Um... you'll want to be careful with that," Luke said. "The limiter's still set to that crazy-high setting, and after that blast, it dropped to about 50% charge, so if you try to use it, it'll shoot another blast like the one I just did."

Bryant glared at him. "Is it gonna blow up in my hand?"

"It shouldn't." Luke shook his head. "I mean... I don't think it will. If it didn't the first time, there's no reason to think it would the second time."

"How about the fact that it didn't do what you expected the first time?" Bryant suggested.

Luke gave a nervous smile and nodded. "The limiter is fixed—as in, it won't move unless I adjust it again, so you should be okay. Probably."

"Uh-huh." Bryant motioned toward the small crater around the sewer grate. "You go first. Help people get to the bottom."

"Sure... No problem." Luke climbed into the opening and descended the ladder.

Bryant gave Hallie an eye roll, and she grinned. "You scientists. You're gonna be the death of me."

"Uh... can someone lower a flashlight?" Luke called from within the sewers.

———

THE BRILLIANT FLASH of orange light from the northwestern quadrant of the city caught Vesh's attention. It also reignited the burning behind his eyes.

He gritted his teeth and blinked it away, as usual. Thus far, the sensation hadn't affected his mission, but if it persisted, it might. At best it was a harmless distraction. But if it grew any worse...

Vesh had to complete this mission and get checked out sooner rather than later. That was that.

Whether or not any of ACM's other soldiers had seen the orange light, he didn't know, but that was of little concern. It was an anomaly, and with precious few leads to pursue, it had shined like a beacon in the night, calling him to it.

Before he could move, Vesh's comms beeped in the uplink in his head, and a generic woman's voice spoke.

"Code Ebony. By order of Admiral Sever, all soldiers must head to the docking bay for immediate return to the Avarice. *Repeat: Code Ebony."*

The comms beeped again, and his uplink disengaged.

A Code Ebony meant that no fewer than two enemy warships were en route, and as such, the *Avarice* was to regroup with the nearest ACM fleet so as to avoid a potentially unwinnable confrontation. It represented a fundamental contradiction of Admiral Sever's mandate to Vesh.

But given Vesh's unique status, he could choose to remain deployed on his current mission rather than return to the *Avarice*. Doing so might invoke Admiral Sever's ire, but if he succeeded in spite of the change in orders, it wouldn't matter. Based on what Admiral Sever had told him, the mission's importance to ACM trumped everything else.

Even if he got stranded aboard this colonist ship, he'd find a way to survive until he could send a secure transmission requesting extraction, or he could steal a transport ship and escape, or he could pursue any number of other potential paths back to ACM's headquarters in the core planets.

The decision was his. Either way, time was short.

Vesh changed his course and headed toward the source of the light.

{: We're all set. :} Keontae's words scrawled across the screen in Justin's hexpod. {: Retreat orders are issued. I handled everything so it looks like this ship's about to be in some major shit. :}

"I can't believe you're pulling it off."

{: Wasn't easy. You'd better believe that. But yeah, it's done. :}

"You wanna jump back in my arm?"

{: Not yet. Lots of movin' pieces here. Gotta keep some of their communications jammed so the captain and the admiral can't talk to each other, can't figure out why their wires are crossed. Just grab me on your way out. There's a surprise for you in the docking bay. I'll handle the rest. :}

"Okay. Thanks."

{: No reason to wait around. Doors will open for you whenever you're ready to move, and only doors I want you goin' through. That way you won't get any nasty surprises as you move. You just gotta get past the brig guards, and you're set. :}

Justin glanced past his feet at the group of prisoners clustered in the common area. "No problem there."

{: Anyone you wanna take with you, now's the time. Anyone left behind ain't gonna make it. :}

"Got it."

{: Then get your ass movin'. Gotta get you back to your girlfriend. :}

"Damn right." Justin grinned and slid out of his hexpod.

When his boots hit the floor, he headed for Val's pod straightaway. She watched him the whole way over.

He leaned close to her and asked in a quiet voice, "You ready to get outta here?"

She eyed him. "This again?"

"Not a joke. Not a ploy. We're ready."

She squinted at him, as if judging his sincerity. "You're serious."

"Have been this whole time."

"Plan?"

"There's a song… hundreds of years old," Justin said. "Perfect for this situation."

Val just looked at him, waiting.

"'Send in the Clowns.'" Justin nodded toward the rest of the prisoners. "Door's open. Someone just needs to walk through."

Slowly, a smirk curled the right side of Val's mouth.

"YOU'RE certain our information is correct?" Captain Jacob Gable asked his first officer.

"Aye, sir," First Officer Reyes replied. "Long-range scans show a fleet of Coalition warships warping toward us. The *Nidus* must've given off some sort of distress signal. The *Avarice* automatically issued a recall to our forces aboard the *Nidus*."

"I thought that had to be done manually."

"There must've been a software update from corporate. It didn't give us an option—just jumped right to it, sir," Reyes replied.

"Yet you are unable to hail Admiral Sever?"

"Correct, sir. His transport is unresponsive."

"He'll figure it out soon enough when our men start leaving him behind." Gable rubbed his chin. Something about this felt off, but he couldn't say what. "Report any other anomalies you notice, no matter how small."

"Aye, sir."

THE FIRST GROUP of prisoners bolted through the now-unshielded doors and overwhelmed the brig guards with their fists in a matter of seconds.

They stomped them into submission, snapping bones and splattering blood across the lobby floor. Then they stripped the downed guards of their weapons and charged into the rest of the ship like a pack of monkeys escaping the zoo.

Justin and Val followed behind at a cautious distance, heading through corridors behind them until a door closed behind the prisoners, separating Justin and Val from them. They skidded to a halt and looked around for alternate paths. A green light flickered down a corridor to their left, so Justin grabbed Val by her wrist and tugged her toward it.

She yanked away sharply. "How do you know we need to go that way?"

"My friend's guiding us. Follow the green light, and the doors we're supposed to go through will open on their own." Justin tried to grab her wrist again, but she smacked his hand away.

"I didn't give you permission to touch me," she said. "So don't."

"Fair enough." He motioned with his head. "This way."

Keontae's green light led them through a maze of corridors within the *Avarice*. As promised, doors that were supposed to open did so, and other doors remained shut or closed as they approached. Without Keontae's direction, Justin would've been lost after the first turn, and thus far, they hadn't encountered even a single ACM soldier.

That changed when the next door opened, this time not to another corridor but to a room. Inside stood racks and racks of rifles, repeaters, grenades, armor, and other weapons and equipment.

An armory. Apparently Keontae thought they'd need weapons on their way out.

But there before them, about to walk out as they were heading in, stood an ACM soldier with a confused look on his face and a handscreen in his hands.

EIGHTEEN

Before Justin could react, Val was already in motion. She lurched forward, wrapped her hands around the back of the soldier's neck, and drove her knee straight into his groin.

He dropped the handscreen and crumpled to the floor, and Val drew the soldier's sidearm from its holster as he fell. One quick blast from his repeater finished him off, and her head immediately swiveled, scanning the room for additional threats.

Justin couldn't believe how quickly she'd dispatched the guy. He gawked at her. "What the hell?"

"I told you," she said, lowering the repeater, "it cost me a lot to learn what I know, and I'm good at what I do."

"Apparently," Justin said.

"Come on." She motioned him inside. "Let's get what we need and get out of here."

WHEN THE FIRST transport fired up and cruised out of the docking bay, Admiral Sever thought nothing of it. Transports between the *Nidus* and the *Avarice* came and went every so often, replenishing supplies and weapons, bringing over fresh soldiers to replace the wounded ones, and so on.

But when the engines of a half dozen more transports hummed to life, Sever grew curious enough to leave the comfort of his personal transport and investigate. As he stepped out of his transport and into the docking bay, a wave of confusion swept over him.

Hundreds of his soldiers were boarding the dozens of transports in the *Nidus's* docking bay, and several of them had already taken off and were already flying back to the *Avarice*.

What the hell?

He stormed over to the nearest transport and shouted, "Someone had better give me a damned good explanation for what's going on here, or I'll have the *Avarice* shoot your transport down the instant it leaves the confines of this ship!"

The soldiers waiting to board the transport froze for a second and then scrambled to drop their gear and salute Sever.

"Forget that bullshit," he snapped. "Answer my question *now*."

They glanced at each other as if dumbstruck.

Sever stomped his foot, and his boot clapped against the docking bay floor.

"Admiral, sir," one of the soldiers finally spoke up. "We received an automated message over our comms ordering us to return to the *Avarice* under a Code Ebony."

Code Ebony? Rival ships were coming for the Avarice? "On whose authority?"

The soldier gulped and looked at his comrades.

"*Answer me*, soldier."

"Y-yours, sir," the soldier replied.

Sever's eyes widened. What the hell was going on? He'd given no such order. Even with a Code Ebony, he would've kept his forces aboard the *Nidus*. Finding that which ACM sought was more important than the entirety of the *Avarice* and its crew.

Whatever was going on, it had been effective enough to draw every single soldier of his forces away from Nidus City and send them back to the *Avarice*. That had to stop right now.

"Belay that order," he barked. "Get everyone off this transport immediately, and stop as many other soldiers and transports as you can from leaving."

This time, the soldiers didn't second-guess him. They sprang into action, abandoning most of their gear behind as they spread along the docking bay.

Sever retreated to his personal transport and tried to hail the *Avarice* onscreen, but for whatever reason, his transmission refused to go through. He waited twice as long as it would normally take to connect, then three times, four times, and five times as long, but the connection wheel on the screen just continued to spin.

He cursed and hurried back out of his transport.

To Sever's dismay, the vast majority of the remaining transports abandoned the docking bay to return to the *Avarice*. The soldiers he'd managed to stop numbered about a hundred, and they'd successfully convinced another transport to stay put, but the rest had all gone.

He noticed Commander Falstaff jogging toward him, and he didn't try to conceal his ire.

"Admiral," Falstaff said with an abrupt salute, "perhaps you can shed some light on—"

"I didn't give orders to fall back or return to the *Avarice*. I didn't give *any* orders at all," Sever snapped. "Something went fritzwire over on the *Avarice*, and an automated order in response to a Code Ebony recalled everyone."

"So we are to stay here?"

"Yes, and I'm sending you back to the *Avarice* with orders for Captain Gable to return all of my soldiers immediately."

Falstaff eyed him. "Why wouldn't you just—"

"The comms on my ship aren't working. I can't get through."

"Admiral, I'd be happy to take a look if—"

"Sending you across the void is a faster, more surefire way of executing my will. I don't need tech support; I need *soldiers*."

Falstaff nodded and saluted. "Aye, sir. I'll leave right away."

"Order the remaining soldiers to rally to me," Sever said. "I'll lead them back into the city myself."

Falstaff's eyes widened, and his saluting hand sank back to his side. "Admiral, are you sure that's wise? For a man of your rank to—"

"Did you lose your *balls* down in that city, Commander? You rarely question anything I command, yet you've protested my orders three times in the last thirty seconds."

"I'm sorry, Admiral." Falstaff's jaw tightened and his posture went rigid. "I only meant to look out for your best interests."

"What's in my best interests," Sever countered, "is to find our quarry, capture it, and bring it to Andridge. If it is what we believe it is, then we cannot delay, and we cannot let it slip between our fingers."

"Understood, sir. I'll relay the orders."

As Falstaff turned and headed for the nearest group of soldiers, Sever returned to his personal transport and entered his private armory. There, he changed out of his dress uniform and into armor like the rest of the soldiers wore.

Unlike the others, however, he donned a special underlayer of body armor on his torso. ACM's outer armor was excellent, but another precaution wouldn't hurt.

Then he strapped a top-of-the-line plasma repeater and its holster to his right leg, clipped a bandolier with some grenades across his chest, and selected his favorite pulse rifle from the collection. Neither the plasma repeater nor the pulse rifle were standard-issue weapons, but as the admiral, he could carry whatever the hell he wanted.

He also pulled the black failsafe orb—the Pilkington—out of his trousers pocket and stuffed it into a magnetized pouch on his tactical belt. He couldn't risk leaving it behind, not with so much uncertainty. Sever patted his pouch to ensure the flap had closed, and he hefted his pulse rifle into his hands once again.

Now armed to the teeth, he ventured out of the transport and approached the remaining soldiers awaiting him. When he came into view, several of the soldiers pointed at him, and the rest quickly turned to face him.

Then, as one, they began to hoot and applaud.

Normally Sever would've disdained such a response, but given the previous confusion, he decided he didn't mind. Even so, he held up his free hand to calm them.

"You men and women are the last remnant of loyal ACM soldiers who rightfully disregarded the false order given over the comms. Reinforcements will soon join us, but let us show them that we don't need their help anyway. Together, we will venture into Nidus City and seek out our targets: a group of scientists hiding somewhere within this ship.

"Our mission is of the utmost importance to Andridge's corporate headquarters. We cannot fail, and so we will succeed. Join me in the glory that comes with securing our company's place in this galaxy forever."

All 200 or so of the ACM soldiers bellowed, "Aye, sir!"

"Follow me." Sever led them past the second-to-last transport, which took off and headed for the *Avarice* with Commander Falstaff on board, and toward the docking bay doors.

As he progressed, he checked an indicator on his wrist. It showed Vesh's location within the city. He would be their starting point, and he looked to be coming toward them, albeit from quite far away.

Soon they would be reunited, and they could seek out the scientists and their quarry together. Soon this would all be over.

THE *AVARICE'S* docking bay beckoned Justin and Val inside, but they both hesitated. Even though they now wore ACM uniforms and carried standard-issue pulse rifles, venturing into the docking bay was still an intimidating prospect.

But Keontae had insisted that they move fast, so they kept moving.

They headed along a catwalk mounted to the back wall of the docking bay, still following the blinking green light overhead. By that point, dozens of ACM troop transport ships were returning from the *Nidus*, and soldiers were disembarking.

It looked like the entire force had decided to return to their ship. The sight amazed Justin. Keontae had done it—he'd actually pulled it off.

Now they just had to get off this damn ship before Keontae did whatever else he was going to do.

Ignoring all the commotion below, they headed to the far end of the docking bay until the green light stopped on the ceiling. Below it sat a ship that looked incredibly similar to the one Hallie and her team had arrived in, only brand new.

"That's incredible," Justin marveled. "He wants us to steal that ship... too bad I don't know how to fly one."

"I know a bit," Val said.

Justin looked back at her. "So do you believe me now? About getting out?"

Val's pierced eyebrow rose. "We're not out yet."

Together, they descended a staircase toward the ship, all while keeping a careful watch on the arriving transports and the soldiers inside. When they reached the ship on the docking bay floor, they quickly discovered they couldn't access it.

But Keontae could.

Justin searched for a console or a panel with a screen of some sort where he could receive Keontae back into his arm. He saw one near a door on the main floor.

"Stay put," he told Val.

"Where are you going?"

"To get that ship open."

Justin headed over to the panel and pressed his prosthetic hand against the screen. It flared green, and his fingers tingled as Keontae made the jump.

"You done?" Justin asked.

[Everything's in motion. We got maybe five minutes to get clear of this place. Ten minutes tops. If not, you're gonna join me as a permanent resident of the afterlife.]

"What did you do?" Justin asked.

[Armed their antimatter missiles. They're gonna blow sooner rather than later. Should cripple the ship, at least.]

"Shit."

"Sir?" a voice said from behind him.

Justin whirled around in time to see a trio of ACM soldiers in full armor. He caught sight of his surprised reflection in their mirrored face shields.

They looked him up and down. He was wearing an officer's uniform—damned if he knew his own rank, though...

The one in the center asked, "Sir, is everything alright?"

217

"Fine, soldier," Justin replied, hoping his voice wasn't shaking too much. "Just dealing with the usual bullshit around here."

That was generic enough, right? He certainly hadn't outed himself as an imposter in only a handful of words.

"Yeah," the lead soldier said. "Hard to know what to make of the admiral's orders."

[I ordered them to return under a Code Ebony,] Keontae explained.

"A Code Ebony is no joke," Justin said. "We have to be prepared."

"But he was so insistent on staying aboard that colonist ship until we found whatever it was he was looking for," the soldier on the right said.

"Yeah, but he wasn't going to tell us what he was looking for, either."

[You can't delay, JB,] Keontae warned. [Once the chain reaction starts, it won't stop until it can't go on anymore.]

"Gents, I've got to be off now," Justin broke into their conversation. "Have a good one."

"You mind explaining why you've got a pulse rifle slung to your back, sir?" one of the soldiers asked. With their face shields down, Justin had no idea which of them was talking unless they moved, and none of them had.

Each of the soldiers held pulse rifles as well. Justin nodded toward them. "You've got yours, and I've got mine. God forbid we should need them, right?"

The soldiers looked at each other again, this time quiet.

"Now if you'll excuse me, I have to—"

Three quick blasts took down two of the soldiers from behind, and the third went down after another two. Val stood behind them with her pulse rifle in hand.

"We don't have time for this," she said. "Let's go."

"Hey! Over there!" A group of soldiers from back the way Justin and Val had come pointed at them and started to run over with their rifles raised.

"Shit." Justin raised his pulse rifle and rattled off a barrage of blasts at the approaching soldiers. Some of his shots hit, and some flew wide.

Val fired, too, and her blasts seemed to hit more than Justin's did. In any case, several of the soldiers went down, but the commotion only attracted more of them, and there were plenty more in the docking bay who could come over if they wanted.

"*Shit!*" Justin kept firing, trying to make his way closer to the ship. If he could just *touch* near the door, Keontae could get it open and up and running for them.

But the soldiers were too many. They were going to pin them down in a matter of seconds... unless the antimatter missiles detonated first.

Then, from behind Justin and Val, a guttural roar sounded, followed by the trill of accelerated pulse rounds searing the artificial atmosphere. A swarm of pulses tore into the approaching soldiers, tearing them apart despite their armor.

When Justin looked back, he saw a blur of chrome flying over his head toward the soldiers. He tried to trace its movements and eventually caught sight of what appeared to be a mech suit bulging with a large man inside.

The mech suit had thrusters in its feet, and it streaked through the air and across the surface of the docking bay floor. It smashed into soldiers with its alloy limbs, leveling them with extreme prejudice, all while firing occasional shots from the plasma cannon mounted on its left shoulder.

Justin finally caught sight of the pilot an instant before he lurched toward another group of soldiers and began shredding their ranks.

It was Bear.

He'd mentioned something about being useless without a mech suit, but Justin had never imagined he'd be this fierce and effective while wearing one—almost like a *real* bear.

Next, a pair of familiar voices shouted from behind Justin—Zed and Ritz.

"Take that, you traitorous bastards!" Ritz's bug eyes practically spun in circles as he fired a pulse rifle of his own into the mass of approaching soldiers.

"Yes. Die now," Zed added loudly, yet without so much as a hint of emotion. He, too, fired a pulse rifle at the soldiers.

Where they'd come from, Justin had no idea, but they'd given him the opening he needed. He rushed to the ship and smacked his hand on the hull. No tingle, so he moved it around until Keontae finally found purchase and zapped out of Justin's metal arm.

The next moment, the access door to the ship hissed open, forming a ramp.

"Val, let's go!" he shouted as she continued gunning down soldiers. "Hurry!"

He didn't think Val had heard him over the ruckus, but she turned around and dashed toward the ship. Ritz followed, running with his head low, and scampered aboard next. Justin didn't care—they'd saved him, so they could come.

Zed tossed a grenade toward the soldiers, and when it detonated, rather than an explosion, it left a huge cloud in its wake. Then Zed hustled on board, and soon after, Bear's mech skated out of the smoke, zipped across the docking bay floor, and clomped up the ship's boarding ramp.

"Go!" Justin yelled, and someone—either Keontae or Val—launched the ship out of the docking bay, through one of the entry shields, and into space.

When Justin made it to the cockpit, he saw *Nidus's* flank fast approaching. But why hadn't the *Avarice* gone down yet?

If it didn't happen soon, the soldiers could just board transports, chase them back to the *Nidus*, and finish the job.

How much longer was the explosion going to take?

THE SEWERS beneath Nidus City weren't at all what Hallie had expected. She'd imagined rivers of sludge flowing toward some sort of automated processing plant, accompanied by the foulest stench imaginable.

Instead, she found soft blue track lights running the length of the sewer ceiling and down every corridor. Rather than an ever-flowing stream of filth, chrome pipes carried the waste along the upper edges of the walls, leaving them ample room to walk freely down the corridors on clean, smooth concrete. And the smell, while evident, was far from overwhelming.

The one thing that made the entire situation nearly unbearable was the temperature. For whatever reason, the sewers vacillated between tropical-paradise-warm and planet-that's-ventured-too-close-to-the-sun-hot at all times.

Sweat beaded on Hallie's forehead and tingled at the base of her neck. She considered peeling her outer layer off but opted not to in case they had to run or otherwise move quickly.

She guessed the temperature stayed high because the ship was burning the waste wherever these pipes came to an end. That heat and the resultant energy could've been repurposed to generate electricity or utilized as-is to warm up the city.

Whatever the case, the uncomfortable warmth and the extra perspiration were small prices to pay to evade contact with the soldiers combing the streets above.

Hallie shifted the satchel on her shoulder. It felt heavier still in the heat, though she couldn't conjure any scientific explanation why that would be the case aside from feeling more fatigued with each passing step.

Bryant walked beside her on her right, and Luke followed them by a few steps on Hallie's left. Every so often, access doors punctuated the walls. At one point, out of curiosity, Hallie got one of them open and peeked inside.

She found tools and equipment, but more interestingly, she found dark, narrow pathways connecting the equipment rooms to each other behind the sewer's main walls.

Hallie grinned. Whoever had designed this ship's infrastructure had done a pretty killer job. If a pipe ever burst, workers could use these access doors to quickly get through the sewers without slogging through sewage spills. Clever, yet simple.

As they approached a junction in the sewer passages, Bryant held out his free hand toward her. "Seriously, Hallie, I'm happy to carry that for you."

Hallie shook her head. "You're sweet to offer, but I haven't been taking AstroFit classes for the last three months to give up now. Sure, it was only one class every two weeks, and I missed a couple of those, but I really learned how to push my limits."

Bryant grinned and didn't lower his arm.

"That was code, in case you missed it," she said. "I'm good, Bryant."

And she was, too. It wasn't like he was any better off, carrying Justin's pulse rifle and his own pack. And he was sweating just as much, if not more, than she was. If anything, she might've been better suited to carry the satchel than him.

Bryant lowered his arm. "If you say so."

As they approached the junction, Hallie noticed that the lights in the corridor branching to the left were out. The path straight ahead remained lit, as did the path that led to the right.

"Which way are we supposed to go?" Hallie asked. "For all my beauty and genius, I'm not great with directions."

Luke chuckled as they passed by the dark corridor. "It should be straight ahead for awhile longer."

"Does anyone need a rest?" Bryant began to turn back to check on the others, and Hallie turned back as well. "Captain? How are your people holding—"

"*Ghk!*"

The sound came from Luke.

Hallie's head spun toward him, and she saw a spike irradiated with red light protruding from Luke's chest.

Not a spike.

A blade.

Luke's body lifted off the ground, inch by inch, as the blade lifted up. All the while, Luke gasped and tried to clutch at his wounded chest, but as he did, the energy blade seared away the flesh on his desperate fingers.

As Luke's body ascended, the blade carved upward, toward his shoulder and neck, the result of the blade cutting through his flesh and bone against the pull of the artificial gravity aboard the ship. Then Luke's eyes rolled back, his hands went limp, and the blade sizzled through the top of his shoulder.

Luke's lifeless body smacked the sewer's concrete floor, eliciting a series of gasps and shrieks from the rest of the group.

But they couldn't see what Hallie saw.

They couldn't see the face staring back at her, illuminated only by the red light from the blade extended from the fiend's right arm.

They couldn't see the reflection of the red energy dancing in his void-black eyes or the bitter scowl he wore.

Then he emerged from the darkness, a violet-skinned phantom headed straight for Hallie.

NINETEEN

V esh had found them. He'd already slain one of their number—one of the men. Now about a dozen others remained.

He'd been right to head toward the flash of orange light, and when he'd picked up their trail and ascertained their most likely path through the sewers, he'd been right to advance beyond their position, faster than their pace, and cut them off.

Now he stood face-to-face with a blonde woman. She carried a satchel over her shoulder that, by Vesh's calculations, had a 67% chance of holding the item he'd been sent to retrieve. The blonde woman stared up at him with horror etched on her face.

Good. If they feared him, that was to his advantage—not that he needed any more advantages. They couldn't kill him, not with the three pulse rifles in their possession or any other weapons they might've been carrying.

He retracted his energy sword into his wrist and drew his pulse cannon from his back.

"Run!" the man standing behind the blonde woman hollered as Vesh reached out for her. His Coalition uniform and his stature conveyed his status as a trained soldier—but he hadn't been trained like Vesh had, and he didn't have Vesh's augmentations.

Then the Coalition soldier raised his pulse rifle.

The latent protective shield built into Vesh's skin augmentations tingled, activating as the barrel of the pulse rifle rose to point at him. By the time the pulse rifle fired its first shot, the woman had darted out of the way, and the shield had fully activated.

The shots pattered against Vesh's shield like raindrops on a puddle, dissipating into small ripples of pink energy. The impacts danced across his skin, harmless.

Behind Vesh's eyes, the familiar sensation of burning began anew, and he blinked hard and fast to chase it away. Now was the worst possible time for any distractions. He was there. He'd found his target. He was about to complete his mission. He couldn't let anything get in his way.

As the burning fizzled to nothing, Vesh lifted his pulse cannon and took aim at the Coalition soldier.

HALLIE DARED to look back at the thing that had just killed Luke. Instead of following her as she chased the *Viridian's* fleeing crew and the two scientists on her team who remained alive, the large purple man took aim at Bryant with the massive pulse cannon in his hands.

Not a man. A monster.

A revenant.

A *titan*.

All of those things in one.

Captain Marlowe and Arlie had already taken up positions nearby, rapid-firing pulses at the titan, but every shot just splattered against some sort of invisible energy shield that coated his whole body and rippled with pink light wherever the pulse rounds hit him.

Bryant's shots hadn't killed the titan, either. Hallie marveled at the science behind it even as its ramifications horrified her.

What did that mean? Who was this guy?

Instead of the massive pulse cannon shearing through Bryant's body, Bryant charged forward and jammed his rifle against the pulse cannon, forcing its barrel toward the ceiling. It trilled with blasts of pink energy, which tore into the sewer ceiling, shredding the concrete overhead. Parts of the ceiling fell in small chunks, and concrete dust trickled down onto them.

As soon as Bryant did it, Hallie knew he was only forestalling the inevitable. The titan twisted and jerked hard, pushing Bryant away. Then, with one mighty kick, he sent Bryant flying into the far wall of the perpendicular corridor, which he hit with an audible *smack*. He slumped to the floor, motionless.

"No!" she yelled.

The titan's attention turned toward Hallie and the fleeing crew of both ships. It leveled its pulse cannon at them and opened fire.

Hallie dove for cover, lucky to find she'd stopped near one of the access doors set into the concrete corridor. She went flat against the concrete adjacent to the doorframe as pulse blasts stabbed at her cover.

"Fall back!" Captain Marlowe shouted from ahead. "Retreat!"

The barrage of pulse rounds coming at her stopped, and she stole a peek ahead.

The titan still stood in place, but now he fired on Captain Marlowe and Arlie's position where they hid near an access door on the opposite side of the corridor. The pulse rounds ate into the concrete, tearing red lines into the wall that soon darkened to black scars. A weapon of that power could shred their concrete cover and reduce it to dust in a matter of minutes.

Hallie could see Arlie, and Arlie could see her. Their eyes met, and Hallie had an idea. With the titan's focus on the others, now was her best chance to try it.

She lowered her satchel and its precious contents and activated the screen to open the door. Like the last one she'd tried, it didn't require any sort of identification to get inside. The door slid open from bottom to top, and she picked up her satchel and ventured in.

The same blue lights swelled to life above, revealing a room full of familiar-looking tools and equipment. None of it would help her. Even if she managed to get close enough, what was she going to do? Hit him with a big wrench?

Hallie discarded the idea. She had a different plan—a better one.

As with the other access room she'd visited, a narrow pathway ran between this one and the two adjacent rooms, one on each side. Without so much as a second thought, she headed down the one toward the titan and the junction.

Power conduits and smaller pipes lined the inner walls, all of it undoubtedly essential in some way to the city's functionality. More than once, spiderwebs clung to her face and tangled in her hair. She tried not to think about it, but perhaps the old adage was right—*no matter where you are in the galaxy, you're never more than five feet away from a spider.*

She shuddered, wiped the sticky netting from her face, and continued down the path.

It ended at a wall, but it banked to the right at a ninety-degree angle. Even through the concrete, she could hear the roar of the titan's pulse cannon incessantly rattling. She took the right turn and soon ended up in the next access room.

Hallie exhaled a long breath. If she was going to do this, she had to be quick about it. There was no turning back.

"CAPTAIN GABLE, SIR," a familiar voice said from behind Gable.

Disdain filled his chest. He turned back and found Commander Falstaff standing aboard the bridge, saluting.

"Commander." Gable saluted back and then lowered his hand. "I thought you would have stayed at the admiral's side like the pet you are."

Falstaff didn't even acknowledge Gable's barb. It gave Gable all the more reason to hate him. "I come with strict orders from Admiral Sever, sir."

Gable sighed. "Very well. Let's hear them."

"All combat personnel are to return immediately to the target ship. The search is to continue as before."

"And why hasn't the admiral conveyed this order to me personally?" Not that Gable cared. He would comply as he always did. What other choice did he have?

When Admiral Sever was aboard the *Avarice*, he commanded the ship. When he left the *Avarice*, he and Commander Falstaff commanded ACM's forces, leaving Gable to sit in the bridge, unaffected by it all. He was all but useless in either situation, so what did it matter?

Never mind that he had more training, more experience, and more brilliance than Commander Falstaff. But then again, why should Sever hear from someone who might actually challenge his ideas?

The whole scenario disgusted Gable, and he didn't mind showing it.

"His comms are malfunctioning. No messages are getting through."

Gable waved him off. "Fine. He'll have his men as soon as we've sorted out what's happening with this order. Our systems are scrambled, too. Go sort it all out on the ground level, like you always do."

"Thank you, Captain." Falstaff saluted and started to leave, but First Officer Reyes's fearful voice seized the entire bridge.

"Captain?!" he called. "Everything's back online, and all of our sensors seem to be functioning normally..."

"But?" Captain Gable faced him, unnerved by his frantic tone. He couldn't solve the problem until Reyes told him what the problem was. More importantly, he didn't want to look weak or inept in front of Commander Falstaff, either.

"...but nothing else is right, sir."

"Explain."

"There are casualties in the docking bay, residual damage in the network from some sort of cyber-attack, reports of prisoners escaping from the brig and boarding a Whip-Class transport, and—oh, God..." Reyes stopped.

"Spit it out, Officer." Gable frowned. All of that was bad, but not insurmountable. Not with the full power of the *Avarice* at his command, even as castrated as he felt in trying to use it.

"C-Captain," Reyes managed to say, "there's something wrong with the anti-matter warheads. They're... arming."

Gable's eyes widened, and he glanced at Commander Falstaff, whose gaze flitted from screen to screen in the bridge.

"Which ones?" Gable demanded.

"A-All of them, sir. They're... they're all armed and activating!"

"Fire them!" A litany of curses rifled through Gable's head, and he glared at Commander Falstaff. Admiral Sever should never have left Gable behind. "Launch them all now! Get them out of the *Avarice* before—"

A flash of pure white light silenced Captain Gable forever.

ARCS OF LIGHTNING ripped through the *Avarice* from the inside out, sending surprise, shock, and then sheer glee spiraling through Justin's chest.

He'd done it. Well, Keontae had done it, but he'd gotten him there.

As their transport docked aboard the *Nidus*, the *Avarice* tore itself apart in a brilliant display of light, explosions, and absolute mayhem.

Glorious. Fucking. Mayhem.

Justin reveled in the sight from the floor of the *Nidus's* docking bay. A lot of people had died aboard the *Avarice*, but they'd made their choice to side with ACM, and they'd attacked the *Nidus*. Now, thanks to Keontae, they'd paid for it.

It felt amazing.

[Hoooo-wee!] Keontae hooted. [Now that's a fireworks display worth watchin'!]

"Damn right it is," Justin replied.

He noticed Val, Zed, and Ritz alternating astonished glances between him and the fractured *Avarice*, now significantly darker as the remnants of the antimatter missiles ate at the edges of the shattered ship in bright white light.

"I mean, damn right it's gone," he told them.

Zed and Ritz nodded. Zed's crazed golden eyes had narrowed as if he was smiling, but it was hard to tell with the bottom of his face missing. Ritz wore a gigantic crooked smile under his telescoped eyes.

"You should've seen it up close," Ritz said as his eyes retracted into his head. "Absolutely breathtaking."

"I'm fine right here." Bear's mech suit skidded to a stop next to them.

He'd seen *Avarice* at the peak of its detonation, and then he'd taken to dashing and looping around the wide-open docking bay in his mech suit, sometimes on the ground and sometimes in midair, just enjoying his newfound freedom. With each movement, the mech shuddered and wobbled as it negotiated with Bear's girth, but it didn't give out.

"Gotta say," Bear said, "my old Farcoast mech was good, but dammit, these ACM ones are smoother than a cue ball in a bucket of grease. Better firepower, too."

With that, he launched back into the docking bay, spinning, spiraling, and gliding with all the grace of a Galaxy Games figure skater.

[If ever a guy were meant for a mech suit, it'd be him,] Keontae said.

Justin glanced at Val. "You believe me now?"

She shook her bald head, still holding her pulse rifle and still wearing a navy-blue ACM officer's uniform. "I don't believe any of this, but I'm here... so I guess you were right. And I definitely owe you one."

"Same," Ritz said.

"And you have my thanks, too," Zed uttered.

"I'm back in my happy place," Bear called between dashes. "So I owe you one, too."

Justin grinned. "Funny you should mention it. I could actually use your help with something..."

WHEN THE *AVARICE* flashed with white light and exploded, Admiral Sever had to double-check to make sure it wasn't a holographic projection on the dome over Nidus City. A look through one of the soldiers' binoculars confirmed it.

The *Avarice* was gone. Destroyed, somehow, from within.

A part of Sever seemed to disintegrate along with the ship. *How could this have happened?*

Only one explanation made sense: an antimatter missile had detonated while still inside the ship. Sever recognized the stark white energy that had rent the *Avarice* into pieces.

According to Coalition Law, the missiles weren't legal, but they *were* supposed to be foolproof and perfectly safe. Countless protocols, both human and computerized, were in place to prevent exactly this sort of thing from happening. The missiles weren't supposed to arm while aboard the ship, and they sure as hell weren't supposed to blow.

Yet they had. And the ensuing chain reaction had shredded the *Avarice* beyond recognition.

Trillions of credits, hundreds of thousands of man-hours, and thousands of lives all gone in an instant. Flippantly. Wasted.

And that included Commander Falstaff, the only man Sever could trust implicitly. *And I'm the one who sent him to his death.*

The sick feeling in Sever's chest blossomed into rage, and he wanted to scream. Instead, he handed the binoculars back to the soldier who'd provided them and clenched his free fist and his teeth.

It had to be sabotage. Someone had called nearly all of his soldiers back to the *Avarice*, and then it had exploded. That couldn't be a coincidence.

Whoever had done it, if they hadn't died along with the *Avarice*, they would die for their recklessness. Of that, Sever would make certain.

For now, all he could do was redouble his focus on the mission. With the *Nidus's* miserable Farcoast army already wiped out and its officers killed, Sever could easily overtake the ship and return it to the core planets or to the nearest ACM fleet.

But first, he had to find his quarry. He had to fulfill his mandate from ACM corporate.

He needed to find Vesh more than ever.

"Enough gawking. We've got work to do. I have a special task for twenty of you." Sever explained his orders, checked the indicator on his wrist, and said, "Everyone else, follow me."

HALLIE WOULDN'T BE quick enough while lugging her satchel around. She hated to leave it behind, out of her sight, but if she didn't stop the titan, it wouldn't matter anyway.

The idea crossed her mind to use its contents now. After all, it was a weapon, and it might be enough to bring down the titan.

But she couldn't. It wasn't really her decision to make. To loose something of that magnitude... the potential consequences could be...

There was still possibly another way, so she had to give it a shot. She couldn't risk the fallout from using the weapon. It was too risky. So she tucked the satchel behind some equipment where it blended in innocuously enough, then she headed toward the access door.

It slid open, and the roar of the pulse cannon raked her ears. How the titan could stand it, she had no idea. If Luke were still alive, she would've asked him why weapons designers had bothered to make energy weapons so loud, especially when they no longer had to.

But Luke was gone, along with who knew how many of her fellow scientists and the *Viridian's* crew... and possibly Bryant. And she was the only one who might have a chance of stopping the onslaught.

Now in the main corridor again, the one perpendicular to the corridor where Captain Marlowe and Arlie were pinned down, Hallie pressed her back against the wall and crept toward the commotion—and the titan—as fast as she dared.

She saw Bryant lying there, still unmoving. *God... is he dead?*

Whether he was or not, she had a plan to execute. There, in his holster, sat the repeater that Luke had modified. Strong enough to shear clean through metal and concrete in an absurdly large blast. Would it be enough to get through the titan's shield?

Hallie honestly didn't know. But that wasn't her plan anyway.

As she moved even closer, she saw the titan's violet-colored right shoulder come into view. He was standing almost sideways to the corridor he was firing into, meaning his left shoulder was positioned even farther into the corridor. It also meant he was more or less looking away from her.

Good.

But the longer she delayed, the more likely he'd move forward or kill either Captain Marlowe or Arlie with one of his shots. Their concrete cover wouldn't last forever, and she imagined his pulse cannon still had plenty of charge in it.

A trickle of concrete dust dropped onto the titan's left shoulder, coating part of it with gray powder. The ceiling above him was still shredded, as if hot metal claws had raked across it and punctured it in dozens of places.

Maybe this will actually work.

With sweat stinging her eyes and trickling down her back, Hallie rushed over to Bryant, praying her shoes wouldn't somehow overpower the deafening sounds of the pulse cannon firing. Whether they made too much noise or not, the titan stopped his onslaught.

He'd realized she was there. How, she didn't know, but that didn't matter now. She had seconds to act, or it would all be over for her forever.

Hallie reached Bryant and yanked the plasma repeater out of his holster. She took aim at the titan's head as he turned his upper half toward her, blinking his black eyes hard.

Then she raised it to the concrete ceiling over his head—the very same concrete his pulse cannon had already turned into Swiss cheese, weakening it.

She hoped it would be enough.

Hallie lined up her shot and fired.

TWENTY

An impossibly bright orange light screamed out of the repeater and carved into the ceiling.

The thunder of crumbling infrastructure shattered Hallie's forced sense of calm. The ceiling above the titan collapsed in an avalanche of concrete, asphalt, and raw sewage from the two pipes that wrenched free and broke open. The deluge pinned him to the floor and then buried him.

Hallie dropped the repeater as soon as she fired it and hooked her arms under Bryant's shoulders and hauled him away from the falling debris. As she did, he stirred and woke up, and for the first time she noticed blood coming from the back of his head. A streak of red marred the concrete as she slid him along.

"What... the hell just happened?" he mumbled.

By now, the avalanche had stopped, and clouds of dust had billowed over them, both stinging their eyes and obscuring their view.

"Oh, you know," Hallie said as she helped him up to his feet. The stink of raw sewage finally hit her nose full force, and it was even more terrible than she'd imagined it could be. "Just handling some shit for you."

Bryant's nose wrinkled. "I'll say."

His footing wobbled, and Hallie used her body to brace him. "Easy there, soldier. I think you have a concussion."

Bryant's focus remained on the gigantic pile of broken concrete. "I bet he does, too."

Hallie huffed. "At *least.*"

"Did you grab my rifle?" He looked down at her with hazy, squinty eyes.

231

"No. I had to get you out of there so you didn't get crushed."

"Oh. Thanks." His head lolled some, and he blinked several times. "I need to go back and get it."

"*I'll* get it," Hallie insisted. She walked him to the nearest wall. "You stay here. Work on righting your internal gyroscope. Lean against this until I get back."

As she approached the pile of rubble, she, too, never took her eyes off it. She'd labeled the big purple guy "the titan" for a reason, and the collapsing ceiling, even though it had to be well over a ton of concrete that fell, might not have finished him off.

She spotted Bryant's rifle and snatched it up, then a voice called to her through the cloud of concrete dust lingering in the corridor.

"Hallie? That you?"

Captain Marlowe.

"Yeah," she called back.

"Is he down?" Captain Marlowe asked.

"I'd say so." She quipped, "Dusted him real good."

"That's an understatement. You even had the decency to bury him." Captain Marlowe emerged from the dust cloud, first as a silhouette, then as his full self, again with a metal stick clenched between his teeth. Arlie followed. Both of them had to hop over the ever-widening lake of sewage spilling onto the floor to reach Hallie. "How's Bryant?"

"Alive. Maybe concussed. Back there, resting."

Captain Marlowe glanced at the rifle in her hands. "You planning on holding onto that for awhile?"

Hallie looked down at the pulse rifle. It weighed less than she'd expected—certainly less than it looked—but it was still heavy. Carrying a rifle and her satchel would be a lot. "No. I figured I'd give it back to Bryant once I—oh!"

Her satchel. She'd left it in the access room. The titan was down, and she needed to go back and retrieve it. It was hers to protect.

"Hold on," she told them. "Or... go check on the others. See if anyone else got hit."

Without waiting for a response, Hallie turned back, hurried over to a still-wobbly Bryant, passed him his rifle, and then headed for the access door.

She found the satchel right where she'd left it, and she snatched it up and slung it over her shoulder again. Relief filled her body all the way down to her toes.

Hallie was glad she hadn't used the weapon. It had all worked out, albeit just barely. She'd made the right call.

Back in the main corridor, the junction was quickly becoming impassable thanks to the raw sewage, so she took Bryant through the access pathways back toward where Captain Marlowe, Arlie, and the rest of the crew might be.

They met up near the access door Hallie had been hiding near, and she did a quick headcount.

Only half of the *Viridian's* crew had survived, and Cecilia was also missing—until Hallie saw Cecilia's familiar form lying limp on the concrete just beyond the other survivors.

Emotion swelled in Hallie's chest and choked her up, both for Luke and for Cecilia. They hadn't deserved this fate. Neither had Captain Dawes or any of the *Viridian's* crew.

Well, maybe the loudmouthed one who had it in for Justin—Lora. But she'd survived and stood there with her arms folded, looking like a powdered gray ghost glaring at Hallie.

Forget her. Hallie looked away. *And forget the others... for now. You're not done yet.*

"I wish we could bury them," Hallie said, resisting tears, "but I know that's not possible. I just hate having to leave them in the sewers to rot."

Bryant touched her shoulder with his hand. "They would understand."

"Can we at least drag them into one of the access rooms? There are racks in there. It's at least a sort of burial."

"Good idea." Captain Marlowe shifted the metal stick to the other side of his mouth. "At least that way, there's some dignity in their deaths."

Hallie blinked back her tears and nodded at him. "Thank you."

WITH ALL THE bodies moved to the racks in the nearest access room, the group ventured out of the sewers and back toward the surface.

Hallie followed Captain Marlowe up the ladder to the street level, glad to be out of the sewers and away from the smell. And from the death they'd left behind. She hoped they wouldn't have to go back down there.

Once the full group made it up top, Angela tended to Bryant's head while the others brushed off as much of the concrete dust from themselves as they could manage. The city around them glowed with a myriad of colored lights and holographic advertisements as it had the first time she laid eyes on it. It almost felt... normal.

Night had fully fallen, and the dome showed only the tranquil stars above them... except for one area of the sky. Hallie noticed a flickering of white light—several flickers, scattered over a wide area, actually—outside the dome.

Bryant had powered binoculars on his belt, and Hallie borrowed them to take a closer look.

There before her eyes, inexplicably, the *Avarice* burned in shattered ruins.

Hallie couldn't believe it. Justin had pulled it off. She had no idea how, but he'd managed to take out the *Avarice*, just as he'd set out to do. It was nothing short of a miracle.

As she listened to the sounds of the city, what few there were, she noticed there weren't any pulse rifle shots or explosions or screams like she'd heard earlier. Where were all the soldiers?

Were they... gone?

No. Couldn't be. They had to have just fallen back or hunkered down for the night.

More importantly, if the *Avarice* had been destroyed... what did that mean had happened to Justin? Hallie feared the worst, but her heart and her rational mind suggested an alternative: If Justin had been able to blow up the *Avarice*, he'd probably been able to get out alive before it blew.

"Guys... I got something here." Captain Marlowe held his fingers up to his earpiece and grinned. "It's Justin."

Hallie couldn't have smiled wider if she'd tried.

"He's asking where we should meet up."

"I know a place," Hallie blurted.

Everyone looked at her—except for Lora, who was downright glaring at her again.

Hallie ignored her. "There's a restaurant. A breakfast place downtown called LaBorn's. He'll know it."

Captain Marlowe relayed the message. "He says that's perfect. Should be there in just a few minutes."

Hallie couldn't stop smiling the whole way there.

And the best part was how mad it made Lora.

THE SIGHT OF LABORN'S, dark inside and stark against the blue glow of the rest of Nidus City, both excited and worried Justin. Even though the place resurrected fond memories, its broken windows and overturned tables and chairs alarmed him.

What a drastic change from how it looked the other morning...

As he stepped over the threshold and his boots crunched on broken glass, he wondered if something had gone wrong with Hallie and the others. Were they delayed? Or captured, somehow, along the way?

Or had Justin's team simply beaten them there?

Four of the restaurant's androids lay on the floor with the overturned furniture and the broken glass, riddled with blackened holes from pulse rounds. Thanks to his encounters with the androids back at ACM-1134, he didn't lament seeing them in such a state. After all, a dead android was one that couldn't try to kill him anymore.

Bear's mech came in last, adding far louder crunches of its metallic feet atop the broken glass. It had barely fit inside the restaurant due to its height.

Justin continued to venture deeper into LaBorn's until a bright light shined in his eyes out of nowhere.

"Don't take another step," someone ordered.

Justin froze, unwilling to raise his rifle. He thought he recognized that voice, but he couldn't be sure.

Behind him, Val's voice answered, "You do him, and I'll do you."

"Easy, Bryant," Hallie said from somewhere beyond the source of the light. "It's Justin. And... a traveling circus. Or something."

The light lowered, and Justin blinked his vision back to normal.

"Probably shoulda seen him coming," Ritz muttered. "What with these augmented eyes and all."

Hallie emerged from behind the checkout counter along the back and rushed over to Justin. She still had her satchel slung over her shoulder, and he still held a pulse rifle, so they exchanged an awkward half-hug that was good, but not great.

[Aw. You made it back to your girl. I love a happy ending,] Keontae said.

As they shared the embrace, Bryant came out from behind the counter next, and then Captain Marlowe and Arlie emerged from the kitchen with only a handful of people behind them.

"You made it," Hallie said, her voice just above a whisper as she released the embrace and stared up at him. Then, louder, she said, "And you blew up ACM's ship? How the hell did you pull that off?"

"Trade secret," Justin said. "Nerdy, technical stuff."

"Is that supposed to dissuade me from knowing more?" Hallie shook her head and put her free hand on her hip. "You do realize that I've spent my entire life studying and mastering 'nerdy, technical stuff,' right? Now I'm more interested than ever."

"Later," Justin said as he scanned the faces of the *Viridian's* survivors.

Aside from Captain Marlowe and Arlie, only Al, Shaneesha, Lora, and two other workers whose names he couldn't remember had survived. Dr. Angela stood among them as well.

"This is it? No one else made it?" Justin's heart ached at the loss of more of his fellow rig-runners.

Captain Marlowe gave a solemn nod. "Ran into trouble in the sewers."

Justin noticed how dirty they were for the first time. It looked as if they'd endured a gray snowstorm.

"Hallie saved us," Captain Marlowe added.

Justin looked at her, and she nodded, smiling.

"What happened?" he asked.

"Long story short, we ran into a purple-skinned giant. He tried to kill us—" Hallie's smile shrank. "He *did* kill some of us... and then I buried him under a ton of asphalt, hence the concrete dust on our clothes and in our hair. Gravity's not the most complex scientific law, but it works on everybody."

"Vesh," Justin said. "You ran into Vesh. Violet skin, kind of translucent? Freaky black eyes?"

Everyone nodded.

"I'm so glad you made it," Justin said. "He was the one who captured me. Not a guy I'd want to mess with again."

"Now you won't have to," Hallie said. "He's buried in the sewer."

"Along with the crew that didn't make it," Bryant added. "From both our vessels."

"Well, we made it," Justin said. "The *Avarice* is gone, and any ACM soldiers left here don't have the strength and resources they once had. All we have to do is outlast them or get past them to the docking bay, and we can get outta here."

"What's with the street performers?" Arlie nodded toward Val and the others.

Justin glanced back at them. "New friends. Meet Val, Zed, Ritz, and Bear."

Each of them waved or nodded when named.

"Found 'em in the brig aboard the *Avarice*. They tried to kill me, then they saved me and helped me escape, so I figured that made us even enough to bring 'em along."

"And we appreciate it," Bear said with a grin from inside his mech suit.

"Gotta say, having a guy in a mech suit's gonna draw more attention if we're trying to move through the city toward the docking bay." Captain Marlowe popped open his metal case and pulled out a fresh metal stick.

"Yeah, but you also got a helluva lot more firepower if we do get into some sorta spat," Bear countered. "Plus, I'm slow as turtle shit without one of these jitterbugs. You want me to keep up, the suit stays on."

Captain Marlowe positioned the stick in the side of his mouth near his molars and chomped down. Then he glanced at Arlie, who shrugged.

"He's actually pretty slick in that thing. Moves like he's gliding on air," Justin said.

Captain Marlowe looked Bear up and down, chewing on his stick. His voice carried a hint of incredulity. "Whatever you say."

"No real reason to linger, is there?" Arlie said. "We should get moving. Don't need to be stuck in one place for too long."

The way she said it might've been yet another jab at Captain Marlowe, but he only nodded. "She's right. Let's head out."

"Good. Along the way, I'll be happy to tell you how I blew up the *Avarice*," Justin said.

[How *you* blew it up?] Keontae grumbled.

Before Justin could retort, Ritz hissed at them with his hands up.

"Wait!" Ritz's eyes were extended, glowing bright green instead of orange and swirling around like mad. "Shit. We're in trouble."

Val's rifle rose to her shoulder seemingly on its own, and she pointed it toward the broken windows at the front of the restaurant. Bear spun in his mech suit, also facing the front.

Captain Marlowe, Arlie, and Bryant followed suit, but they exchanged looks of confusion while they did it.

Justin lifted his rifle, too, but he had no clue why he was doing it.

Then several dozen ACM soldiers quickly surrounded the outside of the restaurant. Their face shields reflected the blue of the city lights, with occasional flickers of other colors, and each of them pointed their pulse rifles into LaBorn's.

Justin swore under his breath.

[Say it aloud, man. I feel the same way,] Keontae said.

"Hold your fire," a voice crooned from somewhere within the ranks of the soldiers.

Justin recognized that voice...

Admiral Sever.

He emerged from the throng of soldiers, carrying a wicked-looking pulse rifle of his own, not wearing a helmet like the others, and sneering at Justin and the others.

"It seems we have you at a disadvantage," he called. "We have the numbers."

"And we have a fortified position and a bottleneck," Bryant called back. "So your numbers don't mean shit."

Justin eyed him. This was a damned *restaurant*, not a fortress. What the hell was he talking about?

[I don't care what that Coalition guy says,] Keontae said. [This is bad, JB.]

Keontae was right. Even with a way through the kitchen, Admiral Sever had undoubtedly posted men there as well.

Justin felt his heart rate increasing. They'd been so close...

"Think again," Admiral Sever said. "You are trapped. There's no way out except through us... and you won't get *through* us. Not even close."

Bryant started to speak again, but Hallie beat him to it. "What do you want?"

"Ah, is that the blonde scientist with the lovely face?" Admiral Sever called. "Never did get your name, darling."

"Dr. Hayes," she answered. "And I'm not your fucking *darling*."

Justin's eyebrows rose at the venom in Hallie's voice.

"Tsk, tsk. Language, Dr. Hayes. I would've expected you to exhibit more self-restraint than that."

"Pretty hard to control my tongue when a bag of dicks like you keeps trying to kill me," she fired back.

Even from a distance, Justin saw Admiral Sever frown. It gave him a small satisfaction, even though their situation remained dire.

"Dr. Hayes, you know what I want." Admiral Sever extended a gloved hand toward her. "Hand it over, and I promise we will kill you all quickly."

"The hell?" Justin called out, "You're not even gonna lie and say you'll let us go?"

"Ah... Mr. Barclay. The man who supposedly knows something about Carl Andridge's death... and who also just admitted to singlehandedly destroying an ACM warship." Admiral Sever added, "Yes, I overheard you mentioning that. And yes, I am exempting you from my generous offer to die quickly."

Justin gulped. It shouldn't have bothered him that Admiral Sever knew, but being threatened over it still unnerved him.

"I don't care what you say," Hallie shouted. "I'm never giving it to you."

"Then, my dear," Admiral Sever said, "I will simply take it."

Shit. Justin knew what that meant. He dove for Hallie with his arms outstretched, letting his rifle fall in the process.

Admiral Sever's rifle snapped up to his shoulder and fired, but the pulse round sizzled past Justin's ear as he took Hallie to the ground.

LaBorn's erupted with the rattle of pulse rifles exchanging fire and shrieks and cries all around Justin. He shielded Hallie with his body and rolled her over behind some of the downed tables and chairs, but they wouldn't make for sufficient enough cover. Hundreds of pulse rounds firing across the restaurant would tear through it all eventually.

But what else could they do?

Justin watched as Val, Bryant, Captain Marlowe, and Arlie returned fire. Zed and Ritz loosed wild barrages of their own, and Bear skidded back and forth across the restaurant in his mech, knocking downed tables and chairs aside as if they weighed nothing. A green shield repelled most of the shots that reached him, but it wouldn't last forever.

Admiral Sever was right. They were trapped.

Even with them returning fire, Justin saw another one of the *Viridian's* crew go down.

It was Shaneesha.

No!

She'd been hit in her gut, and Dr. Angela had rushed to her side to try to stabilize her.

Meanwhile, Lora had snatched up the rifle Justin had dropped and began returning fire along with the others, all while wearing a vicious snarl on her face.

Justin glanced down at Hallie again. She was reaching into her satchel.

THIS TIME, Hallie had no choice. She'd managed to get the edge over Vesh, but there wasn't any "edge" to get in this situation. They were locked down. Hard.

ACM soldiers had already breached the restaurant's perimeter and were steadily advancing forward. Whenever one of them went down, more soldiers popped up in their place.

It was only a matter of time before they were completely overrun.

When Justin had tackled her to the ground, she started reaching into her satchel. She got her hand on the object inside and pulled it out—a chrome capsule, sealed on both ends, longer than her forearm but just as wide as her head.

Am I really doing this? Am I really unleashing this onto this ship?

Pulse rounds dug into the wall just above her head, and she tried to flatten herself to the floor.

Yes. I have to, or we're all dead.

She pressed her thumb hard against a charcoal circle on the surface of the chrome capsule, and it turned green, then red under her pressure. A click sounded, distinct from the ruckus all around her. It was open.

Or maybe we're all dead either way.

"You want it," she shouted, "you got it!"

She tossed the capsule over her head, over the chairs and tables behind where she'd taken cover. A loud hiss sounded from the center of the restaurant as the contents of the capsule dispersed.

It had begun.

TWENTY-ONE

W hatever Hallie had just done, it accelerated quickly.

Before Justin's eyes, a black cloud billowed out of the chrome thing she'd tossed into the middle of LaBorn's. But it didn't behave like a cloud at all—it moved more like a swarm of some sort, glistening from within and moving with a degree of intentionality that Justin wouldn't have guessed was possible for smoke.

He quickly realized that whatever it was, it wasn't smoke.

It separated into five distinct parts, four of which landed on the four downed androids. Within a matter of seconds, the androids rose to their feet as if reanimated, looking and behaving very different from how androids were supposed to look and behave. Their eyes glowed with a haunting pale-green light.

Their metal arms and hands violently twisted and warped into jagged points. Then they leaped toward the nearest ACM soldiers and drove their new weapons into the soldiers' bodies, straight through their armor as if it were only cloth.

The soldiers shrieked and screamed, and they collapsed as the androids stabbed them wildly, again and again.

Keontae gasped. [What the *fuck* is goin' on?]

The sight resurrected the worst of Justin's memories from ACM-1134, and he almost looked away, but he couldn't. His sense of survival wouldn't let him.

Then his eyes punished him for it.

As the androids leaped toward new victims, the fifth part of the cloud attacked the approaching soldiers. It broke into yet even more glistening black parts, and they smacked into the soldiers' face shields and helmets.

The ACM soldiers began clawing at their helmets, screaming and trying to rip them off. When they succeeded, Justin saw parts of their faces dissolving away, replaced by a metallic black film and splashes of blood streaming from their wounds to the floor.

Their eyes went next, eaten away by whatever the cloud was, and were replaced with hollow husks of eye sockets instead. The stuff went after their lips and their teeth, their jaws, and down their necks, but only in patches—never a full slate of metal.

But the worst part was when the soldiers stopped resisting. They didn't fall to the floor. Didn't die.

Instead, they went still for a long moment as metal claw-like structures pierced through the tips of their gloved fingers, knees, and elbows. Then they turned their marred faces toward whatever or whoever was nearest and sprang into an attack.

One of them went for Bear in his mech suit, and another went for Al, who was crouching behind an overturned table.

Bear's mech cannon shredded the mutated soldier who came for him, but it took far more rounds than it should've to bring the thing down.

Al, on the other hand, had no weapons.

Val, Captain Marlowe, and Arlie tried to shoot it down with their pulse rifles, but they couldn't even slow it down. The soldier jammed its clawed hands into Al's chest, and he screamed. Justin shuddered at the sight, helpless to intervene.

Then the downed soldiers, the first ones the androids had killed, started to get up, too. Spikes of glistening black metal stuck out of their wounds where they'd been stabbed, and they rose to their feet with more metal extending from their fingers.

They, too, joined the battle.

It was like ACM-1134 all over again... only worse.

Quicker. More brutal. More visceral.

Justin glanced at Hallie, who lay there, just barely peeking over the edge of the table they were using for cover. Her mouth hung open just like his.

He wanted to shout at her, to demand that she tell him what she'd done. But he couldn't. He couldn't find any words.

Captain Marlowe, however, did.

"Fall back!" he shouted over the clamor. "Into the kitchen! Fall back!"

"He's right," Hallie said. "We have to get somewhere it can't reach us, too."

"Where?" Justin managed to ask.

"The walk-in freezer or refrigeration unit if they have one." Hallie looked at Justin with desperation in her light-blue eyes. "It's our only chance."

Whatever she'd done, she'd known this would happen, or something like it.

She'd known, and she'd done it anyway.

Justin didn't know what to feel about that.

[Move, JB!] Keontae yelled.

"C'mon." Justin hauled her up to her feet, and they ran toward the back of the restaurant again.

As Bryant led the survivors into the kitchen, another mutated ACM soldier leaped at them. It took Dr. Angela down with one set of claws, then it drove its other hand into Shaneesha. Both of them screamed.

Justin swore and cursed, even as Bear, Val, and Captain Marlowe unleashed terrible fury into it with their guns, but they were too late. Dr. Angela and Shaneesha were both dead.

Once they reached the kitchen, Hallie yelled, "To the freezer!"

Bryant found it and shoved metal tables and equipment out of the way to clear a direct path, and then he flung the massive freezer door open. A blast of icy fog billowed out of it, and Bryant ushered everyone inside as quickly as he could.

To Justin's surprise, they all managed to fit, including Bear and his mech suit.

Together, Bryant and Captain Marlowe began to haul the freezer door shut, but before it could latch, an arm tipped with metallic claws jammed inside, scraping and clawing at the door and toward everyone inside.

Then the door started pulling open again, and Justin caught a glimpse of the thing's face. It was Al—or it had been. Like the others, he had no eyes, and splotches of black metal had eaten away at his face. His blackened metallic mouth hung open as he reached for them.

Justin had never missed his energy sword more than right then.

Val, Zed, Ritz, and Arlie unleashed the full fury of their rifles into Al's head and torso, but he still wouldn't relent.

"Move!" Hallie yelled, and everyone moved aside, including Captain Marlowe and Bryant. She held some sort of bucket in her hands.

The freezer door flung wide open, and Al lurched forward.

Hallie doused Al with the bucket, and he froze solid within two steps.

When Hallie dropped the bucket, Justin caught the words "Liquid Nitrogen: Use With Caution" printed on the side.

"Get him out of here, and close the door!" Arlie yelled.

Bear obliged. He activated his mech's thrusters, rammed into Al, and launched him clear across the kitchen. Al's frozen form shattered against the opposite wall.

Then Shaneesha and Dr. Angela came through the kitchen door, equally as malformed.

"Shut it!" Hallie screamed.

This time, Captain Marlowe and Bryant managed to get the door shut and latched, sealing everyone inside. When the door closed, Justin realized a soft blue light glowed overhead. It wasn't much, but it was enough that he could see all of them amid the frozen fog.

And now they were stuck in the freezer.

"As long as this thing actually seals properly, we'll be safe. And as long as they don't think to try to open the door." Hallie wrapped her arms around herself. "They don't like the cold."

"They?" Justin gawked at her. "What do you mean, 'they?'"

"The nanobots. It's new tech. Highly classified, highly erratic. Capable of repurposing metal and other materials to reproduce and multiply," Hallie explained. "Really incredible stuff. But it's fine. They can't hurt us in here."

Justin squared himself with Hallie, suddenly disgusted by her nonchalance about this new brand of horror she'd unleashed aboard the *Nidus*—which was made of "metal and other materials." They might be safe now, but what did that mean for their long-term survival prospects?

"There's still *thousands* of people out there, and we lost some of our own thanks to you setting those bots loose." Justin injected steel into his voice. "What the *hell* have you done?"

Hallie's eyebrows arched down, and she sharpened her tone to match his. "You think I wanted to have to do that? I didn't have a choice. I did what I had to do. And now it's done."

[Yeah...] Keontae said. [And if we ever get outta here, so are we.]

EPILOGUE

Twenty of ACM's soldiers never made it to that restaurant. Instead, they followed Vesh's signal down into the sewers under the city.

The overwhelming stink of sewage almost turned them back, but Admiral Sever had given them orders to find Vesh no matter what, so they had to comply.

But when they got there, they found only brown, ankle-high water and a pile of concrete rubble that had to weigh more than a ton, easily.

"C'mon," the ranking soldier, a corporal, said. "We're done here."

"But he's buried under there," another protested. "Shouldn't we try to dig him out?"

"Probably cost the company a fortune to do what they did to him," another said. "Did you get a chance to see him?"

"You two wanna slog through the shit to try to get him out, be my guest," the corporal said. "He's dead anyway, like the rest of 'em down here. No point anymore. Corporate's gonna have to write this off as a loss, same as they'll do with the *Avarice* and any of our asses that don't make it home. Now let's get moving. We're supposed to rendezvous with the admiral ASAP."

"I guess he's right," one of the soldiers said. "Not much we can do here."

"Yeah," another one said. "Let's go."

As they started to walk away, careful to avoid the sewage creeping ever so steadily outward, the pile of debris shifted.

They turned back. The sound had been unmistakable… and they couldn't have all imagined it at the same time… could they?

Then it shifted again.

Had their eyes deceived them, too? No. Impossible...

But was it more impossible than the alternative? That this thing had somehow... survived?

The concrete continued to shift and move, little by little. Several of the soldiers rushed forward, apathetic to the waste now clinging to their boots, and they began stripping away whatever rubble and debris they could.

Then the rest of the pile burst upward and outward, flinging chunks of concrete and asphalt in every direction. The soldiers staggered back, unable to avoid stepping in the pond of filth around them as concrete dust plumed into the air.

When it cleared, a lone figure stood before them, caked in sewage and concrete dust. Patches of his violet skin were visible even despite his foul coating, and his black eyes burned with the energy of twin stars.

Vesh was alive.

And he was pissed.

SHAMELESS COMMERCIAL

THE WAITING room to get into the afterlife brimmed with thousands upon thousands of soldiers, both from the *Avarice* and the *Nidus*, as well as several dozen noncombatants who'd also perished somewhere along the way.

Fortunately, thanks to the power of fiction and the Spandex-like properties of the fabric of the universe, the pink, hummus-scented room easily expanded to accommodate this series's ever-growing body count.

Among them roamed Fennimore "Jonesy" Jones, no longer imprisoned aboard the *Avarice* but also very dead thanks to Justin Barclay's fist caving in his chest before the ship detonated.

With nothing else to do while he and thousands of others awaited entry into whatever afterlife awaited them, he thumbed through the waiting room's selection of books in a row of Plastrex cases mounted to the wall. He took one out and looked it over.

"I see you are a man of excellent taste," a woman's voice, lilting with a Russian accent, said from behind him.

Jonesy turned back to find a beautiful brunette standing before him—or at least she would've been if half her face wasn't the shining chrome of a cyborg's.

She extended her right hand toward Jonesy, and he'd never been happier that people shook with their right hands instead of their left hands, since the woman's left hand matched the metal of her face.

"I am Dr. Etya Stielbard, but you may call me Etya," she said.

"Jonesy." He warily shook her hand. He looked her up and down.

"You are wondering how much of me is cybernetic?" she asked.

"Sorry." Were Jonesy still alive, his cheeks would've flushed. "...for staring."

Etya waved her hand. "When I was still alive, I used to care about such things. Now, here in the afterlife, I am not bothered. But to address your inquiry, I am still sixty-two percent human. The rest is machine."

Jonesy's eyebrows rose. "What happened to you?"

"It is a long story." Etya shook her head. "Suffice it to say, Andridge Copalion Mines is partially to blame for both our fates, but it is too late to do anything about it now. I would much rather discuss your fine choice of reading materials."

"This?" Jonesy held up the book. The title read *Blood Mercenaries Origins*, by Ben Wolf. "Never heard of it before."

"I have waited in this place for a long time," she said, "and of all the authors whose books reside in this place, none compare to the legendary Ben Wolf."

"He's *that* good?" Jonesy eyed her. "Or are you just reciting lines of dialogue?"

"Yes," Etya replied with a wry grin, but only on the right side of her face.

"Fair enough." Jonesy held up the book. "What's this series about?"

"They are fantasy stories, sword and sorcery, to be precise, set in a faraway world with vastly different rules and extraordinary magic," Etya explained as she pulled three more books from the wall to show him. "I am told they are like a popular game involving dungeons, and also dragons, but in book form. Plenty of action, adventure, and mayhem for readers."

Jonesy found himself nodding. "That does sound enticing."

"They have certainly helped me pass the time while I have awaited the calling of my name so that I might leave this excessively pink place."

Jonesy scanned the walls around them. "Excessively pink" was pretty much the perfect way to describe the walls and the décor of the waiting room.

"I'll give them a try," he said, referring to the books. "Thanks."

"When you finish this series, I recommend you read The Call of Ancient Light series next," she added. "It follows a group of young adults who face down a King and his oppressive soldiers, plus bandits, monsters, and other powerful foes. They are fighting to free an ancient warrior who is prophesied to liberate their world."

Jonesy gave another nod. "Yeah... that also sounds pretty good. Thanks again."

The waiting room door opened, and a voice called for Etya.

"Ah, at long last." She faced Jonesy once more. "Be sure that you write Amazon reviews of these books when you finish. We may be dead, but we still have Internet access—at least for now. See to it that your watchful friend, the reader—yes, you, reader—also writes a review."

Jonesy gave a tentative nod. "Uh, sure. I'll see what I can do."

"It is *very* important that you both write a review." Etya leaned far too close to him for his comfort. Sure, he was already dead, but being that close to a cyborg was still unsettling. "You *must* do this. It is one way to atone for your many sins."

Jonesy gulped. "Okay. I'll do it."

"Good." With that, Etya made her way to the door. When she got there, she looked back at Jonesy one last time. "Do not forget. You *must* write a review."

Jonesy waved at her and nodded, and she seemed to take that as an affirmation. She vanished through the door, and then it clicked shut behind her, leaving Jonesy alone again—but also with thousands of other dead people.

It didn't bother him. He was kind of glad to be rid of her.

He cracked open the first book and began to read, all the while knowing he had to write an Amazon review when he finished.

THIS BOOK IS OVER, BUT THE ADVENTURE DOESN'T STOP HERE!

Get *THE GHOST PLAGUE*, the incredible conclusion of Ben Wolf's Tech Ghost series, now available at **www.benwolf.com/store**.

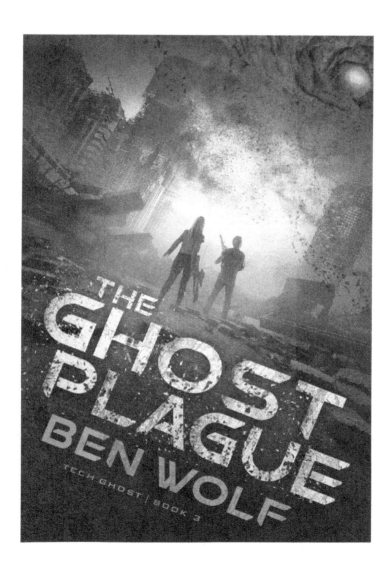

NOTE TO THE READER

Thanks for reading this book. It's because of your support that I can create awesome stories for readers. Without you, I'd have no reason to keep writing!

If you enjoyed this story, please leave me a review on Amazon. You can find them by searching for my author name (Ben Wolf) and the individual titles.

Naturally, you'll want to read more of my books, so I've made it easy for you to find them. I've got both ebooks and print books for sale on my website. Just visit **www.benwolf.com/store** and place your order there.

If you prefer to give Jeff Bezos more money, here are the Amazon links:

Blood Mercenaries: https://amzn.to/2P54qHe
Tech Ghost: https://amzn.to/3vmTaYA
The Call of Ancient Light: https://amzn.to/3CkenWC
Santa Saves Christmas: https://amzn.to/3of1EjS

Lastly, please follow me on social media and join my newsletter (if you haven't already). You can sign up at **www.subscribepage.com/fantasy-readers**, and feel free to join my FB group, **The Ben Wolfpack**, too.

Again, thank you for your support!

ACKNOWLEDGEMENTS

Every published book is the culmination of a lot of hard work, dedication, and support. The author writes the book, but everything that comes after is equally as essential to the success of the book.

First of all, thank YOU for reading this book. I had a blast putting it together, but it was by no means a solo effort.

Second, thanks to my parents for believing in me from an early age and for helping to support my dreams and my growth. I love you both.

Thank you to Jesus Christ for changing my life (and the world) forever.

Thanks to my all-star beta readers, Daniel Kuhnley, Luke Messa, and Paige Guido, for your excellent feedback and encouragement.

Thanks also to my mastermind group. It's a secret group, but you all know who you are. (Insert evil laugh.)

Kirk DouPonce, you are a brilliant artist. The covers for this series are phenomenal. Thank you for your long-suffering patience with me throughout the process.

Dirty Mike Hueser and the BJJ boys, thanks for keeping me frosty.

And thank you to Steve and Rhett at Aethon! Without you, I wouldn't have written this book when I did. Thanks for taking a chance on me.

Last of all, thank you especially to my brilliant, talented, beautiful, thoughtful, and ultra-supportive wife, Charis Crowe. Your flexibility with my weird writing schedule for this series made all the difference in me getting everything done. I love you.

About Ben Wolf

When not writing, I choke people in Brazilian jiujitsu. I live in the midwest with my wife and our cats Marco and Ivy.

Want more of my books?
Order directly from me at **benwolf.com/store** (or on Amazon).

Connect with me on social media, too:

facebook.com/1benwolf
amazon.com/author/benwolf